RICK LAWIN

TEAR
DROP
PASS

outskirts
press

Outskirts Press, Inc.
http://www.outskirtspress.com

ISBN: 978-1-9772-3699-9

Outskirts Press and the "OP" logo are trademarks belonging to Outskirts Press, Inc.

PRINTED IN THE UNITED STATES OF AMERICA

By the same author

Legend of Tierra del Puma

...Some people ain't no damn good
You can't trust 'em, you can't love em...

"Crumblin' Down"-John Mellencamp

CHAPTER 1

1960s
SOMEWHERE IN THE SIERRA

Misery and fatigue caused the man to shiver with each strenuous step in the waist deep snow. The biting wind blew the snow sideways, making it near impossible to see. He stopped again, exhausted. His breath steamed from his burning lungs, his forehead and arm were caked with frozen blood. The torn leather jacket gave little insulation against the frigid mountain air. He blew into his cupped hands; a futile gesture against the icy temps. The duffel bag straps cut into his shoulders, the weight causing him to stumble through the snow. He glanced upwards; the pass was still another steep half-mile climb. He reached in his jacket and pulled out a Snickers bar. Gnawing on the stale candy he peered through the blowing snow spotting a grove of trees. *I can make it there, find shelter, but then what?*

Nobody was looking for him, and nobody cared. As usual, he was alone. Then a thought surfaced in his frozen brain. He dug into his snow-covered pants and pulled out his wallet. His numb fingers fumbled with the sparse contents; a phony identification, several twenties, and a photo. He stared at the small portrait, the woman's warm smile and vibrant eyes transported him off the white tomb of a mountain, if only for a moment. He wondered, would she wait or even care if he didn't show up? God, he wanted to be in her arms. With careful tenderness, he brushed the snowflakes off the photo, closed his wallet, and stashed it back in his jacket. Thoughts of her replaced the cold hopelessness.

His ears pricked when the moaning wind abruptly stopped; replaced by an eerie silence. The swirl of clouds lifted enough to reveal the jagged mountain peak next to the pass. A light wind tumbled down from the summit. It carried no force, just a vagueness of what sounded like whispers intertwined in the breeze. He cocked his ear to listen, but the murmurs faded as the blizzard of wind returned. He considered again taking refuge beneath the tall pines that lay ahead but thought better of it when he spotted animal tracks in the snow. He wiped his dripping nose and eased closer to the fresh prints. *Cougar tracks!* A shiver ran down his spine as he scanned the mountainside, but the animal was nowhere to be seen. Warily, he trudged on toward the pass.

CHAPTER 2

D r. John Walker ran his hands through his thinning gray hair and pushed the large black rimmed glasses back on his nose. He glanced at his watch for a tenth time in as many minutes. Tiny rivulets of sweat ran down his temples and along his round, pock-marked face. Walker was in his 50s but felt himself aging with each passing minute.

The lab was empty except for Walker. The tests wouldn't start until later in the day, maybe. He stared at the silver anodized aluminum briefcase. Small in dimension, it carried years of frustration and success. Walker rapped his fingers on the counter, thinking about the contents. He felt no remorse regarding upcoming events. Rather, anger welled up inside of him. John Walker thought of his lost money and time; not to mention the condescending attitudes of ignorant paper pushers. *Goddamn government bureaucracy. They make it impossible for anyone but the politically connected to play in the defense game.* Once again, he sat waiting. As usual, there were more delays and scrutiny by ill-informed, pinhead bureaucrats. The morass of a corrupt defense acquisition system had burned Walker out. Now, he had found a client keenly aware of the potential of his invention. The Russians were callous bastards, he thought, but they were willing to pay, unlike the arrogant Pentagon political ass-kissers.

Success in the pre-dawn hour was about timing. Walker again looked at his watch. The diversionary fire at the commissary gas station would trigger alarms and chaos. They said other operatives would add confusion by hacking into the power grid. Meanwhile, Walker would leave the installation, drive south a short distance, and meet his contact. The exchange would occur; the device would be delivered, and the money transferred. Nobody would be the wiser for days. Walker tried to dwell on a new life and a villa in the Baltic.

His musings were cut short when the entire building rumbled and the ground gave a sharp jolt. The lights dimmed as a strong rolling wave struck. Walker lived in California and knew the terrifying signature of an earthquake. Debris fell from the ceiling as books and computers slid off the counters. He ducked under a desk and waited as the violent lurching continued. The emergency power kicked in. Lights flickered then died. Walker grabbed the briefcase and ran out the door. Only a few yellow streetlights illuminated the dark military base. A siren wailed, then stopped. An explosion rocked the surrounding area. Walker looked down the street and saw flames. *What the hell, the commissary gas station blew up. That diversion went haywire.* The ground continued to roll, causing power poles to sway as transformers sparked with blinding flashes. A few people at the weapons center ran out in the streets trying to escape falling debris. *Chaos*, he thought, *equated to distraction.*

He jumped in his car and carefully navigated around downed power lines. When he reached the back gate, he noticed the security shack had collapsed. Officers were attending to an injured man. Walker held out his ID card and yelled, "My wife's hurt, she's in the motel. I've got to get to her!"

"Just go," said the officer, waving him on, preoccupied with helping his friend. Walker sped off. Ahead of him lay the communities of Ridgecrest and Inyokern. Steering around cracks in the road and more fallen power lines, he wondered if the quake would alter the rendezvous. He looked in the rearview mirror. Flames from the commissary fire lit up the desert sky.

Walker reached Ridgecrest, where broken windows and crumbling facades littered the darkened streets. He turned south along a deserted stretch of road towards the outskirts of town. The pavement turned into hard-packed dirt, which ended at the county landfill. The stench of garbage was overwhelming. Walker killed the headlights as the full moon revealed acres of trash and demolished vehicles. *Damn, what a place to meet,* he thought to himself. A lone vehicle, a white pickup with a door logo that said, "City of Los Angeles Department of Power and Water," was parked back towards the heaps of refuse. A shadowy figure leaned against the hood. Walker parked his car next to the truck and walked towards the man, noting the hand concealed in the man's dark jacket.

"Walker?" asked the man, in what Walker detected as a slight foreign accent.

Walker approached with briefcase in hand. "Yes, are you Karl?" wanting to confirm his contact, aware that wasn't the man's actual name.

"Yes, I am." He turned the penlight on his face. His beady black eyes carried no friendliness, his expression unreadable in the shadows.

"Uh, ok." Walker said. "My God, that earthquake caused buildings and labs to fall apart. The diversion went bad and blew up a commissary gas station." He sniffed and wrinkled his nose. "And, and this place, this dump stinks. Why in the hell are we meeting here?"

"It is a dump. Dumps stink. This location suits our needs," Karl replied in a curt tone.

Walker blinked, "And this earthquake-it's crazy. I hope you know this will affect my transport if the roads are closed, or worse, if the police move in."

"Things happen." Karl said. "We can't forecast earthquakes." He pointed the narrow beam flashlight at the briefcase. "That is the device, correct?"

"It is. But I want to know, how are we going to get out of here?" Walker's voice filled with anxiety. "Who knows what the highway conditions are like to Victorville, Mojave or even north on Highway 395 to Reno? We damn sure can't go south to LA now. I can't stay here. Your people guaranteed an exit strategy." He wiped the beads of sweat off his forehead.

Karl ignored the question and snapped his fingers. "Open the case."

Walker placed the case on the hood of the truck as he spoke. "Did you hear me? How are we going to get out of this mess?"

Karl examined the contents. Twin polished canisters about 14 inches tall and 6 inches wide were connected by a silver tube. He unscrewed the top to one canister and removed one circuit board from the gold-plated interior. He held an instrument over the component. Seconds later a tiny green light flashed. Satisfied, he glanced at Walker. "All right, we can continue," he said, closing the briefcase.

Walker snatched it back in a huff. "Damn right we can continue. How are we getting out of here, and where's the confirmation of my overseas transfer? Open your phone, laptop, or- whatever and confirm the transfer!"

"No, not right now. Cell service is off because of the earthquake."

"What do you mean? Don't you guys have a satellite phone or something?" asked Walker, his excited voice betraying concern.

Karl remained calm and spoke as if admonishing an adolescent. "Dr. Walker, you have evidence of partial payment when we first started negotiations. It would be unwise to activate an uplink given we are near a weapons test facility that monitors cell or any other frequency. Don't act so ignorant."

"This... this is NOT acceptable," Walker sputtered. "Not at all. A deal is a deal."

Karl again spoke in steely calm. His expression did not change. "Dr. Walker, we will confirm the transfer upon reaching a safe house." Walker started to say something else, but Karl interrupted. "May I remind you not only has this unexpected earthquake altered our plans but so has your mouth."

"My mouth! What the hell are you talking about, my mouth?" Walker said, looking confused.

"Months back you attempted to negotiate a deal with the Beijing people. That has brought another dimension to this."

Walker shook his head, wondering how the Russians found out. "That was months ago. They reneged, gave that typical price quibble crap. They didn't believe what I had. So, I cut them out. It's over."

Karl gave Walker an ominous stare. "Nothing is over in this line of work. It is not typical business. The Chinese have been watching you. We know that and the FBI probably watches them, so the problem lingers." Karl didn't mention that the body of a Chinese surveillance agent had been stuffed into an abandoned railway tank car some miles away.

Walker faltered, searching for words, unsure of his next step. Karl continued, "It is time we go. We will take care of your car. Time and expediency are of the essence. The roads, as you say, could be closed or blocked with law enforcement vehicles and it will be light soon. We will fly out of here by small plane, undetected. Let us go. When we land, you can confirm the electronic transfer."

Walker's eyes grew in surprise. "A small plane-out of here-along *these* Sierras?" He waved his index finger back and forth in front of Karl's face. "No, no that wasn't the plan. I want better assurances, or the deal is off."

"Let me see your cell phone."

"Why, for what?" said Walker as he reached in his pocket and handed over the phone. Karl turned it off and placed it in a lead lined pouch. "What the hell are you doing? I said no deal unless I have my money and safer transportation. Give me the phone back!"

I said, "No phones, no electronics, no traceable signals."

Walker pointed. "Hey, that's my...."

With catlike speed, Karl smashed his right palm into Walker's left shoulder, spinning him around. His forearm flashed across Walker's throat in a chokehold as he yanked him to the ground. Walker had no time to react. He struggled helplessly, grasping in shock at the vicegrip forearms as the air drained from his lungs. His chest screamed and his eyes bulged as his body began to shudder.

Karl tightened his grip. A gurgling sound escaped Walker's throat. His body convulsed, then went limp. After several seconds, there was a sickening crunch of bone as Karl deftly snapped his neck.

Karl stood up and causally brushed the gravel off his pants. He pushed over the dead body with his foot and grimaced. Walker's bowels had let loose.

He dragged the stinking body over to one of the crushed trailers and stuffed it inside, then drove Walker's car into the pile of wrecked vehicles. He pulled out a small package and tossed it underneath the car. In a few minutes there would be another garbage fire in the landfill. Karl grabbed the briefcase and drove towards Inyokern Airport, only a few miles away.

CHAPTER 3

INYOKERN AIRPORT
INYOKERN, CA

K arl reached the isolated side of the unattended airfield. The pilot wanted a non-tower airstrip, but one not so remote as to create suspicions of air smuggling. Inyokern Airport fit the profile. The old former military airbase was now a little used general aviation and sailplane port. A scattering of other businesses dotted the airport, including a parking lot for Los Angeles Power and Water vehicles that serviced the Owens Valley Aqueduct to LA.

Karl drove up to the gate, picked the lock and parked the truck. He wiped down the insides of the pickup then placed the keys where he found them, under the back wheel. He walked along the airport boundary to a large cement apron where a single airplane was tied down.

Eric Necker leaned against the Cessna aircraft, dressed in jeans and a blue nylon jacket. His buzz-cut blond hair made his ears stand out, giving him the look of a 20-year-old military recruit. He approached Karl and glanced up at the black sky that now had a slight tinge of orange on the eastern horizon.

"You're fucking late," he said, lighting up a cigarette then blowing the smoke though his nostrils.

"Walker got delayed because of this earthquake, then he presented problems. It's taken care of."

Necker didn't inquire about details. His job and high pay centered on solid aviation skills mixed with an arrogant and self-confident personality. "So be it. We better get the hell out of here. Daylight is near and the weather north will get crappy."

Karl eyed the plane with uncertainty. "This isn't a twin. It looks old and beat up."

Necker took another drag on the cigarette, flicked it on the ground and crushed it with his boot. "It's over 50 years old, a Cessna 182 with good bones."

"Why this weary looking contraption? There's pressure to get the package delivered. I can't take chances on delays because you couldn't provide a better and faster airplane."

Necker shook his head as if offended by Karl's ignorance of the plan. "You handle your job, let me attend to mine. There is a reason for this plane." He pulled the chocks out from under the wheels. "This aircraft has no record and was hidden in some barn. The ignorant owner wanted to sell it." Necker smiled, "I inspected it and test flew the plane. It is a good machine and suits our needs."

Necker walked around the single engine airplane doing the final preflight. "I changed the tail number." He pointed to large lettering on the wings and fuselage. "Notice the words 'PATROL.' Our disguise will allow us to fly north without attention."

Necker opened the passenger door and pointed to the instrument panel. "No electronics to radiate signals, only a radio, if we need it. My tablet will provide GPS and weather. No uplink." He pointed to another avionic in the panel. "The transponder remains switched off."

"No signal transmissions, correct?"

"That is correct. We will fly low against the mountains. It is doubtful any radar will pick us up. If it does, then Air Traffic Control will consider us another dumb pilot who forgot to turn on the transponder. If people spot us from the ground, they will see a normal power line patrol plane." Necker gave Karl a contemptuous stare. "That's why the old plane and not a fancy twin. Now, do you understand?"

Karl accepted the logic, ignoring Necker's egotistical manner. "I leave it to you. This is your field of expertise. How long is the flight in this, as you say, old, single engine plane?"

Necker climbed in the left seat and adjusted the seat belt as Karl strapped in the right front. "It will take several hours, and we're not stopping for fuel so pee now if you must," said Necker. "Victor or his people will meet us at Blue Canyon Airport, on the west side of the Sierra. It is an out of the way uncontrolled airstrip but accessible to Highway 80. It will appear we are stopping for a break in our patrol duties."

Necker took off, climbed and banked west, crossing Highway 395. Reaching the base of the mountains he tracked northward along the Sierras. Karl looked out the scratched window. The weapons test center glowed with yellow flames from the commissary. Flashes of red and blue lights from emergency vehicles dotted the area all the way to Ridgecrest.

Necker leveled off at 500 feet above ground. The computer tablet displayed GPS waypoints and markers for navigation. He glanced to the right and saw orange slivers of sunlight poking through the black clouds; an ominous warning of impending bad weather. Necker adjusted the aviation radio and listened to the high-altitude sector of FAA air traffic control in the area. Radio chatter seemed light and routine with only an occasional mention of the earthquake.

They flew north along the west side of the Owens Valley, passing over the Sierra gateway towns of Lone Pine and Independence. Off the left wing were the tall, rugged granite pinnacles of Mt. Whitney and other peaks that formed the lofty backbone of the High Sierra. An overcast settled on the tops of the summits. A long flight lay ahead. Karl reached in the backseat for the briefcase and set it in his lap.

"So that's the package," chirped Necker through the metallic sounding headset.

"Uh-huh, that's it." Karl opened the case and pulled out the two joined containers. The tube interior was filled with fiery red crystals and the strange looking circuit boards wrapped with gold sheathing. He eyed the complete assembly with curiosity.

"What's that thing supposed to do?" Necker said, while adjusting the trim of the plane.

"I am not sure. Victor didn't expand on the matter except to say it was a like a magnetron on steroids."

"A what?" said Necker, not understanding the terminology.

"Similar to a small mechanism that powers a microwave oven." Karl held the device in his hand. "It's some revolutionary piece of engineering; small enough to fit in planes and cars, but powerful enough to operate chemical laser weapons. Victor said it produces incredible energy."

Karl balanced the assembly in his hands. "They weigh little. Walker designed a breakthrough. Then his own country tried to screw him. Lucky for Moscow," Karl chuckled, "and unfortunate for Walker."

"Yeah, really bad for Walker", said Necker in a disgusted tone. "He should have stuck with just being screwed by his government. That's to Moscow's advantage, but he sold out his country-a traitor. He would have done that no matter who he worked for." Necker gave the device another once over. His eyes widened, "shit, that's not a nuke is it?"

"No, it's not radioactive. That's what makes it unique. The system is modular, I assume, one part can't operate without the other. The reverse engineering process will be easier with this complete system. We are not privy to greater intelligence details. That's why the urgency to complete the transaction before the Americans or Chinese realize what it can do or where it is."

Necker made a slight heading change with the flight controls. "And the reason this operation has significant risk. Our stipends will reflect that risk."

"More payment upon delivery." said Karl, smiling. "Necessity exceeds hazards. Besides, Necker, you have a history of succeeding despite risks."

Karl closed the briefcase and returned it to the backseat. He looked out the window at the occasional town that intersected with northbound Highway 395. To the west, the towering line of peaks rose straight up into the clouds. "So, where are we?"

"Approaching the town of Bishop. We will stay far west of it then climb as the terrain gets higher."

"Into those mountains?" Karl asked, pointing towards the steep escarpments of the Eastern Sierra.

"Along the edges, the lower portions. We climb over the Sherwin Grade, pass by Mammoth Mountain Airport then climb again near Mono Lake towards Bridgeport."

Necker looked up at the clouds and swore. "God damn Sierras. We have unexpected weather developing."

"A problem?" asked Karl, noticing the build-up of dirty white and gray cumulus clouds towering to the west.

"Nothing I can't deal with." Necker fiddled with a red knob, leaning the fuel mixture to maximize engine performance as the plane climbed.

From the Sherwin Grade, they continued north over a huge ancient volcanic caldera called the Long Valley. As they crossed over Mammoth Mountain Airport, the terrain rose again as the darkening cloud ceiling dropped. However, the visibility beneath the overcast remained good.

The flight droned on as the airplane bounced with an occasional light buffet. Necker pointed. "Over there, east, is Minden, Nevada. To our left, behind those mountains, is Lake Tahoe."

Karl stared at the sheer barrier of mountains as if they were guarding something that lay behind them. "Are we climbing over those?"

"Not now, the weather is lowering, blocking our crossing through Truckee and Donner Pass. We will continue north, pass Reno, and then turn west through a saddle to reach Blue Canyon. The visibility and conditions will be better on that route."

Karl looked at his watch, "We can't be late. Excuses are not acceptable."

"For Christ's sake," said Necker, "Let me fly. I'm very good at what I do."

A short time later the Cessna came abreast of Reno, flying north along the Sierras. Necker noticed his tablet failed to update with the current weather. Tall, ominous cumulus clouds were building up; harbingers of thunderstorms. Dangerous clouds to be near, in, or under. Necker re-tuned the radio to get additional weather broadcasts. The update wasn't good. An early winter squall line had suddenly formed over the Sierra crest. More storms popped up to the east, over the desert.

Karl saw the lowering ceilings as mist and black clouds draped the mountains. Mild turbulence now rocked the plane. "This doesn't seem too good. Can we fly in the clouds or climb over this stuff?"

Necker cursed at the changing weather. "No, that would be suicide in these mountains as these build-ups are too high to get over." Necker gave a nervous laugh. "But, I have options."

Karl turned to Necker, speaking in an assertive tone. "I shall emphasize this again; we must reach Blue Canyon. Any delay will be of consequence. We are getting paid to get this done. We must meet expectations."

Necker looked ahead towards the deteriorating weather. He snapped back; "I'm sick of your persistent reminders about getting this job done. I told you we would get through." Gray tendrils of clouds dropped lower as wind whacked the aircraft. Necker countered the unexpected start of a roll with the ailerons. "If we land at Reno or anywhere around here, it could raise suspicions if the feds realize something is missing from the lab. They will have people waiting there." Necker pointed eastward. "Out there is nothing but desert and restricted airspace. That means military aircraft and radar. It limits our options. We will continue north towards Honey Lake, then turn west. We can reach Blue Canyon from the northeast. I have done this before. I know what to do."

"I hope so," said Karl staring out the window with a look of concern at the lowering cloud bank. "And you will get through these black clouds?"

Necker nodded while concentrating on flying the plane through worsening skies. His mouth was dry. "Yes, I can. I told you we would reach Blue Canyon. I don't let shitty weather alter my intentions. This is workable."

Necker looked at the moving map on the tablet that positioned the aircraft west, near Beckwourth Pass. The display painted better visibility between the base of the clouds and terrain. But what he saw outside ahead didn't match the screen. Necker stayed confident; he knew the mountains and how to sneak through them. And, Karl had made it abundantly clear; failure wasn't an option.

As they flew westward, the clouds tumbled lower. Behind them the pass had closed, obscured by rain mists. Necker suddenly realized he had flown into a blind sucker hole.

They were in the mountains with no way to make a 180-degree turn. The turbulent air seemed furious as the plane shook in the heavy chop. Rain splashed hard on the windscreen. Necker glanced at the outside air temperature gauge. If the temperature dropped further, the rain would turn to ice or snow. With no de-icing equipment, the plane wouldn't fly. He cursed, his brazen overconfidence had exceeded common sense.

Karl looked outside at the deteriorating visibility; an occasional rocky mountain peak revealed itself in the ghostly gray mist. Trepidation played in his dry voice. "This isn't good. Where are you going, can we still make it?"

"No, it's not good, it is unexpected, but I will deal with it." Necker looked again at his tablet. The navigation displays faltered, came back on, then went dark. "Shit." More turbulence racked the plane. Karl bounced upward hitting the overhead. Necker spoke quickly as he fought to keep the plane level. "The fucking tablet is giving me fits. Here, plug the power cable into the cigarette lighter."

Karl fumbled with the cord. The tablet came back on, but the display flickered intermittently. Necker glanced at the screen then stared out the cockpit. "The storm and mountains are fucking up the downlink. It's not painting real time weather anymore."

Karl's eyes searched north. More storm clouds roiled down to the ground as a low mist engulfed the plane. Necker descended to stay out of the clouds, but the visibility was fast disappearing. Karl's voice quivered, betraying a growing fear. "I hope you can get out of this ugliness."

"We turn south," Necker said, casting a quick look at the tablet screen that now glowed with bright red spots; indications of deadly thunderstorms. The screen flashed and went off. Necker noticed the other basic cockpit navigation instruments weren't reacting to the range station he had dialed in. He pulled out an aeronautical chart and handed it to Karl. His voice got loud. "I can't take my hands off the controls, the turbulence is getting worse! Open the map, hand it to me."

Necker looked up just as the airplane entered into a grey dark abyss. His eyes went to the instruments, focusing on the artificial horizon to avoid vertigo. He desperately needed to establish his position in relation to the mountain peaks. His stomach went sour with the realization that they had become trapped in a valley surrounded by mountains with near zero visibility. He saw a touch of ice develop on the wings. He slammed the throttle forward, but there was no way they could climb above the growing storm. Getting lower became impossible. Turning southbound, they unknowingly entered the wall of the thunderstorm.

At the entrance, heavy turbulence ripped at the plane. The aluminum briefcase bounced off the back seat and on to the floor. Necker yelled to Karl. "Tighten your harness!" Rain pelted the canopy, becoming an impenetrable curtain of water. Necker battled to keep the plane level. Beads of sweat dripped from his forehead despite the coldness in the cockpit cabin. He gave another quick look at the sectional chart then tossed it back to Karl. "I'll try to hold this altitude. If we stay in the middle of this valley, we should be okay. Maybe the weather will break a bit. There's a private strip down there, Tierra del something. We can land there and ditch the package. If not, I will fly farther south, there is a uh, break in the western mountains, called, called." Necker's mouth went sour with alarm, as he tasted the rising bile from his stomach. He couldn't recall the name.

Karl struggled to read the chart as the plane bounced hard in the chop. It flew out of his hand as another violent jolt hit the plane. The rain turned to hail. "It's called Teardrop Pass," he yelled, over the roar of ice pellets hammering the plane. There was a blinding flash of light followed by an instant explosion of thunder. The plane nearly went inverted.

"Jesus!" yelled Necker fighting to keep the plane level. "It's all right, I got it now. I think we can still get through it."

A monstrous updraft sent the aircraft wildly upwards, out of control. He pushed forward on the yoke without effect. The plane shot up three thousand feet, then plummeted downward in a viscous down draft. Instantly, the airplane snapped inverted and again thrusted upward, pushed by ferocious air currents. There was another intense spark of lightning. The interior of the powerful cumulus nimbus clouds packed the energy of an atomic bomb.

Karl screamed over the horrific noise, "You arrogant ass, you've killed us both!"

Within seconds the aircraft's wings cracked and buckled. The screeching sound of metal being ripped into shreds became lost within the roaring tempest. The airplane disintegrated. Necker's last moment of consciousness was that of tumbling into a dark gray void, one hand still clutched to a piece of control yoke.

CHAPTER 4

ONE WEEK LATER
AUBURN, CA

Nikolai Cherenkov stared out the picture window, teacup and saucer in hand. A mass of storm clouds obscured the normal panoramic view of the Sierra foothills. The raindrop-splattered window reflected a man in his 50s with white hair, a sharp white goatee and hazel eyes that perpetually darted about, assessing things with a cold, calculated chill. A dark blue tattoo of a snarling wolf covered the side of his neck.

Cherenkov took a slow sip of tea and turned towards the man sitting in a leather chair who stared passively at the fireplace, listening to the steady drum of rain. He, like Cherenkov, was of Russian descent. His jet-black hair accented his saturnine appearance. No friendliness radiated from the snake like eyes and grim countenance. A bond of ruthlessness existed between the two men. Nikolai set the teacup and saucer on the oak table and stroked his white goatee. "It has been snowing in the Sierra for days. We must assume the worst. The plane is down."

Victor Rodin stood and walked over to the table where various documents lay spread out.

"Yes, it appears that way. We know they left Inyokern. Our person confirmed that along with the removal of Walker and the Asian pest. Done well, no issues so far. But the flight remains a mystery. Necker planned to shut off all transmitting devices, cell phones, transponders, everything to ensure no electronic traceability. We waited at Blue Canyon Airport until it was obvious something went wrong. Nothing came but snow and thunderstorms."

"And no reports of missing planes?" Cherenkov said, turning his gaze to the rain outside.

"Nothing, no mention of downed aircraft. Only the news of the devastation caused by the earthquake. That perhaps was a timely blessing, but the weather..." He shook his head in frustration, "... this miserable freak storm that sprung up over the Sierra remains the talk of the media."

Cherenkov turned to Rodin. "This is a dangerous complication. I committed to our Moscow connection that we could complete this assignment. A failure on our part to retrieve this package will have potential consequences to our local endeavors and export industry."

Rodin listened intently to the man known for his profitable and undetectable engagements within the wicked sphere of drugs, sex trafficking, and other activities. The underworld organizations in Russia and abroad respected the reputation of the "Wolf". He lived and functioned by the brutal Code of Thieves and expected the same from his employees. Betrayal or failure, Rodin knew, resulted in death. The code carried no escape clause.

"Nikolai," Rodin said, "We could not control the weather. If others discover the aircraft, our current enterprises remain well concealed and far removed from this Moscow contract. The crew is dead, their bodies buried in snow or eaten by the animals. Necker was contract labor. Karl stood with Russian intelligence, neither closely affiliated with our other investments. Moscow contracted us for delivery service."

"Yes, there is truth in what you say but there remains the word of 'failure.' The latter I cannot allow. They compensate us to succeed and provide overseas immunity on exports and imports. Failure infers weakness and inability to perform. Our other business relationships will question our reliability. We lose trust and face. No, Victor, we must resolve this issue or suffer penalties." Cherenkov's voice carried a fierce resolve that Rodin had often heard and respected.

As the 'Wolf's,' second in command, Victor's loyal obedience was unshakable.

Cherenkov gave a half smile. "So, Victor, what information do we have to solve this problem?" he asked, flipping through the papers on the table in search of something.

"We have no other reasons for the missing aircraft except the sudden change in the Sierra weather. If they had landed somewhere to sit out the snow and rain, then we would have heard. Unless..." Rodin paused.

Cherenkov looked up from the papers in his hand. "Unless what?"

"Unless the FBI knew the plan and arrested them. Or the Chinese intercepted them."

"Hmm, that is doubtful. Our people would have heard something by now. No, Victor, the plane is down somewhere in those wretched mountains. That we must consider a fact."

Rodin pointed to the window as raindrops rolled down the glass. "But where? We don't know their exact flight path or if they altered course. And in this storm, the snow would be heavy at higher elevations."

Nikolai held up a photograph with small yellow arrows on it. "This might assist locating the plane. Our Moscow contacts are eager to retrieve the package. So, they offer limited, discreet support."

"How?"

"This is a satellite photo they transmitted to us. It shows a vague track of something along the Sierra on the day of the flight." Cherenkov held the photo up to overhead chandelier light.

"Notice that very indistinct line. It's what they think might be the path of a plane turning west and then south through the mountains."

Rodin shook his head back and forth. "Nikolai, that's an assumption made by some menial intelligence assistant. The aircraft was small, had no transponder signals. Necker planned to fly low, terrain following and there were massive thunderstorms in the area. We have no idea where the plane went except somewhere north.

Russian reconnaissance satellites are good, but not that good. This is just a wild guess by some low-level analyst, a clerk who wants to kiss the ass of some Party member. They have no awareness of this Sierra Nevada."

"Perhaps, but we have few options except to explore this possibility. They demand this device in the worst way. To them it represents a treasure of technological advancements, so they say. I assume it is weapons related. They are exceedingly impatient to have it in their hands, as we are to deliver it. It involves defense, fortunes, and politics."

Victor exhaled slowly, thinking of the difficult recovery effort. "If you order a response, then we will devise a retrieval plan. But the Sierra snows are deep. This enormous area is inaccessible. We will have to rely on Wade Keeler's expertise of the mountains. Given the international connection to Moscow, is that appropriate?"

"You have a concern because he is not Russian?" said Cherenkov, raising his eyebrows as if surprised by the question.

"Yes, to some extent, though he runs our other operations exceptionally well. His gravel company and warehouses remain ideal storage of vehicles and parts. And he does elevate our diesel fuel sales, but still..." Rodin hesitated and looked at Cherenkov for an opinion.

"You have worked with him for years and has he not performed his duties with effectiveness and discretion?"

"Yes, though some of his..." Rodin searched for the right words, "...assistants are crude and often impetuous with their actions. And sometimes Wade acts like an unsophisticated mountain man with his hunting passions."

"I agree, he and his associates can be coarse. However, Wade understands our code and has never failed us. The man is the filter to our local endeavors. He shares our belief in discipline and the consequence of betrayal. Does he not? He was the one that discovered the stupid fool in the warehouse that skimmed profits on the drugs."

Rodin nodded. "Yes, he did. And he rather enjoyed placing the chains around her neck and tossing her into Clementine Reservoir.

He and his workers do have a zest to inflict pain. Still, I wonder if they are suited for a project that is international, that is, of Russian blood."

Cherenkov nodded, understanding Rodin's concern. "His conduct shows adherence to a strict code and tolerates no compromises in trust and does not accept failure. His loyalty to us during his military service never wavered throughout the investigations. And, his painful physical misfortune is a testimonial to his silence. I suspect that left him with a bitterness towards those that betray and that zeal, as you say, to inflict revenge."

"Yes, you are correct, said Rodin. "I will admit he has paid the price. He does follow orders with few questions asked."

Cherenkov smiled, "and he embraces the other part of the ancient Thieves Code, no wives or children, just lovers." Cherenkov chuckled, "a pleasurable aspect, considering our resources in that matter. Wade will do what we expect of him." Cherenkov gave a sly grin, "Besides, Victor, we own the man, he would be expendable should we so choose. Unlike us, he possesses no visa, and shall we say, no other country to call home."

"Then I will bring him into the recovery project. He knows the Sierra. So, we are back to developing a search plan."

"Here, let us try this." Cherenkov pointed to a forestry map laid out on the table. He ran his finger along the chart. "This area is where they might have gone down, if we believe the satellite track. It is a blend of public access forests and a large private ranch." He tapped his finger on the ranch name, Tierra del Puma. "This covers a wide swath of valleys and mountains. Necker could have continued north on the eastside of the mountains, turned west then back south, southwest. If that is the case, he would fly over this ranch."

Victor Rodin remained skeptical. "If he turned south; there are also mountains and passes to the north."

"True, but more populated. We would have heard if someone located a crashed plane."

"I agree. There has been nothing on the news about a plane crash."

"All right. We gather intelligence until we can access that area. Let us frequent establishments where there could be talk or rumors of missing planes. Wade or his people may know of such places such as bars and so forth. Contact Yeric at our recycle center. Tell him to be alert if someone shows up wanting to sell a strange part. I'll give you a drawing of the device. As the season changes, we can search the area masquerading as recreationists, an off-road club, hunters, skiers, whatever. Hopefully, we can locate and recover the property before others stumble upon it."

"Agreed. Wade possesses equipment to access the mountain roads considering his back-country activities. But this strategy is weak, Nikolai. I am not sure this will gain us anything, except more payouts to him and his crew."

"Cost is not an issue. This plan is an imperative. We have no options at the moment as Moscow presses hard for results. We must proceed with haste to find the device before it involves others. There will be trouble if someone else locates the plane first."

Victor held a sullen expression. "Very well, I will start the effort."

"Thank you, Victor. Keep in touch." Cherenkov patted Rodin on the shoulder. "Do not let anyone stand in the way. Meantime, we wait until the winter storms abate."

Rodin walked to the door and casually looked around the house. "Nikolai, I must say this again, you have a beautiful home. Very private."

"Yes, it is. I have no intruders except for occasional mountain bikers that are easily threatened off. Typical American youth-no respect for a man's private property and ever so lazy. Even the youngsters I hired to brush clear my property were spoiled and useless."

"Most Americans are naïve and think only of themselves." Rodin shrugged.

"How true. I also find it remarkable that one who is not an American citizen can own such real estate as this." The Wolf held a sly grin. "It only takes money, and an occasional trip out of the country to renew the visa status. Take care, Victor, and reach out soon."

At Rodin's departure, Cherenkov turned to the table and studied the forestry map. He tapped his finger on the name of the private ranch, Tierra del Puma, which translated to 'Land of the Cougar.' *Interesting name,* he thought, as the dull rumble of thunder rattled the windows.

CHAPTER 5

Twenty-one-year-old Sean O'Hara gingerly unwrapped the gauze from his arm and grimaced."Fuck, that sucker hurts!" His forearm pulsed from the long bloody gash that needed stitches. But with no insurance and living at home with mom and sister, the medical costs would trash the meager household budget. He sucked up the pain and re-wrapped it with more gauze. The injury didn't hurt as much as the pain of destroying the snowboard that now lay on the floor, cracked in pieces. He knew that snowboarding alone down a remote backcountry avalanche prone ridge didn't rate high in common sense, but the conditions were awesome.

"At least I wore a helmet," he said to his cocky reflection in the bathroom mirror.

He scratched his mop of red hair, thinking about the high-speed collision between the weird metal thing sticking in the snow and his snowboard. He'd been there many times before, and the snow was always perfect on that side of the ridge. Sean admitted to himself *that* side of the ridge and pass lay on private property. But the ranch people never patrolled the remote and treacherous area in winter. The danger didn't bother fearless Sean O'Hara. The fresh snow and wild ride made the long hazardous hike and trespass worthwhile. More so today, considering what he brought home besides a broken snowboard and bloody arm. *I'm both tough and lucky*, he thought, while giving a self-assured grin in the mirror. His optimistic and carefree attitude in life had somehow survived the peaks and valleys of growing up with a minimum of positive paternal guidance.

Sean O'Hara carried a crafty and streetwise edge. However, what he had in natural smarts he lacked in long term focus or ambition. He was content with living for today; enjoying snowboarding and screwing off. Junior college came sporadically, as did his part-time employment at the Decadent Dessert Restaurant in the Roseville Mall. Nevertheless, Sean's affable personality got him through scrapes with teachers and employers. He didn't consider himself flaky, just distracted. He loved his mom and younger sister and forked over much of his restaurant earnings to keep the household afloat. Sean rationalized his shortcomings came from a damaged gene pool called an asshole father. The SOB sat in a Texas prison doing 30 to life for armed robbery and drug smuggling. Sean hated the bastard for running out on Mom, Jessie, and him. Alimony and spousal support didn't exist, and the small O'Hara family suffered. *But maybe that's about to change,* he thought, walking out of the bathroom cradling his arm.

He peeked into his sister's small bedroom; aware she had left earlier in the day. She possessed the only working computer in the house, the one he built out of scrounged and not-so-legal parts. He shook his head with a tinge of sadness, surveying Jessie's untidy space that had few adornments. *Not much to show for a just turned 19-year-old's life.* A few photographs of horses and her own sketches hung on walls. Some soccer team ribbons lay on the tiny dresser next to an artist's easel. Jessie would come home, close the bedroom door and spend hours in her room painting or drawing. She was introverted and quiet. And he knew why. That sibling discussion came with a vow never to bring up the subject again. Sean figured those inner demons affected her self-esteem. She never thought herself pretty given a face full of freckles and red hair. She had little money to mall crawl with her few friends. That too embarrassed her, watching others buy things when she couldn't. The family teetered on a financial precipice. Jessie hadn't found a part-time job yet, which made matters worse. The extroverted Sean worried about his introverted sister. But maybe, he thought optimistically while switching on her computer, he could convert a snowboard crash into money that he would share with his sister.

Sean sat in front of the screen, typed in the password, and up-loaded his snowboard track from his handheld GPS. He studied the map overlay and typed notes where he crashed into the metal box that spilled out the odd-looking thing. Sean opened his daypack and scoped out the broken device. It resembled a banged-up thermos. Judging from the broken tube on the side, it attached to something else. That other half he'd seen careening down the slope. Sean peeked inside the canister and his eyes popped wide in surprise. The interior had circuit boards insulated with what appeared to be gold sheathing. "Whoa, hot damn" he said out loud, hoping it was, in fact, gold. He carefully pulled out the circuit boards and placed them next to the canister, then snapped a cell phone picture of the entire ensemble and scanned a copy on the printer.

Sean rapped his fingers on the desk, thinking his inadvertent discovery had potential value and he knew exactly where to ver-ify that possibility. O'Hara placed the circuit boards in a box and stashed it, along with his notes, in Jessie's closet for safe keeping. His sister understood Sean's occasional scrounging adventures bor-dered within the shadows of legitimacy. Plus, his mom sometimes snooped around his room, curious about his inventory of alleged recyclable computer parts. He tossed the photo and the canister in his daypack and decided to take a quick trip. O'Hara jumped on his old Kawasaki EX motorcycle and headed to the city of Loomis to his favorite and unique recycle center.

Sean turned down a side street to an old industrial park. In the rear of the complex was a small non-descript suite. No name hung above the door, only the address. He peeked through the tinted glass door and rang the bell. Within a minute the door opened half-way, and a man waved Sean in. "Come," he said, in a gruff voice, then locked the door. Sean blinked his eyes and wrinkled his nose, unaccustomed to the harsh odor of cigarette smoke that permeated the shop. The man walked around a counter littered with computer parts. He glanced over the man's shoulder into the back area. Several men were busy disassembling computers, along with what appeared to be a voting machine. Sean knew the routine, parting out electronics then selling components online. He was savvy enough not to inquire about other businesses run by the Russian guy, known as Yeric.

Sean planned his conversation carefully to the oily-looking man who reeked of cigarette smoke and breath that smelled something of garlic. O'Hara figured the man with unkempt black hair covering his ears might be 40. His black eyes, greasy complexion and yellow stained teeth masked his age. He talked with a cigarette pressed between his lips, which made speaking even more difficult given his accent.

"What do you have for me today, Sean?" he said, with an impatient look, running his hand through his stringy hair. "I am busy, be quick."

"I thought you could tell me," he said, removing the canister device from the pack and holding it up. Yeric pulled the cigarette from his lips, exhaled the last puff, and then tossed the butt on the floor.

"And what is that?" he said, taking it from Sean's hand.

"Not sure but look inside."

Yeric removed the towel Sean had wrapped over the top and peered into the canister. He squinted his eyes and studied it. "It is some electronic device. There were circuit boards in here. Where are they?"

"Don't know," Sean said, wary not to divulge too much information on the first negotiation.

Yeric examined the object more closely. "Hmm, this is gold sheathing, thin but, yes, gold." He peeked into one of the small broken fragments of tubing that stuck from the side. Tiny, bright ruby like crystals lined the inside of the tube. Yeric felt his pulse quicken. They had warned him, be alert, they said. Yeric set the device back on the counter. He lit another cigarette, took a puff, and slowly blew the foul-smelling smoke through his nostrils.

"So, you have any idea what it is?" asked Sean trying to temper an eagerness after hearing the word gold. The yellow luster had distracted him from seeing the sparkling stones in the fractured tube. Sean forced himself to play cool.

Yeric waved his hand with a give-it-to-me gesture. "Here, let me see it again."

He felt its weight, then lied. "It must be a piece of satellite that did not burn up." He looked at Sean, "where did you find this?"

Sean slowly retrieved the object from Yeric's hand. "In the mountains where I was snowboarding."

"What mountains, where exactly?"

Sean stayed vague. "North of Truckee on some ridges. So, is it worth anything?"

Yeric responded vaguely in turn. "I would guess the gold wrapping is worth perhaps 500 dollars. Hard to say until I peel it out, verify, and weigh it."

Sean kept a poker face. *Bullshit, he knows its worth more, way more.*

"That doesn't seem very much, considering if fell off a satellite. Maybe the owners of this thing would know?"

"I would think the government would be quick to confiscate it considering it could be from a defense satellite." Yeric exhaled another plume of smoke. "It is best to keep this between ourselves for maximum profit. Leave it here and I will assess the value and call you."

No fucking way! Sean placed the object back in his pack. "I don't think so, Yeric. But here's a photo of it and the circuit boards I pulled from it."

The Russian smiled, "Ah, so you found something else to this; very smart, Sean. And you probably know where the rest of this thing might lie."

"Maybe," Sean said, with a coy, barely perceptible grin. "Study the pictures, call me and we can discuss options. I think we can both make some money on whatever this is. Gold is gold and who knows what else."

Yeric took the photo while flicking the ash off his cigarette. "Very well, Sean, you drive a hard bargain-quite the businessman. I will make inquires and decide if this item and the gold sheathing will, as you would say, fetch a good price. Give me a week. I will call you."

Sean avoided shaking Yeric's dirty hands, grabbed his pack and left. He roared down the street on the old Kawasaki thinking in a few days he would have enough money to get a new snowboard, blow off the part-time job at the restaurant, and add bucks to the O'Hara household. Jessie and Mom would now have some spending money.

Minutes after Sean left the recycle center, Yeric was on the phone. He spoke in Russian. "I think a piece of object you are looking for might have shown up in my shop."

The voice on the other end had no emotion. "Is that so? You have it there?"

"No, the boy who came in with it didn't know what it was. I looked at it and tried to keep it, but he refused. He is a scrounger of electronic parts and wants money for his things."

"And?"

"He didn't trust me to keep it until I made a better offer. He gave me pictures of it and the internal circuit boards. It is a part of something bigger from the drawing you gave me."

"Interesting. And where did he find it?" The voice grew more direct.

"He said somewhere in the mountains, but he knows where. He is aware it has value and wants to deal. I told him not to speak to anyone as it might have come from a defense satellite that fell to earth and the government would confiscate it. He would not make any money. He is smart, eager for cash. He will stay quiet until we can meet again."

"Excellent. I will call back after I speak to Nikolai and others. We will set up a meeting." Victor said and closed the call with a satisfied click.

CHAPTER 6

Sean listened to Yeric's voicemail. "I have located knowledgeable people who are interested in your discovery. It has value. We must discuss issues in private."

Deal time, thought Sean, pulling through the gate of a deserted rock quarry on the outskirts of Lincoln. A few security lights cast shadows on the rock crushers and nearby construction shacks. A dog barked off in the distance, breaking the night silence. Sean shut off his motorcycle and coasted up to the office.

Yeric came out of the building. "Ah, Sean, we were worried about you." He motioned with his hand, "Come, come and hear the excellent news."

Sean stepped off the bike with his backpack. "Had to work late, sorry." He felt a twinge of apprehension looking around at the dark, unfamiliar surroundings.

Inside the construction shack sat another man. Yeric made the brief introduction. "Sean, this is Wade. He is much like you, a collector, an entrepreneur."

Sean O'Hara looked at the guy, thinking he had seen him before. He had a heavy-set body and looked to be in his 40s. A dirty ball cap covered short brown hair and his eyes seemed bloodshot. Sean tried not to stare at the dark bluish scar that ran along the side of the man's cheek. The ugly facial wound registered. *This guy and his buddies got into a drunken brawl at the restaurant. The cops came and threw him out.* Sean grew wary. "Yeah, hey."

"Nice to meet you, kid," said Wade Keeler, exerting a strong handshake.

Yeric continued, "Mr. Keeler has expertise on locating things like valuable meteorites and satellite debris. Wade, please explain to Sean what you know."

Wade sat down and lit a cigarette with a beat-up Zippo lighter. He exhaled a stream of smoke while studying the photograph Sean had given Yeric. "Yeah, uh huh, this thing looks like the part of an old phase B, GPS or GLONASS satellite constellation."

Sean had a baffled look on his face, "GLONASS...what's that?"

"That's the Russian version of the American GPS system. They work the same and are damn near built the same." Wade held the picture up to the light. "Yeah, this part looks about 30 years old. The circuit boards were experimental technology. The big deal back then was to wrap every component in gold sheathing, thin leaf plating, you name it. Designers thought the gold would reduce electromagnetic interference. Countries went ape shit over the concept. Later on, better and cheaper micro insulation got built in. The gold got phased out, too expensive."

"So, it is real gold?" asked Sean, absorbed in the story, but trying to conceal his excitement.

"Big time, with more on the backside of the boards." Wade looked at Sean, waiting for a reply.

"How much is this worth? And I guess I have to figure in your percentage now." Sean said, aware he now had a partner, like it or not.

Wade took another drag on his cigarette. "You're smart, kid. These assemblies had two canisters. Each one had circuit boards tidied up in gold sheathing. The interface conduits had ruby or diamond rods for a phase harmonic; something to do with keeping perfect time. They use quartz now, but the ruby crystals were also experimental. Bottom line is these satellites didn't work too well, so Russia and US just let the orbits degrade and they burned up in the atmosphere over the Pacific Ocean, or so they thought. A few overshot the reentry area and crashed somewhere in the Sierra and in Nevada desert."

Sean got lost in the high-tech explanation but stayed intrigued. "Sounds like a bunch of money in these things."

"Damn right there is. In 25 years, I've only found a fragmented piece of one. I'll tell ya kid, it's every treasure hunter's dream from the sky. You struck gold, literally."

Wade handed the photograph back to Sean. "Judging from this photo I'd estimate we have about 400k in gold and ruby oscillators for both canisters. I need to see the entire package for a better estimate. Yeric says you have one."

"Yeah, I might have part of one" said Sean, working hard to sound casual and cagey.

Wade squashed the cigarette into an empty beer can. "All right Sean, if you want to fuck us around consider this. This is all black-market stuff. The government still considers that device secret. Item two; these canisters are hot."

"Hot, you mean stolen?" Sean said, raising his eyebrows in disbelief.

"No kid, hot as in radioactive hot. They got contaminated by the radioisotopes that power the entire unit."

Sean's mouth fell open, aghast at what he heard. A knot formed in his throat, as he fumbled for a response. Wade saw O'Hara's concerned expression. "Yeah, hot as in making you sterile hot." Wade reached in his pocket and pulled out a small Geiger counter and turned it on. It chattered. "Your fucking backpack is toasty."

O'Hara felt a surging anxiety as he stared at the pack. "Uh, yeah, I brought a board." He was hesitant to open it as his stomach flipped at the word radioactive.

Wade slipped on a pair of gloves. "Here, give me the friggin bag." He looked in the pack and pulled out the single board. "Ah, one board isn't bad, alpha particles only. But three boards could fry your nuts if you aren't careful."

Sean closed his eyes, sick and fearful, wondering if his sister's room was now contaminated from the canister and other boards.

He rubbed his sweaty forehead. *Oh fuck.* Wade reached in his pocket and pulled out a heavy bag and dropped the board in. "That reduces the radiation-it's okay. Relax kid, it won't bite you. Did you bring the other parts so we can bag them too before you go sterile?" Wade said, holding a serious expression.

Sean stuttered for a second, trying to process all that was happening. "Uh, uh, no, that's it, just one board. The other boards are still in the canister I have. I saw the other half, its twin, downslope where I was snowboarding."

"Just where is there?" asked Yeric, joining the conversation.

"Near a ridge around that big ranch. It's all snowed in now." Though alarmed, Sean remained reluctant to reveal all of his secrets.

Wade cracked his knuckles, "Listen, Sean, I can equip my people with gear to locate the rest of this package and ensure the radioactivity doesn't piss all over us. You take us there; we find the other part-we sell the entire package for you. Profits split about 50/50. We're talking over 400k large, divided by two. That's under the table and tax-free cash." Sean's mind was awash with a mix of trepidations and the sweet thought of big easy money.

Wade Keeler added, "Downside here: You run to the Feds and they won't give you a dime. Plus, they'll get wise to your other little enterprise of hawking stolen computer parts. Kid, you got few options. Work with us-just us, and you will be a rich boy."

Sean rubbed the back of his neck and grimaced; overwhelmed by the discussion. "Okay, okay I need to think on this. This is heavy stuff. Let me come back tomorrow." His thoughts spinning around the hazards he left in his sister's closet.

Keeler cast a quick glance over at Yeric and then back over to Sean. "Have it your way." He quickly stood up, walked over to Sean as if to shake his hand and then punched him in the face. Victor Rodin appeared from the backroom, reached behind Sean and plunged a syringe into his neck. Sean O'Hara gasped in pain and fell to the floor in convulsions. He was dead an instant later.

Yeric swore. "God damn it, how stupid. We could have gotten the directions from him. Now what?"

Wade Keeler watched as Rodin pulled the syringe from Sean's neck then spoke to Yeric. "We would have had to beat the shit out of the kid for information and then kill him anyway. We just saved time." Keeler checked the pack to make sure there were no more items or maps.

He turned to Rodin. "We need to make this mess disappear. I'll have my guys lose the body and the motorcycle."

Rodin nodded. "Yes, do it and then we can discuss our next steps."

Wade went outside and spoke on his cell. "Kenny, you and Mason have some work to do. Get over here and bring the truck with the lift gate." Wade stepped back in the office as Yeric and Rodin examined the circuit board. He stepped over Sean's lifeless body and pointed to the other office. "Let's talk in there. Guys will be here anytime to dispose of the kid and the bike."

Rodin smirked, "Wade, that was a very interesting story you told the boy. I almost believed it myself."

"Hell, I almost believed the bullshit too. Now, what's next? We got one board, and a photo of what the kid still has stashed somewhere."

Yeric shook his head, staring at Sean's body. "We could have made him talk first. Cherenkov will be angry."

"I will deal with Cherenkov. He will understand," said Rodin dismissively.

Wade raised his hand, hearing the front office door opened. "Hold it a second, my guys are here. I'll be right back."

Kenny Stovall looked at Sean's crumpled body. "What the fuck is this?" he said, chewing a wad of tobacco, more curious than disgusted. Stovall's 30 something year old thin build was characteristic of too much meth. He constantly pulled on his tangled dreadlocks of black greasy hair or nervously rubbed the unkempt Fu Manchu mustache. He could be mouthy with a mercurial and excitable personality. Though far from bright he followed instructions, if not a bit overzealously. Wade accepted the defects given the guy was loyal but had no problem with dirty work.

"It's a problem that needs to be removed tonight," said Wade. "You and Mason take the body and the motorcycle to Mosquito Ridge Road out of Forest Hill. It drops to the Middle Fork of the American River. There's missing guardrail near a 1500-foot cliff. Pour some booze down his throat and jam some meth in his backpack. Nobody will discover the body for days during this time of year."

"Yeah, no problem, Wade. Why not into the reservoir like the others?"

"Too many campers there right now. Plus, that could generate a missing person's report. Kid has friends, family or something. This way it will look like just another fuck-head teenager on a bike. Just be careful and wait until it's late." Another man, muscular with a shaved head, walked up but said nothing. "Hey, Mason," said Wade. "You and Kenny get this mess out of here and call me when you're done." Mason simply grunted out an acknowledgment.

"You got it man," Stovall said, putting on gloves as he and Mason dragged Sean's body out the door. Wade watched for a minute then walked back into the inner office.

Wade turned to Rodin and Yeric. "Okay, so what's the game plan? We got one circuit board and the photo of a busted canister. We need the entire system, the other parts. Exact location would be nice too. No easy job finding something like this in the mountains."

Rodin nodded. "True, but we now have an approximate area of where the device could be located."

Wade gazed out the window watching Mason and Kenny toss the body and bike onto the flatbed and cover them with a tarp. He looked back at Victor Rodin. "Getting into those mountains right now will be tough. But find the plane and maybe we locate the other part. This will take some time to plan and narrow things down. Until then, I can send Kenny and Mason up there in a snow-mobile for a quick look around. I'm thinking the kid might have been playing around the pass where the plane could have tried to get over. Without more directions it's a crap shoot. At least we can check out the conditions in the area. This is going to get expensive."

Rodin nodded. "You will be well-compensated for your efforts and silence. Money is no longer an obstacle. Moscow backs Cherenkov."

"Good to know. What follows now besides the recon trip?"

Yeric spoke up, "get the boy's address off his driver's license. I suggest we watch the house, and his friends and family. We may learn something more."

Rodin nodded his approval. "Yes, excellent idea." He turned to Wade. "Can you manage that as well?"

"Don't see why not? I'll scope out the kid's home."

Rodin looked at both men. "Cherenkov has made it clear. Apply the required means to accomplish this project. I will investigate other options, perhaps learn more about this vast ranch area which the airplane might have crashed on."

Wade Keeler chuckled, "Good luck with that. The owners of that ranch are pricks about trespassers. I hunt around there and know which roads and trails to use to stay out of sight. We have to be careful." Keeler cracked his knuckles again, "I heard a rumor they let nature freaks and movie companies hike and film in certain areas up there. Not sure how that works."

Rodin cocked his head processing what Keeler just said. "That's interesting. I will follow up on that. How do we contact them for permission, if we pretend to be, say nature freaks or film artists?"

"You might check with those people that run Sierra Puma winery in Auburn. I think there's a connection between the ranch and the winery, not sure. It's a busy place and they host lots of tree hugger seminars to the wine and cheese crowd."

"I will share that information with Cherenkov. Perhaps we can learn something or access the area under a cover of a legal pretense. Yeric, go back to the recycle center. Keep an eye out for any additional items that may show up and note the people who bring them in. I will come by with more information and tasks. Wade, let me know what your people discover both in the mountains and by watching the boy's house."

Yeric looked at Wade with concern. "The body and the bike, are you sure there won't be problems? Your men, they understand what to do, correct?"

"Come on, for Christ's sake. We've worked with Cherenkov for years on all of his business and disposal needs. We don't fuck up." He looked at Rodin. "Do we, Victor?"

Victor Rodin gave Keeler an icy grin. "No, you do not make mistakes. You understand the consequence of failure."

CHAPTER 7

MARCH
NEVADA CITY, CA

The woman strolled along the sidewalk, glimpsing in the windows of the shops that lined old town Nevada City. The cloudless day came with a chilly breeze, but the noonday sun felt warm on her shoulders. She dressed in style, but not opulently so. Her calf length high boots covered portions of her designer jeans and the white pullover sweater contrasted with her navy blue cut away blazer. She glanced around then quickly readjusted her sweater. She smiled, thinking how her husband loved to buy her clothes. However, his definition of form fitting sweaters differed from hers. As usual, she accepted the attire with an appreciative smile, then discreetly exchanged them for something that gave her breathing room.

She continued down the sloped street, admiring the quaint Victorian storefronts that displayed quilts, handcrafted jewelry and artwork, along with a host of other boutique shops. Her nose caught the enticing aroma of fresh-baked cinnamon rolls wafting from a bakery. *That's so tempting, but better not.* Now, as she crested over the 30-year-old mark, the effort to keep a flat stomach got harder. She walked away before her taste buds overwhelmed her discipline.

The woman reached her destination; a small establishment with the front windows filled with airplane models. The faded overhead sign read: PAC Aviation Models. She entered the shop through a squeaky door that jingled an old-fashioned bell. Her eyes filled with astonishment at the display counters filled with dozens of models; die cast metal, wood, plastic, still others in kit form. A variety of scale model military airplanes hung from the ceiling, and aviation posters and aeronautical memorabilia adorned the walls.

The proprietor stood behind the counter, preoccupied with a small model in his hands. He wore a woodworker's apron festooned with pencils and small tools. His weatherworn, wrinkled face spoke of a life outdoors. The half frame glasses tipped the end of his nose and his unkempt gray hair flopped over his forehead. She surmised the man had been a tradesman now in his late 70s.

"Excuse me," she said, when he didn't look up. Thinking the old guy hadn't heard her walk in.

The man glanced up from fiddling with the model. A startled look of bewilderment crossed his face. He squinted and studied the woman's luminous blue eyes and warm smile. He seemed stunned and flabbergasted. It took several seconds for him to answer. "Uh, uh, hello there. Can I help you find something?" he said, as if confused.

She approached the counter. "Hi, I called last week about a custom-made helicopter model."

The man stood transfixed, momentarily lost in thought, but regained his composure. "You did? Sorry, it's been busy, refresh this old man's memory."

If miffed, she didn't show it. She repeated herself. "Oh, okay. I called about buying a special model, not a metal or plastic one. A Mr. Greenwood said he could hand carve something unique and nice. And that I should come in and see his work."

The man smiled. "Well, I'm Cal Greenwood and yes, I recall that chat now. You wanted a helicopter with police markings on it, right?"

She grinned, her dimples showing on her cheeks. "There ya go. My name is Valerie Cahill. You said bring a picture of what I wanted."

"Got it. Step over here and take a gander at these, then we can decide if I can make something." Greenwood motioned her over to a cabinet. He reached in and handed her a finely carved model of a Cessna airplane. The detail was flawless.

"That's beautiful," Valerie said, holding the model as if were priceless. "You made this, and all of those?" pointing to the array of model airplanes.

"I did, young lady. Been a craftsman my entire life." He pointed to the model in her hands, explaining the features. "I make these of hardwood, it takes lots of time and patience. I get orders from corporations wanting models of the aircraft they use."

"Wow, I can see why. They're exquisite."

"And expensive. That's a four-hundred-dollar example in your hand." Greenwood waited for her to set the model down and say, "no thanks." She didn't bat an eye.

"Quality like this always comes with a price, Mr. Greenwood. But I wonder, though, can you carve a helicopter, as I don't see any here?"

"I do a few. Just sold one to a company that makes the actual machine. Let me see your photo. One thing, these projects take time, maybe two months. So, if you're in a rush then it won't work."

Valerie reached in her purse for the photo. "No rush as long as it's perfect, like what I see with all these."

Greenwood studied the photograph and smiled. "Well, this is a first. That's an LAPD chopper, an 'A-star' type. Did your husband fly for LAPD?" spotting the gold ring on her left hand.

"Yes, he did, but now he's kind of retired from the force." Valerie avoided details. Greenwood looked at the youthful woman, thinking the husband, if he was her age, must have left the force early.

"This helicopter must mean something to him," he said, examining the photo then casting a glance back at Valerie.

"I think it does. He isn't into memorabilia, but this whirlybird is special to both of us." She paused as a sly grin crossed her face. "We first met in that helicopter. He gave me a ride in it." She avoided the details of an adventurous flight across the southwest after they had met in a remote New Mexico airport.

Greenwood caught the twinkle in her eyes. "Sounds like an

impressive way to meet. And you want the same tail number on the model, N214LA?"

"Yes, that's special too. Make the model like the photo."

Cal Greenwood held up the photo, "May I keep this?"

"That's why I brought it in. Can you build one?"

"I can. But as I mentioned, it will take time." He scribbled down a price. "If you're comfortable with that, then half payment now and the rest when you see the work. Fair enough?"

Valerie looked at the estimate, filled out the rest of the form, then gave Greenwood some hundred-dollar bills. "That's fair to me."

"Here's my card, Ms. Cahill. Call me in a few weeks. Who knows, I might even finish this earlier."

"Great." Valerie extended her hand. "Thank you, Mr. Greenwood, it's been a pleasure."

"You bet and have an enjoyable day." Greenwood watched the woman leave the store, shaking his head in disbelief.

Valerie hustled back to her car as she looked at her cell phone, flipping through the half dozen texts. She exhaled as her shoulders sagged. As usual, she had a million things to accomplish at Sierra Puma winery. She jumped in the car and sped off, thinking about another hectic day.

CHAPTER 8

APRIL
PROMONTORY POINT
TIERRA DEL PUMA

A mutual trust existed between the horse and rider. Jake Cahill let Rustler, a black mustang with a white blaze on his face, find his own path up the steep, precarious slope. The sure-footed horse was very much at home on rugged terrain.

Within minutes they reached the summit, and the early morning carried a frosty bite. Jake turned up the collar of his heavy ranch jacket, then eased his solid six-foot frame off Rustler. He stretched his arms and rotated his shoulders to warm up. His breath steamed in the chilly alpine air. Jake pushed his sunglasses up over a ball cap stitched with the words, Tierra del Puma. His bright green eyes surveyed the snow-covered mountains that rose across the expansive valley. He gave a nod of satisfaction as he rubbed his chin, feeling two days of unshaven rubble on his tan complexion.

Jake reached in the saddlebag and pulled out a thermos of coffee. He slowly walked out to the promontory of rocks, passing the old fire ring where his ancestor, Nathan Cahill and first owner of the ranch had often camped, two centuries past. Growing up on Tierra del Puma, Jake Cahill also sensed a compulsion to visit the mountaintop. It was here, gazing upon the open space of valley and mountains that gave him a mental clarity; a quiet personal reflection. He perched himself on a boulder and caught the first warm touch of the morning sun. He poured a cup of coffee then let his eyes and thoughts absorb the majestic Sierra landscape.

Well, seasons in change, he thought. It had been a short but heavy winter with some wild storms. Snow still blanketed the peaks, and Teardrop Pass remained buried in white. Left of the Pass, Whispering Wind Mountain stood like a sentry over the valley. Jake silently took in the ancient volcanic peak as its jagged, familiar form triggered a flood of memories.

About a year and a half ago Jake had been a pilot for the LAPD and nearly killed, twice. He left the Department, but not without another violent encounter. Men from the company where his girlfriend Valerie Paige worked, had targeted her for murder. Surviving that fiasco, they left Los Angeles and moved to his late parents' ranch. Jake took another sip of coffee as he considered the other changes in his life. Valerie Paige, now Valerie Cahill had discovered an old diary, written by a pioneer girl named Rebecca Thorpe. Young Thorpe chronicled the treacherous wagon train crossing from Missouri to Sacramento back in the 1800s. The harsh and sad journey had taken them across Tierra del Puma. She wrote of two other girls in the pioneer group. They had formed a bond of friendship and called themselves the "Guardians of the Covered Carriage". And it was at that very mountain, where Jake now held his focus upon, where tragedy befell them. Thorpe had written about the trio exploring the mountain and discovering three small blue diamonds. But then they were trapped in a cave-in. According to the diary, Thorpe's two best friends sacrificed their lives so she could survive. Rebecca Thorpe concluded her journal by wishing that someday she could return to the mountain and spend eternity with her friends.

Through a myriad of coincidences and family generations those blue stones fell into Valerie's hands. From then on, she became overwhelmed with a sense of déjà vu and a pull to return to the mountain. It was as if the sparkle of the diamonds and the winds that tumbled down from the peaks were speaking to her. Valerie soon discovered she had a mystical kinship with Rebecca Thorpe and her friends.

Jake was away from the ranch when Valerie trudged up the unstable mountainside, driven by an inexplicable urge, a timeless sense of duty to deliver the spirit of Rebecca Thorpe to rest with her friends...175 years after the fact. Later, Valerie told Jake of hearing whispers of little girls within the wind, beckoning her upwards into a cave within the mountain. During her perilous ascent she was guided by a blue-eyed mountain lion, supposedly part of the ancient legend of Tierra del Puma, Land of the Cougar. It was unbelievable and unexplainable.

In the years growing up on the ranch, Jake never saw a blue-eyed cougar or any puma willing to be a tour guide. But he and everyone else on the ranch had heard eerie soft sounds mixed within the winds that swirled down from the mountain, so named, Whispering Wind. His late mother often said Tierra del Puma held secrets and where mysterious events occurred absent a logical explanation. It didn't matter whether his wife dreamed her adventure, or it happened. Valerie believed it and Jake accepted it, albeit a tad dubious.

Valerie loved the ranch and connected to it in a personal and powerful way. But she had wanted involvement in something of her own. She had taken the reins of running the Cahill winery, Sierra Puma, located in the western foothills of the Sierras. There she invested her energy and unique visions to expand the business. They soon realized the need for a second home closer by, one with Valerie's own signatures and desires. That was fine by Jake, though Tierra del Puma would always be his real home. Jake Cahill treasured his freedom of open space.

Jake often joked with friends that he and Valerie lived in a democratic household, but she always out voted him. Though far from the truth, Val damn sure had her own perspectives on things as she fast tracked herself to finish a multitude of projects. She had written a novel inspired by Rebecca Thorpe's diary. Hollywood connections from her acting days caught whiff of the novel's popularity and were spinning it into a movie, adding still more demands to her busy schedule. Jake wondered if her frequent absences from the ranch were the reason for his recent uncertain feelings. He had no complaints about their life together, but he sensed a change in Valerie, one that he couldn't explain. He shrugged his shoulders, accepting the fact he was overthinking an issue that didn't exist.

Jake wasn't just sitting on his ass watching life go by, either. Together with his Uncle Walt they had expanded the LA based air charter service to Sacramento; their planes and helicopters were busy with public service contracts. If Jake wasn't working the ranch, then he was airborne. Both Cahills stayed busy though often apart from one another. He glanced at his watch and tossed the last bit of coffee. *Cogitation is over. It's time to saddle up and get productive.*

From the promontory Jake rode to the ranch airstrip and spotted a California Highway Patrol helicopter parked on the tarmac next to the CG Aviation helicopter. Fire and law enforcement aircraft were always welcome at the Tierra del Puma private airstrip. The coffee was hot; fuel available and the bunkhouse open should the weather turn bad. The two officers walked from the helicopter as Jake approached the airfield fence.

He dismounted and spoke to Rustler, "Wait here." The horse turned, stared at Jake, then ambled away to a nearby meadow.

Steve Gavin, the pilot officer, overheard the dialogue between man and mustang. "Cahill, it's obvious neither one of you follow directions. Was he on the LAPD too?"

Years back, during the LA riots, Jake Cahill disobeyed a direct order by landing his helicopter in the street to rescue a couple getting beaten to death by a mob. Those heroic efforts were problematic as whispers of insubordination floated through the LAPD command staff. Steve Gavin got the story while assigned to the LA office during the riots. Later, when Jake resigned from the LAPD, Gavin transferred to the Highway Patrol's Auburn flight operations. The tall, thin officer flew off duty for CG Aviation along with other law enforcement pilots.

Gavin spoke before Jake could make a retort, "Jake, this is my partner Jerry Walker. Jerry, this is the infamous former LAPD pilot I warned you about."

Walker smiled, "So warned. Hi Jake," he said, extending his hand.

"Jerry, do yourself a favor and associate with a higher class of individuals." He turned to Gavin.

"So, did you land here to get a cup of coffee, fuel or to solicit money for the Highway Patrol Ball? Oh wait, I forgot you guys don't have balls!" Jake said, the edges of his mouth twitching.

"You know, Cahill. I would expect that remark from your smart-ass former partner, Logan. What happened to him anyway? I heard he moved up this way."

"Jeff quit the Department when I did. He invested in some fancy restaurants in California and Maui. Plus, he's a general contractor, builds custom homes."

Gavin shook his head. "That's sound like Jeff, enterprises all over the place."

"That's only half of it. He hooked up with my attorney, Natalie Sherwin, they're a couple and business partners living together over in Granite Bay. They have a beautiful home overlooking Folsom Lake."

"Poor woman must be desperate."

"Better to say poor Jeff, as Natalie keeps him on his toes. She doesn't suffer fools. Now they're into my affairs."

"How so?"

"Valerie expanded the winery. Wanted to make it a conference center to attract corporate meetings and organizations. Jeff designed and built the new complex and restaurant."

"Interesting, and how is your bride?"

"My crazy wife is busy and spending a lot of time at the winery. Drives like bat out of hell. She thinks the road sign that says 65 mph represents a minimum speed. I hope she learned a lesson after the last expensive ticket. I said on the next violation she be would be arrested, and I wouldn't spring her bail."

"Uh huh, that's big talk when you're not in front of Ms. Cahill." Gavin changed the subject and pointed to the CG aviation helicopter on the ramp. "What's the Bell 407 doing here with a searchlight and Forward-Looking Infrared system? I thought it was at McClellan Airfield?"

"It was but it's on lease to Treco Security Systems. Jack Treco had some commercial security contracts. We were flying night checks at various truck stops in the Reno area. Now, I'm using it to fly back and forth from the ranch to Sacramento until the contract renews or ends. By the way, you know of any off-duty pilots that can fly it if the contract fires up again?"

"I do, besides myself I can get a few guys for you. Can't beat the stipends, though working for a former LAPD pilot does carry some psychological risks," he said trying to hold a straight face. "You know, Jack's former FBI. He'll figure out you're over billing him on flight hours."

"Jack knows I inflated the lease time, but I gave him a good deal on block rates so we're even. He understands the concept even if he was in executive law enforcement and not street police work," Jake said with a chuckle. "So, what brings you to the ranch, besides to harass me?"

"We stopped by to drop off your stuff."

Jake raised his eyebrows, "My stuff?"

"Yeah, come on over to the aircraft. I have something to show you."

They walked over to the helicopter and Gavin pulled a piece of bent metal from the back seat. It appeared to be about 24 inches by 20 inches of riveted, twisted aluminum and beige plastic. The entire item looked beat up, as if ripped from its hinges.

Jake stared at it. "What the hell, it looks like a hatch, like a baggage door off a small plane. Where did it come from and why is it *my* stuff?" he said in a quizzical tone.

"One of our officers went cross-country skiing last week over near Tear Drop Pass. He spotted this thing sticking out of the snow. He checked the area and found nothing except this piece of busted aluminum. He figures it fell off of an ATV during the summer months, maybe part of a toolbox off one of your ranch vehicles. But as you know, the area is inaccessible right now unless you're on skis. He brought it by our hangar in Auburn. That's when we surmised it's a baggage door off some small plane." Gavin paused, "Look on the other side."

Jake flipped the part over and could see the vague imprint of a partial stencil that said, "CG Aviation."

"I'll be damn," he said. "That says CG Aviation, I think."

"That's what we figured. I assume the CG stands for Cahill-Gipe Aviation. You guys lose an aircraft or at least a baggage door?"

Jake looked perplexed staring at the damaged door. "That's our initials, but no lost aircraft. And we only operate King Air twins and helicopters, no small planes. This is a rear baggage door; maybe off a Cessna or Piper. Odd. Why the hell does it have our brand on it?"

"You tell me. We checked and there are no recent reports of missing planes around here. And no CG ships present, or past are missing, right?"

"No planes or pieces," said Jake, studying the baggage door. "He found this, where, again?"

"Around the slopes of Tear Drop Pass. I assume police officers still have permission to access that area to ski and hike. There's so much snow covering the ground it's impossible to say if it was on a road, slid down from the pass or what. There's been some avalanches in that area."

Jake nodded his head. "They do. But that area is risky and unstable in all seasons. Guys need to be careful." His eyes returned to the broken door. "Man, I don't get this one at all. Mind if I keep the part?"

"By all means that's why we brought it over. For the moment it appears to be your debris." He grew serious, "just glad it's not off one of your planes. And you have no ideas about it?"

"Not a clue. This is strange. I'll ask my uncle Walt about it. He ran CG Air years before I came along. Maybe he knows something. But I can't remember my Dad and Walt every owning a Cessna or Piper."

"It is a weird mystery of sorts. Okay, we have to aviate. Let me know what you discover."

"Yeah, will do." Jake smiled, "Jerry, keep your hands close to the controls. I don't think this guy really knows how to fly."

Gavin chuckled, "See ya Jake, go find your well-trained horse." Within minutes the aircraft departed. A gentle mountain breeze replaced the noisy sound of the helicopter. Jake tossed the baggage door in the back seat of the CG helicopter and sauntered towards the meadow where Rustler munched on grass. "Rustler, get over here." The horse looked up, then continued grazing. Jake shook his head in frustration, walked over and threw his leg over the saddle. "I'm going away for a couple days. You can hang with your buddies in the corral. Maybe they can teach you English."

An hour later Jake returned to the ranch airstrip and did a final preflight of the aircraft. Once buckled in, he flipped on the master switch, pressed several buttons and yelled, "Clear!" Jake never took his eyes off the instrument gauges as the turbine came alive and slowly spooled up its power. Within minutes the rotor blades were spinning. He checked the flight controls and the instruments, then did a quick outside scan. The helicopter was ready for flight. His hand applied a slight upward pressure to the collective, as he slowly depressed the left anti-torque pedal while simultaneously adjusting the cyclic. His smooth, subtle control inputs were second nature, honed by years of experience. With deliberate slowness the front of the skids lifted a few inches above the ground as the helicopter balanced on the heels of the rear skids. Jake held the ship motionless in that position. With another coordinated touch of the controls the helicopter now hovered two feet above the ground. He nudged the cyclic forward, allowing the aircraft to accelerate. Jake felt the exhilaration of flight as the aircraft sped over the green meadows. With a slight aft pressure on the cyclic and a smooth upward pull on the collective, the helicopter climbed skyward.

Jake watched the mountain scenery pass beneath the ship and thought about the baggage door and where the officer found it, near Tear Drop Pass. He looked southwest and saw that the only clouds in the blue sky had amassed at the Pass, obscuring the ridge and nearby Whispering Wind Mountain. There was no way to search for anything resembling parts of a plane, if in fact one was there. He climbed higher and headed westbound. He crossed over the mountains and felt the slight buffet of the wind that blew over the ridge.

Jake's original plan was to fly straight to McClellan Airport, but opted instead to spend the night at the Auburn house. By tomorrow, he would be back at the ranch, without Val, which seemed to be the norm these days. As of late, she spent more and more time at the winery working at a breakneck pace on projects, as if...? That feeling of uncertainly still lingered in the back of Jake's mind. "As if-what?" he said to himself, staring out the cockpit windscreen at the Sierra foothills. He wondered if Valerie's desire to live at the ranch had waned, despite her connection to it. Why, he didn't know. He was hesitant to broach the subject with her, and she never mentioned anything to him. Then she had called last night and said she couldn't come home but wanted him to attend tonight's meeting at the winery. That he recalled, was a pre-planning session for the upcoming gala event concerning the movie production based on her book. Jake dismissed his mental wanderings and returned his attention to flying. He scanned the sky for other aircraft traffic as he approached Sierra Puma Winery.

The hillsides of tidy rows of grapevines came into view. Beyond, on the wide green mesa lay the winery, the new conference center, and the restaurant; all with commanding views of the countryside. Perched on a hill, a scant distance from the complex, was their "other" house. The single story, Tuscany style home matched the motif of the other buildings. Between the house and winery was the helipad. Jake flew two orbits over the pad, executed his approach and landed. After securing the ship he noticed that the red golf cart; his wheels to the house, was missing from the pad. Val had it. With a sense of annoyance, he grabbed his bag and trekked up the hill.

Jake entered the house through what opened to a large great room. "Val you here?" Then he realized she was off somewhere taking care of some last-minute business. Jake shook his head in frustration, looking around the empty house. He sniffed his clothes. *Ugh, first things first.*

The hot shower felt invigorating and helped wash off Ode de Rustler, ranch life, and spilled helicopter fuel. He stepped from the shower, wrapped a towel around his waist and walked back to the master bedroom. He raised his eyebrows in surprise. Valerie lay on top of the bed wearing one of Jake's dress shirts; her long legs exposed from the waist down. She propped herself up on one elbow but said nothing. Her vivid blue eyes watched him approach the bed. Jake took a long delicious stare. He spoke in a serious tone, "That's my shirt you're wearing."

Valerie threw back a cavalier look. "So, take it back."

Jake dropped his towel and climbed in bed next to her. He slowly removed her shirt and pressed his body against hers. "We're going to be late for the meeting."

She wrapped her legs around his and whispered, "I hope so."

CHAPTER 9

Kenny Stovall jumped out of the pickup and ripped down a sign that said, "Private Property-No Trespassing." The black, dirt plastered, off-road truck pushed through the mud and grimy snow, towing a trailer with two snowmobiles.

"How far we goin' in before we see actual snow?" asked Mason, readjusting the wool cap over his shaved head. He snorted hard, cleared his throat with a loud gagging sound and spit out the window. Mason Reems looked older than his 35 years given a pockmarked unshaven face and several rotting front teeth. His short temper and tendency for violence got him prison time and a passion for tattoos.

"Not long," said Stovall, steering the truck over rocks and road muck. "Me and Wade have been up here before killin' bears. This road is rocky shit for miles, but we should hit good snow higher up. If we can't use the snowmobiles, we'll hike in, look around and say we checked the best we could" he said as he hit a large pothole, causing the truck to bounce.

"Just what the fuck are we lookin' for?" asked Mason surveying the wet and muddy forest. "I don't see nothing but trees and mud."

The pickup truck rocked back and forth as they drove further up the deeply rutted road. Kenny glanced in the rearview mirror to see if the trailer was still attached. "Wade said look for pieces of an airplane, maybe a metal briefcase with a metal canister in it. If we find the brief-case or canister then we grab it and get the fuck out of here."

"Oh yeah, a crashed airplane? And what's in this canister? We lookin' for stash or what?"

"Wade said it's something his Russian investors lost. He said an airplane crashed up here in the winter. It went down with their shit onboard. They want it back before anybody else finds it."

"Must be something to do with the dead kid we dumped off the road. Fuckin' Russians, I don't trust them-especially that Rodin guy. He thinks he's better than everybody else." Reems shook his head in disgust. "Always ordering us to do their dirty work."

"Don't sweat it, man. We're making big cash with benefits. Wade said if we finish this job then we can all retire in style and move on. Screw the stolen car racket and being go-fer's for those shithead commies. Wade will be back in a week and pay us more bucks. Even more, if we find something today. These guys want this thing really bad; big paydays headed our way."

Reems spit out the window again, "Yeah, maybe. What does your old lady say about all this?"

Kenny felt the truck stick in the mud and gunned the engine. The pick-up slid around until the wheels caught. "I don't tell her that much, only about our hunting trips. She's too fucked up on pills. I'm kickin' her ass out." He laughed, "She don't know that yet. I got another woman, a younger one."

"Yeah, get the young stuff. I always do. So, how far we goin' in this shit?"

Kenny pointed out front. "We're here. There's enough snow we can park the rig and use the snowmobiles just beyond the broken fence." Kenny turned the trailer around and backed up to the edge of the snow. "Let's unload. Take your piece, just in case."

"In case of what?" said Mason, sticking the gun in his jacket.

Kenny gave a nervous laugh. "For bears or pissed off property owners."

"Fuck them," said Reems, in a foul mood at being in the muddy snow instead of the warehouse chopping down cars.

They were busy pulling the snowmobiles off the trailer when Kenny looked up and saw two men approach on horseback. "Shit, who are these dudes?" He turned to Mason, "Stay quiet, I'll talk. Might be dumb ass ranch cowpokes."

Jake Cahill dismounted from Rustler and started towards the two men. The other wrangler, Eddie Rojas, stayed mounted. He ran his finger across his thick moustache and spoke quietly. "Careful Jake, they look like dirt bags." In a discreet move, Rojas touched the rifle stock in his saddle scabbard.

Jake stood at one end of the trailer, Kenny and Mason at the other, their hands not visible.

"Hey man, what can I do you for?" said Kenny, jumping on the trailer to unstrap the snowmobile. Mason stood silent, catching the tie-down tossed down by Kenny.

"You're on private property. You need to leave," said Jake authoritatively.

"Really, says who, dude? This is US forest. Private property starts on the other road down the hill. You're mistaken," said Kenny, trying to bluff with an arrogant voice. "You need to read your map better, cowboy."

Mason chimed with insolence. "Yeah, we're just heading out on snowmobiles. Go fuck with somebody else."

Cahill listened to the arrogant attitudes as his patience ran out. "You're on my property. Get your shit and split the same way you came in, past the 'Private Property' sign that you assholes ripped off the post and tossed along the side of the road," he said as irritation grew into anger.

"Or fuckin' what?" Mason said in a defiant tone, trying to stare down Jake.

Jake's stark green eyes bored into Mason's. "We can go two ways; you can leave, or I'll call the locals and have your gear impounded. And maybe you guys as well." Cahill felt an altercation coming and almost welcomed it.

"Fuck you, cowboy," said Mason, wiping his dripping nose.

Kenny mumbled to Mason. "Easy, that Mexican on the horse has a gun."

"Yeah, and fuck that Mexican and Mr. Sheriff. Nobody talks to me like that!" Mason yelled, spitting a wad of chew towards the men, trying to antagonize them into a fight. He reached in his jacket for his gun.

Kenny saw the red laser dot appear on Mason's chest. "What the fuck?" Eddie Rojas had his rifle pointed at Mason. Kenny yelled, "Hey, hey! That's assault with a deadly weapon, man! You can't threaten us like that!" Mason froze at the sight of the red dot making little circles on his chest.

Jake glued his eyes on Kenny. "When you get back to wherever you came from go file a police report. What's it going to be? You jerk-offs want a gunfight, or you want to pack it up and call it a day? I really don't give a shit at this point, but one way or another you're leaving." Cahill's voice resonated with a cold steel resolve, one that Kenny knew wasn't a bluff.

"All right, man, don't get so vicious. You're making a big fucking mistake, dude," said Kenny, securing the snowmobile straps. Mason still simmering for a fight, grunted and got in the pickup; the red laser dot following him. As they left, Kenny stuck his hand out and flipped off the two wranglers.

Eddie Rojas kept the rifle at port arms, watching the pickup and trailer leave. He turned to Jake, who pulled out his cell phone camera. "Jake, uh, kind of yanked their chains. Not like you to lose your cool. That could have gone sideways."

Jake Cahill said nothing; aware his temper had clouded his judgment. "I'm sick of assholes on my property. First, I had to deal with crooked developers, now these scumbags. Why the hell does everybody think they can trespass on the property?"

They rode side by side as Eddie spoke. "Those guys were ex-cons judging from the tats on that one guy's arms. These types will always push the limit. This state is overflowing with parolees and people who don't give a damn about others or their property. This ranch isn't immune to intruders anymore. Besides, cap a round at one of these guys and you go to jail. Like I say, this is California. For cryin' out loud, Jake, you were a cop, you know all that."

"Yeah, so it seems," said Jake, shaking his head, finally getting his anger under control. "But so help me God, these kind of people will learn the hard way you don't come to Tierra del Puma without an invitation." Eddie Rojas looked at Jake with a concerned expression. He let the words pass.

CHAPTER 10

MISS DEMEANOR BAR
TOWN OF GRAYHAWK,
NORTH OF TIERRA DEL PUMA

Tourists parked their cars in front of "Miss Demeanor," locals hitched their horses in back. The bar and eatery had been a Grayhawk icon for decades. As the community grew the historic pub became a trendy tourist and college student hang out. Fashioned after an old western saloon, "Miss Demeanor" got its name from the multitude of bar fights where people got arrested on misdemeanor charges. Few tourists knew the rowdy history or caught the double meaning. The owner, a true cowgirl named Sue, long ago recognized that the local ranchers needed their own pub. Located in the far back of the main saloon was a semiprivate bar marked "Mustangs and Bullshitters Only." Doug 'Gunny' Weston, a former marine sergeant and Director of Operations for Tierra del Puma, sat at the bar next to Eddie Rojas, the ramrod for Weston. Eddie retold the story of encountering the jerk snowmobilers.

Rojas took a sip of his brew. "Man, I think Jake wanted a fight."

Doug shook his head, "that sure doesn't sound like Jake. He nor his late father ever lost their cool." Weston looked over at Eddie. "Why were you guys up that way in the first place?"

"Jake got curious about that airplane part the highway patrol pilot brought by and Valerie's at the winery. I think he got bored and wanted to ride. And you're right, I never saw Jake get pissed like that dealing with trespassers." Eddie took another good swig of beer and wiped the froth off of his mustache. "It got edgy, Doug. I had to pull out my rifle and red dot one guy. They weren't your basic dumb ass trespassers. Both copped an attitude."

"Did Jake have a piece?"

"Oh yeah, had it in his waistband. Thought for a second he was going for it. That's why I tried to neutralize things by pulling out the rifle. What's with Jake, he's gotten a little temperamental recently?"

Doug shook his head in disbelief, then raised his hand and signaled to the bartender for two more drafts. "I don't know, Eddie, he seems distracted lately. Maybe he's tired of sleeping alone at the ranch. Valerie's spending a helluva lot of time down at the winery and the Auburn house."

Eddie glanced over at Doug and spoke in a low tone. "Oh man, they aren't having issues, are they? I mean, she isn't playing around or tired of living on the ranch, is she?"

Doug chuckled at that one. "Naw, I doubt that. And make no mistake, she's part of this place. My mystical wife affirms that point. I don't know how, and I don't ask. That said, Valerie seems hell bent on completing projects at the winery. And she's got her book that's going to be made into a movie. Which reminds me, Hollywood will be up here filming this year." Weston sipped his beer. "Yep, the woman is at a pony express full gallop."

"Great, Hollywood is coming," Eddie said with sarcasm, staring at his beer glass. He looked up at Weston. "I agree with your wife about Valerie being connected to Tierra del Puma in weird ways. Your Maria and her family have been on the ranch for generations- they know things that we can't comprehend. Listen to her amigo, she knows better than us."

"Rojas, for a young single guy you act reasonably intelligent."

"That's obvious and why I never joined your Marine Corps. Plus, I couldn't have joined, anyway."

"Shit, here it comes, why?"

Rojas pushed his cap back on his head and said with a straight face, "my parents were married."

Doug gave a guffaw. "You're a sick bastard to say that to your boss. But you and Maria are right. That young lady is wired to the history of this place."

Rojas rubbed his chin. "Yeah," he said thoughtfully. "She and those whispering winds. Doug, you ever listen to those breezes when you're out riding with her? They really do sound like murmurs of little kids, as if speaking to her. And Valerie just smiles and nods as if she understands what's being said." Rojas finished the last of his beer. "She has a sixth sense of something that's beyond my understanding. That said, why is Jake so on edge about things these days?"

Doug grabbed a pretzel from the bowl. "I think he's lonely, misses her." He shook his head. "Ah hell, I don't know. Maybe he's just restless. Jake's always been that way. Plus, trespassers don't help given all the crap that went on in LA with some developer trying to yank the ranch. Then that poaching problem popped up last year, and now some missing airplane might be on the property. You know Jake; he wants to keep Tierra del Puma *very* private and wide open." Weston chuckled, "he needs his personal space, all 40,000 plus acres of it."

"Restless-why? He's got an outstanding woman and Tierra del Puma. What else could a man want?"

"For starters, how about two wranglers who won't sit here and get so drunk they'll fall out of their saddles going home?"

"Too late for that," Rojas raised his glass and called the owner-bartender, "Sue-another round for the ugly Marine and this good-looking cowboy."

CHAPTER 11

RAVINE MOBILE HOME PARK
LINCOLIN, CA

Amber Gaynor washed the two pills down with a gulp of vodka and orange juice. She lit another cigarette and sat back in the overstuffed chair staring at her phone. Her shaky fingers swiped through the listed websites. She stopped at the Department of Fish and Wildlife home page and read the instructions. It said she could download a form or leave an anonymous voice mail. Amber exhaled more blue smoke and tapped her foot nervously, deciding on whether to call the number. She wanted to speak to an actual person about the thousand-dollar reward. She needed the money and wanted to make sure Kenny would suffer. It was time to get even with the bastard.

Amber stared at the smoke-stained celling of the cluttered double-wide trailer. "Fucking jerk," she said out loud. She ran her fingers through her short blonde hair then rubbed her cheek where he had slapped her last night, while in a fit of rage. The bruises on her arms were hard to see because of the tattoos. She felt older than her 40 years, mostly because of the pills and drugs. But those were needed to roll through the day, especially living with asshole Kenny. Shacking with him had become too much. It was always something. If he wasn't high, then he disappeared for days, hunting and working for those other assholes; Wade and that creep Mason. She knew they were into illegal shit but had kept her mouth shut, until now.

When she moved in, Kenny promised that with his job and connections, they would live large with more money and supply to enjoy life. That lasted for a while. Lately, however, he spent more time gone. And when home he was constantly paranoid and agitated; always afraid of being ripped off. Last night broke the final straw. When she bitched about him screwing the woman in the trailer park, he threw a fit and slapped her around, accusing her of spying on him. She threatened to call the police. He laughed, telling her they would take her to jail, given her warrants and meth addiction. "Call the cops, see if I fuckin' care. I own the trailer, you bitch," he yelled. Then it went really to shit. Amber screamed back, saying she would tell the cops about his poaching business with his freak pals. That's when he blew up and smacked her again. He hissed, "you mention that and Wade and me will put a chain around your neck and drop your ass in a lake. Don't even think about it bitch-don't ever." His crazy eyes burned right through her; the threat so deep she thought he was going to kill her on the spot. He grabbed another beer and stormed out of the house and left for the night. Probably to be with his young squeeze, she thought.

Amber considered herself a former dancer, an artist on a pole. They had met at a gentlemen's club in Reno. He seemed okay at first; had money and drugs, a real rebel who bragged he worked for the right people. That was then, now things had changed. She didn't need Kenny's crazy macho man violence or lack of respect. She had to get out. She would split, get her dancing job back at the Reno Gentlemen's Club and find another man. All she needed was cash and the taste of revenge before she left. She took another slow puff on her smoke and dialed the number. After a series of button punching through unwanted selections, she got a person who transferred her again to another person, this time to a pleasant-sounding older man. "Davis, can I help you?" said the calm male voice.

"Yeah, I told the other operator I wanted to talk to somebody about reporting illegal poaching. I read on the website I can get a thousand-dollar reward."

"That's possible based on the case. Did you want to discuss this, or would you be more comfortable making an anonymous report? We have a system for that, forms and voice mail."

She stammered, not sure what to do next. Kenny's cold death threats echoed in her drugged-up brain. "Uh, can I still get a reward if I do that?"

"Maybe. It's based on the violation and crime. Did you still want to talk? What type of poaching are you speaking about?" asked the man, sounding interested.

Amber hesitated, as images flashed in her head of Kenny and Wade tossing her into the icy black waters of a reservoir. "Uh, bears, he and his buddies kill bears for their guts or something. They sell them to some foreign guys, I think, but I'm not sure. How do I get the reward?" she said apprehensively, as fear of Kenny's threats created second thoughts.

"Would you want to provide names or details? We can't promise a reward based on sketchy information."

Amber felt more trepidation as her hands trembled thinking what would happen if Kenny found out that she had made this call.

"I'm not sure now. He, uh drives a black pickup truck, some type of weird off-road thing, all jacked up, big tires. They go up in the foothills. They hide stuff at the quarry outside Lincoln, I think." She paused. "I'm not sure now maybe I'm wrong." *This is a fucking terrible idea. Kenny could kill me.*

"Ma'am can you be more specific with a license on the vehicle, or a name. How are you aware of this? Do you know the people or see something?"

"Uh, kind of, he lives with me at the mobile home park in Lincoln." She stuttered, "I, uh, I better not give you the name. No, not a good idea." she said, her voice filled with apprehension. *I should hang up, but I need the money.* "Do I get the thousand bucks if I just give you the name?"

"No, but after an investigation that leads to an arrest and conviction then perhaps, we can work something out."

"Oh crap, you mean I have to go to court?" she said with a trembling voice.

"No, that's unnecessary. However, we do need more information. Can you refresh your memory and tell me something more than just a black pickup truck? I can assure you this is all confidential. Your name will not be mentioned."

Amber glanced out the trailer window just as Kenny drove up. *Oh fuck!* "No, I changed my mind. Just forget it, I'm wrong." She hung up and nervously reached for another cigarette, lighting it with the one already in her mouth. She heard Kenny walking up the steps and shuddered. The escape plan of going back to Reno vaporized.

CHAPTER 12

Wade Keeler turned off the old Lincoln Highway and then made a left on a dirt road. The big crew cab dually truck kicked up dust as it headed to the entrance of Lincoln Gravel Company. He reached the compound bordered by a high chain-link fence with razor wire. Behind the perimeter several gravel haulers were being loaded with sand and rocks. Off to the left, other big rigs were topping off with discounted fuel. Cheap non-taxable diesel was another of Nikolai Cherenkov's gray area businesses. Keeler admitted to himself that partnering with the Russians was profitable but deadly if one strayed from their principles of loyalty and business.

Kenny Stovall met Wade at the gate. Wade rolled down the window. "What's up?" he said, eyeing the activity in the yard.

"Busy, no issues," Stovall said, chewing a wad of tobacco. "Trucks in and out and we're pumping lots of diesel fuel. Chop shop is busy too."

Wade surveyed the bustle as Kenny spoke again. "The Russians are here, Rodin and that heavyweight guy, Cherenkov. They're in the back in your office."

"Okay. I've been out of town. How did your little recon snowmobile trip go?"

Kenny spit out a wad of chew. "I got a little busy too, but there's nothin' to report. Got jacked up near a section of Lower Pass Road by two cowboys claiming to be ranch security."

Wade twisted a toothpick in his mouth. "Is that so, any problems?"

Kenny hesitated, then hedged the truth. "Nope, we played it cool; apologized and split. We didn't get a chance to check around. The snow is melting fast but there's lots of mud."

Wade nodded, curious why ranch people were snooping so far up in the mountain passes. "No big deal, there's other roads we can access. We'll sneak back later. Let me see what our Russian associates want. For now, you and Mason keep your mouths shut around the rest of the crews. And keep the gate closed except for known customers. We don't need visitors to show up while our friends are here."

"You got it, boss."

Wade drove to the back of the quarry to a set of large interconnected construction shacks that served as his office and storage center for his other activities. He saw the black Mercedes parked in front as he entered the front door. Cherenkov and Victor were inside, staring at the heads of animals mounted on the office walls. Cherenkov turned. "Ah, Wade, we were early, I hope you don't mind."

"No problem," aware he had no control of their actions and wants.

"We were admiring your trophy collection. Impressive. A taxidermist's paradise. Your game hunting is a profitable industry these days, replete with mementos."

Wade grunted, "especially bear hunting. Thanks to your export connections it's been a lucrative pastime."

Cherenkov looked at Wade, "Yes, for both of us." He motioned to the table, "Here, let us sit and talk about other things. How did your man's reconnaissance trip go?"

"Nothing gained. They ran into crappy snow and some horseback riders near Lower Pass Road. They had to blow off the snowmobile search. But now we know the conditions up there. We'll need more time for things to dry up, but I know other roads to use."

"What about those riders?" said Rodin, his voice carrying a concern.

Wade leaned back in his chair, "Kenny said they were from the ranch. Probably checking the fence lines after the winter. That's not unusual, but we need to be careful driving around up there, if that's where we think the airplane or thing is."

Cherenkov held up a map. "We have access to satellite data from our overseas client. Victor, show him the tracks."

Rodin unrolled the chart on the table and pointed to an area circled in red. "It is our opinion the plane is somewhere in this area."

Wade whistled, looking at the marked area. "So that's how you figured it out. Man, that's a sizeable piece of real estate. If the plane broke up in a storm, then pieces would scatter all over hell. Some of those winter storms have gale force winds that blow east. Christ, debris could by everywhere and anywhere. Not just where we tried to search."

Rodin went on. "True, but if you recall, the boy spoke of snowboarding. We presume he might have played near this ridge called Tear Drop Pass given there are access points from the other side." He ran his fingers over the map lines that showed steep rugged terrain. "We think somewhere in here. Either on the forestry side or in this area," he said, pointing to the private property. "If they crashed or came apart near that Pass, then as you mentioned, those winds blew the airplane and package east onto that ranch."

Wade gave a nod of concurrence. "That's the ranch I mentioned, called Tierra del Puma, some 40,000 acres plus with back country. I know the area given I sometimes hunt there on the sly. A conservancy surrounds the ranch. No hunting there either, but I sneak in. Like I mentioned, Kenny and I know all the roads and trails around there. But we have to narrow this search area down, way down. That's a helluva lot of backcountry."

Cherenkov stroked his goatee, "Yes, we will need to define the search area better. However, between what the boy alluded to and this satellite track, our first option is to examine this Tear Drop Pass more closely. Can you access it again without attention?"

"Never bumped into the ranch people before. Kenny's encounter was a fluke, bad timing. As he said, it's kind of shitty up there right now but drying out. The best way of getting in there is working through a maze of forestry roads from the west then down onto Lower Pass Road at the base of the Pass. The snow is melting fast but that can change if we get late season weather."

Cherenkov shifted his gaze to Wade as Victor rolled up the map. "It must be found before others blunder upon it. With melting snow that becomes a strong possibility. So far, we believe no agencies are aware we used an aircraft for transportation. However, that could quickly change."

Wade took the map from Victor. "I assume you want me to go back sooner than later, if I can get into that specific area. I can handle it better as the weather warms up."

Cherenkov spoke to both men. "I have done some research based on what Wade said previously. There might be other options to secure permission to search the area. A man and wife own Tierra del Puma and this Sierra Puma Winery. The winery, as you mentioned, is in Auburn. It is a trendy place. You were correct Wade; they cater to various outdoor groups and host seminars on backcountry activities."

"And how does that help the cause?" said Wade, scratching his chin.

Cherenkov smiled, "We plan to visit the winery, perhaps join their private members-only club and attend some seminars. We might learn when the ranch will allow tours." He raised his index finger. "However, from what I understand, they permit limited access to production companies to film scenic shots for movies and commercials. Victor will approach the owner pretending we are an overseas production company seeking permission to make a documentary about this famous section of the Sierra."

Wade Keeler looked baffled. "What do you mean famous? These are friggin' mountains, not the pyramids of Egypt."

Cherenkov chuckled, "Wade, you must read more books. The ranch owner's wife, the CEO of the winery, wrote a book about pioneer women crossing the famed High Sierra in this area. It is very popular. It seems women find this story, 'Guardians of the Covered Carriage,' spellbinding."

"I don't read books-especially chick novels. But I see your angle. You want to snag permission so we can search the place under a legal pretense, right?"

"Yes, but we must prepare alternate plans regardless of securing authorization. That requires your resources and expertise. Victor can assist on continued surveillance of the O'Hara family to determine if the boy shared his discovery. Yeric said he had police encounters and dealt in stolen computer parts. Given that, I do not think he ran to Momma and told his story. But we must be sure."

Victor cut in. "We will need more manpower to do this. Wade, can your people handle this as well?"

"That won't be a problem. But then you'll need people to cover our other operations, the chop shop and the diesel fuel sales. Kenny, Mason and I can cover the search and surveillance."

Victor got a nod from Cherenkov, then spoke, "That will not be an issue. I will visit the winery and also be available to help on other matters. We need to stay in close contact. We will access that land one way or another."

"Yes, we will" said Cherenkov. "It's best we start as soon as possible." He stood up to signify the meeting had concluded. "I must emphasize, apply any means to accomplish this but do not expose or compromise us." Cherenkov eyes grew cold. "People who should not know things must not talk."

The men walked towards the door when Cherenkov placed his hand on Wade's shoulder. "Wade, perhaps some of your fellow hunters have interest in one of our latest international investment endeavors- safari adventures and youthful female escorts. I'm sure rugged men of their caliber would enjoy such travels. It is what you say, a stag adventure." He smiled, "All at a discount."

Wade Keeler returned the smile. "After this project, I might take the trip myself."

"Excellent idea. Keep in touch. Contact me through Victor."

Wade Keeler watched the men drive away and grimaced as he touched his face. The pain was back. He rummaged through the cluttered desk for a bottle of pain killers. Over-the-counter meds were useless against the deep scar etched along his cheek. He swallowed two pills and washed them down with cold coffee. It was a routine done for years that came with angry memories.

Keeler had a throw away childhood with no parental guidance. His parents were divorced. He lived mostly with his old man who didn't give a shit about kids, given his interest in stolen cars. He taught Wade that business, but not much else. Wade failed most of his high school classes but excelled as an intimidator with a reputation to organize ruffians and hoods for illegal adventures. After one too many brushes with the law, Wade left the neighborhood. He joined the Army and soon discovered a talent for working the system. His success as an entrepreneur blossomed when he got assigned to supply. It wasn't long before Sergeant Keeler gained a unique position to discreetly sell government property to a group of civilians interested in everything from ammo to uniforms. He worked the scheme, made good money, and cultivated connections that would serve him well when he left the service. Keeler was shrewd and knew how to cover his tracks, or so he thought.

Things blew apart when a snoopy lieutenant with her uppity, academy ring attitude took her job too serious. Accusations were made and evidence fabricated that pointed to Sergeant Keeler being a crook. Keeler's commanding officer, who's star was on the rise, somehow got vindicated of everything, even the failure to complete standard audits. The system protected the academy boys and girls. But Wade Keeler, ever the savvy and shady businessman had concealed his investment program well. His shifty entanglements were never proven. Instead, he got transferred and busted in rank. With every shot of booze his hatred grew towards the snotty young officer who ruined his underground portfolio and career. Keeler found out she wasn't done fucking up his life.

One-night Wade sat off post in a bar when he spotted the lieutenant and her wimpy boyfriend sitting at a nearby table. Keeler's drunkenness manifested into anger. He stumbled over and told the woman she was a piece of shit for what she had done to him. When her boyfriend stood up to defend his girlfriend's honor, Keeler simply pushed the dumb fuck millennial to the floor. Wade turned around just as the whore lieutenant broke a bottle and shoved it in the side of his face. Keeler went to the hospital and ended up scarred for life. Politics and the system once again prevailed. The officer and her boyfriend were the victims, said the cops when they turned Wade over to the military. Keeler got kicked out of the service with a bad conduct discharge. There were no veteran benefits or "thank you for your service" comments for the bitter Wade Keeler.

Civilian Keeler reconnected with his former client of contraband. They respected his silence not to implicate them in the scandal that cost Wade his stripes, job, and face. He had been tested, they said, and demonstrated faithful adherence to the rigid Code of Thieves. The Russian organization became his new employer. They provided a bonus because of his loyalty and keen ability to manage their illegal businesses. Several months later Keeler learned that the bitch lieutenant and her cocky ass boyfriend were killed in a hit and run accident. That gift of revenge came with an obligation to do whatever the Russians wanted. Wade rubbed the scar of his disfigured face. He thought of the woman at the warehouse that skimmed profits at the quarry, and the kid Sean that had tried to play him for a sucker. Both got what they deserved. Keeler's revulsion toward betrayal ran deeper than any physical wound.

CHAPTER 13

N atalie Sherwin sat at the large dining table dressed in workout pants and a sweatshirt with the words 'Stanford' embossed across the front. Her long blonde hair, parted down the middle, was pulled into a ponytail. Her fingers ran lightning quick across the laptop keyboard as she stared at the computer screen, thinking of the research needed before work today. She paused from her work and stared out the bay window. Natalie nudged over 30, holding a tall and athletic figure. Her close friends kidded her about resembling a model for Surfer Magazine. Appearances notwithstanding, her intellectual acuity and clarity said 'lawyer.' Natalie Sherwin was an attorney for the prestigious law firm of Sherwin and Barer. *That* Sherwin was her father, Robert. The law was a passion with Natalie, having decided on the profession at the age of 10 years old. Throughout her life men came and went. None of them ultimately could handle her often razor-sharp wit and her focused preoccupation for law. She sipped the bold breakfast tea, enjoying the panoramic view of Folsom Lake, when her eye caught the figure of a man jogging back up the long driveway to the house. Watching him huff and puff up the steep incline gave her a moment of reflection. She had finally met a man who made her realize there was more in life than just the practice of law. *Such strange karma* she thought, considering how they had met.

Jeff Logan, or Jeffery as she called him, was her "fake" brother's best friend and former flying partner on the LAPD. Her so-called fake brother, a forever friend and legal client, was Jake Cahill. Both he and Natalie were only children and their parents; the Cahill family and Sherwin's were close friends. Generations of Sherwin's had represented generations of Cahills and their investments, including the legacy ranch Tierra del Puma, the Sierra Puma Winery and CG Aviation charter service. The parents hoped Jake and Natalie would become a couple, but the romantic attraction didn't exist. However, a close friendship developed between them at a young age. That created what Natalie coined as "fake" brother and sister. The bond became stronger when Jake's parents died in an auto accident, leaving Jake the unprepared sole heir of family investments. Natalie, now an attorney and close friend, represented Jake on legal matters and shared personal perspectives about life.

Natalie had bumped into Officer Logan at the hospital when Jake was recovering from a sniper's bullet. Their first encounter was marked by an instant polarization of personalities. Yet, amazing as it could be, something clicked between the two. Beneath a facade of sarcastic toughness lay a chemistry that developed into a relationship. Jeff Logan quit the LAPD when Jake did. He and Natalie bought a house together in Granite Bay, near Sacramento. Jeff stayed busy designing custom homes and investing in restaurants in California and Hawaii. Natalie continued with the law firm and handled all the legal ends of their combined business ventures. They were close by to their best friends, Jake and Valerie, now Mr. and Mrs. Cahill. Natalie watched Jeffery finish his run, pondering what the future held for Mr. Logan and Ms. Sherwin.

Minutes later Jeff walked in the dining room, out of breath, toweling his face and short blonde hair. His 6-foot physique spoke of a discipline for exercise. Both he and Natalie enjoyed the outdoors which for Jeff meant surfing in Hawaii during their business visits. He bent over and kissed her cheek. Natalie feigned a dodge. "Jeffery, you stink and are sweating all over me."

"Small price to pay to live with an athlete," he said, draping the towel around his neck.

"Give me a break," she said, touching his hand with hers. "You are so full of shit. You sound like Jake."

"Ah, the great men that we are."

"Only because you have superb women who guide you through life," she retorted.

"I might concede that one counselor," he said, kissing the top of her head. "I thought you would be at the law firm today?"

"Not today. It's fieldwork, pro-bono stuff. Going out to Roseville to assist a lady in need of legal assistance."

"Pro-bono work? What's gotten into you? You're Jake's fake sister and you charge him for your services. Is that just to compensate for this freebie legal stuff?" Jeff waited for the typical acerbic reply.

"Jeffery, the time I spend dealing with Jake's issues has gone far beyond billing. Thankfully, he married Valerie. Poor woman, I don't know how she does it? That has to be genuine love."

"Too bad ole' Jake isn't more like me, problem free and emotionally stable. Is that what you're saying?" Jeff said, holding back a grin.

"Oh God, one of you in the world is sufficient. And you are NOT normal."

"Natalie, may I remind you, the term 'normal' is a setting on a washing machine. That said, this unstable person has to drive out to the winery today to inspect the last touches on my renovations to their restaurant and conference center. You want to meet me there? We can have a drink with Val and Jake, if he's there? And I guess we better set a date to visit the ranch in the next few weeks. That should be marvelous fun smelling horses," he said sarcastically. Logan preferred water over horse ranches.

"I'm not sure when I'll finish this meeting, but I'll text you when I get done. Jeffery, you'll enjoy riding mustangs and hiking the high country. You owe it to Jake to see the ranch."

"If you say so, but a cowboy I'm not." Jeff looked over her shoulder and peeked at her laptop. "What's the case, if you can talk about it?"

"It's a single mom with some serious financial issues along with aggressive bill collectors and landlord. She called the Firm unaware of the cost of legal services. But my Dad and his partner are believers in helping those in genuine need. She fits the profile, and I got the case. Hopefully, I can get her some relief from the creditors."

Jeff bent down and kissed her on the cheek. "Nat, you're a wonderful person despite being an attorney and what others say about you," he said drolly.

"Wow, thank you for that vote of confidence," she said, rolling her eyes.

"I'm going up to take a shower and then hit the road. Say goodbye before you go." He turned and headed up the stairs. In a few moments Nat heard the shower running. A wicked thought flashed in her mind. She headed up the stairs, tossing off her clothes with each step.

Two hours later Natalie arrived at the Roseville Business Center where she had rented an office suite for several hours. It was a compact space with a desk, two chairs complete with a view of the parking lot. Known for her impeccably stylish attire, Natalie opted to dress down today, wearing plain blue designer jeans and a peach colored shirt. She was scribbling notes on a yellow legal pad when a woman tapped on the open door. "Excuse me, are you Ms. Sherwin?" she asked with a shy, uncertain tone, as if intruding.

Natalie stood and walked over to the woman and shook her hand. "I am and you're Ms. O'Hara, correct?"

The woman gave a nervous smile, "It's Nancy, I'm sorry if you had to drive all the way from Sacramento. It's just I have to get back to work in Lincoln after this meeting."

"It's not a problem at all. That's why I chose this place. Please, have a seat, can I get you a cup of coffee or something before we start?"

"Oh no, I'm fine. Thank you anyway."

Natalie, a quick study of people, looked at Nancy O'Hara and concluded the lady was embarrassed about sharing her problems with an outsider. She had short red hair with a tired-looking face and weary gray eyes. Natalie deduced the O'Hara woman was in her 50s and worn down in life by a multitude of trials and tribulations but attempted to conceal her desperations with a positive attitude and a smile.

"Ms. O'Hara, I looked at the notes you gave us. I need more details, if you don't mind?"

Sensing the woman's discomfort at discussing personal financial matters, she added, "Nancy, this is an attorney-client relationship. Our conversations are confidential. Understand?"

"I understand." She reached in her old purse, pulled out a roll of dollars. "It's only 150 dollars. I know Sherwin and Barer want something down. I can pay more later."

Natalie gently pushed the money back to her. "Ms. O Hara that isn't necessary. Let's see if we can resolve your legal concerns. Okay?"

Nancy O'Hara breathed a sigh of relief, knowing the money meant groceries on the table. "Thank you."

"Tell me, in your words what I can help you with."

"Ms. Sherwin, I'm a single mom. Been that way for a long time. Years ago, my former husband left us, ran out, ran away, and then got arrested for drugs and attempted murder in Texas." She hesitated. "He wasn't a pleasant man, an alcoholic drug user who got physical with me and the kids. Then he vanished. There was no alimony or spousal support, just bills."

"And he's still in prison?" said Natalie scribbling notes on the legal pad, silently hoping the loser, wife-child beater got Texas fried in the chair.

"I assume so. We never communicated. I received a letter from the prison system saying they denied him parole and sentenced him for life. That was years ago. I've been working two jobs to make ends meet; one at the market and the other as a waitress. My son Sean is..." She blinked her eyes several times to fight back tears. "He had just turned 21, lived at home, had part-time jobs that helped with the bills. He got killed last month in a solo motorcycle accident. The police said it was alcohol and drug related. I don't understand.

Sean wasn't like that." She looked at Natalie and sniffed. "I'm sorry to ramble, it's difficult to accept this."

Nat swallowed hard, attempting to remain professional and not let her emotions interfere with the job at hand. "Nancy, these things are tough, nor do they just go away."

Nancy O'Hara blotted a tear away and continued. "I have a daughter, Jessie, she's 19 and isn't taking this very well. She and Sean were close. She has always been a quiet girl, not a lot of friends. Now without her brother it's gotten worse, she's really withdrawn."

"It must be difficult for both of you. Ms. O'Hara."

"It's very hard, but we can get through it. What makes it harder are the ever-increasing financial burdens of medical bills, rent increases and just trying to keep food and clothes in the house. The landlord isn't the most understanding person in the world. Now my hours are cut back at the restaurant. I was hoping you could ask these bill collectors to allow me some flexibility. I can pay, but I just need more time. Jessie wants to work if she can find a job. That will help too."

"Did you bring some utility bills and letters from creditors and landlord? If not, I can give you a form to fill out or I can run down the information." Natalie wrote more notes on her legal pad.

Nancy O'Hara reached in her purse and pulled out a stack of invoices and letters wrapped in a rubber band. "They keep coming like the phone calls. It's never ending."

Natalie accepted the overdue bills "I'll get on this, Ms. O'Hara. We'll get these companies and the landlord to provide some extra time or a payment plan." Nat thought about the contingency fund that her Dad created to help people like Nancy O'Hara through tough times. The law firm paid the bills and then adjusted the client's invoice with a note that said, PAID. Natalie saw this case as one that needed that special attention.

"Ms. O'Hara, did you say your daughter was looking for a job?"

"She wants to, but lost motivation. It's been a bad few months even before we lost Sean. Money and things are tight. She spends so much time alone now. But she's smart and willing to work," Nancy O'Hara said, trying to put on an upbeat spin about her daughter.

Natalie listened, tapping the end of her pencil against her teeth, thinking. *Sounds like serious teenage depression. I can't dismiss this dynamic.* A thought bubble appeared in her mind-the Cahills.

"Ms. O'Hara what does your daughter like to do, does she have any work experience?"

"She helps at the restaurant with kitchen cleanup and some-times works the register. She's good with numbers and comput-ers. Oh, she's a skilled artist, does sketches of horses. She even took riding lessons a long time ago." O'Hara paused as a sadness crossed her face. "When there was some money to do that. It was a Christmas present from her brother, Sean."

Nat wrote the information down. "That's good to know. I have some friends that own the Sierra Puma Winery in Auburn and the Tierra del Puma Ranch north of Truckee. They hire seasonal help; people to work around the vineyards. Some kids, 18 and over, can take part in the wrangler program. That's where they spend weeks at the ranch working with horses and outdoor projects. They stay in dorms. The owners run the program under strict mandates."

Nancy O'Hara's face lit up. "Jessie would love that; ranch for sure, but also anything at the vineyard. Is it possible to get her a job?"

"I'll check and get back to you. They support programs for young people. Give me Jessie's information, full name, birthdate, social security number and whatever you can provide. I'll pass that along. Ms. O'Hara does Jessie have any criminal record or issues the owners should know about?"

Nancy O'Hara scribbled down all of her daughter's information on the legal tablet. "No, Jessie's never been in trouble. She doesn't do drugs or smoke. She has her driver's license, but no car. But I can drive her to the winery, I know where that is. If she gets a job, maybe she can carpool with someone." She hesitated, "I can't loan her the car, I need it. So that might be an issue."

"Let's not worry about that right now. First, we take care of the bills. That will happen as soon as I get back to the office. I'll en-quire about a job for Jessie and get back to you as soon as possible.

However, discuss the idea with your daughter to make sure she's agreeable to this. She must take an interview. The owners don't believe in the online application processes. They're big on meeting face to face. Working for these people is fun with good pay, but they expect integrity, tenacity, and a full day's effort. That said, there's a waiting list for these jobs."

Nancy O'Hara exhaled a sign of relief and smiled. "Thank you, Ms. Sherwin. I hate asking for help, but...."

"Nancy, you are not asking for help or receiving charity. We all need some back up when things get off the rails. We good?"

"Yes, we are." She glanced at her watch. "I better go to work." She stood up and hugged Natalie. "Thank you again," she whispered.

After Nancy O'Hara departed, Natalie tapped her cell phone but then stopped. *Knucklehead fake-bro Jake is probably flying or on horseback somewhere. I'll call Val and get an answer right now. We can chat tonight regardless if Jake is at the winery or not.* She grinned as she dialed Val's number. *Val and I will tell Jake exactly what he needs to do.*

CHAPTER 14

CG AVIATION OFFICE
MC CLELLAN AIRFIELD
SACRAMENTO, CA

Walter Gipe folded his arms across his chest and watched from the inside of the office as the helicopter touched down on the tarmac. The pilot deftly lowered the helicopter into the small parking rectangle and then shut off the engine. Watching Jake do his post-flight inspection made Gipe wonder just where time had gone. It didn't seem that long ago that he was banging a pencil on his young nephew's head, yelling instructions as Jake struggled to master the art of hovering. Walter Gipe, now in his 60s, had always been Jake's aviation mentor. Jake had changed over the years, but Walt still sported a "one each-standard" military crew cut. His stance reached about 5'11" with a waistline that said he spent too much time at a desk or in a cockpit.

Walter A. Gipe was the brother of the late Elizabeth Cahill, Jake's mom. Decades ago, Jake's Dad, James, a former naval aviator, and Walt, a retired Coast Guard pilot, started Cahill-Gipe Aviation, or CG Aviation. Gipe was half owner of the business, a well-respected air charter and cinema service based at Van Nuys Airport and in Sacramento, at McClellan Airport. When James and Elizabeth died in an auto accident, Jake inherited half ownership of CG Aviation along with all of Tierra del Puma ranch and Sierra Puma Winery. Upon leaving the LAPD, Jake returned to the ranch but continued flying for CG Aviation and assisting Walt in managing the Northern California flight operations.

Jake walked in the office as Walt pointed towards the helicopter parked on the ramp. "The skids of the helicopter are several inches out of landing spot," he said with feigned seriousness.

Jake causally glanced back at the helicopter. "No, they're not. Your vision is poor."

"Bullshit, I can see two beetles fornicate at 1000 feet."

"Then how come you can't spot that mosquito on your arm?"

Walt glanced down and swatted the bug away and pointed to the item in Jake's hand. "Always the smart ass. What's the piece of junk you're holding?"

Jake held up the part. "It's part of a plane, a baggage door, I think. It comes with a story to it."

"Where's the rest of the plane?"

"That's the story. There is no rest of the plane."

Walt raised his eyebrows and cocked his head. "No rest of the plane? I'll bite, enlighten me, nephew."

Jake filled Walt in on the circumstances of discovering the aluminum fragment up near Tear Drop Pass. "Gavin, over at the highway patrol Air Ops, brought it by the ranch. We both agreed it came off a plane. Look at the faded lettering. It says CG Aviation."

"I'll be damned," said Walt, looking at the faded writing. "Well, we're not missing a plane or parts."

"That's what I told Gavin. But why was this thing sticking out of the snow near Tear Drop, with our name on it? I bet it's off a small plane."

Walt flipped the part over several times, eyeing it. "That it is. But CG never owned one. The only small plane in the family is the Stearman your Dad owned. I assume it's in the hangar at the ranch and in one piece." He chuckled. "Unless you busted it on landing..."

Jake recalled the memorable days when father and son would fly the open cockpit biplane over the ranch. The World War II trainer had a nasty habit to ground loop on landing. "It's in one piece.

I flew it the other day. And to your amazement I landed without incident."

"Ha, your luck always exceeds your skill, Jake." Gipe studied the piece of baggage door. "I have no guess why our name is on this...whatever the hell it is." Walt glanced back to the hangar. "I bet Wingnut could figure this out."

"Is he here?"

"In the hangar, he and the guys are finishing an inspection on one of the King Air's. I'll go get him." In a few seconds Walt's booming voice echoed in the hanger. "Wingnut get in here for a minute."

Chief of Maintenance, Randy "Wingnut" Thompson was in his 40s and had a quiet wry personality. He resembled a long-lost beach comber with his lanky frame, long blonde hair and scruffy beard. Thompson spent his entire life in aviation maintenance. Once discharged from the Coast Guard, Walt Gipe recruited him to work at CG aviation. Randy gained his moniker when he fell off a wing injuring his groin. From then on, he became "Wingnut" to fellow mechanics and friends.

Randy cautiously eased his way through the office door. His brown eyes darted around the office, half expecting to be a victim of one of Gipe's typical horseplay jokes. He noticed Jake standing next to Walt, both looking at something. "I'm impressed. The entire brain trust of CG Aviation is here," he said drolly. "How you doing, Jake?" extending out a calloused hand. "What did your flyboys bust this time?"

"Hi Randy, good to see you too. Nothing. Thought you could help us with a puzzle." Jake retold the story of the airplane fragment.

Wingnut furled his eyebrows and examined the aluminum hatch "Yeah", he said slowly. "That's a baggage door off a light plane all right. Sure is beat to shit."

Walt piped in. "Can you identify what type of plane it came from?"

Wingnut's eagle eyes missed nothing when it came to aviation maintenance. He scrutinized the part, flipping it over several times.

"There's a small hard-to-read part number that could be traceable." He scratched a fingernail across the lettering. "The wording, 'CG Aviation' is a stencil, looks like cheap spray paint. And you say this thing was just sticking up in the snow, no other parts?" he said, looking at Jake with a quizzical expression.

"That's all. The officer searched the area and didn't find any other parts. I tried to fly over there, but clouds obscured the ground. Plus, there's still snow up there."

"And CG never owned or operated a small plane. Am I getting this right?"

"Correct," said Jake. "I checked the NTSB, FAA and the Civil Air Patrol. There have been no reports of lost planes, accidents or missing planes in that area. You might be able to refine that data search with a part number or something."

"Yeah, maybe. This thing is old but hasn't been exposed to elements too long." said Wingnut. "The plastic inside lining isn't badly faded nor is the white exterior paint and pin stripe. The twisted aluminum frame and hinges still have a shine to them. Man, hard to say. Maybe some dumb shit found this in a junkyard and used it as a saucer sled."

"Possible, I guess," said Jake, "guy found it near the base of Tear Drop Pass. Could have slid down from the top." Jake glanced at Walt for comments.

"Randy," Walt said, now more serious. "When you get the time can you run down some history on this? This is curious, since our name is on it and they found it on ranch property."

"Sure, be interesting to sort it out. Man, this thing got torqued around," said Randy, running his hand over the twisted and torn aluminum door.

Jake scratched his chin. "It did, as if the plane got eaten by a thunderstorm and spit out."

"Now that makes sense," replied Walt. "That part of the Sierra Crest is a birthing crib for nasty thunder bumpers, summer and winter. But who in the hell would be dumb enough to fly through a thunderstorm?"

Randy gave a dead pan stare to both pilots. "Yeah, who could imagine some dumb ass pilot with get-home-itis thinking he could beat Mother Nature. Gee, like that never happens."

Jake and Walt glanced at each other and chuckled at the spot-on remark.

"Point taken," said Walt. "Try to find out something about it, if you can."

Randy grabbed the baggage door and headed to the hanger. "Do you want me to drop everything to play detective? Can I at least eat my lunch?"

Walt pushed the mechanic out of the office. "Finish the 100-hour inspection and have your lunch. Just don't eat on the airplane wing, Mr. Wingnut," Walt said, laughing.

"Screw you, Gipe. But nice to see you again, Jake," he said, walking back into the hangar.

"Be interesting to see what Randy discovers," said Jake. Then added, "Better go. I have some errands to run, then get back to the winery."

Walt shuffled some papers on his disorganized desk. "I'll snoop around and check if there's another CG Aviation or used to be in this area. Changing gears for a second. Are you taking that US Geological Survey charter up to Mt. Lassen? That's coming up soon."

"Sure, should be fun if it's with the same guys that flew before." Jake pointed to the helicopter on the ramp. "Are they asking for a helicopter, 'cause if so, Jack Treco still has that one on a first right of refusal basis. He's got some ongoing security contract with it."

"They need the King Air. There're no off-site landings this time. They're doing some over flight monitoring and then want to land up in Siskiyou County for other projects. Jake, if you get a chance, reach out to Treco-see how long he wants the helicopter. Our other birds are out on contracts."

"Will do, he's been out of town, but I'll swing by when he gets back and check. He enjoys chatting, kind of like you," Jake said with a smile.

"That's because we have something to say. You should listen to us wise old pelicans more often. Say hi to Jack but remember he's former FBI; records everything you say."

"Knowing Jack, he couldn't find the button to turn on a tape recorder."

Walt chuckled. "Gotcha, and by the way, how's my beautiful niece-in-law?"

"Valerie's good, full speed, and non-stop. She's on some supersonic mission to expand the winery and open the new conference center. Plus, her book is shifting into a movie which means dealing with production business. She spends most of her time at the Auburn house." Jake paused, "Be nice if she could get back to the ranch once in a while since the season is changing." He reached for a set of car keys hanging on the wall. "Going to borrow a company car, be back in two or three hours."

Walt sensed a mild frustration in his nephew's voice about his wife. "Jake, give her some maneuvering room. She loves the ranch but wants to make her own mark on things. She's still adjusting to life away from the LA crap."

Jake walked from the office talking more to himself than to Walt, "yeah, whatever, I'll call you later."

Cahill left McClellan Airport still wondering about the mysterious airplane part, then turned his thoughts to something more enjoyable. He looked forward to the upcoming geological charter flight. He once told Valerie he should have gotten a degree in geology instead of engineering considering the time he spent in or over the mountains. "So, go back to school," she said, as if that statement solved the issue and would satiate his interest in rocks. He smiled, thinking of Val's typical 'just do it' mantra. Jake's passion for the open country and the freedom of flight negated any desire for a return to academia.

Jake reached "The Java Buzz" and parked next to a dark green 'California Department of Fish and Wildlife' truck. He walked in the busy shop, ordered his coffee and walked over to a man in his 50s, sporting a trim and fit appearance in his Department uniform. His clear brown eyes met Jake's. "You must be Jake Cahill," he said, offering his hand then pointing for Jake to have a seat. "I'm Paul Davis, we chatted on the phone last week about your illegal hunting problem on the ranch."

"Hi Paul. Thanks for meeting me. I'm sure you guys are busy."

"That's an understatement. Too many violators and not enough time or resources." Davis held up his cup of coffee and stared at it. "Did you know this is no longer a medium size?" he said, twisting the paper cup around.

"I'll bite, what the hell is it?" Jake said, surprised by a sudden change in conversation.

"It's a 'Grande'. I asked for a regular size cup of joe and the young lady behind the counter said she only had this. I'm old school, Jake. Never thought the word medium would be obsolete."

Jake chuckled, "Yeah, new generation with a special language. I grew up with cowboy coffee, which meant when Dad got home on leave, he would put grounds in the coffee pot. Made me appreciate K cups, cream, and these shops." Jake took a sip of coffee. "I wanted to meet face to face to get the status of what Fish and Wildlife is doing about these scumbag poachers coming on my ranch. Last year I found three gutted out bears on the edge of the ranch and forestry land." Jake shook his head in disgust. "It's sickening what these assholes have done."

Davis set his cup down. "More than sickening, it's a perverse business. Wish I could say we were doing more, but like I said, resources and budgets are tight."

"What you're saying is that you haven't found these creeps or put extra wardens on patrol up there. I said last year you had permission to stake out on the ranch after I reported finding these eviscerated bears. Nothing came of that. This is bullshit, Paul," said Jake with a stern expression.

"Jake, it is. But this is also California, home of poachers, illegal fishing, and just about any other violation concerning wildlife. Hell, we have jerks that go up in the forest and blow away songbirds just so they can eat them. We find people with fish 10 times over the legal limits. They fish out streams and lakes and leave their trash and garbage on the shore. And talk about out-of-season killing sprees; try the deer population. Hell, when people can't find an animal, they shoot the road signs." Davis shook his head, "In this state if a critter walks, swims, crawls or flies then some shithead wants to kill it. And the Department hasn't the means to cover all the areas. We're working a case on the American River where some homeless campers killed lake otters to eat. We're stretched to the max and a low priority in the state budget." Davis paused. "I'll get off my soapbox now. Shouldn't bitch to a taxpayer, but I seem to remember you were on the LAPD. You can understand what's behind my ranting. It's as frustrating for us as it is for you."

"Paul, bitch all you want. I get it. But I also want to catch these bastards. Life in prison would work for these scumbags. But that won't happen in this state. If caught they probably would get a fine and probation." His voice shifted into an icier tone, "too bad I can't bump into them and they point a gun at me. I could blow away the problem really quick."

Davis saw a hard-grim expression on Cahill's face and tried to neutralize the conversation. "Yeah, well, whatever, hope it doesn't come to that. These are poachers in the bear business."

"Bear business?"

"We think there's a local group of poachers who go around killing bears and carving out the gall bladders. The organs are an aphrodisiac in parts of Asia, so they say. There's huge money in the business if you can export the organs out of the country. Lots of bears up near your ranch. They're easy kills when Momma has cubs."

Jake shook his head, "what scum. If you know about this, why can't you detail more guys to work the case?"

"Like I said, all about resources and leads. Most of the time all we have is the carcass, perhaps some tire tracks. But there again they hike in, make a kill, and hike out. Boot tracks don't help too much either. That said, we're trying to cobble together a case as we get more info." Davis shook his head, "I had one weak lead; a woman in the area who claimed she knew of guys killing bears for money. She wanted a reward for her information." He sighed, "That went nowhere. She went off the radar and never called back."

"That happens. I had an uncover assignment while on the LAPD and saw that frequently. People want to spill their guts to get even with an employer or get revenge on a former lover. They either cool down or get killed. It's tough to develop a confidential informant. What about high-tech surveillance gear? Can you guys deploy that around the ranch?"

"Tell me about it. We're limited on both. And the surveillance gear we have isn't that sophisticated for this need. It would help to have a few more snoop toys and leads. Sorry, but those are the issues."

"Makes sense," said Jake, taking another swallow of coffee. "Not sure if this will help but a couple weeks ago, I ran two jerks off the ranch near Tear Drop Pass. They were pulling a trailer with snowmobiles. Said they were going snowmobiling, which was crap. There are plenty of easier places to access over on forestry's side. They acted like tweakers with attitudes. Now I wonder if they were casing the area for bears."

"Could be. Did you get a look at their ride, a license, by any chance?"

"They were in some off-road abortion of a pick-up. Looked like a bastardized mix of truck and old military parts. It was dirty black, except for the rusted right front corner panel. They lifted it, had heavy shocks with oversized tires, and winch on the front. Vehicle looked like total junk but functional. The license was covered in mud, but it had California plates." Jake pulled his cell phone and showed a picture of the vehicle. "I almost got in a fight with these guys, so the picture became a last second thought as they left. You can barely read a few numbers on the plate."

Davis stared at the image and tried to expand it. "Yeah, it's sketchy. Text it to me. I can try and have somebody play with it." Davis thought for a second. "This is interesting considering the woman who called said her guy drove some black, jacked up, off road ride.

Jake chuckled, "That narrows it down to only a thousand or so vehicles."

"At least a thousand, but most are city polished and waxed. Built for show not mud. But if I recall she mentioned something about the guy or guys worked in a quarry so a dirty pick-up might fit the profile." Davis shrugged his shoulders. "The woman didn't sound like she was all there. I think she had more interest in getting cash so it could be a scam on us." He sighed, "but one never knows. I'll examine your photo and check my notes again. We might get lucky. I'll have to secure some better surveillance equipment if there is something to this. Most of our gear is already deployed along with other wardens."

"Paul, I'm friends with a guy that does trick things with surveillance technology. It's Treco Systems in Roseville, just down the road. Warren Treco is retired FBI and runs a high-end discreet security system business. He works with corporations and government agencies." Jake reached in his wallet and gave Davis a business card. "Call him. Maybe the Fish and Wildlife can cut some deal with Warren. You can mention my name, if it helps."

Paul took the card. "Worth a try. I'll pass it up the bureaucratic food chain of command. Between that, my feeble lead, and your vehicle description, maybe we can get traction on this."

"All we can do is try. Reach out to me if I can help."

Davis finished his coffee. "Thanks, Jake, good talking to you. I'll stay in touch." He glanced over at that counter. "Wonder if I can get a reload of coffee?"

"Only if you speak 'Grande'."

CHAPTER 15

AUBURN
SIERRA PUMA WINERY

essie O'Hara stood at the front entrance of the Sierra Puma Winery and watched her mother drive away in the old Subaru Forester. At barely 19, Jessie thought about the independence of having her own car. That, she realized, was a dream. Now that Sean was dead and with Mom's job on the brink, there wasn't much money left for the remaining family members-her and Mom. She wiped the tear that ran down her cheek thinking about Sean's death. Her brother and confidant now gone. The heartache wouldn't go away soon, if at all. Jessie brushed a piece of dirt off her old best jeans she wore for the interview, still thinking about Sean. She was convinced he didn't just run off the road. The cops wrote the accident off as just another intoxicated, brainless teenager. They were wrong. Her brother was smarter than that. Well, most of the time. And the broken scrap he stashed in her closet remained a puzzle. What was it and why did he write about seeing more parts near the big private ranch? She wondered what was so interesting about a bunch of smashed junk, unless it had value. Her brother often sold things that had questionable legitimacy. She kept that aspect of Sean's enterprise a secret for fear of lending credence to his lack of common sense. She loved him too much for that. Jessie became confused by the strange and sad events that engulfed her thoughts. "Not a perfect day to interview for a new job," she whispered to herself.

Jessie tried to act enthused when Mom found her a potential job but hoped she wouldn't screw up the interview. She recalled Mom's last words before stepping from the car this morning; "Sweetie you will do fine but try to smile more." Easy to say, but hard to do. The depression always lurked in the recesses of her mind. It had been there for years, now made worse by the loss of her brother. Jessie forced the dark shadows aside. She pinned on a false smile, took a deep breath, and walked through the wooden doors to the winery.

She entered a large open lobby with a massive stone fireplace and enormous windows with views of the vineyards, rose gardens, patios, and outdoor eating areas. The wide tile hallways and curved archways gave the winery an open, airy ambiance. The boutique, a coffee bar, and a tasting room all connected to a large restaurant. The building had a fresh and vibrant look to it. There was another corridor with a sign pointing to a conference hall where construction crews were coming and going. Jessie wandered around, basically lost. Tourists sauntered by chatting and carrying gift bags. *At least they know where they're going,* she thought. She reached the end of the wide corridor. She hesitated, unsure which way to go. A young man passed going the other way. He seemed to be about her age, maybe older. He was long-legged, tall, dressed in jeans, with a blue and white western shirt, and dusty cowboy boots. His brown hair suffered from hat head with a cowlick that stuck straight up. He stopped as if forgetting something, then did a quick turnaround and approached her.

"Hi, you look lost, can I help you?" he said, with a friendly smile.

"Hi," she said, embarrassed at his direct brown eye contact. "Uh, I guess so. I'm looking for..." she glanced at the paper her Mom gave her. "For a Ms. Cahill."

"Oh yeah, Valerie, she's the CEO, the boss of the outfit." He pointed, "Up the stairs, I'll take you there."

"Thanks, this is quite a place." she said, following him up the stairway.

"It sure is. You here for a job interview?"

"Yes, but I hear it's hard to get hired."

He smiled, "It is, but it's great work either here or up at the ranch. I double duty between both. But I'll take the ranch and horses anytime. Today, I'm here playing drone pilot," he said. "They pay me to fly my drone over the winery for marketing pictures, but I'll be back at the ranch this afternoon."

"Sounds interesting," she said, surprised by his outgoing effervescence.

"Great job-great people. Well, here you go. See that lady over there and she'll take you to Valerie. Good luck on the interview. You'll do great. Besides, you have the looks for it! See ya." In a flash he disappeared down the stairs.

A trim-looking woman in her early 40s with short brown hair approached her. "Can I help you?" she said, with a pleasant smile.

"Hi, I'm Jessie O'Hara, I have an appointment with Ms. Cahill for a job interview?"

"Oh sure, hi, I'm Erin, kind of second-in-command around here. Let me show you to her office." They entered a large open and bright room. "Well, she seems to have slipped out again. That's Val, always into something. She's expecting you though and will be here in a minute." Erin pointed to the round table in Valerie's office. "Here, have a seat and make yourself comfortable." Erin looked out the window and saw a red golf cart speeding back toward the office. "Here she comes if she doesn't crash the golf cart, again," Erin said with a chuckle then left the office.

Jessie gazed at the memorabilia and photos that hung on the wall. There were pictures of three women on a movie set. Jessie recognized them, the stars of the TV show "High Corporate." She watched the show and enjoyed the self-assured attitude of the women characters in the story line. She looked at the other pictures. A woman stood on the skid of a helicopter wearing a ball cap and sunglasses, giving the typical aviator thumbs up. There were other photos of the same woman, standing next to a man, his arms around her waist. Another picture showed the same woman sitting on a horse, backdropped by mountains. And in another, the same woman was smiling and holding up a book with the title "Guardians of the Covered Carriage." Jessie knew the book; a popular novel about a group of intrepid women pioneers who battled the harsh elements of the Sierras, along with heartbreak to reach Sacramento. Jessie read it, captivated by a story of undaunted courage and friendship. She heard a rumor it was to be a movie with the "High Corporate" actresses. Then she realized, *oh my God, the owner of this winery is Valerie Paige Cahill, the movie lady and the author.* Jessie's stomach filled with butterflies with a sudden flash of nervousness. She was about to get interviewed by the same woman! Jessie hoped she wouldn't make a complete ass of herself.

Jessie nervously wiped the sweat from her hands onto her jeans when she heard a voice. "Hi, sorry I'm late. You must be Jessica O'Hara." Jessie turned as Valerie approached and extended her hand. "I'm Val," she said with a warm smile. Her cat like vivid blue eyes seemed to ignite the room with energy. Oddly enough, Jessie felt a calm reassurance in the woman's presence.

"Hi, it's Jessie. It's a pleasure to meet you." Then she blurted out, looking at the photographs. "Is that you? I mean, you're the same lady, right, the writer and movie star?" she said, then feeling a flush of embarrassment by asking the question.

Valerie gave a grin. "Yep, that is I." She pointed to the pictures. "The ladies in the photos are the real actresses, Gwen and Lindsay. Me, just a part-timer, but we became good friends." She pointed to another picture, "I wrote the book-and what a challenge. It was inspired by some legends of the Sierra." Valerie kept her genuine connections to all of it very private.

"I read it and really liked it!"

"Thank you for that." Valerie pointed. "And that's me standing on the skids of an LAPD helicopter. That's the first time I met my hubby, Jake. Guess you could call it a first date." She grinned, thinking back to the day they met. "And that's my horse, Tidbit. I ride him at the ranch up at Tierra del Puma."

Jessie got distracted from Val's pictures. She cocked her head. A flashback played in her memory, thinking of Sean's GPS and notes he left in her closet. "Did you say, Tierra del Puma, the big ranch? You own that too?" she asked, struck by the coincidence.

"It belonged to my husband's late parents. That's our home when I'm not working here. We do agriculture work, socialize wild mustangs, and guide trips into certain sections of the backcountry. But my hubby likes to keep things quiet up there." She smiled, "He gets a little weird about that. You know how guys are about things." She said laughing, making Jessie feel more at ease.

"Wow, that's exciting." Jessie said, feeling envious of this woman who carried herself with warm poise and confidence. Val's clothes had something to do with it, she observed. Valerie dressed in brown leather ankle boots, skinny jeans, and white silk blouse covered by a cashmere sweater. Her brown hair fell to her shoulders, and from what Jessie could tell she wore little makeup. Then again, Jessie thought, Ms. Cahill had a perfect, natural complexion, not a face full of ugly freckles.

"So, Jessie, you're looking for a job, right?" Val asked, guiding her to the round conference table.

"I am. My Mom spoke to a Ms. Sherwin, who said you were hiring part-time seasonal help."

"Natalie is a close friend of the family and our attorney. She made the referral about you, so you already passed a lofty standard. She's an excellent judge of character."

Jessie forced a smile, trying not to act self-conscious. "Thank you." Then added with a sudden burst of eagerness, "I can do anything you want me to. I know how to work hard and I'm a fast learner," speaking with a sureness that she hadn't felt in a long time.

"I'm sure you can but let me explain a few things then you make the call. The jobs are a mixed bag of tasks. You might work in the the winery, but not wine tasting," she said with a grin. "Chores include cleaning, inventory, and rolling barrels, you name it. Or, the next day you would work the boutique, the restaurant, in the conference center or running errands for Erin or me. We want you to learn everything about the business. You need to hone your multi-tasking skills, hustle, and be a quick study on things. You work

10-hour days with days off. Hours are flexible if you get someone to cover for you. Being late, cutting out and not notifying us, or being lazy will get you tossed out the door. We're a team here. Everybody has each other's back. We don't tolerate poor attitudes or rudeness from employees or for that matter, any customer."

Jessie nodded, feeling a sense of enthusiasm. "I can do this," she said with a liveliness in her voice.

Valerie smiled, "Now, the other aspect to this job, the ranch. We have a program where men and women about your age work on the ranch doing everything. When I say everything that means cleaning out barns, corrals, fixing fences, checking trails, cleaning airplanes and once qualified, riding horses. We socialize wild mustangs for adoption, so they need people on their backs before we let them go. That also means you might have to ride into the backcountry when we guide groups into fly-fishing streams or take production companies to film scenic backgrounds." Valerie paused, waiting to see the expression on the teenager's face. "You with me so far?"

Jessie beamed a smile, "I am, it all sounds unreal."

Val smiled back, "You stay in a dorm during the time you're there. You get time off. Grayhawk is nearby and is a fun town with lots to do. Or, you can drive home or sometimes bum a ride in the helicopter. The work is hard, the pay is good and just like here, the standard of conduct high."

Jessie's eyes blazed with excitement thinking, *outdoor work in the mountains and riding horses-wow.* That, she thought, was a perfect job.

"I get the part about cleaning barns, but airplanes and helicopters?"

Valerie grinned, "My husband and his uncle run an air charter service out of McClellan Airport. They operate helicopters and airplanes. They sometimes keep an airplane or helicopter at the ranch airstrip on a government contract." Val chuckled, "Jake's a former LAPD helicopter pilot. He grew up around aircraft and ranch life. He can't stay out of the cockpit or the Sierra. You'll meet him. The aircraft on contract must be kept clean and fueled. That's the aviation side of things and one of your duties."

"That sounds crazy exciting."

Val grew serious, "The jobs at the ranch are coveted positions, as you probably deduced. But it's not all ranch and horse work. We often bring people back down here to work as needed. You might have seen one of our ranch hands walking around, Tim Fremont. He's been with us a couple years. Somehow, he keeps weaseling his way back. You can't miss him. He's tall, with your typical cowboy appearance, who can't keep his hair combed. He's one of the best. I suspect Jake would hire him full time after he gets out of college."

"I think I met him; he gave me directions to your office." *Kind of cute,* thinking to herself.

"That's him." The sound of a helicopter interrupted their conversation. Valerie pointed out the window to the helipad. "Ah, you get to meet my hubby, Jake. He's on the way to the ranch." Valerie tapped her fingers on the table. "Hmmm, let's do this. I'll have Tim show you the workings of the winery and vineyard. Erin will fill you in on the pay and HR issues. Jake has to take Tim back to the ranch, so you can fly with them, see the place, then he will bring you back afterwards. You good with that?"

Jessie's eyes widen with disbelief. "Sure, but did you say fly in a helicopter?" she asked, her eyes filled with anticipation and trepidation.

"If that's okay, but if you don't enjoy flying-no biggie. It's not a job requirement."

"It's more than okay!" *Don't let me hurl.*

As if reading her mind Valerie smiled, "Don't worry about projectile vomiting. Jake is an amazing pilot. You'll have fun. But if you toss your cookies, turn your head out the window. Jake hates it when people puke on him." Valerie heard Jake's laughter in Erin's office. "Speaking of which. Let me grab him before he harasses all the other employees."

Jessie stared out the window, unable to grasp the strange happenstance between Sean, Tierra del Puma and now her going there.

That's really weird, she thought. Jessie looked back into the outer office just in time to see a man wrap his arms around Valerie and plant a huge kiss on her.

Jake Cahill walked in the office holding Valerie's hand. Jessie saw his radiant green eyes and a million-dollar smiled focusing on her. His short brown hair seemed to match his tan face and lean frame. He reached out and shook her hand. "Hi Jessie, I'm Jake, the other half to this business." He glanced over at Val and smiled, "That is when Valerie lets me. She just informed me you might work for us," he said with an approving wink of the eye.

"Uh, I guess so. That would be great."

"If Valerie and Natalie Sherwin gave you a thumbs up, then it's our gain."

Jessie smiled, feeling good for the first time in months and struck with a tingling feeling of excitement and optimism.

"Jessie, you good with flying to the ranch for a quick tour? I'll have you back in a few hours. You have to be on payroll for insurance, so you get paid to fly. That's always a plus. Afterwards, you and Val can decide when and where you work. We good?" he said with a charming Jake Cahill smile.

Valerie grinned watching how Jake instantly put Jessie at ease, making her feel part of the operation. She turned when Tim Fremont tapped on the door. "Excuse me, Val, Erin said you wanted to see me. Hey Jake, I saw you fly in. We headed back to the ranch?" Fremont said with enthusiasm. Tim loved flying and occasionally Jake let him sit in front and get free flying lessons.

Jake put his arms around Tim's shoulders. "The good news is yes, and you are to show Jessie, our new employee, around the winery then give her a safety brief on the helicopter. She's flying back with us. The bad news is you're sitting in the backseat on the way back to the ranch. I want to see if Jessie is a better pilot than you," he said, tossing a grin at Jessie.

Tim Fremont smiled, suddenly not caring that much about flying, taking more interest in the new hire. He motioned with his hand. "Come on Jessie, I'll show you the place and tell you how

Jake really flies. You won't need a sick sack; we have buckets over at the winery."

Jessie raised her eyebrows in apprehension as Jake spoke up. "Don't listen to him. He got kicked in the head by a mustang."

After Tim and Jessie left the office, Valerie sat at her desk pouring over a stack of documents. She looked up at Jake. "Natalie filled me on Jessie O'Hara; a pleasant girl, but shy and insecure. She lost her brother about a month ago in a freak motorcycle accident. Her Dad is some creep doing life in a Texas penitentiary. She lives with her mom and they are damn near bankrupt. I think a job here or at the ranch will help her," her eyes connected with Jake's, "you agree?"

"I do. She seems okay to me. Let's see how she handles things. Maybe she can split her time between the ranch and here. That way Tim won't try to jump her bones."

"Cahill, what a thing to say!" she said half grinning, having noticed Tim's poor attempt to conceal his interest.

Jake walked over to Valerie and rubbed her shoulders and neck. "Speaking of which, why don't I hustle back, drop off Jessie and whisk you away to the ranch for a few days. The Auburn house keeps you too close to the office. And too busy," he said, nuzzling the back of her neck.

She reached over and touched his hand. "I can't. I have vendor meetings tomorrow. Plus, I have more prep for this preproduction conference gala. And now some Russian guy is coming by to talk about a film permit to make a tourist documentary or something. I can't Jake. I just can't," she said, trying to let him down gently.

Jake stepped away from her. "Sierra Puma is almost on autopilot. Erin can handle all this. She knows how you want things. The meadows are filled with wildflowers. Tidbit misses you not riding him. I miss you not being up there. You spend more time here than there. The ranch needs both of us-together."

Valerie dropped the papers in her hand and looked up at Jake. "Yes, the winery is running well, but there are some projects I need to finish. And yes, I want to be at the ranch. It's..." she paused, then said in a lower voice. "It's part of me but I need to get things done here. We have a major event coming up. A lot of important people will be attending this dinner meeting including Mark Parnell, my former producer, who was also your parents' friend. He's the one turning my book into a movie. Gwen and Lindsay and other cast members and crew will be here as well. He's also bringing the board of directors from his wilderness conservancy. I can't, as you say, put things on autopilot for a few days. Things are getting hectic. This is important to me, Jake. I need to be involved with these projects."

"And your choice to wear yourself down. Val, you look beat." he said, his voice sounding discouraged.

Valerie exhaled loudly. "Yes, by my choice, if that's what it takes. Speaking of autopilot, you could stay here more often. Our foreman, Doug Weston and Maria have been at Tierra del Puma for years. They ran the ranch when you were on the LAPD. They can handle things. You could help Walt more in Sacramento." Valerie leaned back in her chair feeling frustrated, not wanting to argue with Jake. It made her uncomfortable.

Jake shook his head in resignation not wanting to embark on a path to an argument. "Okay, whatever Val, I better go fly." Valerie didn't want Jake to leave feeling the way he did. She stood up but then felt a tinge of dizziness and steadied herself against the desk.

"Whoa, you okay?" he said, as a look of concern crossed his face.

"I'm fine." she said, rubbing her temples and walking up to him. "I've been battling sinus allergies that won't go away. I got up too fast." She hugged him. "Jake, once all this wraps up then lets' go to the ranch and ride. I love you; you know that."

He held her in his arms. "I love you too. It just seems you're in the fast lane and getting worn down." He sighed, "I love you even if you are making me go crazy."

She patted his cheek with her hand and smiled. "Be careful on those airwaves, flyboy. Hurry and come back today." A few minutes later Valerie watched out the window as Jake departed in the helicopter heading east, towards Tierra del Puma. She returned to her desk and read the odd request wondering why a Russian film director was interested in Tierra del Puma. *Guess I'll find out. Better tell him we take dollars, not rubles.*

CHAPTER 16

AIRBORNE
THE SIERRA FOOTHILLS

essie had sensory overload staring out the helicopter as the ground quickly passed beneath her. The land appeared close-up and personal. She could see over a hill, peek into a river canyon, or watch as the foothills transitioned into the taller Sierras. The exhilaration of flight and panoramic views was an elixir. The lofty perch created a pleasant disconnect from earthbound problems. She understood now-flying was magical.

Jessie adjusted the headset volume to soften Tim's enthusiastic narration on the points of interest. She sensed an attempt to impress her with his knowledge of the area. She glanced over at Jake. He seemed focused on pilot duties but held a slight grin, listening to the "Tim Fremont Tour Guide Service." Jessie returned her gaze to the front of the helicopter. Sean's notes caused her to interrupt Tim's lecture. "Where's Tear Drop Pass?" she asked, glancing at Jake.

He peered over the rim of his sunglasses at her at the unexpected question. "How do you know about Tear Drop Pass? Are you a hiker?"

She avoided details of her late brother's mountain escapades. "I think I read about it in your wife's novel, 'Guardians of the Covered Carriage'. I wondered if those were real places."

Jake didn't answer right away. Valerie's fictional story was inspired by a historical diary and intertwined with her own emotional connections to the area and people. He cautioned her on writing the novel for fear that every idiot in the world would trespass into Tierra del Puma looking for evidence of the legend. Her response: "Jake you're getting a bit paranoid about people coming to the ranch." *Maybe she's right,* he thought to himself. He pointed out the front windscreen. "Over there, just off to the right. There's an old volcanic mountain called Whispering Wind. On the left is a dip in the ridge. That's Tear Drop Pass."

Jessie spotted the pass and the mountain peak. "I got it. The novel says there were whispers here, voices of pioneer girls. That's eerie," she said, engrossed in the scenery ahead of them.

Jake spoke with a passive indifference trying to deflect the comments. "It's fiction. I grew up here. Winds blow down from mountains all the time. You hear what you want to hear," he said in a matter-of-fact tone, not wanting to discuss the strange peculiarities of the land.

Jessie's mind was not on a story but Sean's GPS tracks and notes. "Can we fly by it?"

Jake thought about the airplane part and the recent encounter with the jerk trespassers. He agreed to the request thinking he might spot something or someone. "We'll fly over the pass, not the mountain peak." Without mentioning the missing plane or the prior confrontation Jake solicited a second set of eyes. "Tim, as we fly over check out the snow levels and see if there are any tracks that lead onto our side of the Pass."

"Sure, are we looking for anything specific?"

"Not really but the area is avalanche prone so we should at least do a fly by to make sure nobody is down there."

The westside of the pass was calm and cloudless allowing Jake to descend the helicopter to catch a better glimpse of terrain. The aerial search proved fruitless. Jessie gazed out at the rugged mountain pass, lost in thought. Somewhere down there Sean had his final adventure and left his sister with a disquieting mystery. They crested the ridge and flew through a canyon gouged by ancient glaciers that opened into an expansive valley. Jagged boulders gave way to pines, aspens, green meadows and the meandering Little Truckee River. Jessie took a quick breath, awed by the verdant scenery. It was as if they had crossed over a barrier and stumbled upon a pristine vale lost in time. Jake pointed out the front of the helicopter. "There's some of your responsibilities and duties."

Jessie looked down and saw a heard of mustangs at full gallop along the river's edge. She closed her eyes and imagined herself riding horseback through a field of wildflowers. "This is unreal" she said over the intercom, captivated by the beauty and energy of the land.

"Welcome to Tierra del Puma," said Tim Fremont.

Jake flew through the valley as Jessie kept her face pasted to the cockpit window. A few minutes later they touched down at the ranch airstrip. Standing at the hangar was Doug "Gunny" Weston, and his wife Maria, the medic and all-around den mom to the ranch.

Jake made introductions. "Doug why don't you and Maria take Jessie over to the ranch offices and introduce her to other wranglers. Explain the job requirements and the standards. Tim and I will refuel the ship." Jake saw Tim's disappointed expression. "On second thought, Tim, you go with Jessie and Maria. Doug and I need to chat on matters. Come on back in a couple hours. I have to fly Jessie back to the winery to complete some paperwork, if she takes the job."

Jessie gave a broad smile, "I'm taking the job, wherever and whatever it is."

After they had left, Jake filled Doug in about Jessie's background. "See how she fits in. She made mention of having horse riding experience, whatever that means. After you or Eddie check those skills, then explain the rules-no riding without a partner, always in a pair. No exceptions."

Doug nodded, "Will do. How are things at the winery?"

Jake rubbed the back of his neck as if to remove a kink. "Busy. Val's in a terror to get things done. Not sure when she's coming back to the ranch. Which reminds me, regarding her book-soon-to-be movie, that production crew will be up here in a few weeks.

Figure that's going to be a pain in the ass. We need to have both parking areas and guest cabins available. Plus, plan on some extra wranglers to babysit them. I'll know more after this upcoming gala that Val's hosting at the winery."

"Jake, it will be fine, we won't let..." using his fingers as italics, "...*those Hollywood types* trample the property or wander about. We'll just take their money."

Jake gave a friendly tap on Doug's shoulder. "Leave it to a Marine to square things away. By the way, I dropped off that airplane part at CG Aviation. Walt is going to do some background history on it. Maybe the rest of the plane ended up at Tear Drop Pass. I did a quick fly over and didn't see anything, so who knows? It's on the back burner for the moment as we're getting busy with charters."

"I'll be interested in hearing the story," said Weston. "So, what else is going on?"

"I spoke to the game warden about those dead bears we found last year. He said it could be part of an international poaching ring. Apparently, bear gall bladders are an aphrodisiac in Asia-worth big money if you can export them. As usual, budget issues don't allow for more follow-up. Finding poachers is getting to be a low priority in California," said Jake, his voice filled with cynicism.

"Jesus, these poachers are a bunch of sick bastards. The Fish and Wildlife guy have any clues?"

"Not too many. I gave him the partial license and description of that junky off-road vehicle and the creeps Eddie and I ran into near Tear Drop during the fence line check."

"Eddie mentioned that. He also said you got pissed and nearly got into an altercation with those guys. It got tense; he had to pull out a weapon. What's that about, Jake? It isn't like you." Doug said, looking eye to eye at Jake.

"Yeah, kind of pissed. Tired of arrogant and rude jerks coming on the ranch. Kind of lost my cool."

"Is that it or is something else bothering you? I don't want to pry, but you and Val okay?"

Jake looked towards the mountains, then back at Doug. He

ran his fingers across his forehead as if pushing away a headache. "Yeah, we're both fine, Doug. She's overly occupied with all the things starting to happen around the winery. And I need to spend more time on the ranch than at the Auburn house."

"You're including Val in that statement, right," Doug said.

"I am. All is good, but thanks for asking," said Jake wanting to drop the subject. "So how about a ride to the admin office? We need to review those Bureau of Land Management mustang contracts and nature guide tour permits. Plus, we better work on plans on how to accommodate these folks from Holly-weird," he said. "I need to give Val an outline about the film preparations up here. Then I have to fly our new employee back to the winery. It's a busy day."

"You bet, and we tried."

"Tried what?" said Jake climbing in the cab of the dirty ranch pickup.

Doug sounded serious. "We tried teaching Rustler to speak English so he would listen to you better. Didn't work so Eddie tried Spanish-that too was no-go. Rustler's being obstinate because you're not spending enough time riding him. This is his ranch too, you know."

Gunny drove down the road as Jake stared at the meadows, "I don't blame him."

CHAPTER 17

Yesterday busy, today chaotic, thought Valerie. She sipped the super-charged latte, as Dwight Stewart, the operations manager, discussed inventory and shipping issues. With that logistical brush fire extinguished, she raced the golf cart to the top of the hill overlooking the vineyards. There she studied the land, comparing it against the aerial photos that Tim Fremont had taken with the drone. Valerie removed her aviator glasses and looked beyond the vineyards onto the adjoining property. The land once deemed watershed was now getting bulldozed and subdivided into a future housing tract. She knew development was nearly unstoppable, given the number of real estate investors seeking to buy the winery for its premium land. "Not in our lifetime," she said out loud. Valerie glanced at her watch. She was already behind schedule. The golf cart sped back to the winery.

Valerie quick stepped towards her office while perusing a thick document detailing plans for the upcoming pre-production dinner and gala affair for the movie making of her book. For Valerie, it represented far more than a dinner. It would be a validation of her efforts both as a writer and CEO of Sierra Puma Winery. Marc Parnell, the keynote speaker was a renowned actor and executive producer of the film. He had known Val when she was a part-time actress and was a longtime friend of Jake's late parents. Along with producing the film, Mark planned to pitch his wildlands conservancy organization. Other distinguished board members of the conservancy would be attending as well as Valerie's actress friends. Val wanted the event to be flawless-every detail perfect. She looked up as Jessie O'Hara came by pushing a service cart. "Jessie, I haven't seen you around here for a few days. Been at the ranch?"

Jessie smiled, "For a while, but they sent Tim and me back here to help with your upcoming dinner party. It's crazy here today with everything going on, but I like staying busy."

"That's good to hear. It might get crazier as the big day approaches. So, how goes ranch work? Enjoy cleaning those horse stalls?" Val said, wrinkling her nose.

"Just part of the job, but worth it when I get to ride horses. It's so incredible" she said with a wide grin. Valerie noticed the teenager smiling nearly every time she saw her.

"Cleaning stalls and fixing fences is all part of the job, but I agree, riding a mustang is the best part of ranch work," Val said.

"I even rode Tidbit. Hope you don't mind. Doug Weston said he needed a woman's touch. He and Tim took me and some other wranglers on a ride along the Little Truckee River. It's gorgeous with all the wildflower filled meadows surrounded by the mountains. It's so special."

Valerie closed her eyes for a second. Far away whispers were beckoning her back to the ranch. "Yes, Tierra del Puma is beautiful this time of year," she said wistfully. "I need to get back there."

"But I'm glad Doug drafted Tim and me to come back down and help prep for the big show. I want to see my mom. She misses me since I'm living in the ranch dorm. Oops, I guess it's called a bunkhouse according to Doug Weston."

Valerie smiled, "the Gunny is big on proper terminology." She glanced at her watch, "I better run, people are waiting for me. You take care."

Val did a quick check of her attire while climbing the stairs to her office. She wore a long sleeve blue jersey turtleneck with brown straight slacks. She hoped her running shoes didn't clash too badly with the outfit. Today comfort beckoned over style. She pushed her hair back and double checked to make sure there were no specks of dirt on her clothes. When she entered the outer office, Erin, her executive assistant, stood up. "Hey Val, this gentleman has an appointment."

"Yep, sorry, I'm a few minutes late. Busy here today," she said smiling, catching a glimpse of the man standing near the door dressed in a black sport coat and dark shirt. She noted his appearance; his eyes lacked warmth and were uninviting. She sensed something hidden behind his visage.

His accented voice cut the brief lull in conversation. "Ms. Cahill, I'm Victor Rodin, I spoke to your assistant on the phone," he said, extending his hand in a perfunctory manner.

"Hello Mr. Rodin," she said, returning the handshake. She noticed his eyes scanning her body-an instant turnoff.

She motioned him towards the office table. Victor waited until she sat down, then followed. Valerie flipped open her folder and read the notes. "Mr. Rodin, I understand you want to do some filming at Tierra del Puma, is that correct?"

Rodin cleared his throat. "Yes, but first may I ask if you are the correct person to discuss this request with?"

"Yes, I am. Sierra Puma and Tierra del Puma are both owned by my husband and me. We take film or tour requests here or at the ranch office. We don't issue permits until we meet the people. Our ranch is private, and we only grant authorizations for nature walks, fly-fishing tours or filming in designated areas."

"What do you mean by designated?"

"It's a working ranch and there are places off-limits. Much of the area is rugged and inaccessible except by 4-wheel-drive or horseback. Filming is only allowed in preselected areas. What are your needs? I wasn't sure reading your message."

Rodin handed her a business card. "I represent a media documentary company in Russia. They produce films about unique people and places around the globe." He pointed to the book cover poster mounted on the wall. "Your novel is a best seller in Russia.

People are fascinated by the story of intrepid pioneer women crossing the famed Sierra Nevada."

Valerie listened intently, scribbling notes and thinking, *we're already making a movie-what gives?* "Mr. Rodin you do know a movie is currently in the production works, right?"

"Yes, but ours is short documentary not a motion picture. We intend to focus on specific locations in the Sierra Nevada that were a catalyst for your book and the Hollywood production."

Valerie scribbled more notes, still unclear on the marketing value of such a film. "So, you're an independent film company, doing specialized productions, right?"

Rodin nodded, "Yes, exactly, specialized is a good description."

"And when did you want to do this?"

"Ms. Cahill, we would like to start as soon as possible."

"Well, that might pose a problem. The snow is still hanging around and it's muddy in the designated film zones."

"Actually, we are interested in getting footage of the area called Tear Drop Pass where the more dramatic aspects in the book took place. We would like, as one might say, to get some boots on the ground to survey the area and enhance our artistic perspectives about filming."

Valerie furled her eyebrows and jotted down a note on her legal pad. 'Tear Drop Pass?' and underlined it-twice. She placed her finger across her lips. "Hmm, that might be out of the question for a couple of reasons. There's still snow up there, and it's a rugged remote section of the ranch. I'm not sure the few access roads are open or passable. And, we have never permitted people up there because it's unstable and prone to rockslides."

"I see," said Rodin, placing both hands on the table and leaning forward. "With your permission, we could quickly scout the area, perhaps in a day. This would enable us to accurately evaluate the scenic potential of the area. The current snow conditions up there are perfect to capture the grit and realism of your novel. We are amiable about financial arrangements. Our clients are motivated and enthused about this project. They want to be the first company in Russia to produce a unique film that many will view. And, I'm sure it will elevate your book sales. They will not balk at a reasonable price point. As one might say, time is money in our case." Rodin kept his eyes on Valerie, waiting for a response.

"Well," she said, exhaling a slow breath. "This is unusual, so I need to run it by my husband. He handles the ranch side of things. I know you want a quick answer so let me do this." Valerie stood up and leaned into the outer office. "Erin, have Jessica O'Hara come up for a second. She's downstairs."

Erin piped in, "She's right here."

Jessie popped her head in. "You need me, Val?" Jessie glimpsed at Rodin sitting at the table.

"Jessie, when or if Jake lands, run over to the helipad. Tell him we need to chat."

"Sure, on my way."

The name O'Hara instantly clicked with Rodin when he saw the red-haired teenager. He said nothing but gazed intently at her. Val returned and sat down, distracting Rodin's thoughts. "I'm not sure when Jake will return. He spends a lot of time flying these days. When he lands, I'll discuss your request with him. At the very least he needs to survey the road conditions before deciding. That could take a day or two."

Rodin nodded. "Of course, I understand. We will be positive and prepare to access the area with proper permission. Let me add, there will only be a few of us-not a total production team. We possess equipment and experience to quickly be in and out without assistance. This will not be our first encounter in remote areas with less-than-perfect conditions. Filming in Siberia makes this easy," he said with a partial, forced smile. He stood, "Ms. Cahill I shall not take any more of your time. We do not want to pressure you with a hasty decision, but our needs are on a tight schedule. I look forward to hearing from you."

"Sure. I'll get back to you as soon as possible. Thank you."

Valerie watched out the window as Rodin walked to his car. She tapped her fingernail on his business card, mulling over his request.

"There wasn't any mention of Tear Drop Pass in the novel, only the name Tierra del Puma. Did I misunderstand the guy ? And how did my book become a bestseller in Russia so fast?" She decided to do a quick follow-up on the request after she dealt with the endless issues already overwhelming the day.

Once in the car Victor Rodin called Cherenkov. "The woman, Valerie Cahill, is hesitant to grant permission. She is undecided about allowing our little film company to visit the area. She would have to check with her husband who runs the ranch. That may take some days. But there is other news."

"That is?"

"In passing, she mentioned the name of a young woman who works at the winery."

"And how does that affect us?"

"She said, Jessie O'Hara. I saw the girl. She has red hair." Rodin didn't need to explain the possible connections to Sean O'Hara. "That could mean potential ramifications."

"Yes, that would be serious if there is a relationship to the boy. Especially if he shared certain things with her. This requires an immediate resolution. Notify Wade and have him elevate the surveillance on the O'Hara residence. Find out who lives there. The situation is changing. We must access the area much sooner than later, with or without permission. There is mounting pressure from overseas. We need results or lose money and creditability. I shall not lose either one."

Rodin spoke as he navigated around a car. "We have a large region to search and I believe it will take more than a day. Despite what I told this Cahill woman."

"Yes, I realize that," said Cherenkov. "It is necessary to find this boy's maps or sketches that he claimed to have. He wasn't stupid. I'm sure he kept a record. If need be, give Wade and his people a loose leash and find any links to what the boy might have said or left behind. Do what's required to locate the information. It will save time." Cherenkov's voice became a low growl. "This change of events may require a frank discussion with this O'Hara girl. We do not need additional impediments to our project." Cherenkov hung up.

Rodin pressed the speed dial on his phone for Wade Keeler. When Wade answered, Rodin relayed the order as if it came from Rodin himself. Keeler snapped back, "Victor, I told you we had that covered," he said in an irritated voice. Wade Keeler grew weary of Rodin's often condescending manner to people who weren't of Russian blood. He calmed down then added, "We got information for you."

"And what that might be?" said Rodin impatiently.

"We checked the house. It's a small rental place in Lincoln. There's mother and a daughter living there. The daughter's name is Jessica O'Hara." There was silence on the other end. "Victor, you there?"

"I must call Cherenkov back immediately. You will have additional work."

"All right, then call me with the next step. My people are ready to roll." Wade cut the connection.

CHAPTER 18

The growl in her stomach made Valerie look at her watch. She went downstairs to the restaurant, picked up a small salad, and returned to her cluttered desk. She distractedly picked at her late lunch while looking at the stacks of papers. She blinked her eyes several times trying to focus on the myriad of projects that needed her attention.

She glanced at Victor Rodin's business card, wondering again how her book became so popular in Russia. An idea flashed in her head. She picked up the phone and called her editor. Within seconds Kim Becker answered. "Hey, Val, what's up? You're calling to say you're writing another book?"

"Hi Kim, I wish, but time and energy are elsewhere with business projects and the screenplay dynamics. We're having a large get together at the winery to kick off the filming. Mark Parnell, the producer is the speaker and wants to pump up enthusiasm for the production and also promote his wilderness preservation organization. Why don't you fly out and join us?"

"Love to but I'm swamped here. Our New York office is crazy busy at the moment. I'm at home and still working. Thanks anyway."

"Well, if you change your mind, we have a guest cottage for you." Valerie shifted subjects. "Kim, some guy stopped by here, said he was with a Russian film company. They want to film sections of

Tierra del Puma and do a documentary relative to my book. He said the 'Guardians of the Covered Carriage' was a best seller in Russia. Is it?"

There was a moment of silence of the other end as Val heard the keyboard clicks of Kim's computer. "Val, we haven't promoted your book in Russia, and it hasn't been converted to any language- it's only English. Your book is exceptional and is selling nicely, but it's not on the New York Times bestseller, yet." She chuckled, "Hopefully, the movie won't dampen book sales."

Val tapped her pencil on the desk, digesting what Kim had said. "Well, this is weird. Why would this guy say that about my book then?"

"Who knows, maybe his company is trying to develop a special angle on making a film. Oops, Val I have to run, Steven Smith is on the other line. He may have another bestseller in the works. You better write another book. Ciao."

"Sure, if I ever get the time. Take care." Valerie pushed away her half-eaten salad, wondering why Rodin wanted to make a movie of a bestseller that wasn't a bestseller. She decided to call the man to clarify her questions. There was a slight delay in the connection, then a male voice came on the line. "Mr. Rodin's office."

"Hi, Mr. Rodin, please."

"He is not here. May I ask who is calling," said the formal voice.

"This is Valerie Cahill at Sierra Puma Winery. He came by to discuss a film permit. There's been some delays with that, and I had a few more questions. He doesn't answer his cell."

"Mr. Rodin is unavailable. I will make sure he gets the message and we have your call back, correct?"

"Yes, you do. Please have him call me. Thank you, bye."

Cherenkov hung up from his special trunked phone service, then dialed Victor to relay the conversation.

"The bitch." Rodin hissed into the phone. "It's time for other options. But if you want, I will call and play nice one more time. I doubt it will do anything but raise her suspicions. I noticed she has an acting background. Perhaps she made inquiries about our so-called film company."

"That is possible. Let us wait on that decision for a while. Time is growing short, and the backcountry will open soon. We will plan to search the area-with caution. Call Wade back. Tell him to keep listening and make preparations."

"I will give him the order." Rodin clicked off.

It was after 5 pm and Valerie sat in her office handling more unexpected business issues. She pushed the hair back from her face and rapped her fingers on the cluttered desk, lost in thought. Inquisitiveness still lingered in her mind about Rodin and his unusual film request near Tear Drop Pass. She gave a long-tired sigh deciding there were too many other things that needed her immediate attention. The unusual permit application would have to be deferred until after the upcoming festivities. She walked into Erin's' office and fixed herself another cup of coffee.

"A little late in the day for a caffeine blast, isn't it?" said Erin, clearing her desk for the day. "That's not like you, Val."

"I know." Valerie said, slowly sipping her coffee. Her wan face showed more than just afternoon weariness. "Erin, are you good with handling things here after we pull off this event? I need to get back to the ranch for a few days."

"Val, sure I can. You need to slow down before you go crazy. Or, as Jake says, crazier," she said, grinning. "I've got your back."

"Thanks." She glanced out the window and squinted her eyes trying to identify the two employees in the parking lot. She grinned, thinking Jake might be right.

Not having a car, Jessie accepted Tim's offer to drive her home. "It's on the way, no problem," he said, smiling. Jessie knew it wasn't but was starting to enjoy his company. As they drove along Tim adjusted the radio volume in his pickup then asked, "You want to go get something to eat? I guess we're going back to the ranch in the morning. Things are getting nutty bouncing back and forth from winery to ranch."

Jessie looked over at him, hesitant to get overly friendly. "I haven't seen my Mom enough, so I better not." She saw the disappointment in his eyes. "But, if she's at work then that would be fun. Can I text you later?"

His face lit up. "You bet." He dropped her off at the house in Lincoln and sped off.

Jessie walked in the house carrying a large backpack of clothes and gear. "Hey Mom, I'm home." There was no answer. On the untidy small kitchen table lay a note. 'Jessie, I had a chance for a double shift tonight. I'll be home after 1 am. How about we go to breakfast tomorrow? You can tell me about your job. Love Mom'. Jessie looked around the empty house; loneliness echoed off the walls. She pushed aside the gloom, dug out her clothes and dropped them in the washer, and then walked back to her bedroom. Her inquisitiveness about Sean's last adventure had amplified given the coincidence of working at Tierra del Puma and flying over Tear Drop Pass. It was where he found the *thing*.

Rummaging through the closet, she located Sean's box with his handheld GPS, notes and the strange-looking canister. She picked up the GPS and turned it on. It came to life with a 'battery low' warning light. She brought up the menu of recorded hikes. The tiny display revealed an overlay of Sean's tracks in the mountains. She zoomed in on the map and confirmed what she noticed on the first examination. Jessie stared at the squiggly lines, attempting to determine where Sean had hiked when the screen image faded, and the GPS died.

"Crap." She searched the room for the charging cable with no results but remembered he uploaded his hikes onto the GPS website. Her brother often logged his snowboard and mountain biking excursions with detailed map profiles and comments. Jessie switched on the computer. The old machine was agonizingly slow to load. She got up, checked her laundry, and returned to see the website pop up on the screen. After typing in a password his Tear Drop Pass exploit and notes appeared. She expanded the illustration and leaned closer to the screen. *Wow, he did hike over the Pass and snowboard on the ranch side.* She examined the path of tracks and the note that showed where he crashed and what he hit. Another comment popped up, "Other piece farther downhill, I think. Not going there because of avalanche danger-no way!" She swallowed hard reading her brother's final entry.

Jessie shook her head, confused. She printed out the entire map and his notes. Nothing came out of the printer except a faded sheet of paper. She closed her eyes in frustration. *Now the printer is out of ink.* She tossed the illegible paper on the floor then rummaged through her desk for another ink cartridge. Finally, a clean copy emerged from the noisy printer.

Jessie looked over at the box with the odd-looking broken device, convinced it was some electrical or computer part. Sean had scribbled an address on the side of the carton. She knew that location as her brother often took his not-so-legal computer and electrical junk there to pawn. Jessie took the device and print outs and stuffed them in her backpack. She felt a sad compulsion to retrace her brother's last adventure and discover what had piqued his interest, and maybe got him killed. She wasn't sure of a connection to his death, but she sensed a duty to her big brother. That, she hoped would give her a purpose, something Sean would have wanted her to do. Jessie closed her eyes, feeling the approaching wave of depression. She thought about taking the anti-depressants prescribed to her right after Sean's death. They really didn't help, she thought, just a bandage to cover the other issues. Instead, she texted Tim. "Mom's not home until super late. Want to come over and hang and watch TV?" She knew the potential implications and didn't care. It was better than being alone with the demons of sadness.

The text came back in a second. "Sure. I'll get a pizza. Okay?"

"Yes, but no anchovies!"

Late that evening Wade and Kenny drove by the O'Hara residence. No lights were on and a Toyota pickup was parked in front. "Don't know who owns that," said Kenny, glancing around Wade's shoulder. "But somebody's there besides that teenage kid. The old lady drives a beat-up Subaru."

Wade grunted, "You and Mason scope out the place. Keep track of the kid and also who her old lady meets up with. I'll call Rodin tomorrow to set up another meeting." Wade slowly drove down the darkened neighborhood.

The next morning at 9 am sharp, Tim drove up in front of the O'Hara residence. Jessie stood out front with her backpack. She tossed her gear in the bed of the truck, then climbed in the cab and smiled at Tim. "Good morning."

"Good morning to you too," he said with a bright smile as they drove away. Tim looked back and saw Jessie's mom's car parked in the garage. "What time did your mom get home?"

"About 15 minutes after you left. It's all good, I tidied up the bedroom. She won't know." Both grinned with no words spoken.

Tim broke the awkward silence. "Erin from Val's office called me. They want us back at the ranch today. She also said a bunch of us would have to come back to the winery to help with Valerie's upcoming gigantic party."

Jessie smiled, looking out the window at the passing traffic. "Wranglers to waiters. I'd rather be a wrangler, but it will be neat to see some movie stars."

"I guess. Erin said we can take the company shuttle up to the ranch. I want my truck up there so I told her we would drive." He looked at Jessie, hoping she would agree.

"That's fine, Tim. I appreciate the ride. The shuttle doesn't always stop at Starbucks," she said, grinning. An idea crossed her mind. Sean's notes mentioned the recycled center where he planned to hawk his strange discovery. "Tim, can we make a quick detour before getting on I-80?"

"Sure, where to?"

"It's an industrial park in Loomis, not far. My Mom said there's a Habitat for Humanity place there. She wants to get another kitchen table. I just want to see where it is." Jessie never spoke to Tim or anyone else about her brother or her life growing up. Nobody would understand.

In a few minutes they drove into the industrial park. She directed Tim to the rear of the complex to a set of offices off by themselves.

"Jessie, I don't see any sign about a donation center. Are we in the right industrial park?"

"Stop for a second, maybe it's this place." Jessie rolled down the window and looked at the office suite with no name. At that moment Victor Rodin and Yeric came out the front door.

A chill went up Jessie's spine. *That guy was in Valerie's office. What's he doing here?* She regained her composure and touched Tim's arm. "You're right, Mom got the wrong address, Lets go to the ranch."

As they approached the highway, Tim answered his cell phone. "Okay, Jessie is with me. We're coming back."

Jessie was still thinking about the man at the recycle center when she heard her name. "What's up?"

Tim turned the pickup around. "Change of plans. Valerie needs us back at the winery for last-minute projects and to explain our duties for this big conference, dinner or whatever it's called. We go back to the ranch after the party. Wish they would make up their minds," he said, frustrated.

Jessie half listened. Disjointed thoughts swirled in her mind about the bizarre coincidence of seeing Rodin at the winery *and* recycle center. She became perplexed by the ever-increasing twists that centered around Sean's findings. But she knew it now; Sean was reaching out to her. Jessie didn't understand but felt compelled to follow her brother's haunting footsteps into the mountains. She sighed and looked at Tim. "I wish we could go back to the ranch right now."

CHAPTER 19

WEEK LATER
CG AVIATION
MCCLELLAN AIRPORT
SACRAMENTO, CA

Jake retarded the throttles on the King Air as the main landing gear touched the runway. He let the aircraft coast down the runway as CG Aviation was at the other end of the field. With enough energy left in the roll out, Jake easily steered the plane off the runway and came to a stop on the ramp. He shut the engines down then exited the cockpit and walked through the cabin to assist the clients off the plane. The 'clients' were geologists from the US Geological Survey who were on a scientific charter to study Mt. Lassen and Mt. Shasta, both volcanoes. Shasta was asleep, Lassen on a century old snooze; both were worthy of studying and monitoring. One man shook Cahill's hand. "Thanks again, Jake. We'll charter the helicopter on the next flight for some off-site work near Lassen."

"No problem, just let me know. Say, you guys will tell me if Lassen uncorks, right?" Jake said jokingly." I may want to sell my ranch before it's a lava field."

The older geologist, with silver hair, hefted up his gear bag, "Lassen hasn't erupted since 1917. The area is bubbling, but so far, no indications of another light off. I think you're safe. Speaking of your ranch, we would like to do a little exploring on Tierra del Puma. You have some interesting geology in those hills. Be nice to update our science of the area, especially that mountain peak, Whispering Wind."

Jake considered the request. As always, he was reluctant to let anyone explore the mountain, given Valerie's mystical connections and feelings to the area. "Yeah, maybe someday." He changed the subject. "I'll look forward to flying you up to Lassen. Sounds like fun."

As the geologists walked from the plane one turned and said, "Jake, you seem pretty interested in all of this. Why don't you hike around with us with on the next mission? Beats sitting around at base camp playing gin rummy."

"That sounds like a plan. I'll make sure I'm on the schedule. Thanks again." The two geologists shook Jake's hand again and headed to their car.

Jake stood on the ramp as another King Air taxied up and shut down. He saw Walt in the left seat and Randy the "Wingnut" in the right seat. He figured they were returning from a maintenance test flight. Then Randy strolled down the flight stairs, not in his usual mechanic overalls, but in blue jeans and kaki shirt, topped with an old fedora hat.

"What the hell is that on your head, Randy?" asked Jake.

Randy smiled, adjusted the hat over his mop of blonde hair. "That's 'detective' to you Jake."

"Come again?"

Walt approached carrying his flight bag. "Detective Wingnut here and his personal pilot just returned from the Lone Pine Airport in the Owens Valley."

They all walked back towards the office as Jake nodded. "Yeah, I know where it is. What were you guys doing over there? That's a long maintenance hop."

Randy looked at Jake. "Looking for the rest of a plane."

"What the hell are you talking about?"

"Walt and I think we found out where your mysterious baggage door came from and who used to be CG Aviation."

They entered the office as Jake pushed up his sunglasses. "Now this I want to hear."

Walt placed his arm around Jake's shoulders. "Make yourself useful for a change and grab us some coffee. Our resident aviation detective will fill you in on the details."

Jake brought over several cups of java. "How did you end up at Lone Pine?"

Randy propped his feet up on Walt's desk, and sipped his coffee. "This is one interesting story, Jake."

"Go for it. I'm listening."

"I ran the part number on the baggage door. As far as I can tell it tags to an older series Cessna 182, maybe late 60s or 1970s era."

"Wow, old plane," said Jake.

Walt chimed in, "Vintage but a damn good airframe and engine with good horsepower. Basically, the same plane today, but they added lots of fancy electronics and bigger price tag. A rugged bird with fixed gear. The retractable gear models came out later."

Randy flipped through his notes and continued. "With that, I did another check of possible stolen 182s. That was a dead end; the FAA needs a tail number. So, Walt and I did a general data search on the words CG Aviation. Bingo. Many years ago, there was a Charles Goodman Aviation in Lone Pine. Better known in the company's brief history as CG Aviation."

"Really?" said Jake, surprised and intrigued with the discoveries.

"Goodman lived in the Owens Valley near the airfield," added Randy.

Walt interjected. "Charles Goodman ran a one-man flying business doing aqueduct and power line patrols. That was 40 plus years ago. He had a contract with the Los Angeles Department of Power and Water. Back then, people in the Owens Valley watched helplessly as Los Angeles ripped off their water resources. Some locals tried to sabotage pipelines and aqueducts. Thus, the contract for airborne security patrols."

Jake shook his head in amazement. "How did you guys find all this out?"

Walt went on. "We got curious about all this, so we flew over to Lone Pine and snooped around. Even spoke to a relative of the late Charles Goodman. It gets better." Walt flipped on the desktop computer to Google Earth and zoomed in on Lone Pine Airport; a quiet, non-controlled, rural airport nestled near the Sierras. There were a few hangars with several planes and gliders on the ramp. "Randy snooped around and met an old mechanic who remembered servicing a 182 and recalled when it got taxied off the airfield."

"Taxied off the field?" said Jake, scratching his head, confused.

Walt ran his finger over the airport photo, tracing a dirt road that went off airport property to several rows of houses covered in trees and off Highway 395. "These houses have some big barns, big enough to stash a single-engine plane like a Cessna 182."

Jake stared at the satellite photo. "How and why did it end up there?"

Randy chimed in. "Charlie Goodman lost the DPW contract. He owed back taxes and was afraid the plane would get repossessed. So, he stashed it in one of those old barns." He pointed on the screen, "That one there, a distant relative owned it. The plane sat in the barn for years, then Goodman died. Years later this relative also died and bequeathed the house to his son, the current owner." Randy smiled, "Not the sharpest guy I ever met-got some brain cells missing. Anyway, the dude didn't know what to do with the old aircraft. Months ago, some guy slides by and says he's interested in buying it. The relative shows him the plane. The guy inspects it, then takes it around the patch. He lands and gives the guy 30k cash-no questions asked. The guy says his name is Joe and will be back to get the plane. A few days later, no plane."

Jake rocked back in the chair. "Crazy. So, no theft of the plane?"

Walt shook his head, "Nope, that's the bizarre part. This distant relative, he uh, like 'Wingnut' alluded to, is the type you might have arrested when you on the LAPD. Probably a meth addict and cooks the stuff. Not real bright and hinky of the law. But suddenly he has 30,000 bucks, no paperwork, and no strings attached. He doesn't have the brainpower to figure out the value of the old Cessna. What does he care? He's got 30k, no questions asked. And he has a house with an empty barn for his other not-so-legal activities. He's the type that doesn't want police snooping around the place." Walt looked at Randy and grinned. "This freaky guy connected with

Randy for some odd reason. Must have figured they did prison time together or something," he said with a grin.

Randy raised his brows. "Yeah, he did time, for sure." He looked at Walt with a stern expression. "MY prison time was working in the Coast Guard with you as my commanding officer."

Jake tapped his fingers on the desk. "Hmm, so no stolen plane but maybe an altered tail number I assume the original registration goes back to the dead guy and a defunct company with our initials. Thus, no crime, no report and now no plane. But where the hell is the rest of the aircraft?"

Walt pointed with his hand eastward. "We suspect in the area where the officer found the baggage door. The aircraft is probably in pieces around the ridges of Tierra del Puma. Like you said, the new owner was a smuggler that never made it over the mountains."

Randy chimed in. "I agree, that's why no theft or lost report. As Walt said, it probably got eaten by a thunderstorm and spread all over the Sierras."

Jake recalled the days he flew undercover as an air smuggler. "Most drug runners crash and die without notice. Nobody cares about them unless the cartels want their dope or money back, which usually isn't the case. And rarely is the aircraft reported missing, for obvious reasons. So, this plane, if one is there, is spread out in fragments.

"Yep, all over canyon and pass," said Randy.

Jake took a deep breath then exhaled, "All this is interesting. But for now, let the bones of the dirtbag and the plane stay in the mountains until it's safe to get up there. It's muck and avalanche prone right now. I've got too much going on at the winery and ranch, and here with more charters popping up to do any follow-up."

Randy stared at the floor listening to Jake's seemingly passive interest after all the investigative work he had accomplished. "So, I guess we wasted time on this. Kind of figured it was important," said Randy in a dejected voice.

"It is, Randy. Now we know a plane is up there, thanks to you. And it wasn't an aircraft with a missing family onboard.

That's excellent research. I plan to tell Gavin at Highway Patrol Air Operations so they can recon the area. Sorry, Randy, keep the fedora on, we might need your detective services again. And, I'll do a few fly overs of the area on the way to the ranch. Never know, we might spot something."

The Chief of Maintenance grinned, "No problem, Jake. You seem loaded up and busy. Guess this super shindig that Valerie's putting on at the winery is taking a lot of time."

"Yeah, it's hectic at the moment. Afterward, when conditions improve, maybe we can all hike up there and locate the remnants of the plane, its cargo and the decomposed pilot that flew it, whoever the hell he was." Jake glanced at his watch, "I better run back to the winery."

Walt looked out the window. "Are you taking the helicopter?"

"Uh-huh, we still have some hours left before it needs an inspection. I'll stop by and chat with Jack Treco to reaffirm his need for it." Jake said his goodbyes and went out to the flight line.

Once the helicopter departed Randy turned to Walt. "Jake seems preoccupied with stuff. Is he okay?"

Walt cleared his desk and scratched the side of nose. "I think he's concerned Val's gotten too absorbed with the winery business. He misses her not being at the ranch, that's all."

"Makes sense. Jake is grounded to Tierra del Puma. He would never leave the place again. I know Valerie enjoys the ranch and working the vineyard gig, but she'll be back up there. So what's his hang up?"

"He doesn't fully understand her pressing desire to prove something to herself by making the winery business something special. I'm guessing that might be a reason. One never knows with Jake."

"She sure has built the place up, that's for damn sure. And she was an actress and wrote a novel. Those are pretty impressive achievements. Sounds like the lady already made her mark of success."

Walt stared out the window at the tarmac. "I agree, she's done an outstanding job with the winery enterprise; better than Jake or his parents ever did with it. Given that, maybe Jake is afraid she might want to live in Auburn and work the business instead of the ranch." Walt sighed and shuffled the papers on his desk. "Not my business, best to let them sort it out."

"Gee, Walt, you sound like a wise old guy. Well, old anyway."

CHAPTER 20

A WEEK LATER
TRECO SYSTEMS
ROSEVILLE, CA

Jake parked in front of the office suites located less than a mile from the FBI office in Roseville. That made sense, he thought, considering Warren Treco was a retired Bureau man. He walked into the modern building, then down the hallway to the door marked with a number-nothing else. Warren Treco's company handled only corporate or government accounts. His expertise, law enforcement contacts and high-tech equipment made Treco Systems a high demand service. Some cases required airborne transportation or discreet aerial surveillance and for that he chartered with CG Aviation.

Within seconds of pushing the buzzer on the locked door, Chuck Taggert, a business partner of Treco's motioned Jake in. Taggert, in his late 50s, was also former FBI. "Hey, Jake, what brings you around? Looking for money? Are we delinquent in our aviation bill?" he said, smiling.

"Nope, all good as far I know. I was in the neighborhood and wanted to ask Warren about the helicopter you guys have on lease. Is he around?"

Treco's loud voice boomed from a back office, "Chuck, I told you don't let that guy in here. He's former LAPD, a security risk. Aw hell, it's too late now, send him back here." Warren Treco had a trim and neat frame topped with thinning gray hair giving a hint of being in his 60s. He dressed in dark slacks with and a tieless white shirt with the sleeves partially rolled up. Coupled with his tortoiseshell frame glasses he had the stereotypical appearance of an accountant or attorney. Jake assumed one or the other given he was former FBI. Treco spoke little of his past career except to say he chased criminals through a computer and traveled a lot. Warren walked over and shook Jake's hand. A well-dressed Asian woman sat quietly in one of the office chairs. He smiled at the lady, then glanced back at Treco. "Warren, am I interrupting something?"

"No, not at all. Joy and I were just traveling down memory lane. Jake, this is Joy Lee. She's with my old alma mater." Jake caught the inference-FBI. "Joy, this is the guy I mentioned in a disparaging manner, Jake Cahill, former LAPD, but don't hold that against him. He runs CG Aviation. We use his aircraft despite the fact he screws us on the billing."

Joy Lee gave a courteous smile. "Nice to meet you Jacob," she said, with an air of formality. "Actually, Warren speaks highly of you, both professionally and personally. I understand you have interest in the Sierra Puma Winery. It's a very nice establishment. I've been there many times."

"Thank you. My wife is in command of the winery. She's done an amazing job. I'm just a flyboy or cowboy depending on what day it is."

Treco chuckled, "Jake here is more than an aeronautical cowpoke and grape picker. He owns Tierra del Puma, the ranch north of Truckee. He's got the most beautiful countryside in the Sierra. Makes one wonder how a former LA cop scored that. I'm sure all obtained through illegal means and shake downs."

"No, not totally, I purchased it with the winning number off that five-dollar lottery scratcher you gave me as a Christmas present. The one that had four lines already scratched off."

Warren grinned, "He's also a liar, Joy. I only scratched off two lines. Jake, you want a cup of coffee?"

"Thanks, but I'm caffeine loaded already." Treco's office had a sparse appearance, adorned with a few pictures on the wall of mountain scenery, a plaque with an FBI logo and a credenza with family photos. Jake looked at the clutter free desk with only a computer on it. "Warren, you could do surgery on that desk. Do you ever put things on it, such as pens or paper?"

"It only looks clean. The drawers are like my brain, messy. So, what's up with you?"

"Busy, running between the ranch, the winery and McClellan Airport."

"How's that lovely lady of yours?"

"Val's good and busy with endless activities. With any luck, she's hoping to break away and get some down time at the ranch soon."

"That sounds good. How's the weather in God's country?"

"Snows melting and wildflowers blooming. Spring is here and we're getting busy with more wild horses arriving."

"That reminds me," said Treco, "my granddaughter is now in love with horses. Mind if I come up sometime and take some pictures of the herd, flock or whatever they call a bunch of horses?"

"No problem. Bring her along if you want. We have some colts running around. Plus, we can give her a riding lesson."

"I would if she wasn't in school. So, what's up, you wanted to chat about something?"

"Excuse me," said Joy, "perhaps I'd better run."

Jake considered her position on the FBI might subtly help shed light on the plane crash mystery. "Joy, please stick around. I have a story you might find interesting. But first let me give Warren the news."

"Here it comes, what news?" said Warren, raising his eyebrows with suspicion.

"Real quick, you still want the helicopter for your contract over in Reno?"

Warren examined the computer screen and then gave a furtive glance to Lee. "Hmm, I don't think so. The client's needs have changed but let me confirm that again later. Why do you ask?"

"The helicopter is coming up for a maintenance inspection. I've been flying it since you took it off standby. But if you have plans to use it, then I'll hanger it at the ranch and save the hours. It's the only CG helicopter with search light, moving GPS map, and Forward-Looking Infrared Radar gear."

"No problem-fly it. I'll let you know if we need another helicopter with those fancy options. That way you can bill the hell out of me."

"Well, it makes it a perfect law enforcement ship. We had a similar helicopter on the LAPD. The difference was radios and the logo. Neither of which you need, especially the police logo."

"No, that we don't need. So, what else did you want to waste my precious time about, Cahill? I'm a busy man," he said, leaning back in his chair.

"Yeah, I can tell you're overworked. I have a mystery for you, if I'm not interrupting your nap time." Jake glanced at Lee, who chuckled at the sarcasm between the two men.

"I'll try to stay awake-go ahead."

Jake kept his missing airplane story brief. When he finished, he looked at Treco and smiled, "So, there ya go. Weird. The CG Aviation logo is interesting though we never owned a single-engine aircraft. I know you like puzzles and this is good one."

Both Warren and Joy listened intently to the story. "Hmm, that is interesting; did you guys check with the FAA and law enforcement about a missing plane?" asked Warren.

"Affirmative, and no plane of this make and model missing, lost or overdue in the Sierras in the past ten years. I'm assuming the plane slammed a mountain or broke up in a thunderstorm on a drug run. That area up there is a crumbling avalanche zone. The plane probably got covered up in snow. But now a few parts are exposed because of rockslide movement. Air smugglers work alone. The aircraft would never get reported. Walt's doing more follow-up, mostly for curiosity's sake." Jake stood up, "Anyway, that's why I stopped by. I know you have a thing about mysterious occurrences or was that the occult?" he said with a grin.

"It's detective mysteries and space aliens Jake, I gave up voodoo when I transferred back from the Caribbean. But this *is* curious. What's your next step?"

"I'll look around when and if the geology stabilizes. Gives me an excuse to ride the mountains. Besides, I hate trash on the ranch, broken aluminum, or dope."

"Jacob, may I ask, why do you think it's a smuggler's plane?" asked Joy Lee, absorbed in the story.

"I did some air smuggling at one time," he said with a straight face.

"Excuse me?"

"When I was on the LAPD, I worked undercover with a joint task force dealing with narcotics and drug cartels. Since I flew airplanes and spoke Spanish, I assumed the role of an air smuggler. It was edgy work with a limited life expectancy. After a few things went sideways I got transferred to the helicopter unit and patrolled over LA" Jake didn't elaborate further. "But I learned a lot about air smuggling. That's why I think it's an old doper plane. Again, *if* there's a plane up there." He shrugged his shoulders. "Who knows, but like Warren said, it is a fascinating puzzle."

Lee smiled, "Yes it is, another mysterious tale of the High Sierra."

"One of many, Joy. From lost gold mines to the ghosts haunting the tunnels of the first transcontinental railroad across Donner Summit. All those legends and history, just up the road."

"Yes, the Sierra holds enthralling history of people and things." Joy stood up, "I better return to the office before I get captivated with another curious story." She extended her hand, "Nice to meet you Jacob. Good luck with your airplane mystery."

"Thank you. Look forward to seeing you again."

A few minutes later, Treco walked Cahill to the door. "Yeah, odd deal about your airplane part. Let me know what you find." Treco chuckled, "Hey, maybe the plane had a bag of money in it. But remember, Jake, if you find it don't launder the bills through me. Take care."

Jake turned, "How do you now I haven't already?"

CHAPTER 21

FOREST HILL, CA

Paul Davis stopped at the market in Forest Hill for a cup of coffee. The grocery store was an icon of the area. Locals, cyclists, bikers, river rafters and tourists all stopped at the market for supplies. For Game Warden Davis it was just coffee. He was pleasantly surprised when the young man behind the counter understood the word medium size coffee. *So much for designer coffees shops, I'll stick with old stores for my java.*

He walked out of the store, coffee cup in hand, and sat on the stone wall that overlooked the deep canyon where the American River tumbled and plunged 2000 feet below. The historic river was where the Gold Rush began. Small sections of the river remained wild and scenic, but Davis wondered how long that would last given California's voracious thirst for water and reservoirs. He changed mental gears and considered the day. It was half gone and so was his patience.

Earlier, he met another warden and the local sheriffs farther up the road. Hikers had found two eagles shot and killed. Then they stumbled upon an abandoned pot and meth lab. The small camp was littered with deer carcasses and turkey remains; all shot out of season. Davis and his fellow officers completed the investigation, realizing it was an exercise in futility. Next, the EPA showed up and determined the area was permeated with spilled barrels of toxic chemicals. The environmental hazard would require cleanup. At that point, he finished his work and came back down the hill. He had other calls to handle, probably equally frustrating as all were absent a conclusion. Paul Davis shook his head in resignation-getting burned out. Retirement to Idaho couldn't come soon enough.

He stowed his mental complaining and reached in his pocket for the computer printout of vehicle license plates and registered owners. After his discussion with Jake Cahill he completed the tedious work of attempting to match the last number on the license plate on Cahill's photo along the description of the vehicle that he had provided. A remote possibility existed of connecting Cahill's observations and the ramblings of the confused woman informant who wanted to report a bear poacher. So far, results were nil. He would check another address in Lincoln that held more promise, given it was close to a quarry; something the woman mentioned in her babbling. It was worth a follow up. He noticed a Placer County Sheriff's car drive up. He knew the deputy, Matt Plahy.

"Hey Game Warden, how goes the day?" said Plahy, sitting in the patrol SUV adjusting the volume on the police radio.

"It goes, Matt, day by day. You probably heard about the pot and meth farm up the road. No suspects, just dead animals and toxic waste. You were smart to stay away."

"I heard but got busy with a dead body call at Lake Clementine."

"Another drowning?" Davis asked, half interested, taking a final sip of his *medium* coffee.

"Don't think so. A kayaker discovered the body. Victim is female, maybe in her 40s, blonde hair and some tattoos. Had her hands tied behind her back. Doesn't take a super sleuth to figure out we have another homicide. I'm betting drug related." He smiled, "Just another busy day in them *thar* hills. I can hardly wait for the summer rush of tourists and idiots." Plahy typed something on his vehicle computer screen. "Got a call, take care Paul."

"Watch your back out there, Matt, and be safe."

Thirty minutes later Davis drove by an old trailer park on the outskirts of Lincoln that matched the address on the license list. The trailer in question was at the rear of the complex. The registration info came back to Kenneth Stovall. *Not Mr. Clean,* thought

Davis having checked Stovall's record that listed prior jail time for battery and a host of other minor crimes. The Fish and Wildlife truck was a standout, so he chose not to drive into the trailer park and blow a potential lead. Just then a black, lifted, four-wheel-drive vehicle roared out of the trailer park and headed west. Davis going east looked in the rearview mirror and did a quick 180 turn and followed the oddball contraption from a distance. He recalled Cahill's description "an abortion of parts." That's what now sped down the road. Several miles later, the vehicle exited off the highway and turned down a dirt road that led to a well fenced in quarry. "Well, I'll be damn, the rambling woman on the phone got it right," Davis said.

CHAPTER 22

MAY
PROFESSIONAL OFFICE SUITES
ROSEVILLE, CA

K enny Stovall watched from across the street as the red Porsche SUV pulled up in front of the offices and a woman stepped out of the car. "That's the classy looking bitch attorney we saw before," Kenny said to Mason, noticing the woman greet a red haired, older woman. "And that's Nancy O' Hara, the dead kid's mom. Shit, they're at it again." The two women disappeared into the office suites. Kenny picked up his cell and pushed speed dial to Wade Keeler.

Keeler sat in his office at the gravel pit sharpening his skinning knife. With slow and methodical movements, he ran the blade over the stone, then touched the edge with his thumb, drawing a drop of blood. He smiled, admiring the glistening sharpness of the large knife; the perfect tool for skinning bears. He sat the knife down and looked over at his rifle, handgun, and pack. Wade mentally reviewed his gear. Cherenkov or Rodin would call wanting to explore Tear Drop Pass for the device. Without more details, Wade figured the search for the missing plane and its cargo would be a tough and risky effort. But it was also an opportunity to find bears, groggy from hibernation. They were easy targets. And there were plenty of bears in and near Tierra del Puma. Good fun and easy money, thought Wade, seeing his cell light up.

"What's up?" he said to Kenny while working the knife over the sharpening stone.

"I'm in Roseville. The attorney bitch met with that O'Hara woman, again. Me and Mason think they're planning something, man. I bet she found the kid's package and working to cut a deal with the lawyer," he said.

"Maybe, keep watching them. Let me know if anyone carries a package. Try and get into the O'Hara's house and see what you can find. I'll call Rodin."

"Will this fuck up our mountain trip?"

"I don't think so. It could actually speed up things. The critical pieces are still missing. But wet weather is forecasted so we aren't leaving tomorrow, that's for sure. Keep watching these broads and then let me know what you find in the house. Just be careful. I'll have more information by then." Wade hung up and went back to his knife, admiring his reflection in the shining blade.

Kenny spoke to Mason, "Wait here, I'll be right back." He got out the of the truck and walked over to the shiny new car, thinking the attorney might have left something important in the ride. Stovall approached the car, gave a casual glance around, and then cupped his hands to see through the tinted window. He felt a tap on his shoulder and then heard a voice.

"Hey, shithead. Get away from the car."

Kenny turned and saw a tall guy with short blond hair staring at him. The guy had a good build and stood just far enough away as not to take a punch to the jaw.

"Did you hear me? Get away from the car," the man snarled.

Kenny surveyed the man. Hitting the guy could be a losing proposition.

"Relax, I was just checking the ride. It's a nice Porsche, never seen one like this. I'm thinkin' of getting one."

"Yeah, right, you couldn't afford the smell of this car. Get going or I'll call the police."

Kenny came on strong. "I haven't done a fuckin' thing so back off!"

"Most assholes say that. I wonder how many traffic warrants go with your name?"

Kenny was tempted to pull out his piece, but Wade had cautioned him about bringing attention to the operations after the snowmobile trip. "I'm going. What a suspicious prick," he said, walking away towards his pickup.

Jeff Logan watched the man as Natalie walked out of the office. She looked surprised. "Jeffery, what are you doing here?"

Logan looked at Nat then refocused on Kenny strolling away. "Hi babe. One of my construction foremen dropped me off. I thought we would drive over to the winery together. I need to do a final inspection of the dining and conference center before Valerie's big event." He held a stare across the street.

Nat tossed her briefcase in the car. "Excellent plan, it will be nice to see Val and Jake, if he's there. What are you looking at?"

"Some dirt bag was looking in your car for something inside to rip off."

"Great. Just great. And in broad daylight," said Nat, following Logan's eyes. She saw the man get into the dirty pickup and noisily roar off. "That truck looks familiar. I could swear I've seen it over at the law office. Maybe I'm wrong," she said casually, tossing Logan the car keys. "You can drive, I have to answer a bunch of emails." Her mind was back on the law.

Logan kept his eyes on the truck, processing what Nat had said. "Yeah", he said slowly, "lots of strange off-road types around. I wouldn't worry about it. Just keep an eye open when you're out and about."

CHAPTER 23

WEEK LATER
QUARRY YARD
AUBURN

"I am weary of delays," said Cherenkov. His eyes darted from one man to the next as they sat around the green felt poker table inside the Keeler's quarry office. "Tell me exactly what is going on. Wade, you begin."

"We got in the O'Hara's house."

"Without being noticed, I hope," said Victor with a tone of condescension.

Wade glared at Victor and snarled. "No, we bulldozed the fucking house. What the hell do you think we did?"

Cherenkov raised his hands. "Enough. We do not need this bickering. Both of you have worked together for years. Do not let current frustrations derail our efforts. This is a project of immense importance. I need both your talents. Is that clear?"

Victor and Wade stared at one another, then both nodded.

"Yes, I understand," said Rodin.

"And you, Wade?"

"Yeah, I got it." Wade swallowed his ego. The Russians controlled his businesses and didn't tolerate disrespect. He glanced at Victor Rodin with a partial expression of conciliation. "Victor and I are good."

Cherenkov smiled, "Excellent, continue Wade."

"Anyway, Kenny broke in and Mason covered the outside. Straightforward job as the house is old with broken windows. No alarm, no dogs. He looked around and didn't find any hardware, but he located some other things." Wade held up the crumpled paper. "It's a faded print out of a partial map where this Sean kid went snowboarding and found part of the device. I can't make out anything else except it looks like he was on the ranch side of this Tear Drop Pass. I figured as much; he lied to us to keep his discovery a secret."

Rodin rubbed his chin, pondering the implications. "We must assume the sister knows or possesses what her brother found. Which also means, given this diagram, she may know the whereabouts of our package."

Wade nodded, "It looks that way. She probably made another copy and snagged the stuff her brother found and then split. She doesn't live there all the time."

"And where does she live? Nearby?" asked Rodin.

Wade went on, "She works at the winery, but we also learned she's a part-time hired hand at that Tierra del Puma ranch; lives up there in a dorm, most of the time. Occasionally, she comes back to work at the winery, stays with mommy, then returns to the ranch. It makes sense that she's got directions and the device. I figure she's going to look for the rest of the package and then cash in on what she thinks is her late brother's treasure."

Cherenkov stroked his goatee. "It appears then she knows where to go."

Wade cracked his knuckles. "That's my take." He reached in his pocket for a pack of cigarettes, lit up and slowly exhaled a puff of smoke. "There's more," he said.

"Which is?" asked Rodin.

"We found out that the mother, Nancy O'Hara has been seeing a lawyer since her little boy had that terrible motorcycle accident," Wade said causally.

"So, it is likely the daughter discussed matters with the mother. Perhaps, they know of its value and seek legal counsel to ensure a financial reward," Rodin said.

Wade shook his head in the negative. "I thought so too but

Kenny found couple things in the house that changed my mind on that. It gave me an idea."

Cherenkov rested his chin on his folded hands. "And what did he discover?"

"Besides the shitty copy of the map, he found a letter from a law firm. It was addressed to the mother and signed by the attorney that Kenny and Mason followed around. She works for a high-power law firm in Sacramento."

"What was in the letter?" asked Cherenkov.

"The O'Hara woman is on the edge of bankruptcy, lots of debts and bills. She reached out to a lawyer to get the bill collectors off her back. The letter was signed N. Sherwin and simply confirms they got her some relief. There's no legalese regarding items or treasure. Plus, Kenny kept watch on this attorney, Sherwin. She and the old lady met a couple of times at an office in Roseville. They never exchanged any packages."

"What about the mother, did they follow her in case she moved something to another location?" asked Rodin, with unease in his voice.

"Yeah, Victor, they did. My guys aren't total idiots. They do what they're told. Give it a rest."

Cherenkov raised his hand again, "Continue, Wade."

"The woman works two jobs. She's got no social life, doesn't go many places except work. Guys double checked her bedroom, the garage and her car. They never spotted any package. I really don't think she has any idea what her little boy did or brought home. But the sister is another story. This Jessie kid is probably aware of something but is keeping it secret." Wade chuckled, "She doesn't want to tell mommy that their precious Sean was a fucking crook and dealt in illegal computer parts and junk."

"That seems to be a plausible assumption," said Cherenkov, then adding, "We must assume the sister has a part of the component and directions to the rest." Cherenkov sighed, "This is a complication."

Rodin nodded. "Then we need to retrieve what she has including her brother's map. But that too comes with risk."

Cherenkov stroked his goatee. "Yes, but so does losing the device while it was in our custody, after the client had gone to great risks to acquire it. And, we had been paid to safety transport it. A failure of this magnitude will have poisonous effects on our reputation. It is imperative we find it and complete the transaction."

Wade stubbed out the remains of his cigarette in the ashtray. "There's some serious issues here, but I have a plan." He glanced at both men. Cherenkov waved his hand in a let's-hear-it manner.

"The kid has some sort of map and one piece of the device. If we go into the mountains without directions then it might take days to find the other piece, if at all. And, even if we find it, we still need the stuff the girl has. We need all of it and fast, right?"

Cherenkov nodded. "That is an absolute. Our Moscow clients will not pay for a part. They are insistent for a complete device."

"That's what I thought. Here's my idea. I know the back roads in that ranch area. Kenny and I have snooped around there many times. The weather is improving and some of the roads are accessible with heavy-duty vehicles, which I have. I say we bag the kid, her brother's stuff and the map. That's insurance in case she's already been up lookin' around. We can't waste time with some bullshit lie she could throw at us. She shows us where it is and then we get rid of her." Wade looked at Rodin, "You agree?"

"That presents problems, but it appears to be a quick option. Once we obtain all of the devices, we dispose of her."

Cherenkov spoke in a clear, cold tone. "That might be required as we must not have loose ends, or people that can talk. Actions must produce total results absent entanglements. Victor, tell me more about this teenager."

"As I mentioned, she must be 18 or older to work at this winery. She has red hair and a face full of freckles. Nothing more I can add."

Cherenkov rapped his fingers on the table. "Hmm, she might fetch an acceptable price for our overseas services." He sighed, "We shall keep that option open, but for now recovery of the device is more vital. Do what is necessary to extract the information, however, do not abuse her or leave marks. She might prove useful later. Is that understood?"

"Yes, I believe we can accomplish all this without damaging her, if she cooperates. Otherwise we will have no alternative but to apply force," said Rodin, glancing at Wade.

Wade nodded his agreement and looked at Cherenkov. "Works for me. I'll get the equipment together and let Victor know when we're ready to make it happen. Snatching the kid and then getting up to the ranch area is about timing."

Rodin added, "Wade and I will examine the best opportunities to pick up the teenager and transport her and our people to the mountains." He looked at Wade. "What contingency plans exist should ranch employees come upon us?"

Wade stretched his arms. "We'll take a team of five and two vehicles. Kenny, Mason, and I can figure out the best roads to slip in and out of the area. That part of Tierra del Puma is way off the beaten track from the rest of the ranch. It's remote as hell; I doubt anybody gets up there this time of year. Kenny's confrontation was a fluke, but we need to keep eyes open. If company shows up, then we drug the kid and cover her with a blanket. We feign an excuse, say sorry, just four wheeling, trespassing by mistake and leave. This time we put on different license plates. At least we have part of the device for whatever good it will do later. If that happens then the only option is that we sneak back and leave two guys hiding up there. They search the area, and with luck, along with the map, find the rest of the stuff and hike over the pass with it."

Cherenkov rubbed his hand across his face and frowned, "This all sounds possible, but I am concerned about what happens when this girl disappears. Now there will be two family members missing. That could bring attention or leave a trail back to us."

"That trail may prove difficult, Nicolai," said Rodin. "The girl is unaware of us. At most, she may know that her brother sold parts at the recycle center. But so have hundreds of other people, many of her brother's age. We just ensure Yeric cleans the building of items that would raise suspicions on our other investments. The trail would end there."

Wade casually cleaned his fingernails with a pocketknife, then spoke. "I don't think a dead brother and then a missing sister will be such a big deal."

"Explain that further," said Cerenkov.

"The girl uses drugs. Kenny spotted a bottle of anti-depressants in her room. It's apparent she's bummed out that big brother is dead. The family's broke. They live in a dump...hell, the list goes on. So, we bag her and leave a bottle of pills in the car. We make sure the car is on some side road, as if abandoned. Easy assumption; the kid got depressed and disappeared. The cops will search for a while. They'll put her picture up in rest stop bathrooms between here and Reno or throw up an Amber Alert, but I doubt it. Hey, it's just another depressed and confused teenager that committed suicide. Who gives a shit about that? And the cops don't have any connection to us. We just need to make sure she isn't found alive or we get her out of the area into your servitude program."

"Wade is correct, this can work, risks and all," said Rodin. "We continue with the plan. Take the teenager; move her out of country or eliminate her."

Cherenkov nodded his approval. "All right but this will be accomplished without evidence that falls back upon us. Let us move forward." He stood up to signal the meeting was over.

Rodin turned to Wade, "I'm glad we have resolved our personal differences. We will work out the timing to pick up the teenager before she becomes a problem."

"Will do. I'll check the weather and get Kenny and Mason to pack the right gear."

"Excellent, call me if you need help."

Rodin drove as Cherenkov stared out the front window as if lost in thought then spoke in Russian. "It has been arranged. You, Yeric and I shall have safe passage out of the country once we retrieve the device."

CHAPTER 24

THE EVENT
SIERRA PUMA WINERY

T he evening festivities roared into full swing. Most of the ranch wranglers, including Tim Fremont had exchanged western wear for black pants and white shirts. Tim, Jessie, and another wrangler, Summer, peeked through the kitchen door portholes into the conference dining area. It was packed and boisterous. People sat at every large table laughing, talking, and tasting the Sierra Puma wine. "Wow, how cool," Summer said in amazement, "that's Gwen Rodgers and Lindsay Taylor sitting across from Valerie. They're actresses and best friends. They all worked together on the TV show, 'High Corporate.' "

"Let me see." Jessie pressed her nose against the small window. "I've seen that other lady with the long blonde hair parted in the middle."

Tim glanced through the porthole. "That's Natalie Sherwin. She's the attorney for the Cahills and a longtime friend. The guy next to her is her boyfriend, Jeff Logan. He flew with Jake on the LAPD. He owns a bunch of restaurants, one in Hawaii. He's also a contractor who designed and built this conference center."

Jessie nodded, recalling her mom had met the lady attorney who then connected with Valerie and got her the job at the winery. She looked again, "Who's the senior citizen woman with the silver hair?"

Summer looked at Jessie with an expression of surprise. "Jessie, that old lady is a retired US Supreme Court Justice, Maureen

Sullivan. Duh-didn't you take a civics class in high school? She and that older guy speaking at the podium are part of the conservancy group that works with the Cahills at the ranch."

Jessie smiled at the barb. Her mind was never in a classroom. "Oh yeah, I remember," she said hoping the lie wasn't obvious.

Tim pointed to the man on the lectern. "That's Mark Parnell. Valerie said he was a famous actor turned producer. He's making Valerie's book into a movie. That's why all the people are here; most of them are part of the production group. Val said she might play a part in the movie. That's pretty decent, huh?"

The three chatted and watched the party when Erin came up from behind. "All right ladies and gentlemen let's keep rolling and clear the tables. And remember, nobody asks for autographs or selfies from these people." Erin tapped Jessie on the shoulder, "Jessie, run up to Val's office and grab a blue binder off her desk. It's something to do with scripts she wants to give Mr. Parnell. Here's the key to her office. Hustle up." Erin peeked through the porthole at Parnell still talking on the stage. She shook her head, "That guy never takes a breath."

Jessie reached Val's office and walked over to the untidy desk-top of papers and documents. Sitting next to the blue binder was a yellow legal tablet with the name 'Tear Drop Pass' and Victor Rodin's name written on it. Jessie's eyes zeroed in on the words. Valerie had written in big letters "Tear Drop Pass" and "why there?" She had scribbled other questions and comments; "Book not translated to Russian. No Russian film company and who is this Rodin?" Valerie had made additional annotations about Rodin's legitimacy and motives to access that part of the ranch.

Jessie snapped together a connection as she locked on the notes. *I saw that guy in Val's office and at the recycle center.* She pondered the strange link between Rodin, her brother and Tear Drop Pass. Her inquisitiveness got interrupted by yells and shrieks coming from the dining area. Propelled by a surge of curiosity, Jessie ripped the notes from the legal pad and stuffed them in her apron, grabbed the binder, and ran downstairs towards the commotion.

Mark Parnell, a gray haired, distinguished looking man stood at the podium lavishing praise upon Valerie for her indefatigable energies towards making Sierra Puma a superb establishment. He gave a humorous recognition to "what's his name", her husband, Jake. Parnell had been close friends with Jake's late parents. Decades past, he and his wife spent time at Tierra del Puma vacationing, hiking, and fly-fishing the scenic backcountry. Then it was a youthful Jake Cahill who served as their wrangler and guide. Parnell spoke of the upcoming movie about Valerie's book and thanked in advance the production crew and actors associated with the effort. Parnell then shifted gears and pitched his pet project, the wilderness conservancy. People listened and laughed at the often-heard jokes as they reached for the wine bottles.

Valerie, dressed in a stunning blue evening gown listened to Mark chatter on. She became distracted by a light touch on her leg. She cast a glance at Jake, dutifully listening to Mark's endless monologue. Valerie thought about her husband. *He's been so patient with me; I love this man.* She felt the gentle caress of his fingertips move up her thigh; his touch teasing and sensual. Val smiled, thinking that later tonight she would return that sensuality with passion. She reached over and rubbed the back of his neck while holding a sly grin. Jake turned to her, smiled briefly, and returned his eyes to the podium. Valerie furled her brows in puzzlement noticing both of Jake's hands were on the table. Yet, she continued to feel the soft touch on her upper thigh. She slowly raised the tablecloth and discreetly peeked under the table. Gazing back at her behind a black mask and dark eyes, was a raccoon. "Son of a bitch!" she yelled, pushing away from the table causing her chair to fall backwards on the floor. The startled raccoon darted from beneath the table. People screamed as others looked around trying to figure out the sudden turmoil. Seeing the raccoon race across the room, some guests jumped on their chairs.

Natalie Sherwin stood on her chair yelling, "Jeffery, what the hell kind of contractor are you to leave holes in this place so a damn raccoon can sneak in?" Jeff Logan couldn't control his laughter as he helped Nat off the chair. Jake pulled his red-faced wife off the floor.

Parnell, ever the consummate actor of ad lib, pointed to the fleeing raccoon and yelled. "Stop him, it's the Paparazzi!" Tim and Summer, guided the confused animal out the door, followed by a round of loud applause.

A blushing and embarrassed Valerie looked at Jake. "I thought that was you rubbing my thigh."

Jeff Logan caught the remark. "Wait, Val, are you saying Jake has the hands of a raccoon? Wow, that sounds sexy as hell!" More howls radiated across the room. Nat glowered at him, then burst out laughing, "Jeffery you are so insensitive, but funny."

Jessie O'Hara reached the dining area to catch the last act of the debacle. She handed Erin the binder. "What happened?" she asked, staring into the dining room where people were settling down.

Erin wiped tears of laughter from her eyes. "You might say we had a surprise guest. Summer and Tim escorted him out." Jessie grinned, and then disappeared into the back of the kitchen to the employee's closets. She took the notes from Val's desk and stashed them in her backpack that held the rest of Sean's items. A wave of guilt rolled over her, thinking about stealing from a woman that had been good to her. Her need to know about Sean and Rodin exceeded common sense. Emotions overrode logic. She pushed the shame to the back of her mind and returned to the kitchen.

It was after two in the morning when Jake and Valerie finally returned to the house. Jake, exhausted, fell in bed and asleep in minutes. He felt Valerie pushing on his shoulder. "Jake, are you asleep yet?" He moaned, trying to push the first spirals of sleep from his head. "Kind of, what's the matter?" he said groggily.

"Jake, you have to make sure no more raccoons sneak in the buildings. That was scary."

Jake gave a sleepy nod. "Okay, sure. I'll call your handyman, Gene. I think he does animal removal on a part-time basis. Tomorrow Val, tomorrow, okay?"

"Okay."

Rick Lawin

Valerie shook Jake's shoulder again, "Jake, are you asleep?"

He moaned, "Not anymore. Now what?"

"Gene won't hurt the critters, will he? I don't want that raccoon hurt. Okay?"

"Yeah, sure. He won't. Good night." Jake rolled on his side.

A few more minutes ticked by. Valerie pushed her body tight against his. She purred softly in his ear. "Jake, darling, you're not *that sleepy, are you?*"

148

CHAPTER 25

TIERRA DEL PUMA

The hassles of the winery shindig were over, and Jessie felt glad to be back at Tierra del Puma. Ranch work hadn't stopped since her return. The young wranglers stayed busy all day and into the evening doing maintenance from fences to stables. Mustangs required riding and grooming. The days were long and filled with chores, but her thoughts were never far away from the baffling connection between Sean's discoveries and the man named Rodin.

Today, the wranglers, under Doug Weston's supervision, had finished repairing fence lines early. Because of their extra efforts, he gave them the afternoon off. Jessie discreetly headed over to the barn where Tidbit was stabled. She threw on the saddle and stuffed Sean's map, the broken canister along with Val's notes in the saddlebags. The afternoon weather appeared threatening so she jammed in a rain jacket aware the Sierra weather could be all four seasons in two hours. She wasn't exactly sure how to reach Tear Drop Pass but at least she could explore a bit. Jessie was convinced that whatever Sean had found, others wanted. And they had killed him for it. Her confused emotions at least were aligned on this point. She felt compelled to bring the pieces of the puzzle together. It was an obligation to Sean. Jessie led Tidbit out of the barn when Weston's truck drove up. She swore under her breath. "Shit. Great timing."

Doug stepped out of the cab with a scowl on his face. "Jessie, what the hell are you doing? I didn't give you permission to go solo riding. I thought you were at the dorm?"

Jessie blushed, feeling stupid and embarrassed. "I was just going to ride Tidbit over to the airstrip, not going far," she said, holding the reins, as the horse seemed to sense a problem and tried to tug away.

Doug came on firm. "Jessie, it doesn't work that way and you know it, so don't bullshit me with that excuse."

"I'm sorry I wanted to ride and just think. I didn't intend to..."

He raised his hand, cutting her off. "Save the 'I'm sorry' crap. That doesn't wash with me. There are rules about new wranglers riding without a partner. It's about safety and insurance. You were told the rules and chose to bust them."

"No excuses, Gunny," she said, knowing Doug was a Gunnery Sergeant in the Marine Corps and went by that moniker for a good reason-like now.

He locked her eye to eye, his voice unforgiving. "If the Cahills find out you busted the rules, you're gone-period. Which reminds me."

Jessie closed her eyes, thinking, *That's it, I'm out of here. My own fucking fault, again.*

"Valerie needs a bunch of you guys back at the winery for another damn function, some wilderness conservancy dinner. The shuttle is leaving right now. That's why I came looking for you." He pointed, "Here it comes. I'll stable Tidbit. Get your butt on the shuttle. If this afternoon's storm drops snow on Interstate-80 it could be chain-up time, so no time to waste." Before she could reply or empty the saddlebags, he grabbed the reins. "Get moving. If you need to stop at the dorm for your gear, then make it quick. I can't deal with freak weather and more delays. I'm busy enough around here without more screw-ups and your stupid rule-breaking stunts."

Jessie sensed Doug's irritation about losing ranch hands and then dealing with her violations. "Okay, Doug." She kept looking at him, biting her lower lip, wondering if she would be coming back to the ranch after her screw up. "Are you going to tell Jake?"

He raised his hand and cut her off. "Just go, Jessie."

"No more problems, I promise," she said, her stomach queasy, speculating if Weston would open the saddlebags.

"We'll see about that, just get a move on!"

Weston led Tidbit to the stable, removed the saddle and hung the saddlebags on the post. He patted the horse. "You know, Tidbit, just when you think you know these kids, they do something stupid." He looked up at the horse, "just like me when I was young."

CHAPTER 26

Agent Richard Foster leaned back in his chair, "So, what's a copyright crime specialist doing here? You aren't busy enough, Joy?" he said with a grin.

Joy Lee casually brushed a piece of lint off her pantsuit. Her jet-black short hair accented her inquisitive brown eyes. She was trim and looked younger than her 40 years. "My literary piracy case is on hold. I want to run a thought by you regarding the buzz from upstairs in National Security. I stumbled upon something that might have a correlation with an active investigation."

"What case are you referring to?"

"The theft of a top-secret package out of China Lake Naval Weapons Center, back in December, during that big earthquake down there. The LA office has the case. I understand the few leads they had didn't pan out. The case is still open."

"Correct, we're not involved other than getting updates in the monthly intel briefings. What's your interest? That's a leap from piracy to espionage."

"I had a chat with Warren Treco the other day. He does some consulting for us from time to time. His commercial security and investigation businesses are doing well. Not bad for a retired FBI agent. Better than living off the pension plan."

Foster grinned, "Good ole Warren. We worked together for

years. And what brought him into this? He sure as hell isn't privy to espionage briefs anymore." Foster grew serious, "You guys aren't discussing things that are off limits, are you?"

Lee gave Foster an icy stare. "That's an insult, Rich."

"Sorry, Joy, but obligated to say it."

"Actually, I was talking to Warren about an old case of copyright law. He was an expert on that. A friend of his named Jake Cahill came in the office. He was a former LAPD pilot. He and his uncle own CG Aviation out of McClellan and Van Nuys airports. They have airplanes and specially outfitted helicopters and often do security contracts for Treco and law enforcement agencies. A top-notch outfit, according to Warren."

Foster nodded while typing in the name CG Aviation on his computer. "Go on."

"Mr. Cahill owns Tierra del Puma, that huge ranch north of Truckee. He and his wife also own the Sierra Puma Winery in Auburn on the old wine trail road."

"I know Sierra Puma winery, classy place. My wife and I often go up for a weekend dinner. In fact, I think we met Mrs. Cahill once or twice."

"You probably did, as she spends a lot of time there. She handles the winery business. Her husband works the ranch and flies charters. They have two homes; one in Auburn near the winery, and the main house at the ranch. Warren Treco speaks highly of the Cahills."

"Uh huh, that's nice of Warren. I'm sure the Cahills are decent people. Where's this going exactly Joy?"

"Cahill was telling Warren about a cross-country skier finding a piece of an airplane way up in the mountains on ranch property."

"What type of part?" Foster asked, now more curious.

"According to Cahill, it's a baggage door off a small plane. It somehow ended up in a remote area called Tear Drop Pass. It had a faded logo that said 'CG Aviation.' "

"And that means?" said Foster, spreading his hands, trying to follow Lee's direction of logic.

"Cahill said *his* CG Aviation doesn't own small planes and never lost a plane or a part."

"Okay, and why is that interesting to the Bureau?"

"It gets better, Rich," she said, holding a wry smile. "Cahill and his aviation people got curious about this thing. They did a little background work and discovered a part number on this busted up baggage door. It tags to a 50-year-old plus single engine, Cessna 182. Then they check more records and guess what?"

"It's an old small airplane that crashed in the Sierras. What am I missing here, tell me?"

"There's no data, or evidence regarding missing or stolen planes of that make and model for a 500-mile radius or over the past decade. They searched the records of the FAA and National Transportation Safety Board with no results."

"I'm not seeing any connection if you're inferring it ties to the China Lake case," Foster said with a bit of impatience.

"Hang on a second and you will. Cahill discovered that some old man at Lone Pine Airport owned the plane. That's a little used, non-controlled rural airport off Highway 395 in the Owens Valley. The guy's name was Charles Goodwin. Years back he ran a one-man, single plane operation and contracted with the City of LA doing aqueduct and power line patrol through the area." She paused and refreshed her memory with the notes of her tablet. "His little company was CG Aviation, CG as in Charles Goodwin." She watched Foster fiddle with his computer and added, "Notice where the airport is in proximity to China Lake...you with me now, Rich?"

Foster typed in Lone Pine Airport on the map search. He leaned forward and looked at the surrounding cities. China Lake Naval Weapons Center lay due south. He rubbed his hand across his chin, "I'll be damned." He looked up, "Fill in the gaps to this."

"Cahill said that Goodwin removed the plane from the airport to conceal it from the bank and repossession guys." She pointed to the map on the computer. "Years later he dies. The plane sits there and gets inherited by some distant relative, who's an ex-con and meth cooker, so says Cahill. The idiot doesn't have a clue what the aircraft is worth or how to dump it. Then some guy shows up and offers hard cash for the plane-no questions asked. He takes the deal. A few days later the plane disappears. There was no FAA registration transfer, no bill of sale."

"What's the logic path you're seeing here, Joy?"

"That transaction took place just before the China Lake heist, maybe a month before. Mr. Cahill has no awareness of that connection. He thinks a smuggler used the plane, ran into foul weather, and T-boned the mountains in the dead of winter. Those mountains are on his ranch."

"Hmm, did you confirm Cahill's research?"

"To the extent there have been no reports of stolen aircraft, no FAA change of registrations, no reports of crashes or missing planes-nothing. Cahill mentioned the tail number. It came back to the prior owner, Goodwin. I verified all that based on Cahill's conversation with Treco. I assume Cahill knew I was FBI when Warren introduced me as a former colleague. He didn't care, just chatted openly as if this was a curious but unimportant issue. Personally, I think he wanted me to explore the possibilities."

"I'm sure he figured you as law enforcement. When you say no missing planes, what's the time frame?" Foster asked.

"Good question. There are hundreds of missing planes in the Sierra Nevada, dating back to World War II and before. With the climate change and mild winters, so-called aviation wreck hunters are discovering crashed aircraft that were once covered by snow or water. Add to that, the age-old rumors of missing planes carrying bags of money or drugs and you can see why this wreck hunting has become an outdoor hobby." She chuckled, "Seek and ye shall find."

Foster rapped his fingers on the desk. "And you think this plane or part thereof somehow connects to the theft at China Lake? That's thin given the LA Office still feels the leads point south and out of the country. And, from what I'm told, they did an aviation check after the theft. Nothing turned north. If so, we would have heard about that, as well as the Reno office. This notion to connect an airplane fragment to the China Lake event is a bit shaky."

Joy nodded, "It is iffy. And yes, Cahill thinks it's probably a smuggler's plane. But he can't be sure because of the conditions up there. It would be hard to spot from the air or on the ground. He said that area was difficult and impassable. I think his chief concern is about treasure hunters trespassing on his ranch. He's got a real attitude about privacy."

"I can understand that. People don't respect private property these days. Did you check with DEA or Customs about any buzz on air smuggling around here?"

"I did, Rich, there are no reports associated with this part of the Sierra Nevada."

Foster rubbed the back of his neck. "Well, we know there haven't been any bank robberies or hijackings over that area." He smirked, "Or guys parachuting from airliners with bags of money." Joy nodded at the reference to the old unsolved D. B. Cooper case in the Pacific Northwest. A man had parachuted out of an airliner with a bundle of currency and disappeared forever. Over decades the case became the basis of conspiracies and TV documentaries. Foster went on, "But, I can understand drug-runners."

"True, and that's why Cahill leans towards the smuggler angle. He should know."

"Well, it's obvious you've done homework on this. Fill me in on this Cahill and why he knows about smuggling. You obviously have some background on all of this?"

Joy opened another file on her tablet. "Tierra del Puma is a family legacy ranch owned by generations of Cahills. As I said, the current owners are Mr. and Mrs. Jacob Cahill. His wife is the former Valerie Paige. Jake Cahill inherited the ranch, the Sierra Puma Winery, and portions of CG Aviation. That was after his parents got killed in Mexico during some botched cartel assassination. They were innocent bystanders. Cahill worked for the LAPD at the time."

Foster furrowed his brow, thinking aloud. "All right so he flew for LAPD and lost his parents in a tragic crossfire. How does this play into things?"

"Cahill flew undercover for a multi-agency task force acting as an air smuggler. So, he knows all about that line of work. But then he got in an inflight shootout with a cartel hit man and blew the guy away. Task force disbanded and LAPD transferred him to their helicopter patrol unit, the Air Support Division. Then, during the LA riots he made some gutsy landing in the street and rescued two people who were getting beat to death by gang members. He and his partner made an incredible rescue, however Cahill got shot in the chest, but somehow landed his bullet ridden helicopter in a field. Called heroes by the press, but not by LAPD. He'd been ordered not to land. Sergeant Jake Cahill wasn't entrenched in the police culture. You might say he had a personality conflict. The high command had the personality and he had the conflict. A smart and brave guy but definitely not a company man." Joy Lee continued, "Around that time he met Valerie Paige; a part-time actress who also worked for Flyn Developments."

Foster raised his hands. "Whoa, hold it, are you referring to Bryce Flyn, the hot-shot developer who got connected to that money laundering scheme that went down after the riots? The state politician, Pritchard got implicated in that too. That was a major case in LA."

"Yes, the same, and it gets more complex. Ms. Paige became the target of an attempted murder plot because of what she found out at the Flyn Development Company. Jake Cahill, once again, ended up in a shoot-out with the bad guys, killing one of them."

"Jesus, the guy must live under a cloud or something." He chuckled, "But he certainly saved the taxpayers some money."

"He comes across sharp. A man who had a sense of duty."

Foster held a quizzical expression on his face, "What do you mean he *had*?"

"Cahill learned the LAPD and some government agencies never told him about the connection between an undercover flight and his parents' death. Add to that, the men that tried to kill Ms. Paige had also shot up his helicopter during the riots. He was understandably pissed when he discovered the cover-up. After that, he resigned from the LAPD. He and Ms. Paige moved up here and married. Jake now spends his time with his uncle, Walter Gipe, running CG Aviation that they co-own over at McClellan."

"But he's not a team player anymore." It was a statement from Foster, not a question.

Joy Lee gave Rich a hard stare, "Would you be if your employer and the government lied to you about facts concerning the murder of your parents?"

Foster pursed his lips, "Yeah, I see your point. Let's leave that for a moment. Tell me where and how there's a China Lake connection in these weeds of vagueness."

Lee smiled, "If you recall LA gave our office and the Reno shop an assignment to check for a freight theft ring along Highway 395. We used Treco's company to check possible leads, such as truck parking lots and rest areas. That's why he contracted with CG Aviation and how I met Jake Cahill. Nothing materialized on that case. However, that made me think about how the China Lake device could have gone northbound via another form of transportation, like a small plane. And now Cahill thinks he may have found pieces of a small plane in the mountains."

Foster scratched the back of his neck. "According to my briefings, this object wasn't missed for days. And only after they found the physicist's burnt remains and car in a nearby landfill. It was chaos down there. The thieves couldn't have timed it better. Continue with your line of thought on this."

"I agree. And going south from the weapons installation to Los Angeles either by vehicle or by plane would have been near impossible. Emergency traffic jammed Highway 395 and the police blocked the roads. The airwaves were filled with emergency and media aircraft. It was an unexpected turn of events for the suspects. But the thieves had a back-up plan-fly north and avoid any roadblocks."

"Okay, could be possible, I'll concede that point."

"Plus," Joy said, "no plane could fly south near Edwards Air Force Base with FAA radar coverage blanketing the area. We would have seen some rabbit tracks on the screen. And the thieves were smart enough to figure that possibility."

"So, you're thinking an aircraft went north."

"And I'm convinced they didn't fly northeast. Most of that is desert and military operation airspace covered by radar." "But," she said, raising her index finger, "if a plane was used then maybe it went north, straight north, using the Sierras as concealment. That's why I'm intrigued by this airplane part that Mr. Cahill found."

Foster tapped his fingers on the desk. "Let me be the devil's advocate here. Why use a small private plane for such a major, high end theft?"

"Because a twin-engine plane or a jet might have popped up on somebody's radar. A low-level helicopter would give off a noisy sound print, and it doesn't have the non-stop range. And if it landed for fuel it takes kerosene, jet fuel, which might not be available at a small remote airport. A small plane, however, would fit the bill. It has range, uses aviation gas, and not as loud or unique as a helicopter signature."

Foster nodded in the affirmative. "Sounding better, go on."

"Well, here's a possible scenario. How about a low-level flight against the steep eastside of the mountain range and in crappy weather? They could go unnoticed; risky flying for sure. There isn't any low-level radar coverage along that path. The earthquake caused confusion which provided a good distraction for the northbound flight. I think it's worth a check out."

"Sounds reasonable but still, the intel points south and then out of the country. The basic description of the package is similar to an aluminum briefcase; easy to conceal and transport by any means. And a small plane just doesn't fit the profile for an important heist."

"That's the beauty of the plan," said Joy, energized with more conviction. "There are small airports and dozens of dirt strips in the Owens Valley where a small plane could depart, stay low, and go north. By hugging the Sierras, they could stay outside controlled airspaces like Reno. To the east of Reno, is more military airspace painted by radar. Seems the only flight path option would be low level along the Sierra. Maybe they continued north, but then again, they would need fuel. There are remote strips out there but also more military airspace. Turning west at some point makes better sense. Add to that, the urgency to get the package to its destination, wherever that was. But the weather got nasty, so maybe the pilot gambled and tried to cross over the mountains." She sighed, "I don't think the plane ever made it across the Sierra. It crashed in the mountains, maybe on that ranch."

Foster rubbed his hands, thinking. "I'll share this with you. This scientist guy attempted to reach out to a Beijing agent several months prior. The Asian operative suddenly went missing, never seen again. Then the scientist's body ended up as charcoal in a dump and the device now gone. LA still says it all points southbound, not north. But they also admit nothing has materialized."

Lee cocked her head in surprise hearing about the missing operative. She paused as if to refocus her thoughts, then spoke slowly, "Then all the more reason to run down this airplane fragment angle. I think it's part of a smuggler's plane, but it wasn't smuggling dope."

"Perhaps. Enlighten me again on the size of this ranch." He said, zooming on a satellite photo of Tierra del Puma.

"It's expansive, well over 40,000 acres. The ranch is surrounded by conservancy land and national forest. Lots of rugged back country. It's an immense piece of real estate."

Foster studied the map, tapping his fingers on the screen. "I would say so. It's too big to search for something that may not be there. The old 'needle in a haystack,' and we aren't even certain if it's the *right* haystack." He looked up at Lee, "This is still a thin lead given it lacks corroborating details. But you seem tenacious about this. What's your game plan, without depleting the resources we don't have?"

"Warren and I should drive up to this ranch and talk to Cahill."

"To what, appeal to his sense of patriotism?" asked Foster.

"Something like that, after we establish a rapport with him concerning this case. Given his past experiences, I can understand a reluctance to play ball with the feds. But since he cued me in on it before, it tells me we may have some wiggle room. However, if we mouth off with a national security search warrant threat, he'll just toss us off the property and go right to his attorney, or worse, the media. That's a dynamic we don't need. This is a sensitive matter that we're trying to keep a lid on. I say we level with him and see what happens."

Foster leaned forward, "Level with him by how much? We won't say, 'Jake, buddy, this is a top-secret device ripped off from the weapons test center. But don't worry, it's not a bomb.' We'll need discretion on this."

Joy smiled, "True, but we tell him who we are and that there's a sensitive piece of government property that might have been on the plane, if one is buried up there. It's not radioactive, but for national security reasons we need to keep things quiet. My gut feeling says he's not totally antigovernment. I think it's all based on the right approach, such as being honest."

Foster folded his arms. "All right, here's what we can do. This is a weak lead, but I concur, there's adequate justification to keep our ears open. Ask Warren if he would go up there with you and help break the ice with this guy. Give Cahill the truth but avoid sensitive details. Ask him to keep his eyes open and call us if he finds something. Make sure he understands this needs to stay just between him and the Bureau. Meanwhile, you work the lead and see what else pops up. I'm out of town for a while but reach out if you need me."

"Will do," she said, standing up.

"Joy, you put a lot of work in this idea. But I'm still dubious. Nobody would take such a high risk to steal a top-secret device then fly across the Sierra in a little plane into poor weather. Too simple. Too stupid."

"Uh huh, too simple, you say? Tell me again how Klaus Fuchs stole the atomic bomb detonator plans from Los Alamos during the war. A simple chicken-shit mail drop, was it?" She smiled and walked out the door. "Be in touch Rich."

Rich Foster grinned as he shut off his computer. *She does have a point.*

CHAPTER 27

TIERRA DEL PUMA
CAHILL RANCH HOME

Val made her way downstairs in her red bathrobe and old UGG slippers, sweeping her hair back in a ponytail as she followed the aroma of fresh coffee into the large, well-appointed kitchen. Jake stood over the stove stirring eggs, stopping to look up as she made a beeline to her coffee mug. "Well, good morning." he said. "About time you met the day."

She yawned, then poured a cup of coffee and wrinkled her nose. "The coffee smells great, even mixed with the smell of burned toast. I'm surprised the smoke alarm didn't go off."

Jake took the skillet off the stove and dished, or rather scraped out scrambled eggs on a plate alongside the well-done toast. "Hilarious. Here's your breakfast. Don't get too spoiled by me making breakfast for you."

She sat down at the counter and smiled. "Or too selective about the menu."

Jake ignored the jab with a smirk and leaned over the kitchen island. "So, are you re-adjusting back to ranch life after all the madness at the winery?"

She slowly sipped her coffee, appreciating the mountain scenery through the expansive windows. "I am." She yawned again. "I feel so lazy. Must be the altitude."

"Or you ran yourself ragged. What was the urgency with all the renovations?"

"The winery is my responsibility. I had goals to accomplish sooner than later. But now I need some outdoor time and to get back into an exercise routine." She eyed Jake's flirty glance as he copped a peek down her bathrobe. "And not just in the bedroom, Cahill."

"Just trying to help you, that's all. So, how about we take a hike along the Little Truckee River and have a picnic? Tomorrow we can saddle up the horses and ride up to Tear Drop Pass."

"Now that sounds like fun." She stared at the blackened toast with a raised eyebrow. "Jake, did you know that at one time burnt toast was a universal antidote?"

"Thank you for sharing that bit of information. Tomorrow *you* can make breakfast."

"I will. But the eggs are fine. Though I like them over easy."

"They started out that way, but I lost command of the spatula."

Valerie set her coffee cup down and grinned. "Flyboy, you are a culinary genius in the kitchen. I'm curious, why Tear Drop Pass tomorrow?"

"Remember that airplane part, the one Gavin from the Highway Patrol dropped off?"

Valerie nodded. "Vaguely, but I got sidetracked with all the haps at the winery. Refresh my memory. Or, as usual, you probably neglected to tell me everything." She pushed aside her breakfast plate. "Did you ever find out where it came from?"

Jake grinned. Ever since they met, she had accused him of being reticent on details. "Yes, and no." Jake filled her in on the particulars and the puzzling fact that the plane, a possible smuggler's aircraft, now lay in pieces somewhere near Tear Drop Pass.

"Wow, that's strange," Val said, refilling her coffee and pouring more in Jake's cup.

"It is, considering the plane got sold to some unknown guy and never got re-registered. It's not listed as stolen or reported missing. That said, I'd like to ride up there and check around. You interested in riding with me?" he said, with his perfect Jake Cahill smile.

She looked at him with a look of false surprise. "Oh, we have to ride together, really?" She set her coffee cup down. "Tear Drop Pass seems to have international notoriety these days."

Jake cocked his head. "Why, because of your book? I don't recall that in your manuscript."

"It's not, that's what's rather peculiar. Before the party at the winery some guy stopped by, a 'Mr. Rodin.' Said he represented a Russian film company that wanted to do a documentary regarding some aspects of my book. He specially mentioned Tear Drop Pass." She used her fingers to show italics; "'Your novel is a best seller in Russia, ' is what he said."

Jake furrowed his brow. "Huh. What's that about?"

"No idea. I held off giving permission since it's off limits and I wanted to chat with you. You and I never connected. And you're right, there's no mention of Tear Drop Pass in the book. It gets weirder. I called Kim, my editor, and she said it never got translated into Russian. So, I call this Rodin back and some other guy, I guess his secretary, said he was out of town. I told him we couldn't permit access to the area, but we could discuss options for filming at other spots."

"What happened?"

"He never called back. I checked online and got no hits on this so-called production company." She smiled. "Kim also mentioned my book wasn't quite at the best seller level, yet." Valerie chuckled. "It won't be if the movie flops."

"How could it fail if you're going to be in it?"

"I haven't decided about that. That's why I gave Mark some production notes. I really don't want a return to acting. It's less stressful being on the sidelines as a technical advisor." She looked at him. "I don't want those crazy schedules. I'd rather be here."

Jake touched her hand. "I fully support that idea. Odd though, why would some Russian movie consultant show up at the winery and be so specific on filming at Tear Drop Pass? Suddenly everybody knows the name. When I flew Jessie O'Hara to the ranch she asked if we could fly over Tear Drop. Told me that she read about it in your book. That's when I thought, hey, wait, you never mentioned that... I don't think." Jake scratched his cheek in consternation.

"I have no clue why a 19-year-old part-time employee would ask that, especially since she told me she read the book. She's rather young to have dementia," Val replied.

"I don't know either. Maybe this Rodin guy has some awareness of the age-old rumor of a plane that crashed up there; thinks it's carrying money or drugs. I bet he's connected to some bullshit treasure hunter reality show. They want to film their discovery and sell it to a network. But I still don't understand why Jessie O'Hara would mention it, unless she's a part of this scheme and working with this Mr. Rodin."

"I kind of doubt that." Val said, finishing her coffee. "I'm sure Jessie heard the name somewhere else. She doesn't strike Natalie or me as a scammer."

"No, she doesn't. But I don't buy into coincidences either. Some weeks back Eddie Rojas and I were in that area checking fence lines and ran into a couple of dirt bags pulling a trailer with snowmobiles. They said they were recreationists. Of course, they claimed they were on forestry land. They copped an attitude but finally left. I figured they were possible poachers after talking to Fish and Wildlife about those dead bears we found last year. But who knows, maybe they were part of this treasure-seeker group."

Valerie peeked over her coffee cup at her husband, who seemed angrier than normal at the property transgressions. "Everything go okay up there?"

"Yeah, things got resolved," he said with annoyance in his voice. "I'm just sick and tired of people trespassing through our ranch." He waved his hand dismissively. "Whatever. Let's ride up there tomorrow and see for ourselves what the attraction is all about. The last time I checked, Tear Drop Pass was still part of Tierra del Puma."

Valerie glanced out the window at the jagged peak adjacent to the pass. The scenery evoked memories of her near hypnotical ascent up the rocky peak. Her guide, a mountain lion with crystal blue eyes, had led her to a cave filled with the haunting whispers of little girls. Since that time, she often heard those whispers mixed in the mountain wind. She was convinced they spoke to her. So crazy and strange, she thought, yet oddly reassuring.

"Val, you still here, or are you back in time?" Jake said softly, aware of her belief to a mystical connection to the past.

She turned and gave a wistful smile. "I'm here. It's been a while since I was up there." She raised her hand. "I know it's a dangerous place, but I still think about returning." She looked at Jake in earnest. "It wasn't a dream, Jake. I climbed that mountain, heard the voices and saw that lion."

Jake nodded knowingly. "I still remember reading those words in Rebecca Thorpe's diary of her final request to someday rest with her companions. And the discovery that you and she have an ancestral kinship. In some profound way you brought her spirit back to be with her friends, 175 years later. Pretty amazing."

She directed a suspicious glare at him. "Are you patronizing me?"

"No Val, I'm not. There's something special that connects you with those pioneer kids."

Her head dropped lightly on his shoulder. "Sorry, my emotions are getting a bit irrational these days. Guess I need a dose of Jake Cahill's therapy called 'wide-open space.' " She looked up at him and smiled. "Time for fresh air. Let's go walk along the Little Truckee River. Tomorrow we can explore Tear Drop Pass and search for a pirate's treasure, or at least a pirate's airplane."

Jake glanced at his watch. "We better hit the trail, as they say on the ranch."

"Let me go change. Remember we have weekend plans too. Natalie and Jeff are driving up tomorrow afternoon. Jeff wants to ride a mustang. I think it's more like Natalie's forcing him to experience the mountains, and not just Hawaii beach life."

Jake gave a quick laugh. "It'll never happen, but we can try."

Valerie studied the mess in the kitchen. "Tomorrow we need to get back early so I can make dinner. I don't want you to poison our best friends with your lack of culinary skills."

"Hey, Logan's fine with burnt toast as long as there's some bourbon to wash it down."

Jake's cell rang as Valerie returned upstairs. He looked at the number. "Well, Warren, you're telling me you can't pay the bill for the helicopter this month. Work been slow?"

"Jake, to the contrary, my client wants to continue the security contract for another couple weeks. Keep it at the ranch, just in case we need to work the Reno area."

"If you say so. I'll probably be the one to fly the mission unless Gavin or the guys over at Highway Patrol can get some vacation time. Either way it's here and ready."

"Great. I might drive to Reno tomorrow. Thought I would stop by the ranch, take some pictures of the mustangs for the grandkids. Will you be around?"

"Should be by late afternoon," said Jake, casting a glance out the window at the blue sky feeling anxious to get outdoors. We plan to take a ride around the ranch, maybe up to Tear Drop Pass and see if I can find any more parts to this mystery plane."

"Ah, still at it. You're possessed with that conundrum, I see."

"A little bit. If there's a plane up there, which is doubtful, it probably broke up in a thunderstorm. I'll hike around for curiosity's sake. That said, I'm not sure how much I want to tramp in snow-covered rocks looking for pieces of a smuggler pilot and his plane. It's still hazardous up there." Jake sighed. "But I'm willing to try."

"That's an interesting angle. I once worked with a Drug Enforcement agent. He said there's an age-old rumor about a smuggler's plane filled with money that crashed in the local Sierras. Never found it-still missing."

Jake chuckled. "That's total bullshit propagated by conspiracy nuts. I grew up here and that story is as old as tales of ghost prospectors and their burros roaming the hills. But the smuggler airplane rumor seems to be back in fashion."

"Oh, how so?"

"Some guy came in to see Val over at the winery representing an independent Russian film company. He wanted to film parts of

Tierra del Puma related to Val's novel such as the Tear Drop Pass area. Problem is that section of the ranch wasn't in her book. She told him no. He never called back. We figured the guy is part of a treasure hunter group following up on that High Sierra airplane rumor. Earlier in the season I caught some guys sneaking around up there. They claimed to be snowmobiling and were lost. Total assholes. They were either poachers or part of this treasure-hunting group."

"That is interesting," said Treco. "Typical these days. Make a low budget movie about searching for the long-lost treasure. Then market it to some reality show. For some people the fame, good or bad, is better than fortune."

"Ha, that's exactly what I said to Val. It is curious though. First, we find the piece of an airplane, and then these clowns start showing up. I'm getting tired of people thinking they can trespass on the ranch."

"I don't blame you, but how do you secure 40,000 plus acres? Can I sell you some security systems?" Treco said with a chuckle.

"I'll just train our mustangs into watch horses."

"Watch horses?"

"Yeah, like watch dogs only with a bigger kick."

"Good luck with that. Okay, the helicopter contract is solid. Let me know what riches you find."

"You bet. Take it easy, Warren. We'll look forward to seeing you tomorrow. We have a nice guesthouse replete with a bottle of our private reserve wine and an easy access bathtub. I'll give you a good senior discount."

"Screw you Cahill." Treco said laughing ending the call.

CHAPTER 28

Jake led Rustler out of the barn and ruffled his mane playfully. "Listen to me today." Rustler snorted and turned his head. Jake stuffed his gear in the saddlebags along with a .45 caliber semi-automatic pistol. In all the years growing up on the ranch, he never needed a weapon. But after surviving several shootings while on the LAPD, he knew the day he quit carrying a piece was the day he would need it. He looked over at Valerie. "You and your steed about ready?"

"In a second." She gave Tidbit an apple slice, then placed her gear in the saddlebag. "What's this?" she said, pulling out a raincoat.

"Yours?"

She examined it more closely. "No, it's got Jessie O'Hara's name on it."

Jake slung his leg over the saddle. "She probably forgot it when she and the gang went riding."

"Uh huh, but what the hell is the rest of this stuff?" Val said with a puzzled expression, looking at a wrinkled map, an odd canister, and pages off a legal tablet.

"What are you talking about?" Jake dismounted and walked over to Valerie.

Valerie recognized the yellow pieces of paper. "I don't believe it. These are notes off my desk! And this is some map of Tear Drop Pass."

Jake peeked over her shoulder at what appeared to be a circuit board in a can. "What the hell is that thing?"

Valerie absent-mindedly handed Jake the device and map as she flipped through the tablet pages. "Jessie rifled my desk and stole these!" She looked up at Jake. "That girl is a damn thief!"

Jake studied the metal device then asked. "Your notes? What notes?"

"My notes that I wrote during my meeting with Mr. Rodin about filming up here." She shook her head in confusion. "I really don't get this at all. Why would she want these?" Valerie exhaled a breath of frustration. "Damn, this really pisses me off. She betrayed my trust, *our* trust!"

"Why would she do that?" Jake handed the map back to Valerie as he examined the metal container.

Valerie shifted her gaze to the map. "This is some type of print-out with marks near Tear Drop Pass." Val squinted to read the small handwritten scribbles. "These are notations made by her brother- what's his name-Sean. The kid that got killed on his motorcycle according to Natalie." She studied the map more intently. "It's got plot marks where this, whatever it is you're holding, was found and the location of some other parts. This is screwy."

Jake looked at the map. "Maybe she's working with this Rodin joker after all, and the brother was in on it too. These people *must* be treasure hunters of some sort." Jake shook his head. "Pretty shitty of that guy to use teenagers as spies. Now I know why she asked me about Tear Drop Pass when we flew to the ranch. And, apparently why this Russian guy wanted access to the area. What a bunch of low life con artists. Jesus, what people do for a buck."

Valerie angrily threw Jessie's rain jacket on the ground. "She lied to us, Jake. She used us when that jerk didn't get permission to come on the property."

Jake stuffed the material and device back in the saddlebag along with Jessie's jacket. "Well, maybe there *is* an airplane up there. If so then we've been out of the loop on that. That said, all the more reason to discover what's piqued everybody's interest about the crash."

Valerie wasn't listening as she threw her leg over the saddle. "I'm going to fire her ass. I want to see her expression when she finds out we caught her. Where is she today, the winery? Wonder what she and her buddies are ripping off now?"

"Val, cool down. I don't know where she's working. Doug is in the hills with some wranglers. There's no cell service in those canyons and I didn't bring a radio. We'll call him later and then get this figured out." Jake saw Valerie's irritated scowl at being duped. He tossed her an affable smile. "Hey, we're supposed to be on a relaxing ride today. We can look around at the pass and then decide what this is all about. Obviously, something is up there and attracting a lot of attention."

She patted Tidbit. "Whatever, let's just go." Valerie said, still peeved. She trotted off.

Jake followed alongside, noticing clouds building along the mountain tops. "We may get some non-forecasted rain, or even snow today." Valerie didn't respond as she guided Tidbit around the pines and occasional patches of dirty snow.

CHAPTER 29

FRIDAY
LINCOLN, CA

Jessie had borrowed her mother's car. "It's a short day at the winery, Mom. I'll be back before you go to work." She avoided the words, "my last day." *What else would you call it when you steal documents from your boss and break ranch rules?* Jessie glanced at her reflection in the rearview mirror as she nervously tapped her fingers on the steering wheel. *What was I doing?* Her mind swirled like a dizzy carousel; passing people, places and events. All of them telling her that Sean's death was no accident. She had convinced herself that she alone could solve the riddles of odd coincidences concerning her brother's demise. Jessie now realized her clandestine detective work was flawed from the start. *Why didn't I just tell somebody about all of this?* But there was the rub. She lacked the ability to trust or confide in anyone, except Sean. Jessie glanced in the mirror. *Should have just told Valerie about this, been honest. But as a brand-new employee? Pretty dumb.* Jessie cursed her lack of judgment and common sense. *It will devastate Mom that her only daughter, now her only child, lied and lost her job.*

She drove on feeling the weight of depression with the words she kept repeating. *I stole from a woman who trusted me.* Jessie bit her lower lip; aware she lacked the courage to drive to the ranch and speak directly to Valerie. Instead, Jessie O'Hara took the easy way out. She would leave a letter of resignation on Val's desk and then simply disappear forever.

Jessie was supposed to be at the ranch today and spend several weeks there. For a short time, it was wonderful therapy, the freedom of it. It was hard outdoor work, but worthwhile; riding horses, interacting with people her age, all happy and full of vigor. Her nightmarish memories stayed away from Tierra del Puma. But that escape was now gone forever. Jessie wiped tears from her eyes and tried to concentrate on driving. Clouds of gloom obscured the day of sunshine, along with her awareness that a pickup truck had begun following close behind her.

Wade Keeler had the team park behind the offices at the quarry. He clicked off his cell and turned to Rodin and Yeric. "Kenny and Mason said she just left her house, driving mommy's beat-up car. She's alone and taking her normal route up to the winery."

"Very good," said Rodin. "Wade, once we secure the girl, you and Mason come with me. Kenny can drive with Yeric and show him the back roads. You're confident we can access that area?"

Wade lit another cigarette. "Yep, it's open. Still rough and muddy but our trucks can handle it." He looked at Mason. "You stash the kid's car after we grab her. You good with that?"

Mason ran his hands over a bald and tattooed head as he nervously tapped his foot. "Yeah, yeah, not a problem," he said, biting his fingernail. He pulled out a gun and checked the magazine, then stuck it back in his waistband. He looked at Wade and Rodin. "My insurance. Just in case."

"I will ride in the back with the girl," Rodin said. He held up an ice pick while placing a small leather pouch in his pocket. "She will understand what we expect of her." His eyes focused on Mason. "You will not touch her, you understand? After she talks and we secure both pieces of the devices, then I will give her the injection. Do you comprehend my orders?"

Mason spat on the ground and wiped his dirty hand across his face. "I got it, man. Don't worry about me."

Wade did a final check of the equipment in his big crew cab truck. The weapons, packs and cargo blankets were all in place. He pulled the large skinning knife from the sheath on his belt and eyed the razor-sharp blade. "Well, time to go huntin'."

CHAPTER 30

FRIDAY
THE BAGEL BAG
ROSEVILLE

Warren Treco sat in the corner of the bagel shop, gazing out the window at the string of cars in the drive-through. He smiled knowing he would never wait in a long line just for a cup of coffee. That, he thought, was true caffeine addiction and/or a generation thing. He spread a dab of cream cheese on the fresh bagel as Joy Lee entered the shop and approached the counter. Her blue jeans and white shirt topped by a leather jacket were not her typical workday clothes.

"Good Morning, Joy. Try the bagels," he said, finishing the last of his.

She held up a bag. "I will, this is our road kit for the drive." Lee did a quick glance of the other customers then sat down.

Treco took another swallow of coffee. "Obviously you're serious about this trip today, aren't you?"

Lee spoke in a hushed tone. "Yes, the lead may have potential, but it first mandates establishing a rapport with Jacob Cahill."

"Your boss called me before he left town. Wanted to reaffirm I was okay with being the ice- breaker of sorts. He said you would enlighten me a bit more on the dynamics of all this."

"Rich agreed that we level with Cahill. That's after you help with introductions. Then I will explain to Mr. Cahill that a piece of sensitive government property is missing. And, the aircraft part he found might be from the plane transporting the item. We need not elaborate further except to say it is not a radioactive bomb, and public attention must be avoided."

"Missing in this case is synonymous with stolen. So, let's start with that truth. And what are we asking him to do, exactly?"

"Yes, point taken, we should say stolen. We ask that he keep an eye out for pieces of the plane or cargo. And that he contacts us if he discovers anything."

"Ask him, not demand, right?"

Lee nodded. "Correct, we will not pressure the man. It would be idiotic to insult his intelligence with the threat of a search warrant. Such actions would blow back on the Bureau and lead to potential media exposure. We don't have the resources to search all of that rugged terrain based on a small piece of airplane. Thus, we need his assistance. I think Cahill will cooperate. For obvious reasons, we can't share every detail, but at least provide him with enough information to appeal to his sense of duty."

Treco rubbed his chin, pondering Lee's words. "And I assume I'm not privy to those specific details behind this missing...uh correction...*stolen* government property."

Joy adjusted her jacket and felt the firearm strapped on her waist. "Sorry Warren, even if you were still on the job you wouldn't have authorization on the metrics of this. It's top level. In fact, even I'm not cleared for all the particulars."

"The standard need to know. I get that, but will Cahill?"

"We'll find out. I did some background checking. Did you know that Cahill held a Secret clearance working on the LAPD and government task force? And that his late father, a naval aviator, flew missions for the CIA? My assumption is Jacob Cahill seeks honesty before dealing with government agencies again."

"That is interesting about the family. And what about his wife? You think he would talk to her about all of this?" Warren dropped his voice. "Joy, I can read between the lines, this is an espionage case."

She gave a wry grin at Treco's deduction but didn't comment. "He probably would tell her something, but not the entire story.

Plus, we can't stop him from doing that anyway. Warren, this entire lead is based on a weak assumption and small possibility that we locate evidence of a downed plane. We might have nothing."

Treco briefly scanned the room then spoke. "Uh huh, your weak assumption might be stronger than you think if I'm connecting the right dots together."

Joy raised her eyebrows in mild surprise. "Oh, how is that?"

"I recently met with a Department of Fish and Wildlife agent. They're working on a poaching ring that kills bears for their gall bladders; prized aphrodisiacs in Asia. They've cobbled together some preliminary evidence on the players. They think there's a possible connection with a Russian export service that uses local hunters. And these poachers, according to their limited intel, have been working near Tierra del Puma. Fish and Wildlife are in the process of contracting my surveillance services. Coincidentally enough, Jake told me he ran off two guys snooping around the backcountry a few weeks ago that were claiming to be snowmobilers. But he got the vibe that these guys were either poachers or treasure hunters reviving the decades old rumor of a lost smuggler's plane. You were present when he said the baggage door part seemed pretty new and there were no reports of missing planes. He has no clue about the angle you're working on." Treco took another sip of coffee. "All this sounds like pieces of a puzzle that could fit together."

Joy leaned closer to Treco and spoke in a hushed voice. "Are you implying a connection between these poachers, this Russian business *and* the missing plane?" A thought flashed in her mind. *The Southern California lead was a planned distraction by the thieves.*

Treco grinned. "Hey, you tell me. I'm just an old dog retired agent."

Joy tapped her chin with her finger. "There's always been Russian mafia action associated with prostitution, drugs, chop shops and under the table diesel fuel sales. But there's no intel that relates back to this case. Never heard of a poaching ring either. Warren, if I may ask, how did you discover this information?"

"Just popped up," Treco said, pushing his plate aside. "Earlier, the Fish and Wildlife guy had met Cahill about poaching issues on the ranch. Cahill suggested they call me for tech gear. So, they called inquiring about a contract for aircraft and some surveillance equipment. They operate on a tight budget and lack the advanced airborne technologies that could help surveil suspects in the mountains. That's what prompted me to think of a connection. A long shot, but you never know."

"Fascinating." Lee contemplated the idea that the espionage case now steered towards a Russian involvement. Her quick mind searched for more substance to validate the idea. "Who did they want surveillance on? Did they yield that bit of information?"

"They didn't say. But they mentioned something about starting out at a quarry operation outside Lincoln, east of the shooting range. It's set back from the major road, protected by a security system. I did a little, shall we say, pre-contract assessments. The guy that runs the quarry is Wade Keeler. He's an avid hunter, always in the backcountry. Got cited several times for shooting out of season and for being drunk and disorderly at a restaurant. I suspect that's why the Fish and Wildlife want my services. That's all I know." Treco smiled. "Hey, why am I explaining this to you? If I recall, the FBI are the experts at evidence gathering."

"Warren, as your many years with the Bureau should tell you, we are not privy to everything. There are other criminal activities going on in this country. Television creates the fantasy image that we know and see everything. And like every law enforcement agency in the country, we are desperately shorthanded."

Treco leaned back in the seat. "Yeah, I get it. Hell, who wants to be in law enforcement these days? But speaking of television. Cahill said some movie producer met with his wife, the CEO of the winery. Guy wanted to film a documentary about her book using Tear Drop Pass as background. She declined the request. Jake said that area never got mentioned in her book. He figured just more treasure seeker infatuation given the age-old smuggler rumor. Get this, the guy said he was with a Russian film company."

Lee glanced out the window at the passing traffic, then looked at Treco. "Now that is indeed significant. And perhaps more than a happenstance, given the missing plane angle. Seems to me these events reinforce the need for follow-up. Especially now that other people, including Russians, seem interested in this Tear Drop Pass." Lee rapped her fingers on the table. "Hmm I wonder if this illegal hunting and film business is a cover to locate the plane and the package. All the more reason to chat with Jacob Cahill. We need to form a consensus whether this is about poaching, treasure hunting, or something relevant to our case. I think it leans to the latter."

Treco finished his coffee. "Point taken. I told Jake that I might drive up to the ranch today on personal business. I didn't know you planned to tag along until this morning, but it doesn't matter. We can try and convince him to play ball and help us out. This is all for Mom, apple pie, and the American Way. Am I catching this right?"

"In a matter of speaking, yes. We tell him the truth. Any offer of a consulting stipend would be an insult. From what I can tell, the Cahill's don't need another source of income nor would they be interested in becoming, um…"

"Government spies…" interjected Treco.

"Or informants. Therefore, we level with the man. He checks out the area and reports what he finds, if anything." Joy sensed a tinge of professional excitement in thinking her hypothesis was going to prove out. But she wanted more details before reluctantly having to relinquish the case to another agent, as was the M.O. when anything big showed up on the radar.

Warren Treco smiled. "I'm in on that premise." He stood up. "Shall we take a drive? It's a couple hours up the road. Can we take your SUV if you have an all-wheel drive? I'm not sure of the road conditions on the ranch."

"You just don't want to get your Audi dirty. Yes, we take my car. It's paved roads to the ranch airfield, and to the Cahill ranch house. Only side access roads are dirt."

"You went up there all ready?" Warren said surprised, as they strolled out of the coffee shop.

Joy smiled. "Warren, being the FBI, we have a secret portal to charts that I will share with you. It's called Google Maps. Just load the app on your expensive cell phone. Of all people who should know, Mr. High Tech Security Consultant."

"I'm getting old. I'll have my granddaughter show me how this damn phone works."

CHAPTER 31

Jeff Logan tossed his suitcase on the bed next to a pile of clothes. He held up a pair of paddleboard shorts as Natalie walked in. "Jeffery, we're going to the Cahills to ride horses and hike, not paddleboard. You're going to look ridiculous on top of a mustang wearing yellow board shorts."

Logan cocked his head and looked at her. "Really, you mean these won't go with cowboy hat and boots?"

Natalie shook her head in exasperation. "Oh God, I know Jake expects you to pull a stunt like that, but just for once humor me. Be normal, okay?"

"No boarding up there, huh? I think Blue Star Lake is a magnificent place to paddleboard." Logan tossed the shorts in his suitcase. "That's one of the nicer places on the ranch."

"It's an ice-cold alpine lake. And by the way, you are not putting a board on top of the Porsche. The Cahill's don't have paddleboards-they have horses. Accept the idea we're spending a weekend in the beautiful mountains, not in Maui. This trip has been planned for weeks."

"Complete with smelly horses and dust to trigger my allergies. How wonderful."

"Give me a break. You're too much." She said, rolling her eyes in mock annoyance. "By the way, did you inspect the winery dining hall to make sure no more raccoons or other critters could get in?"

Jeff folded his clothes and placed them in the suitcase. "I did. Can't figure out how the little bastard got in. Somebody must have left a door open or something. I spoke to Valerie's handyman, that former military guy with the off-duty snake removal service. He and that Fremont kid did an inspection too. Anyway, no holes or entry points. Nat, I build good structures-critter and slither proof. Not my fault if some moron left a door open. And hey, the raccoon enjoyed the party! Val likes animals besides her fantasy mountain lion too."

She glared at him. "Don't joke about that with her. She's sensitive to those matters. And I believe her. Valerie has a strong vibe to that ranch legend. I hung around that place growing up. I'm not sure it's a myth."

Jeff raised his hand. "Hey, I never said she was dreaming or smoking dope...I'm *kidding*. I know she senses a tie to some mystical beast and spirits. I would never hammer Valerie." He paused, then smirked. "Jake I'll give crap to, but never Valerie."

"Just remember that when you get on one of your joking modes that sucks in Jake. You two guys can go off the deep end sometimes."

"Comes from working together in a police helicopter cockpit with the dimension of a good-sized refrigerator. You go nuts after a while. Change of subject, when do we leave today for the great outdoors?"

"I have to run into work for an hour. Then we can go."

Jeff nodded as a different thought popped in his head. "You ever see that guy in the oddball looking truck again? The idiot I chased away from your car when we were in Roseville with Mrs. O'Hara?"

Nat picked up her suit jacket. "Strange that you ask. I thought I did once or twice afterwards, but black off-road trucks around here are a dime a dozen. Every Sacramento flatlander thinks he's a mountain man with his badass pickup on stilts." She gave him a quick kiss on the cheek. "Gotta go. Be back soon."

"Nat, that's lifted, not stilts. Hurry home."

"Whatever," she said, going down the stairs.

Logan watched from the window as Natalie drove off. He rubbed his chin, thinking of the encounter with the asshole that cased her car. He walked over to the nightstand and pulled out his .40-caliber handgun that he had carried on LAPD. Jeff checked the action and sat it on the bed.

CHAPTER 32

Jessie's thoughts wandered as she drove down the empty stretch of road. A truck suddenly pulled alongside, jerking her back to reality. The passenger frantically motioned to her to lower the window. The man yelled. "Hey, you're leaking oil, big time! There's smoke coming out of the engine! Get off the road before you catch fire!" Startled, she quickly pulled off the highway onto a dirt levee road. The truck and another larger pick-up followed behind her. Jessie stopped and jumped out of the car as Kenny raced up to her. "Wow, your car is on fire."

"It's not..." Jessie turned to motion at the front of the car just as Kenny slipped his forearm around her throat. Rodin held an ice pick to her face. His voice was low and menacing. "Be silent and do what you're told, and I won't jam this in your ear." Jessie froze, fear and confusion flooded her body. Her panic-stricken eyes followed the movement of the ice pick until Kenny shoved her into the backseat of Keeler's truck.

Wade did a quick search of Jessie's car, retrieving her phone and small pack. He pointed at Mason. "Move the car behind the trees, let it roll into the drainage ditch. Use gloves and drop the bottle of pills on the front seat. Kenny, you and Yeric go in your truck. Mason, Rodin and I are right behind you. Don't stop until we hit the forestry road before the ranch unless I call." In less than two minutes the two vehicles departed.

Keeler swung the pick-up back onto the main road as Mason, riding shotgun, checked for traffic. Rodin sat in the backseat with Jessie, her mouth and hands covered with tape. Terror filled her eyes as she fought to breathe. Rodin waved the ice pick in front of her again. "Look at it carefully. I will stick this into your eye unless you give us all the things your brother found in the mountains, including his maps. Do you understand?"

Jessie was on the verge of vomiting as the tears streamed down her face. Rodin growled. "I said, do you understand me, girl?" She nodded as Rodin ripped the tape off her face. She winced as blood seeped from her lips.

Rodin stroked her red hair as he slowly waved the ice pick. "Now, let us converse, young lady."

Mason leaned over the seat. "I can see why Cherenkov is interested in her; she's tempting," he said touching her knee.

Rodin glared at Mason for mentioning Cherenkov's name. "Enough. I will handle this." He turned to Jessie. "Now talk."

Jessie panted trying to catch her breath. "I don't have those things. I left everything at the ranch."

Rodin pulled on her ponytail. "*Where* on the ranch, with who?"

"Nobody. I stuffed them into the saddlebag of Mrs. Cahill's horse. I was going to ride up to Tear Drop Pass, but they sent me back to the winery. I don't know where they are now. Please, believe me," she pleaded between gasps.

Wade glanced into the rearview mirror at Rodin. "I told you so. The kid knows what's going on and was heading up there. We'll get into or near Tear Drop and look around, but we need the goddamn map, the clean copy. Otherwise, we could be there all day. And we need the part she has or had."

"Yes, we do." Rodin said. "We'll continue on. I'm sure Jessie will help us." He stared at her. "After all, you must have seen his last footsteps on the little map. We have plenty of time before we get to the ranch to refresh her memory." Rodin focused his cold, snake like eyes on the terrified teenager. "And where is this stable that Mrs. Cahill keeps her pony?"

Jessie gulped for air. "It's on the ranch near the airstrip and bunkhouses."

Keeler swore. "That's fucking great, we could meet a shitload of people. We need to find a way to get in and out without notice. Maybe this Cahill woman already grabbed the stuff and is holding it. Where the hell is she today?"

Rodin glared at Jessie. "Would you know her whereabouts?"

Jessie cried out. "I don't know. I think at the ranch today. She's on vacation. Please, I'm not sure."

"So be it. You will call Mrs. Cahill and explain you must have your things returned. Tell her it is personal." Rodin touched her earlobe with the ice pick. "Very personal."

Wade broke in. "What if this Cahill bitch already knows about the device or suspects something? She's already figured you were lying when you dropped that bullshit movie idea on her."

Mason chimed in. "So, let's grab her too and drop the body in a lake."

Rodin thought for a second. "That might be required. We can deal with that after our little red hair guest makes the phone call." He gave Jessie back her cell. "Call Cahill and talk." Rodin pushed the ice pick into Jessie's ear. "If I suspect you are lying or sending some secret message, I'll plunge this into your brain. Do we agree on things?"

Jessie's voice broke into a whisper. "Yes." Her hands quivered so badly she could hardly hold her phone.

Valerie and Jake had worked their way along a steep game trail towards Tear Drop Pass. As usual, Jake let Rustler find the best path as Val and Tidbit followed. There was no talk between them as they enjoyed their own thoughts in the majestic and rugged scenery. Val's cell chirped, breaking the forest silence. She looked down and saw the caller. "Jake, hold up a second, it's Jessie O'Hara. I don't want to lose cell reception." Val pulled back on the reins as she answered the phone. "Hello Jessie," she said in a business-like manner. "It's so nice of you to call. Are you in my office rummaging through my desk, again? Can you at least leave the pictures on the wall?" She instantly regretted the snide remark.

Jessie's voice was weak as she tried to conceal her fear. A fleeting thought crossed her mind. *Talk formal, maybe she'll know something is wrong.* She felt the pressure of the ice pick in her ear. "Mrs. Cahill, I need to talk to you in person, privately."

"You're damn right we need to talk. I can barely hear you, speak in the phone. Where are you?"

"Mrs. Cahill, I'm on my way to the ranch. I was driving to the winery, but they said you were at the ranch. It's important I talk to you. I need my things back, the items I left in your saddlebag, they're personal. Are you at the ranch?"

"Jessie, I'm on my way to Tear Drop Pass to find out why you're so interested in the area. And why you have a map of our property and some damn device that I assume came from your brother's illegal romp on our land. Are you working for Mr. Rodin; part of a treasure hunting team, a snitch, maybe? I'm disappointed in you Jessie. I thought we were friends. You betrayed my trust. We'll talk later when I get back to the winery office. Have a wonderful day."

Jessie's voice choked with emotion. "Mrs. Cahill, please, I'll meet you up at Tear Drop. I can explain things better if we meet up there. I borrowed a friend's truck. I know the roads up to the base of the pass. It's important, Mrs. Cahill. Please bring my things. Please, give me a chance. It will all make sense."

Valerie pressed the phone against her ear; as the reception faded in and out. Jessie's voice sounded faint. "Nothing you just said makes any sense. I can barely hear you, Jessie. Obviously, I can't stop you from trespassing. I doubt you can get through on the roads or even if I'll be here. Don't waste my time or yours."

"Thank you, Mrs. Cahill. I'll be there in less than two hours. Please wait for me. I'll explain. I'll..." Rodin tapped the cell phone off, having heard both sides of the conversation. "What does she mean that you and I are treasure hunters?"

"I don't know."

Rodin slapped her hard across the face. "Don't lie to me or you will scream in pain!"

"I stole notes from her desk when you came to see her. I recognized you from when Sean took me to that recycle place. I saw you before. I connected you to the thing that Sean found. And why you wanted to film at Tear Drop Pass, so you could look for the other part. Sean told me it was valuable, people wanted it. You killed him, didn't you?" She choked between tearful sobs.

Wade shook his head in disgust and frustration. "Rodin shut her up or stuff a fucking rag in her mouth. I can't handle that goddamn blubbering." Wade punched the steering wheel. "Jesus Christ, now the Cahill woman is involved. Has to be the case. Shit, we need to get rid of her too. And where's her old man? That's another problem."

With icy calm Rodin turned to Jessie. "And what about that, Jessie? Where would Mr. Cahill be today? Don't lie to me." He made tiny circles with the ice pick inside her ear.

"I don't know," she cried. "He usually flies during the week. He mentioned something about flying north this week. I'm not sure. Please believe me, that's all I know."

"Goddamn it" Wade said, shaking his head. "All right, if he's there then we gotta take him out too. Ah, shit what a fucking mess. We're in too deep to back out now." Wade yelled again. "Rodin, I told you, stop that kid from whining. Slap her or tape her mouth shut."

Rodin stared at Jessie. "You want Mason to kiss you? If not, then shut up." Rodin turned to Wade. "The recovery is an imperative. We will do what it takes. It might come to eliminating all of them, or we take hostages to ensure an escape out of these mountains. Cherenkov will have transportation and a getaway plan for us."

Wade glanced over his shoulder at Rodin. "Uh huh, for you guys. What about us non-Russian people?"

"We do not betray loyalists. If there are complications, then you will have options."

Wade gunned the big dually, passing a semi-rig as he sped up Highway 80, keeping a scant distance from Kenny's truck. "Yeah, nice to hear. I've got my own back-up plans just in case."

Rodin recalled Cherenkov's private words. Acquisition by any means necessary and no witnesses. Completion of the project was critical. At this point, blood ties exceeded employment loyalty. The plans were set. He and Yeric would travel out of country.

Jessie slumped in her seat, overcome with fear and fatigue. She accepted the fact they would abuse her and then kill her. Rodin looked over at her as he pulled out a syringe. "Jessie, tell us the truth or enjoy a relaxing sedative. Does this Cahill woman ride horseback alone when her husband is away?"

Jessie cringed seeing the syringe. Her jaws chattered, trying to speak. "Mrs. Cahill often rides alone, it's her therapy."

Roding smiled. "Well, we all need therapy, don't we?" He placed the syringe back in his pocket. "There, we need not worry about a sedative right now. Let us talk further about things and enjoy the drive."

"Shit." said Mason. "This could fuck up plans. We don't know who's up there with that bitch. You can't trust this little crybaby."

Wade raised his hand. "Chill out, Mason, there's five of us. Whoever is up there expects the kid-not us. I'm guessing the Cahill guy isn't there. Besides, we have the element of surprise and fire-power. Things might get messy, but it's going to work out just fine."

Rodin looked at the panic-stricken teenager then spoke to Keeler. "Call Kenny and Yeric. Make sure they know the husband or others could be up there."

"Right." Wade reached for his cell. Rodin placed a bottle of wa-ter on Jessie's lips. "Here, take a sip. We won't be stopping so if you drink too much then pee in your pants," he said trying to extract as much humiliation out of the girl as possible. Jessie already had.

CHAPTER 33

LOWER PASS ROAD
BASE OF TEAR DROP PASS
TIERRA DEL PUMA

Valerie stared at the cell phone. "Damn it. I lost her-poor reception. She kept saying it's personal and important. She wants to meet us here at Tear Drop and explain everything. Maybe all this drama relates back to her late brother. I don't know. It's weird."

Jake glanced back at Valerie. "Good luck with that. Her car won't get up that service road. Not in these conditions, not in any condition."

Valerie scooted Tidbit up alongside Jake. "A friend loaned her a truck. She sure sounded overly formal calling me Mrs. Cahill."

"She's trying to suck up to you. Hoping you'll understand why she stole your stuff for this Rodin asshole." Jake smiled. "Or scared you'll file theft charges."

Valerie guided Tidbit around some boulders and muddy holes. Her anger shifted to a curiosity. "I guess. Still, something seems amiss. Maybe I was too callous with her. That isn't like me."

"I'll remind you of that when you bitch at me."

"Oh, poor you. Like I do that so much."

They reached the base of the pass and dismounted. Jake looked up canyon around the tall Ponderosa pines and the occasional drifts of snow. "Let's see why everybody's so interested in this place."

Jake glanced over Valerie's shoulder as she studied the map. He pointed at the tick marks on the map. "That's up towards the crest. Getting there will be rough. Hell, I still don't know what I'm looking for besides more airplane parts."

Valerie pulled the device out of the saddlebag. "The other part of this?"

Jake pushed his ball cap back and gave the canister a closer inspection. "Does appear it's a part of something." He pointed to the bright foil inside the canister. "Whoa, now that's a reason to want this thing. I bet that's gold shielding. Maybe this is a piece of some high-end electronics. The gold wrapping is worth some bucks." He squinted his eyes and peeked into the small broken conduit that protruded out of the device. "And if those red stones are rubies, then I can understand why everybody is hot to find it-whatever it does or did. But where did it come from? Given what we see and know, I don't think this missing plane was smuggling drugs or money."

Valerie scanned the forest. "And where's the missing airplane?" She placed her hands on her hips and turned to Jake. "I don't understand why we never heard of a plane crashing up here, but Jessie and this Rodin guy did."

"Me neither. Now I'm guessing the plane was used in conjunction with some kind of heist. I'd say this device or invention is worth a fortune, together or in pieces. Who owned it and who stole it is the big mystery, at least to us anyway?" Jake shook his head. "This is well beyond a scavenger hunt. That too is perplexing when you consider the Russian guy's interest and Jessie's connection. I'm not sure how they're mixed up together. And why isn't law enforcement involved if this thing is so valuable?"

Jake eyed the slope toward Tear Drop Pass, then glanced back at the map in Val's hand. His fingers traced the line made by Sean O'Hara. "If the plane crashed around here, then it smacked the ridgeline and parts slid down the hill. The pilot tried to sneak over the pass to beat the weather." Jake thought about the damaged cargo door. "I'm convinced this airplane flew into a thunderstorm and disintegrated. That's why parts are all over the place-not just one heap of metal." He waved his arm across the canyon, "Pieces are scattered through the area. I'm betting the lighter parts might have blown or slid down here during winter."

Valerie set the canister on the ground. "Okay, flyboy, so now what? And that doesn't answer why Jessie and this creepy Rodin might be a team." She looked at Jake. "Maybe Jessie's brother found something and told her about it. Then Rodin, whoever he really is, somehow got wind of the discovery. He wants to locate the other half of this thing before Jessie does. He thinks she might pawn it." Valerie tapped her finger on her chin. "That makes more sense considering the O'Hara family needs money. And why she's hell bent on getting up here."

Jake acted as if he hadn't heard Valerie. His eyes and thoughts focused toward the mountains. "I'm thinking the heavier parts of the plane are further up the canyon. But the other part of this device may be around here. That jives with the map drawing." He looked at Val. "I bet those snowmobile jerks were part of Rodin's group. That's just a guess. But what I am certain of is that a crashed plane is scattered about and lots of people want the cargo, including our wrangler."

Valerie shivered. "Ugh, a crashed plane means there's a dead guy around here."

"Well, yeah, Val. That's usually the case when a plane slams into the ground." He kept a straight face and teased her. "But I'm sure the animals ate most of the guy's guts by now."

"Very amusing, Cahill," she said, scrunching her nose. "I'm not eager to find body parts. You wander up farther. I'll take a short walk around here. If we do find something, then what?"

"We take it to the Feds. They might know something. I sure as hell don't want to hang on to it. But I also don't want a bunch of people searching our property for pieces. We have enough trespassing problems."

Valerie gave Tidbit another apple slice. "Okay. I'll stick close by."

"Whatever makes you comfortable." Jake checked his cell phone. "I've got one bar so we might be able to connect. I should have brought the handheld radios."

"Why didn't you?" Valerie asked accusingly, knowing her husband had simply forgotten to pack them.

He gave her a sheepish look. "We never use them when we ride together."

"Lame excuse, darling, stick with I forgot."

He grinned. "Okay, I forgot. I'll work up the side of the canyon as far as we can go. You check around here, maybe start at the stream. Snow runoff could have pushed parts down the mountain." Jake turned serious. "Val, you might find bones or something. If that bothers you, then stay put. I'll be back in about forty-five minutes if Rustler can get me through the rocks and snow. If you spot something call me. I'll ride back."

"I'm a big girl, I can handle it." She raised her hands. "I assume Jessie will be here in a little while too if she can make it up the Lower Pass Road. But if she calls again, I'll tell her we left for the house. I still don't get why she has to meet me here. This entire affair is getting bizarre." She touched his cheek. "Be careful up there and call me. Don't get into one of your obsessive-compulsive modes and forget about the time."

"Thank you, Dr. Valerie, for that psychiatric assessment." He clicked to Rustler and started through the pines and rocks. "Val, be careful walking on the snowdrifts."

"Got it. And don't let that damn horse wander off! Tie him up for a change."

Jake waved but didn't look back as he spoke. "Never happen."

Valerie tied Tidbit to a nearby sapling and surveyed the surrounding forest. The wet ground mixed with clumps of snow. Gray clouds blocked out the sun, giving a chill to the mountain breeze. She zipped up her windbreaker and followed Jake's suggestion by working along the edge of a fast-running stream, looking for anything out of the ordinary. According to Jessie's map the missing items could lay somewhere between Lower Pass Road and halfway up the pass.

Valerie had only walked a short distance when her eyes caught sight of the broken end of a ski pole protruding up through a mound of dirty snow. She bent down and pulled on the pole, but it was stuck solid. She kicked at it then gave another yank, causing it to break free. The "pole" was a piece of aluminum tube attached to an aircraft control yoke. The decomposed remains of a human hand still gripped the yoke. "Shit!" Val jumped back, dropping the yoke and body part. Goose bumps crawled on her skin. She clutched her chest and tried to slow the rapid thumping of her heart. "God bless it." Val caught her breath then at stared the part with a morbid fascination. She exhaled and spoke in a low voice. "I don't need this crap." She warily looked about and saw bits of aluminum scattered on the ground. Leaving the decomposed hand and control yoke in the snow, she walked farther into the forest, ever mindful that more human remains could be scattered about. It was eerily quiet, as her boots crunched over the snow. She tried to call Jake but there was no cell reception. "Figures," she said, stuffing the phone in her jacket.

She moved cautiously along a faded game trail and spotted more debris. *What happened to the plane?* Valerie shuddered, unnerved of being alone amidst an airplane crash. *Enough is enough, Jake can sift through this field of metal and body parts.* Valerie started back to the road when she spotted the remnants of what appeared to be an aluminum case. She warily looked down, making sure no human remains were attached this time. The briefcase top was missing but inside, still strapped in the molded insulation, lay the twin component of what Jessie had left in the saddlebag. Her eyes widened. *I don't believe it.* Her attention got diverted by the sound of a vehicle grinding its way along the road below. She decided not to show Jessie the discovery until they talked. She set the briefcase near a fallen tree and started down the hill.

CHAPTER 34

TEAR DROP PASS

J ake tediously worked upwards toward the pass. There was less snow along the canyon walls, but reaching the sides required plodding through a mixture of snow and thick brush. The climb was time-consuming and difficult. He reached a thicket of tangled buck brush and decided to hike the rest of the way. Jake dismounted and wrapped the reins around the saddle horn. He patted Rustler, "Stay here." As usual, the horse ambled away several feet to munch on fresh grasses popping up out of the snow.

Cahill pushed his way through the heavy growth, getting face slapped by limbs every few feet. In some areas he broke through the snow, stumbling in the deep slush. Finally, the thicket gave way to a tarn of glacial rubble. He elected to rock hop rather than trudge through the mud. He perched on a large boulder and caught a splotch of something bright red. At first glimpse he thought it was a snow plant; a colorful harbinger of spring. Upon closer inspection it was a piece of red plastic, the broken remnants of a rotating beacon off a small plane.

Jake scanned the steep chutes of rock debris that had slid down from the mountains. Many of the stones balanced precariously atop each other, as if ready to tumble farther down the hill. He figured more airplane parts could be sequestered behind the large outcroppings. He continued on, hoisting himself over the enormous volcanic rocks. Within minutes he was sweating and out of breath. He lifted himself over another rocky berm and spotted an aircraft wing wedged between two boulders. Jake rock hopped over to the mangled remains of the aluminum airfoil. The flaps and ailerons had been ripped away from the twisted wing. There were other metal fragments scattered about, but no fuselage or tail. The excitement of discovery pushed him forward to locate the rest of the aircraft, more importantly, the cargo. Cahill climbed on, unaware of the time and distance that separated him from Valerie. After stumbling over more rocks, he eyed what resembled an engine and prop about 50 yards ahead. He hastily started towards it when the snow gave way, plunging him downward into a crevasse.

The fall was instant, with no time to brace his landing. Jake hit hard on his shoulder and rib cage. He let out a loud "Oomph," as the air rushed from his lungs. He lay on the ground, dazed. His shoulder ached, but he could breathe without pain. With deliberate slowness he stood up and tried to get his bearings. To his surprise he had fallen into a wide and long volcanic fault line that cut horizontally across the canyon. The sky was 15 feet above him. Jake followed the fracture, hoping to find a way out of the deep trench. He pulled out his phone and saw the cracked face. *Damn it. Not that I could get reception down here anyway. And no radio.* He kicked himself for doing exactly what Val had chided him about.

Jake plodded through the winding fault and then stopped with a look of astonishment. The bent wreckage of a small airplane lay in front of him. Its paint had long faded away, exposing dirty and dull aluminum. The plane's nose pointed upward, resting on the crushed tail. The wings were crumpled forward. Jake noticed the engine and prop were still attached to the fuselage, and the cabin area intact. It appeared the aircraft had slid tail first into the crevasse. He peeked in the cockpit, prepared to see the bleached bones of the pilot, but it was empty. Rusted and broken analog gauges sat askew on the instrument panel. The seats were reduced to rusty springs. Jake folded his arms and stared curiously at the carcass of the old plane. He stepped forward as his boot crunched on something metallic.

Cahill bent down and picked up a small metal circular device and brushed off years of dirt. In an instant he recognized the vintage item. It was an E6B flight computer or "whiz wheel;" a small circular slide rule dotted with numbers. The little handheld device was used by an older generation of aviators to solve a myriad of aeronautical problems dealing with time, speed, and distance. The quintessential gizmo had long ago been replaced by digital calculators. Jake flipped the E6B over and squinted to read a scratched-on inscription, but mud and time made it unreadable. "Very cool!" he said out loud, stashing it in his pocket.

A realization flashed through his still slightly jarred brain. *"Wait a minute. This is a complete airplane! It's got both wings, tail and engine! What the hell?"* Yet, he had just found another wing, the one in the rock field. Puzzlement crossed his face as he rubbed his chin. Not one, but two small planes had crashed in Tear Drop Pass. One, an old but complete wreck lay jammed in a crevasse, the other was spread all over the mountains. Jake tempered his curiosity when he looked upwards and saw ominous clouds passing overhead. He squeezed around the wreck and discovered a mass of jumbled rocks providing a pathway out. With grunts and groans he made the painful climb toward the top.

CHAPTER 35

LOWER PASS ROAD

Valerie worked her way back to where Tidbit was tied. She could hear the engine growl of a truck grinding its way up the road. She anxiously tapped her foot, wondering why Jessie was so emphatic about meeting at Tear Drop Pass. She tried again to call Jake but with no success. She glanced back up the canyon, shaking her head. *Damn, he gets so distracted.*

Val stashed the cell in her jeans, just as two pickup trucks rolled around the corner. The bigger pick-up nearly hit her when it slammed on the brakes. She jumped back and yelled. "Hey, watch it jerk!" Wade Keeler leaped from the driver's seat and slapped Valerie to the ground. Kenny and two others came up from the other pickup as Rodin dragged Jessie from the back seat of the truck.

Valerie was stunned and confused, trying to figure out what just happened. Keeler wrenched her up off the ground. "Stand up, bitch." Before she could say anything, Rodin pushed Jessie next to Val as Kenny, Mason and Yeric surrounded the two women. Jessie appeared pale and comatose. Puke covered her clothes. Rodin looked at Valerie and shook the ice pick in front of her. He spoke in a low growl. "Mrs. Cahill, suppose we start by asking, are you riding alone today?" He touched her chin with the point of the ice pick. "I prefer honest answers, or I shall make a hole in your cute dimple?"

Valerie suddenly caught off guard by the violent encounter, thought fast. "My husband and some ranch hands are coming up to meet me." She took a deep breath, feeling the sharp tip of the ice pick on her chin.

Rodin pushed the ice pick harder, drawing a drip of blood. "I somehow doubt that." He pulled Jessie in front of her. "Our young lady here casually mentioned that Mr. Cahill is flying today-lucky for him." Wade and Kenny suspiciously scanned the surrounding forest while Mason and Yeric walked along the trail following Val's boot prints, searching the ground. Rodin gave a sardonic grin. "May I call you Valerie? We were much too formal when we met at the winery. Too bad you didn't allow us to access this area. That, my dear, would have made things far less complicated for you and this young lady. Now, where are the things that Jessie left with you?" He looked over at Tidbit. "Oh, that's right, on the horse."

Wade walked over to Tidbit and opened the saddlebag. "Here it is." He grabbed the map and canister and then gave Tidbit a hard kick in the side. "GET!" Valerie grimaced as the horse jumped and bolted off. Kenny laughed, watching the startled animal race away.

Wade handed Rodin the map and device. "Okay, that part we got, what's next?"

Yeric looked over Rodin's shoulder. "That's what her brother showed us in the picture. I knew he had all of it the day he came to recycle shop! The cocky little liar."

Mason trotted back over, out of breath. "Her tracks lead back in the snow, up the hill." He spit out a piece of tobacco at Valerie's feet. "I bet you found something didn't you, good lookin?" He patted her cheeks with his dirty hands. Valerie pulled back as Mason chuckled. Jessie stared blankly at the ground, as if shell-shocked.

"How about that Valerie?" Rodin said, his eyes meeting hers. "You find anything that will save us time and buy you some options?"

Valerie stared back, concerned Jake would walk into a trap. She told the truth. "I found whatever you're so damn interested in about a hundred feet back in trees. It's in a broken aluminum case. I dropped it there when I heard noise."

Rodin added pressure to the ice pick against her chin. "I hope you aren't lying. I hate women that lie." He patted Jessie on the head. "Isn't that right girl?" Jessie nodded in fearful silence. Rodin looked at Yeric and Mason. "Find it, then we depart." He looked at Valerie. "You and the teenager will take a ride. Won't that be fun?" He turned. "Wade, you and Kenny watch these pretty ladies while I go with Yeric and Mason." Rodin handed Kenny the ice pick. "Here, it helps to keep them attentive and submissive."

Valerie stared at the ugly scar on Wade's cheek. "What the fuck you are looking at, bitch?" Keeler hissed, slamming her against his truck. Kenny laughed as he shoved Jessie to the same spot next to Val.

Both women had their faces pushed into the hood of the pick-up. "Don't look at us, don't move, and keep your mouths shut!" said Kenny, stuffing the ice pick in his jacket. He turned away to watch the others search the forest. "What's next, Wade?" he said, rubbing his hands together, anxious about the getaway plan.

Wade spoke in an undertone inaudible to the women. "The broad gets dumped somewhere in the hills. The teenager gets drugged and transported away for other duties. You, Mason, and I will split and disappear with Rodin's guys. It's all worked out." Wade pointed. "I think they found the package. Shit, how lucky can we get?"

Valerie slowly raised her face off the hood. She peeked over at Wade and Kenny. Both men were engrossed at watching Rodin and the others. She glanced at Jessie and whispered. "Jessie, can you hear me?"

Jessie turned her head slightly; her eyes glassy and red. She whimpered in disjointed phrases. "My brother... he, he found it and... they knew he did." Her words choked in tears. "They kidnapped me when I was driving to the winery. They're going to kill you and take me somewhere. I'm so sorry. It's my fault, I don't know what's'... I'm so..."

"Shush, that's enough," Valerie whispered. She glanced back at the two men still distracted with the discovery. She cocked her head and saw that Tidbit had ambled back, now standing off in the trees. Valerie whispered. "Jessie, listen to me. When I tell you to, run and jump on Tidbit. Get back down to the airstrip. You've got to ride and get help. Do that, don't look back. Ride." Jessie sniffed and nodded, unsure of Valerie's next move. She put her face back down on the hood and waited.

CHAPTER 36

TEAR DROP PASS

J ake finally clawed out of the steep walled fissure. Instead of returning downhill via the rocks, he opted to slip and slide down the snowfield to the brush line. Once out of the slush he pushed through the dense barrier of bushes in hopes of finding his horse. About twenty feet into the tangled mess, he stopped. Rustler had somehow crunched through the thicket to meet his rider. Jake climbed on the sturdy mustang. "Guess I'll keep you after all." The horse snorted and headed back towards the Lower Pass Road.

Kenny and Wade's attention remained focused on the action of the men returning from the forest. Rodin had found the damaged briefcase. Valerie canted her head sideways, watching as Kenny inadvertently backed closer to her. She eyed the ice pick that dangled out of his jacket pocket. It was inches from her hand. Wade stood next to Kenny, directing the men to place the device in the other pick-up truck.

Valerie took a deep breath and nodded at Jessie. In one swift movement she yanked the ice pick from Kenny's jacket. Startled, he twisted around just as she plunged the ice pick into his groin, pulled it out, then jabbed it in Wade's thigh. Kenny's horrified screams echoed across the canyon as he dropped to the ground. Wade yelled, "Goddamn it," falling to his knees pulling the pick from his thigh.

"Ride Jessie!" Valerie pushed Jessie towards Tidbit and then sprinted to the side of the road. Wade Keeler pulled out his gun and fired at Valerie; the rounds flying wild. Within an instant she tumbled down the muddy embankment and disappeared into the trees. Wade cursed and limped after her, blindly firing into the forest. Mason spotted Jessie on Tidbit and fired several rounds at the fleeing teenager, then made a futile attempt to chase after her. Rodin saw Kenny rolling on the ground, screaming in pain as Wade had disappeared after Valerie. He yelled to Yeric. "Get in the other truck, we must leave-now!"

"What about those guys?" Yeric yelled, tossing the devices in Kenny's pickup truck as he jumped in.

"The fucking fools made mistakes that leave us with no choice. You drive!"

Jessie was galloping away when she felt the excruciating pain deep in her side. She leaned over in the saddle to hide from more rounds. "Take me home Tidbit, please take me home!" The mustang's ears flicked back and at the command did an abrupt turn and scooted down the steep embankment. Jessie clung to the saddle horn as the plucky horse sprinted along the narrow trail. Blood began to seep down Jessie's side as consciousness faded in and out.

Jake approached Lower Pass Road when he heard the gunshots. They were close and numerous. He froze, knowing the direction of the shooting. He jumped off Rustler and pulled his weapon out of the saddlebag. Gun drawn; he quickly but cautiously worked his way down the hill. Cahill reached the road just as two men raced away in one truck. Jake spotted Mason Reems looking panic-stricken as Rodin and Yeric drove away without him. Mason started running towards Wade Keeler's dually when he spotted Cahill in the pines.

Jake tried to process the deadly situation, wondering where Valerie and Jessie were. *Are they in the truck? Don't let the guy get in it.* Mason pulled out his gun and fired at Jake but missed. Jake reacted and double tapped two rounds from the .45. The first one missed, the second hit Mason in the throat, blowing away part of his neck.

Cahill warily advanced towards the dead man while scanning the area. He stared at the bloody remains with a look of surprise.

The same fucking guy on the snowmobile! Adrenaline and confusion pumped through Jake's body. *What the hell is going on? Where's Valerie?* Agonizing groans came from the other side of the truck. Jake snapped back; gun ready. He cautiously walked over and saw Kenny lying on the ground holding his blood-soaked groin. The man looked up at Jake and pleaded. "Help me, man. She stabbed me in the nuts."

Jake tried to control his anger-fed emotions. "And you, you're the other prick with the snowmobiles. Your asshole buddy is over there missing his throat. Where's my wife and the teenager? Just who the fuck are you and why are you here?"

Kenny acted as if he hadn't heard Cahill's question. "God, help me man, I'm bleeding, it hurts bad."

Jake stepped on the man's groin. "Where's my wife, asshole?" Kenny screamed as his face contorted in pain. Jake pushed harder. "I said, where's my wife, you piece of shit?"

Kenny panted out the words. "She-stabbed me-then jammed the ice pick in Wade's leg. The bitch-jumped over the side of the road. Wade went after her, ok? Help me-I can't take the pain much longer!"

"And the teenager?"

"She split on the horse! Please, I'm begging you man-do something!"

Jake took a deep breath, trying to put it all together. He looked over and saw where somebody slid down the hill. He turned back just as Kenny pulled a gun from his waistband. Jake fired into his chest, killing him instantly. Jake Cahill stepped over the body and followed Valerie's tracks and whoever was after her. His entire being was filled with hell-bent rage.

CHAPTER 37

Doug and Maria Weston stood with Tim Fremont and Eddie Rojas. All were scanning the countryside, trying to figure out the location of distant gunfire that echoed across the valley. Doug cocked his head, listening to reports. "Those are handguns. One sounded like a .45, Jake carries one." He turned to Rojas and Fremont. "You guys know where he went today?"

Eddie Rojas swept his eyes towards Tear Drop Pass, "I think he and Valerie rode up there. I saw them saddle up and head in that direction. Not sure, we didn't talk. I only saw them from a distance."

Tim Fremont spotted Tidbit trotting down the dirt road. "Jessie!" he yelled, seeing her slumped over in the saddle.

"Oh my God." Maria said racing over to where the sweat covered horse had stopped. Tim and Eddie lifted the semi-conscious girl off the saddle and gently laid her on the ground. Jessie's face was pale and gaunt, her breathing shallow. A mass of sticky blood covered her side. Maria pushed the men aside and spoke in a commanding voice. "Tim, get the med bag. Eddie call 911-now!" Maria pulled up Jessie's shirt. Her eyes showed a look of shock. "She's been shot! Eddie, tell 911 they need a medevac chopper here, now!"

Doug knelt down beside Jessie. "Can you hear me, Jessie, what happened?" He gently touched her face. "Jessie, can you hear me? We'll get you to the hospital. What happened, can you talk?"

Jessie's consciousness floated in and Weston's voice echoed

in her ears. She raised her hand and whispered in a feeble voice. "They took me to Tear Drop Pass. Val was there. We tried to get away. Val stabbed one of them and ran." Jessie wheezed out more. "They shot me-as I tried to get on Tidbit. I..." She struggled for words. "I didn't see Jake. Please help...Valerie." Jessie's voice faded into a mumble.

"Jessie? How many? Jessie...?" but Jessie said no more.

Fremont squeezed Jessie's hand as Maria applied bandages from her triage kit. Doug looked over at Rojas. "Eddie, get some guys and two of the backcountry rigs. Grab my weapon from the truck and the ammo pouches. Make sure everyone is packing." He looked at Tim Fremont, whose eyes were glued on Jessie as he held her limp hand. "Tim, stay with Jessie and Maria. Explain to the cops what happened. We should have a medevac chopper here soon." He looked up at the threatening skies near Tear Drop Pass, then added, "I hope." He turned and headed for the pickup, twirling his hand, signaling for the other wranglers to load up.

Through the woods, Valerie kept running and slipping down the wet slope. She exhaled hard as her heart pounded against her chest. She reached a large fallen tree when another gunshot sliced the air and a piece of the trunk exploded in her face. She leaped over the log and flattened herself on the ground. Keeler hobbled towards her yelling. "I'll get you for this bitch!" Valerie rose up and sprinted away. Adrenaline filled every aching muscle in her body; but she couldn't run any faster. Her energy was ebbing away. More bullets shattered a branch above her head. She winced and forced herself forward. Keeler fired again, but the gun just clicked. He dropped the magazine and searched his pocket for another, but realized the clips were still in the truck. "Fuck it." He pulled out his skinning knife and limped after Valerie. He was going to enjoy this part.

Valerie ran hard again, dodging more fallen trees, jumping over rocks; afraid to stop and look back. She needed to get closer to the meadows near the base of the old volcanic mountain. She knew that area. She stopped, bent down, trying to catch her breath and closed her eyes in utter exhaustion. "Oh no, no" she whispered, between gasps. She had forgotten about the steep-sided creek that separated her from the meadow. She couldn't get down the cliff. She turned and a chill ran down her spine. Keeler stood two hundred feet away, the enormous knife blade glistened in his hand. He growled. "You're gonna watch me as I cut out your intestines!" He moved in closer, flipping the knife from one hand to the other.

Valerie darted to the left, then disappeared behind the trees and boulders. Her energy was spent; she could go no farther. She'd lost sight of Keeler but could hear his heavy breathing. It was here, beneath the tall Ponderosa pines, that Valerie Cahill would have to stand and fight. She grabbed a handful of rocks lying at her feet. *If these don't work and I die, then that bastard's DNA will be under my fingernails.* She thought of Jake, wondering if he got shot in the hail of gunfire that still rang in her ears.

Keeler closed in as blood seeped from his wounded thigh. "Go ahead, throw your little rocks. Then I'll gut you like I do the bears." He dodged the last of her poorly thrown granite missiles. "But first, your pretty face needs a little work."

Valerie's heart raced with fear. Her plan: kick at his wounded thigh, hoping it would drop him. Keeler took another step forward, now gripping the knife in one hand. He approached slowly, savoring the look of fear in her blue eyes. Valerie stood frozen in the silent forest, waiting for her end. The pine trees rustled with a gentle breeze. Everything was oddly silent except a familiar sound, whispers mixed in the wind. She had heard them before, their presence calmed her. Keeler, now only yards away paid no attention to the swirl of air. He stopped and wiped the sweat out of his anger filled eyes, then raised his knife and moved in to seal her demise.

Something flashed by in a blur of speed. Keeler screamed, flinging his arms wildly as the knife fell from his hands. Effortlessly the mountain lion dragged his thrashing body away. Valerie watched as the cougar and its prey disappeared into the forest in nothing short of a moment. She blinked her eyes several times, trying to assure herself it wasn't a dream.

She gave a long exhale as her shoulders sagged with total exhaustion. The whispers in the wind had ceased. Only Valerie's heavy breathing broke the forest silence. She sat down on a rock, unsure if she could ever stand up again.

Jake had followed the tracks, weapon at the ready. Then he saw her, limp on the rock. She looked up and gave a weak smile, tried to stand, but her legs buckled. Jake caught her in his arms. "Are you okay? Where's the other guy?"

"I'm okay, just beat to hell." She pointed. "It dragged him off that way, towards the ravine."

He looked at her with a puzzled expression. "It?"

She nodded. "They heard me; they sent the puma." She hugged him again. "Please, don't ask Jake, not now, it happened. It was here."

Jake gently sat her back down on the rock. "Stay here for a second."

Valerie panted out. "I'm not going anywhere, trust me."

Cahill followed the bloody tracks to the cliff edge. He looked down and saw Keeler's mangled body disappearing into the fast-moving stream. Jake glanced across the ravine and suddenly spotted the solitary cougar. Its laser blue eyes were sparkling like jewels, staring directly at him, its tail twitching in the air. He blinked and the animal vanished. Cahill stood motionless, astonished at what he had just seen. He hustled back to Valerie, now aware his wife's mystical connection to Tierra del Puma wasn't a dream.

Valerie was standing but braced herself against the rock. She looked at Jake with concern etched across her face. "Jessie got away on Tidbit. Where is she?"

Jake put his arm around her as they walked along. "I don't know where she is. I was coming down from the ridge and heard gunshots. When I got there two guys split in a black pickup. Some other guy shot at me. I shot back and dropped him. Another dirty-looking creep was lying on the ground moaning. Said you jammed an ice pick in him, and his buddy went after you. He mumbled something about shooting at Jessie as she rode away on horseback. The SOB pulled a gun on me. He's dead too. They were the same ones I saw on the property weeks back. What the hell is going on? What are we into?"

"Jake, stop a second. I need to rest. My legs ache and feel like rubber. That Rodin guy I told you about; he was here with a bunch of goons. They had kidnapped Jessie. They wanted the map and that canister she had-*we* had. As we suspected there was another piece of it up here. I found it while you were up canyon. They planned to kill us for it but got distracted from watching Jessie and me. That's when I jabbed them with an icepick and told Jessie to run." She looked at Jake then hugged him as tears ran down her face.

"I was so worried you got shot. Jake, I don't understand. And poor Jessie, I hope she made it to the ranch."

Jake held her tight and brushed the hair from her face. "And I worried that something happened to you." He paused, then said with a touch of awe, "Val, I saw it, the cougar. It's real!"

She sighed. "I told you that. So are the whispers in the wind. I heard them. They spoke to me."

"But..."

She placed her finger on his lips before he could respond. "Darling, some things up here are unexplainable. Please leave it at that." She fell limp in his arms. "Whoa, I'm exhausted." She forced a smile. "Jake, remember when I told you that I'm not a woman who needs rescuing?"

He steadied her in his arms, "I sure do."

"I've changed my mind. Would you rescue me?"

He gently picked her up in his arms. A few minutes later, he stopped and grinned. "Well, every knight has a steed." Rustler had followed Jake down the hill. "Damn horse is smarter than he lets on." He helped Val into the saddle. "You ride and I'll walk."

"This damsel in distress thanks you, kind sir." They reached the Lower Pass Road and turning the corner were met by the leveled rifles of Weston, Rojas, and several other wranglers.

Doug Weston ran over and embraced Valerie and Jake. "Thank God you guys are okay. Jake, Val, what in God's name happened here? We heard gunfire down at the airstrip. We didn't know who was coming up the road...glad we didn't have to shoot you. What's going on? Who are these dead shit heads?"

Eddie Rojas stared at the bodies. "These are the same guys we encountered up here before with that oddball truck and snowmobiles. Looks like they didn't listen to your warning."

"Yep, except they were here with three other guys this time, two I didn't recognize. They split in that same truck we saw before. Another guy chased Val down the hill but fell over a cliff. He's dead." Jake avoided the details. He turned to Doug. "You better call the sheriff and..."

Val interrupted. "Doug, where's Jessie?" she said with a worried look.

"Oh shit, you guys don't know." Weston had a grim look. "She's been shot. Came riding back to the airstrip hurt really bad. She could barely tell us what happened up here before she passed out. Maria worked on her while waiting for medevac."

Weston looked at Valerie. "Val, she's lost a lot of blood. Maria stabilized her the best she could. The sheriffs are probably staging at the airfield. They can't get up here in their vehicles. We'll take them in our off-road rigs."

Valerie covered her mouth. "Shot? Oh my God, this can't be!"

Jake stared down the dirt road. "Did you see the other two guys in the truck on your way up?"

Valerie cut in. "One of them was that filthy creep, Rodin. He tried to stick me with an ice pick. He did the same to Jessie when they kidnapped her and then slapped her to pieces. That fucking bastard!" The anger had replaced her pain and exhaustion.

Doug and Rojas both shook their heads. "Nope, didn't see anybody," said Doug. They must have turned off and tried to go southwest. Christ, there's a maze of roads in that part of the forest."

Jake handed Doug the reins to Rustler. "Somebody can ride him back to the airfield. I'll take one of the trucks. Call 911 again. Explain they need an air unit to search for these assholes, weather permitting. They could be anywhere up here. Tell them they're armed and dangerous. We have to get to Jessie."

Weston nodded. "Go Jake, I'll leave Eddie here with some wranglers and then follow you down to the airstrip in a few minutes."

Valerie had regained her stride and ran to the truck as Jake jumped in the driver's seat. He did a quick 180 turn and flew down the rough trail.

CHAPTER 38

NORTH ON HIGHWAY 89
NEAR TIERRA DEL PUMA

Jeff Logan sped along the highway, taking little interest in the mountain scenery that flashed by at 75 miles an hour. Natalie looked up from answering messages on her cell phone. "Jeffery, slow down, it's a Porsche SUV not a Carrera. Enjoy the mountain panorama."

Logan nodded. "Right, sure. I can see trees and pine sap at the Cahill ranch," he said noticing the dark ominous clouds building over the mountains. "Besides, I don't want to be driving in the rain or snow. I thought the weather was forecasted to be clear and sunny."

Nat looked at the peaks that bordered Tierra del Puma. "I thought so too but I've visited the ranch enough to know the weather here is unpredictable. Jake's mom once said that according to legend the ancient spirits who roamed upon Tierra del Puma would brew storm clouds when they sensed an evil presence."

Jeff did another quick glance of the sky. "So, what the spirits are saying is that I'm evil and trespassing on their land. Okay, that works for me. Let's turn around and tell the Cahill's to meet us in Maui. There are more cheerful spirits over there."

"Good try, Jeffery. There's a difference between evil and crazy. You fit the latter. Besides, all these legends and myths add to the aura of the ranch. That, and it's beautiful. In some ways, I'm attached to this place, well...by association. Not like Valerie is, but still, I like to come up here."

"That's right, you and Jake are so called 'fake brother and sister.' Heard that story from Jake many times over when we were flying for LAPD. In fact, he said I couldn't date you because you were A: his fake sister and B: his attorney. Guy almost passed out when I showed him pictures of you and me in Hawaii. But how did you deal with being isolated up here playing mountain woman when you said you wanted to get into law at the tender age of ten?"

Natalie gave a wistful smile. "Mom and Dad were close to Jake's folks. They dragged me up here to visit and spend vacations. I didn't like it at first. In fact, I hated it. But Jake and I were near the same age, so we hung out. I had no choice. Jake was so filled with imagination about this place. His late grandpa was quite the storyteller. What campfire yarns he could spin. I got sucked into the lore and magic of Tierra del Puma." She gazed out at the mountains. "It was so sad when Jake's folks got killed. Dad's law firm turned over the legal duties of the Cahill family to me. I was reluctant at first, wanted more high-end action and challenges of corporate law." She sighed. "But recalling the enchantment of this land, Jake and his wonderful parents, well, here I am, the legal gatekeeper."

Natalie stared out the window and continued. "Then I got involved in CG Aviation, the winery and protecting the ranch from that slimy LA developer and his politician buddies. Seems like that fiasco was only yesterday."

Logan glanced over at her. "Nat, it was, what, about a year and half ago and that fiasco turned lucky for me," he said, thinking how events led them to one another.

She placed her hand on Logan's leg. "Well, thank you Jeffery. If it weren't for my fake brother, I wouldn't have met you. I consider that a win...most of the time."

"Yeah, you really scored, didn't you?" he said with a grin.

She threw up her hands in mock frustration. "God, you are so full of yourself."

Logan made a sudden hard left turn off the highway, causing Natalie to grab the side of the door. "Where the hell are you going?" The SUV bounced along the dirt road.

Logan slowed down to ease the car over the rocky washboard road. "This is the entrance to the ranch, right? Damn, they ought to pave it!"

"Jeffery, this isn't the way, it's a forestry road. There's a mess of these dirt roads on this side of the ranch. The road to the airstrip and their house is farther up Highway 89. I told you that earlier. You know that. Where's your brain? Slow down, you'll get my car filthy or worse."

"Oh, right, can't dirty up the princess's car, can we?" he joked, while looking for a turnaround spot. Large pines and rocks bordered the road. The ground beyond the trees looked soft and muddy. He spotted another dirt road disappearing through the trees. "Ah, maybe a turnout down there."

Just then Yeric and Rodin came barreling around the curve nearly out of control. Logan saw the truck speeding towards them. "Who are these idiots?" Something instantly clicked. Alarm bells rang in his head just as he saw the passenger stick a gun out the window. He yelled. "Nat, get down!"

Natalie started to say "What are you talking..." Logan slammed her head down in the seat as the bullets exploded the windshield. Logan threw the car in reverse, looking in the rearview mirror as he sped backwards. He quickly glanced forward and ducked as more rounds came through the windshield. Jeff pulled his gun from the side panel and returned fire. He spun the wheel hard, whipping the car around. He reached the highway and looked in the rearview mirror. Nothing was there.

Yeric felt a sting on his cheek from the bullet that had come through the windshield and grazed him. He held his hand on his face. "Fuck, I'm bleeding. Did you hit them??" he said while turning the truck around.

Rodin snapped another clip into his small assault rifle. "I hit the car, but it continued to the highway. They were obviously looking for us since there were armed. We need to get back into the forest and go west. More people will be searching. Can you drive?"

Yeric looked in the mirror at the gash on his face. "Yes, I think so, but we must contact Cherenkov!"

"Can you find your way through this goddamn web of shitty roads? We can't afford to get lost again."

Yeric wiped blood off his face. His eyes stung from bits of windshield. "Yes, yes, I have it now. Kenny showed me-I can get through."

Logan sped down the highway towards Tierra del Puma. He reached over and pulled Nat up from the floor. Bits of windshield were tangled in her hair. There were small cuts on her forehead. "My God, what just happened?" she said, fighting to catch her breath.

"You okay?" He glanced at her face, checking for blood.

Natalie trembled, trying to regain her composure. "I think I'm okay," she said, brushing bits of windshield from her face. "Who were those freaks? What the hell did we do?" Her hands shook as she touched Logan's shoulder.

Jeff kept driving and glancing in the rearview mirror. "I don't know who those assholes were. We got lucky and need to get to the ranch. Call 911. Tell them what happened and give a description of the suspect's vehicle. Advise them there are two male Caucasians in a dark pick-up, armed and dangerous-do not approach without backup. Tell them the encounter took place on that forestry road." He paused. "Shit, I don't know the friggin' name or number, just say the south side of Tierra del Puma." Logan's police instincts ran at full bore. "That truck was black like the one I saw when some creep cased your car. Jesus, that can't be a coincidence. And, call Jake, let him know what happened too."

Nat's hands shook while trying to dial her cell phone. "What, the same truck, are you sure?" She looked out the bullet-cracked windscreen and pointed. "Here, turn left, then another left to the airstrip and their house."

"Yeah, now I remember." Logan made a nervous laugh. "How could I forget?" He smiled at her. "Might be time I invest in a long-term caregiver to keep me straight on things, one with a legal background."

She squeezed his hand. "I second the motion."

Jake and Valerie reached the airstrip and parked in front of the hangar. Maria Weston and several wranglers were talking to a group of sheriff's deputies and highway patrol officers gathered on scene. None of the law enforcement vehicles had off-road capability to reach Lower Pass Road. Officers were talking on radios, calling in assets and discussing plans to hitch rides with the wranglers on ranch vehicles. There was a sense of organized chaos to it all. Maria spotted Jake and Val and ran up to hug both of them. "Thank God you're both all right." She looked at Valerie's muddy face. "Val, what happened?"

Valerie wiped splotches of mud and blood off her forehead, then brushed the debris off her hands. "It's a messy story. Where's Jessie? How is she?" Her voice struggled to keep from breaking.

Maria stared at both of them, her solemn expression telling of the next words. "She's pretty bad off. I triaged her the best I could. They airlifted her out. Tim Fremont went with them. The paramedic onboard said they had to go to the UC Medical Center in Sacramento. Val, she's critical." Maria then shifted her eyes to Jake, not wanting to see heartbreak in Valerie's eyes.

Cahill's face showed no emotion. He looked toward the mountain peaks then turned back and met the sad eyes of Maria Weston. "Maria, you did all you could. Jessie left here alive because of you. The Highway Patrol helicopter will get her to the trauma center." He turned to Valerie who shook her head back and forth in total disbelief.

"What's going on here?" she said in a frustrated voice filled with anger and disbelief. "Why her, why me? Who are these violent people? I don't get it. What did we do?"

Maria put her arms around her. "I do not know. This is evil upon the land."

Jake remained lost in thought staring at the CG helicopter parked on the tarmac. He spotted Logan and Nat drive up in their shot-up car. "Holy shit!"

Valerie turned, aghast at what she saw. "My God, *now* what?" She ran to Natalie, who struggled to get out of the car while still brushing bits of windshield out of her hair.

Jeff Logan saw Valerie's smudged and bloody face and that Jake wore a weapon. Groups of officers milled around, gearing up for a trip into the hills. "Jake, what the hell is happening here? We nearly collided with a black pickup ripping down a forestry road. The ass-holes shot at us-almost killed Nat. We're talking homicidal mani-acs. I capped off couple rounds, but they split back into the woods. They're somewhere on the ranch. We called 911." Jeff looked around at the gathering of law enforcement. "That was quick, I see the cops got here already."

Jake had a steely calm in his voice. "Jeff, the cops are here be-cause I just dumped two guys up on Lower Pass Road where they tried to kill Valerie and shot one of our employees, Jessie O'Hara. She got medevac'd to Sacramento in bad shape. Two other guys got away in a truck and ran into you."

"Huh? Jesus, what's going on?" said Logan shaking his head, baffled with Jake's explanation. He thought for a second, then add-ed. "A couple weeks back I'm pretty sure I saw that same truck in Roseville driven by some dirtbag trying to case Nat's car. Man, this makes no sense."

Jake nodded. "It's a can of worms. Best I can figure it's a gang trying to retrieve something buried in Tear Drop Pass. And at least two of them are still on the loose armed and ready to kill again."

Natalie was explaining to Valerie about the incident but stopped when she heard Jessie's name. "Jake, did you say Jessie O'Hara got shot?" She turned back to Valerie and said with shock and confu-sion in her voice. "Would somebody please tell me what the fuck is happening?!"

Valerie hugged her. "I can tell you what little we know." She looked at Jake. "But first we need to be with Jessie. Somebody has to call her mother."

Natalie regained her normal steady composure. "I will." She looked at Val. "Or we will."

A total sense of bewilderment fell upon everyone as they attempted to figure out the next move. Several officers spoke to Jake and Logan about the events. Jake half-listened and nodded. He turned away and looked up at Tear Drop Pass. His gaze shifted back to the helicopter sitting on the ramp. He looked at Valerie, Jeff and Nat and thought of Jessie O'Hara. All were nearly killed and Jessie dying. Two of the fanatics were on the loose. "Excuse us for a second," he said to everyone and pulled Jeff aside.

Cahill glanced around then spoke in a hushed tone. "Jeff, we take that helicopter and find these bastards. They won't take the highways, not after trying to kill you guys. They'll keep on logging roads and try to get back wherever they came from, which is probably on the west side." He looked skyward. "And I don't see any air units buzzing around." Jake pointed to the helicopter, "We use my ship and go find them."

Logan nodded in agreement. "Okay, but then what? We locate them and call in the troops, right?"

"No, Jeff, we kill them." Logan stared at Jake. In all the years of friendship and working together on the LAPD, he had never heard Cahill speak with such a powerful desire for revenge.

"Jake, uh, clear your head. Let's go find them first. We can deal with other things as they come up."

Valerie approached Jake. "Natalie and I need to get to the ER and be with Jessie and her mother. Can you fly us there? We'll go clean up at the house and come right back."

Jake looked his wife. "No. Jeff and I are taking the helicopter to search for these guys. They're probably running loose on the backcountry roads. No police air units have shown up and the weather might turn bad before they do get here. I want to find them now before they escape." Valerie read something ominous in her husband's eyes. Without further comment she walked away.

Jake turned to Logan. "The ship is fully equipped and has a searchlight, all 30 million candlepower's worth. The gear is better than what was on our LAPD copters. Come or stay, Jeff, I don't care.

You decide if you want to fly with me given what I told you." Jake started towards the helicopter.

Logan caught up to Cahill and punched him in the arm. "Stupid ass remark, Cahill."

CHAPTER 39

AIRBORNE
TIERRA DEL PUMA

Jake strapped into the right-side of the cockpit and started the helicopter as Logan buckled in the left seat. Within minutes the helicopter became airborne, flying low and fast over the forest. They climbed higher and headed toward Tear Drop Pass. Cahill adjusted his headphones and spoke over the intercom. "They went south and ran into you. I suspect they turned around and are trying to take the power line access road over the ridges. Those run south of that pass and mountain peak that's ahead of us at 12 o'clock."

Jeff looked out the canopy with the stabilized binoculars. "Hope you're right, because I can't see anything through the trees."

Jake raised the collective lever and eased the helicopter upward as the terrain rose beneath them. "No, you won't, its heavy forest but things thin out higher up the mountain, above tree line. I bet they already crossed over the lower ridges. We can shortcut things by going through Tear Drop Pass." He pointed at the canyon and saddle ahead. "After clearing the pass, we descend and turn southwest. There's a ridgeline with a service road to the power lines. That's where we'll locate them or farther west."

Logan nodded as he studied the moving map display, which didn't show the backcountry roads. "This GPS isn't too useful here. It's your land Jake, so you're the pathfinder. But how are we getting over that pass considering the cloud build up in front of us." Jeff looked behind them. "And it's lowering behind us too."

Jake did a surprised double take out the window as clouds began to form. "This damn bizarre weather. How did that change so fast? Clear one second then out of nowhere-clouds."

Logan watched tendrils of mist meet the rising terrain as the helicopter entered the pass then spoke. "Got some options, Cahill?" Jake swore to himself. His zeal to find the truck exceeded aeronautical common sense. A sickening pit grew in his stomach as he looked at the foreboding wall of gray that encircled them.

CHAPTER 40

APPROACHING THE RIDGES
TIERRA DEL PUMA

Rodin and Yeric made several wrong turns that dead ended. Finally, they crested one ridge and headed west. Rodin looked around. "We may get lucky. The weather is turning bad." He punched his cell and anxiously waited as the number went through various filters and transfers. Cherenkov answered. "You have it, all of it?"

Rodin had difficulty talking as the truck bounced over rocks. "Yes, but there are problems." He avoided names. "Our uh, contractors made mistakes and got eliminated. It is just Yeric and I. We must expedite our departure plans."

"So be it. It is arranged. Come to the rendezvous spot. You will be met there." Cherenkov clicked off.

Yeric wiped the caked blood off his face as he drove recklessly over the rough road. "What are the plans?"

Rodin braced himself in the shaking truck. "Cherenkov said to reach the rendezvous point as quickly as possible. It is between Grass Valley and Nevada City. I know where it is." Rodin glanced upward at the angry looking clouds. "Let us hope the weather gets worse."

Jake reduced the speed of the helicopter to a crawl. Climbing over Tear Drop Pass was now a dubious proposition. They were creeping upward as if in a slow-moving elevator. The helicopter passed in and out of the mist. Jake split his attention between the cockpit instruments and looking outside. The stark contrast between black volcanic rocks and snow gave him depth perception. He needed ground reference for his eyes to send accurate signals to his middle ear for spatial balance. Absent the visual cues there would be no safe passage through the cloud filled mountain canyon.

Logan cracked open his door and peered down beneath the skids. "Jake, tell me there are no big-ass rock formations ahead of us. We're only a few feet above the ground. Hey...uh, we just flew over a piece of airplane, a wing or something, did you see that?"

Jake manipulated the controls to keep the helicopter in a flat attitude while ascending to match the rising terrain. "We found a crashed plane up here today. It was carrying something those bastards wanted. That's what started this nightmare."

Jeff looked down as more wreckage debris passed by. His voice carried a gallows humor. "Great, we're over an airplane graveyard. Oh wait, we're a helicopter. I feel so much better." He kept staring downward. "More rocks below. You're sure there aren't any tall trees up here?"

Logan's remarks eased the tension in the cockpit. "Well, Jeff, not real tall ones that I remember." Jake countered on the controls as the helicopter shuddered with a buffet of wind.

Logan stared out the front. "How close are the rotor tips to this mountain side? Losing a blade would complicate things," he said with more sarcasm.

Cahill held the helicopter level, just high enough to keep the rotor blades from hitting the steep slope. It was a precarious maneuver; a hovering mountain climb fraught with disaster. Another slight bump of turbulence jostled the helicopter. Jake added more power to compensate for the sink rate and noticed the clouds were thinning out. He glanced at the altimeter. "We're on the lee side of the pass so there's a downdraft, but we're nearing the top."

"That's delightful news, right, Cahill?" Jeff looked down through the chin bubble. "What the-we almost hit a signpost!"

Cahill saw it too and gave a half grin. "That's the old pioneer marker denoting the crest. We just cleared Tear Drop Pass."

"Uh huh, now I know why the pioneers called it Tear Drop. I wonder how many tears were shed getting over this piece of real estate?"

Jake saw patches of blue sky mixed with the gray clouds. His muscles relaxed. He felt that his entire body had lifted the helicopter over the pass. Clouds bunched up along the side of the mountains, but the visibility had improved, at least for the moment. Cahill banked the helicopter southwest toward the dirt road that descended to lower elevations. He glanced back at Tear Drop Pass. It was now obscured by gray mists. He thought of Valerie and her connection to Tierra del Puma. *Did we get through this because of that?* He wondered too about those whispers in the wind and the puma that seemingly vanished in the forest. His mental replay got interrupted when Logan pointed and spoke.

"Jake, over there at 10 o'clock! There's a vehicle on that ridge line." Logan looked through the stabilized binoculars. "It's that pick-up going like a bat out of hell! Throw some heat into the engine and go!"

The truck bounced in the rubble of the perilous switchback road leading to the top of the ridge. Yeric concentrated on driving as the road snaked along the boulder-strewn ridge. Its twisting path crossed under power lines in a southwest direction. Rodin yelled over the roar of the engine. "Yeric, stay on this road. It will run the ridge and then drop lower to the west. We can get down into the forest and disappear. You must go faster."

Sweat ran down Yeric's forehead, stinging his eyes and the gash on his cheek. His knuckles were white from gripping the steering wheel as the truck hit more rocks. He pushed his stringy hair from his face. "Goddamn it, I *can't* go faster. This road is terrible, there are boulders everywhere. If we bottom out it's over. The engine is already smoking, it may have taken a bullet from that guy in the SUV."

A cloud deck had reformed over the ridge. Jake pointed out the canopy. "We have to go under those clouds over there. The ceiling looks pretty good so this can work." The helicopter swooped beneath the clouds.

Logan nodded. "Doesn't look all that comfortable, but not as bad as what we just crawled over."

"No, thankfully that's behind us." Jake glanced up at the darkening overcast. The occasional patches of reassuring blue sky had vanished.

Jeff noticed Cahill's web belt with weapon hanging on the back of the seat. He recalled Cahill's vengeful words before takeoff. Jake caught Logan's look. "What are you thinking, Jeff?"

"I wonder how you plan to land and shoot these bastards, and if you considered the consequences."

"Are you having second thoughts? Even after they tried to kill Nat and you?" Jake's voice carried a touch of ire to it.

"Don't give me that crap, Cahill. These guys have weapons; we have one gun, a .45 which isn't too accurate from a moving helicopter. Shooting out the window of an aircraft is movie fantasy. I'm not a SWAT sniper sitting on a skid bench with an assault weapon." Logan pointed out the canopy again. "They're still on the ridge; I don't think they made us yet." Jeff saw the cloud deck dropping. "Thought you said we had plenty of space to play under the clouds?"

Jake processed Logan's spot-on remarks about tactics. And once again they encountered nature's fickle hand of worsening weather while pursuing the fleeing pickup.

Logan watched as they closed the distance to the truck. "We gotta be careful here, they have a big gun, remember? We don't have a lot of options."

Jake noticed the graying skies. "It's getting pretty dark outside, maybe we can distract them with the searchlight. With any luck they might crash the truck. I can see it smoking."

"Man, that's a stretch."

"If we don't do something, they'll get off the ridge and disappear into the trees. We aren't getting any favors from the weather."

Jeff watched the truck bounce wildly over rocks nearly out of control. "We can try the searchlight for whatever good that will do." He placed his fingers on the switch. "This thing works, right?"

"Oh yeah, brand new and powerful." Jake saw the huge power lines that spanned across the road. The tall stanchions on either side of the road looked like giant robots with their tops obscured in mist. Jake pushed the helicopter downward. "We have to stay low and do it this way-here we go."

Logan looked up as the massive power lines flashed overhead. In an instant the wires were behind the aircraft. "I don't recall ever doing THAT when we flew at LAPD."

"You were asleep when I did." Jake kept his eyes glued out front.

Rodin looked behind them and saw the approaching helicopter. "Company!" he yelled excitedly. "They are too low and do not see the power lines. They will crash!" Rodin watched in amazement as the helicopter zipped under the wires. The rotor blades kicked up dust vortices as the helicopter sped down the road, rapidly closing the distance.

"What, what is it?" Yeric yelled. He glanced in the rearview mirror then forward, swerving at the last second to avoid hitting a large boulder. Sweat blinded him in one eye.

"Just drive and keep us on the fucking road!" said Rodin. "I'll handle this-be ready!" Seconds later the helicopter came up behind them. He yelled. "Now! Slow down, now!"

Jake misjudged the closure rate and approached too fast. Logan saw Rodin lean outside the window and point a gun. He yelled, "Gun! Break off, break off!" Cahill peeled off into a steep left bank. The helicopter fell below the ridgeline. Jake stayed low, paralleling beneath the ridge. Logan cursed. "Damn it. The asshole is capping rounds at us."

Yeric shouted over the screeching noise of the truck engine. "Where did the helicopter go?" He nearly lost control of the pickup as it skidded around a sharp curve.

Rodin saw the helicopter roll over the ridge. "I hit it. I hit the cockpit! It went over the side and crashed. Drive faster and get off this fucking road!"

Jake slowed the helicopter and stayed below the ridgeline. "I know that road. They have to go through a boulder field. It's now or never. You ready to try it again?"

"Yeah, we can try unless they let loose with more rounds." Logan repositioned the searchlight.

"Here we go." Jake climbed slightly and popped over the ridge. The battered pickup lay ahead, speeding through the massive boulder field. Jake lowered the nose of the helicopter. They were three feet off the ground and accelerating. The pickup raced on, swerving violently to miss large rocks. Jake slowed the helicopter to avoid another overshoot. Within seconds the helicopter closed the distance to the pickup. Jake yelled. "Do it Jeff! Light it up-now!"

Another crashing jolt racked the truck as it bottomed out and the engine started to howl. Rodin looked upward, searching for the helicopter. "I hear it but..."

Yeric glanced in the rearview mirror just as Jeff turned on the searchlight. 30 million candles of blinding brilliance flooded the car. He yelled trying to shield his eyes against the intense light. "Fuck, I can't see!"

Rodin could almost feel the intense light. He looked forward just as the pickup slammed into an enormous granite boulder. The truck crumpled as Yeric flew through the windshield. Rodin got instantly decapitated as a massive hulk of sharp rock splintered the cab.

Jake pulled up at the last second as pieces of truck struck the belly of the ship. He flew past the boulder field and put the helicopter into a steep climb, then pivoted the ship 180 degrees back toward the crash. "Put the wreck on my side," said Logan holding the gun out the window.

Jake slowly hovered forward so Logan would have a straight shot at whoever might have survived the crash. But the carnage was complete. Logan surveyed the mess, "Holy shit, there's nothing left. Looks like one guy is missing his head. The guts of the driver are splatted all over the rocks. Can we set down somewhere?"

Jake scanned the area and found a postage stamp size open space just big enough to land the helicopter. He hovered over the spot. "Jeff look aft, is the tail clear of those rocks?"

Logan cracked his door, looked back along the fuselage at the tail rotor. "Tail clear, but don't back up."

Jake set the ship down with a solid thump. He rolled off the throttle. Logan was already out the door.

CHAPTER 41

RANCH AIRSTRIP
TIERRA DEL PUMA

J oy Lee and Warren Treco reached Tierra del Puma and encountered a dozen sheriffs and highway patrol vehicles. Officers
stood around the tarmac, while others loaded up in the ranch
trucks. An air of urgency and disarray covered the scene.

"What's going on here? Looks like some police staging area,"
Warren said, puzzled by the mass of law enforcement.

Joy pulled to a stop near the hangar, taking notice of the groups
of officers with rifles. "No clue, but clearly something is happening."

An exhausted and grim-faced Doug Weston approached the
driver's side of the car. "Who are you people?" he said in an unkind
voice.

Joy produced her FBI credentials. "Lee of the FBI and this is Mr.
Treco, former FBI. Where is Mr. Cahill? What's going on?"

"The FBI? Great, that's all we need is a bunch of feds. You plan
on clueing us in on what the hell is going on?"

A sheriff's deputy stepped in front of Doug and intervened,
pointing toward Tear Drop Pass. "A shootout and attempted murder. We have two, maybe three dead suspects up there. One victim
is a 19-year-old girl who got airlifted to Sacramento. We're not sure
what started it and are still trying to piece it together. You have
some information about this?"

Joy glanced at Treco, then back to Weston and the deputy. "No,
we don't. And where is Mr. Cahill?"

Weston cut in. "Jake and a friend are in a helicopter looking for the shooters. We're trying to get more air assets, but the weather up there isn't good. So, what's your business here or did you just happen to stop by to adopt a mustang?" he said, with an edge in his voice.

The deputy again pushed Weston aside so he could finish the story to the FBI in law enforcement terms. "So far that's all we know...and that's why Cahill and his friend departed in the helicopter to locate the remaining suspects. This is a tangled mess. We still don't know the details or motive behind the shooting and attempted murders. Some of the officers are heading up the hill to meet the ranch personnel still at the scene. Now you're up to speed."

"Damn." Treco said softly, stepping from the car. "We're friends of the Cahill's. I charter his aviation service. And Ms. Lee is a friend of mine. We stopped by on the way to Reno just to say hi. This isn't an official visit." Warren shook his head. "Sweet Jesus, what chaos, and this happened where?"

Weston edged in again and pointed. "Up there at Tear Drop Pass. Some of my guys are there guarding the scene."

Lee cast a serious look at Treco. Both keyed in on the words 'Tear Drop Pass.' Doug Weston pointed to Valerie and Natalie returning from the ranch house. Both had cleaned the blood and dirt off their faces. "Those women are victims and were damn near killed. They can fill you in on details. I've got to get these officers up to Tear Drop. It will be four-wheel drive or horseback. Maybe you FBI types can do something helpful and reach Cahill on a radio, we can't. He's airborne, west of here if the weather didn't force them to land."

Lee got on the cell and called her office. Treco stepped towards Weston. "Doug, you know me. Warren Treco, we met before. I use CG Aviation on consulting gigs. You got a minute?"

Weston stared at Treco. "Yeah, Warren, I remember you. Sorry for the attitude, it's been chaos here. Didn't mean to give you crap or to the lady fed," he said, casting a glance at Lee still on her phone.

Treco gave a come-on-over-here nod with his head. Once alone, Treco asked. "Doug, you have any idea why all this took place up in Tear Drop Pass?"

Weston shook his head, "All I know is that Jake and Valerie went up there this morning to check out this missing airplane rumor. Then Jessie showed up at the airstrip with a bullet in her side barely able to talk. She mumbled words about being kidnapped by these scumbags and taken up to Tear Drop. Apparently, these animals were searching for something and didn't mind killing for it. They shot Jessie and Valerie somehow escaped by rolling down a hill. I don't know how Jake got in a shootout, but damn glad he did." Weston stared at Treco. "And of course, neither you nor the FBI woman know anything about this, but you just happened to show up here. That's pretty good timing isn't it?"

Treco debated on telling Weston the truth but decided under the circumstances it wasn't the right time. "Doug, I don't know anything about this. But then again, CG Aviation does security work for me, so maybe it's related to a job we did. Somebody wants to get even or something. I really haven't a clue."

Weston stared at Treco. "Warren, you should be a D.C. politician. I hope you aren't going to sell that bullshit to Cahill." Doug Weston shook his head and walked away.

CHAPTER 42

CRASH SCENE
POWER LINE RIDGE ROAD

Logan walked around the demolished vehicle. He turned to Cahill. "Who were these guys, Jake?"

"I have no idea. But they wanted something from that airplane crash. Whatever they took is probably in this trash heap." Jake shook his head in disgust, looking at the mangled corpses. "Good riddance."

It took ten minutes of digging through the wreckage to find both items which had buried themselves under the dash. Jeff reached in and pulled out the devices. He had a quizzical look on his face. "What are these things? They look like a couple of thermos jugs with circuit boards wrapped in gold or something."

"No clue, but they were willing to kill to get them." Jake scratched the top of his head. "Now, why do I think it involves the government or governments?" He looked skyward. "It's starting to clear up. Let's get back to the ranch and figure this out."

Jeff met Cahill's eyes. "And what do we say about this?" He pointed to the bodies and destroyed pickup.

"The truth, we followed them and discovered this mess."

"And the searchlight?"

"I don't think anybody needs to know how these bastards lost control."

Logan nodded. "Agreed. Let's roll."

They looked up and saw a highway patrol helicopter circling overhead. Jake walked over to his helicopter and flipped on the radio. "Patrol helicopter orbiting, this is 53 CG on the ground below."

"53 Charlie Golf this is CHP 50. Jake, this is Gavin. You okay, buddy? Why are your skids on the ground?"

"All is good. We found the shooters. They apparently crashed into a boulder. Both dead."

"Roger that, Jake. Looks like a mess down there. We dropped off Jessie O'Hara at UC Medical in Sacramento. She's in surgery. Got a call to bring back some federal agents. They want to land down there and check out the scene. Any room for me?"

"Negative. I have the only parking spot and it's small. But, I'm about ready to depart. You can have it. Just push your nose all the way forward in the landing area so you don't hit your tail. The wind is out of the west, light and variable."

"Copied. Uh, Jake, my passengers want to chat with you."

"Not now. I'm heading back to the ranch, then to the hospital. That's my employee they shot."

"Okay. One last thing, they ask you not to go through the wreckage. It's some type of evidence. I don't get it, but that's what they request."

"Whatever. Watch the weather on the eastside. Tear Drop Pass is in a foul mood, the visibility is in and out."

"Thanks, Jake, see you at the ranch."

CHAPTER 43

RANCH AIRSTRIP
TIERRA DEL PUMA

Jake orbited the airfield, noticing more cars and people had gathered around the flight office. They all looked up as if expecting his arrival.

"Looks busier than when we left," Jeff said, as the helicopter landed on the tarmac. "I see Nat and Valerie are over at Nat's car." Jeff chuckled. "She's pissed about her car being shot to shit. So much for being traumatized."

Jake rolled off the throttle, "Yep, that's Natalie." He glanced over at Logan. "So, what is she, Jeff, besides your roomie and business partner?"

Logan watched Nat as she waved to him. "I think the word will be fiancée. Let's leave that between us until the chaos settles down." He jumped from the helicopter and jogged over to a smiling Natalie.

Jake completed a quick post flight inspection of the helicopter as Valerie came over alone. She had washed the blood and mud off her face and changed into clean jeans and shirt. "You clean up well," he said putting his arms around her.

She slowly released his embrace. "We heard you found them. The highway patrol pilot, Gavin notified the sheriffs over the radio. He said those monsters got killed when their car crashed. And you landed at the scene minutes afterwards." She waited for a response, but none came. "Jake what happened?" Her eyes held steady on his.

Jake Cahill's silence told her what she didn't need to know. "They crashed. They died. Leave it at that."

She hugged him again and pointed over to the white SUV. "Warren Treco is here, along with a lady FBI agent. They want to talk about something."

Jake glanced over Val's shoulder. He motioned Lee and Treco over to the helicopter. "Val, let me talk to them, alone."

"Cop talk, right?"

"Yeah, something like that."

She kissed him on the cheek. "Don't punch out the FBI agent, she's a lady. Besides, she might kick your ass." Val smiled and walked back toward Natalie and Jeff.

Jake leaned against the side of the helicopter with arms folded as Lee and Treco approached. "Well, what a coincidence that a former FBI agent and I assume an active FBI agent are here. Just one of many odd things happening today, I suppose."

Warren gave a half grin, noticing the dirt and sweat on Jake's face. "Actually, it is, Jake. You okay? You look beat."

Jake wiped the grime off his brow and ignored Warren's remarks, looking at Joy Lee. "It is Joy Lee, right? I seem to recall you had more than a passing interest about my airplane part story over at Warren's office."

"Yes, I did. Mr. Cahill, as I think you intended me to." She displayed her FBI credentials. "May we talk?"

"We can chat here or in my copter office." He opened the back door to the helicopter and pointed. "Notice the nice leather seats, bench and club; cozy, but private. Shall we?"

They climbed in the passenger compartment and Jake closed the door. His startling green eyes locked on to Lee. "Okay, before we start let me make one thing crystal clear. If I hear some government bullshit from your lips, then your ass is off the property. And that includes you too, Warren. I've been down this road with federal task forces and the alleged big case shit when I was on LAPD. Got lied to before, but no more." His voice carried a sharp edge. "Today I damn near lost my wife and a 19-year-old kid got shot. They, whoever they are, nearly killed my best friends, and they tried to kill me along the way. And this was for something in the wreckage of a small airplane. A plane never reported missing or overdue. And I foolishly assumed it was a smuggler's run." He glared at Lee. "But now you're about to tell me something different, right, Agent Lee?" he said.

Joy Lee felt Cahill's simmering anger. "Yes, I am Jacob. And believe it or not, our presence here is in fact, a coincidence. We have no idea what transpired. We came up to discuss something with you. But it appears the subject of our discussion and the events that have just occurred are connected."

Jake held his eyes on Lee while contemplating her words. "All right so tell me why you drove up here. Add some veracity, if you don't mind."

"I will tell you the truth as far as what we know. You certainly deserve that given your past experiences." She glanced at Treco. "Warren is here because I asked him to come with me so you would see that we both wanted you to understand what this is all about. That said, even Warren isn't privy to everything I am about to say." She sighed. "I'm aware of your background on LAPD. I also know your department and other agencies kept you in the dark about many things including the circumstances of your late parents' death." She paused, eyeing Cahill's tightly drawn countenance. Lee continued. "But I believe you still have a sense of duty and honor. As did all your family through generations. You will cooperate if we provide the truth. Am I right?"

Jake held her stare then looked out the window at the mountains that surrounded the ranch. Those natural barriers could not stop responsibility. As with all Cahill's before him, there was an obligation to duty. His expression never changed, but his voice and attitude did. "Okay Joy, fill me in, explain why this happened."

She gave what could have passed for a partial smile. "Jacob, I will if you promise me to keep this information confidential. This story cannot be public. That is an absolute. Your wife, friends, and your attorney are out there. They too suffered in this horrible event.

Yet, what I tell you must not go to them. However, given attorney client privilege and spousal confidentiality, I really cannot enforce that request."

Jake spoke with a tone of finality. "It won't be a problem."

Joy Lee stayed silent for a moment then continued. "Months back a device got stolen from the China Lake Naval Weapons Center." She raised her hand. "It was not an explosive nor radioactive. It was a prototype of something. What it does is a secret and handled by our National Security Section."

Jake shook his head. "A prototype of something ripped off from a military weapons test center. That 'something' is obviously connected to a weapon system. You want to try again, Lee?"

"That is all I was told, Jacob. I work white collar crime and stumbled onto this clue because of your airplane story back at Warren's office. I'm not connected with the National Security operations."

Jake had a look of confusion on his face. "White collar crime? Explain that."

"My assignment at the Bureau is literary piracy. I know, makes no sense. When you came to Warren's office, I was there to chat about an old case of illegal copyright violations." She smiled at Treco. "Warren handled such cases while with the FBI. Then you happened by the office, told your story and things changed."

Jake grinned at Treco. "Wow, a literary geek G-Man and now a security consultant. Quite the transition, Warren."

Warren shrugged his shoulders. "Everybody needs a change," he said smiling. "Continue, Joy."

"The device got stolen at the time of the December earthquake in the Owens Valley. It was total disarray down there. Our LA Bureau had some leads that indicated the device went south. But they kept our Roseville office in the loop with some checks just in case new evidence pointed north. At that time Warren was working on truck cargo theft and using your helicopters. So, we asked him to advise us of any unusual movement of certain vehicles that we felt might be involved in the transportation of the device. We did not provide him with the specifics. Ultimately, our leads concerning a northbound passage proved unfounded. Everything pointed south, by some conveyance. The background intel is not open for discussion."

Jake nodded his understanding. "You're alluding to a potential compromise of a secret defense project."

She hesitated, not commenting on Jake's statement. "Let's just say that is why we speak today, in private, with hopes this never goes public or..."

Jake finished her sentence. "Or leaves the country."

"Your words, not mine." Her expression confirmed Jake's assumption. "The recovery and investigation were going nowhere. But then you told Warren and me about your mystery airplane part and the research about the plane taken from Lone Pine airport, which turns out to be a few miles away from China Lake." She paused as if to collect her thoughts. "That caused me to think about how clever it would be to fly the device north, in a small plane disguised as a power line patrol aircraft. No big aircraft, no transponder signals, and low along the Sierra. To what destination remains unknown. My supervisor agreed this could be a potential lead. He authorized me to drive up here. The plan was to solicit your help in searching your property for more of the airplane and perhaps the device. Warren came along today to help convince you we would not prevaricate the truth. We wanted your help." She looked outside at the flurry of law enforcement activity. "We drove up today and ran into this commotion. As I said, that was a coincidence. Can you fill us in on what happened? We received the basics from one officer and Mr. Weston. I might add, he wasn't pleased to see the FBI."

Jake chuckled. "Yeah, Doug isn't a fan of government people on the property. And chaos it is. This started with a young woman who had a brother, now dead. Probably murdered after he discovered something on Tear Drop Pass while snowboarding. My guess is he somehow interacted with these creeps and the Russian guy. You'll have to interview Jessie O'Hara about that. We recently hired her as a seasonal wrangler. She could have put things together after she learned about her brother's discovery. I can't speak to any of this with certainty."

"Russians? Are you sure about that?" Lee asked, glancing at Treco, recalling their earlier conversation about poachers and a Russian connection.

"Like I say, ask her if she's still alive." Jake's anger resurfaced. "Those fuckers shot her, tried to kill my wife and my friends and me! There are three dead guys in Tear Drop Pass and the other two are meatloaf in a car crash on a ridge road." He raised his hand. "But it gets better, Joy. One of those dead guys by the name of Rodin visited our winery weeks prior, pretending to be a Russian movie director. He wanted to film a documentary about my wife's recent book regarding this area. He specifically requested to film at Tear Drop. The problem is my wife never mentioned Tear Drop in her book. She told him no. There's always been rumors of a smuggler's missing plane around here loaded with money. We figured he was another jerk treasure hunter, scamming us to access the property, and that Jessie played a part in this too." Jake wiped more grime off his forehead, staring at his dirty hand. "Guess we were wrong on that account. They kidnapped her and brought her up to where Valerie and I were looking for aircraft parts. Then the shit hit the fan."

"What made you go up there today?" Joy asked, attempting to corroborate what Treco had told her earlier.

"As I had mentioned to Warren, I was up there weeks ago and ran into two guys in a junky 4-wheel truck pulling a trailer with snowmobiles. They were trespassing, claiming to be out for a spin or some other bullshit. I chased them off. I spoke to a Fish and Wildlife guy and he thought they could be part of a poaching ring operating up here killing our bears." Jake shook his head, "They were here today, but had company with them. And they damn sure weren't bear hunting."

"The same two men that you shot?" asked Joy.

"Yeah. It's obvious now they were up there the first time casing the area for whatever was onboard the plane. And what Jessie O'Hara got from her brother."

Warren scratched his cheek, trying to fit things together. "Jake, how did they know where to find the items that O'Hara had?"

"Jessie apparently found a map from her late brother's trek at Tear Drop Pass along with the things he discovered. I guess she wanted to search the area for reasons unknown. She stashed the stuff in a saddlebag and planned to take my wife's horse up there. Something came up and she got sent back down to the winery and forgot the gear." Jake exhaled a lengthy breath. "Today, Val and I rode up there to look around because of all this interest in a missing plane and Tear Drop Pass. That's when Val discovered the articles in her saddlebag."

"So, you were already up there when these men showed up?" said Joy.

"We were. I hiked farther up the pass to look around and Val stayed near the road searching for airplane pieces and for the other half of whatever this thing is. At some point, maybe down in Auburn, these creeps kidnapped Jessie and forced her to call my wife and asked to meet on the road below Tear Drop Pass. I assume they wanted this stuff that Jessie had and the parts which Val found near the road. They showed up, grabbed everything and tried to kill Valerie and Jessie."

"What happened next?" asked Treco, glancing out the window at the officers departing in trucks heading up to Tear Drop Pass.

Jake walked Treco and Lee through the details. Cahill omitted seeing the lion, simply adding that the SOB chasing Valerie was last seen floating down a roaring stream. Jake sensed the body might get discovered later, mangled by teeth and claw marks. He could easily explain that a cougar probably found the carcass and chewed on it. After all, he thought, this is Tierra del Puma. But for the moment he held back that and one other detail.

Jake wrapped up his narrative and glanced at Warren, then shifted his gaze to Joy. "Talk to Jessie and the others for better information. All I can add is these assholes left with both parts of this secret thing." Jake briefly described the helicopter search and spotting the crashed truck. "From what we could tell they must have lost control of their pickup. It's a bad road up there with lots of rocks and potholes. We landed and saw that one guy got decapitated and the other mixed into granulitic mush." Jake shook his head. "A real tragedy. Wish I could have seen it."

"So, you got there after they crashed. Did you do anything at the scene?" asked Lee.

Jake raised his eyebrows as if offended by the tone of the question. "Like what, cover the bodies, get a DNA sample? Hey, I'm not a cop anymore, just a concerned citizen. They're dead and I'm good with that. We made sure nobody else was integrated in the metal and then lifted off just when your FBI buddies flew over in the highway patrol helicopter."

Lee ignored Jake's acidic remark. "Then the entire package must be in the wreckage."

"Could be. So, tell me again, Joy, you're here to find this equipment which is all about what?"

"For the reason I just mentioned, national security." Jake studied her expression. Lee made no other comments and stepped out of the of helicopter with cell phone in hand.

Warren Treco looked at Jake. "I didn't intentionally get you involved. You did that at my office when you told us the story of the missing airplane. She cobbled this together on her own. And by the way, Jake, you knew she was FBI. You wanted her to take an interest or at least give you some insight."

A thin smile played across Jake's face. "I suppose in a way I wanted some subtle law enforcement perspective."

"Then why in the hell did you just give Lee and me the third degree about being part of the big bad untrustworthy government?"

Cahill looked out the window watching Valerie talking to Natalie and Jeff. He thought about Tierra del Puma and his late parents. He sighed and spoke with a weary slowness. "Because, after what happened today the past revisited me. Back when I worked undercover for the government task force, nobody in those agencies ever bothered to explain why my parents were killed or why Valerie got targeted for murder. It was impersonal to them. Just another big important secret government operation. I was only told afterwards by an LAPD commander who had the balls to level with me." Jake shifted his gaze back to Treco and spoke in a weary voice. "Warren, it's really hard to have faith in the system these days."

"I get it, Jake. But Lee's a straight and dedicated agent. She's been right with us and wouldn't lie to you. Neither did I. The helicopter contract was for truck theft. But the Bureau asked me to report any out of the ordinary activity, whatever that meant. So, we good here?"

"We are. I think I understand all of this. But it's these government bureaucracies that bother me. And I still think something isn't right with all of this, there's more going on. I don't know what, but something seems askew." Jake let out a deep sigh and rubbed the back of his neck, "Hell, I'm either too cynical or too suspicious about people. No wonder I prefer ranch life over the city."

"I understand and know where you're coming from. Hopefully, they'll find whatever they're looking for and it will be out of your life. And that Russian connection, if true, adds another dimension to the word national security and espionage. Oops, that's just an opinion of course."

Both men stepped out of the aircraft as Lee approached. "Jacob, our agents at the truck crash scene didn't find the devices. Do you think they were tossed out somewhere?"

Jake rubbed his chin. "Maybe. It's rugged up there and inaccessible in some places. Even the local law enforcement had to bum rides in ranch vehicles. It will be tough to search that back country. It might require horses." Jake grinned. "The FBI provided equestrian training to you, right? I can't rent my mustangs to a bunch of city slickers."

Joy Lee missed the humor. "We can deal with that. But, you're right, it will be necessary to get personnel up there and conduct a search."

Jake snapped his finger. "Wait, I just remembered something." He turned and opened the helicopter cargo hatch and pulled out a canvas bag. Lee and Treco looked at the bag with a puzzled expression.

"I might have omitted a detail in our conversation. I wanted to make sure I wasn't being lied to again. When Jeff and I landed we found this." Jake opened the canvas bag. "Are these what you want-ed? They seem to fit together."

Lee raised her eyebrows in surprise staring at the items. Without saying a word, she took both canisters and set them on the hood of her car. Jake and Warren watched in fascination as she used two cameras to photograph the devices, inside and out. Warren shook his head. "Typical FBI. They have an array of sophisticated photo systems way better than James Bond. Somebody in their National Security Section is studying her uplinked photos to confirm this is the real deal. Redundancy in equipment and detail all the way."

Within a minute Joy Lee returned with a smile across her face. "Jacob, you have a flare for the dramatic, but thank you."

"My wife accuses me of the same thing. So now what?"

"Our agents are finishing up at the truck crash site. They will return and then head to the other crime scene. We might request your assistance and additional statements from you and Mrs. Cahill. I'm sure the local law enforcement will have an equal amount of inquiries. However, we will work with them as not to compromise the security and confidentiality on this matter. Perhaps you could fly me to see Jessie O'Hara. It's imperative we interview her."

"Negative on that, sorry. You can hitch a ride on the highway patrol helicopter. Doug, our ranch supervisor, can help your people. I'm taking my wife and our friends to the hospital. We have to be with Jessie." Jake smiled and then strolled away.

Treco turned to Lee. "Told you. Pretty tough guy."

Lee watched as Valerie put her arms around Jake. "So is his wife with an ice pick."

CHAPTER 44

AIRBORNE TO SACRAMENTO

N at and Valerie sat in the backseat of the helicopter; Logan in the cockpit with Cahill. Jake switched on the intercom. "After we get airborne, I'll relay some of my conversation with that FBI woman, what little she told me. You can probably guess this has something to do with the theft of some government property. Had nothing to do with treasure hunters."

Natalie came on the intercom. "Ha! Whatever she told you is a bullshit cover-up story. This has clandestine government fingerprints all over it. Fake brother, we have been down this road before." Before Jake could reply Nat spoke again. "We were nearly killed by a bunch of murderers. We were expendable pawns in this entire occurrence. I'll be damn if I'm going to sit on my ass and play dumb. I'll get to the bottom of this if it takes years." Jake said nothing, knowing Natalie would do just that.

The helicopter lifted off and Jake made an easy climb towards Tear Drop Pass. No one spoke as the scenery, albeit breathtaking, evoked fresh recollections. Jake broke the silence. "Amazing, now it's clear and not a cloud in the sky."

Logan shook his head thinking a few hours ago they were flying in mist only feet off the ground. "Yeah, strange, but I'll take it."

Valerie's soft voice came on the intercom. "It's not so strange, Jeff." Jake gazed out the cockpit window, understanding her words. Just then he caught a fleeting glimpse of the crevasse he had fallen into. During the bedlam he had forgotten there were two planes that lay in the pass. Jake felt the little E6B flight computer in his pocket. He was sure it too had a story to tell.

They crested the ridge top and Jake made a slow left-hand orbit over the old pioneer summit placard. "Nice to be above the sign and not level with it," he said over the intercom. There was little conversation as they flew directly to the UC Med Center. Each person held the same thoughts; hoping Jessie O'Hara was still alive.

Logan worked the radio notifying the hospital of their non-emergency landing. Jake made a recon of the helipad then executed his approach. Once on the ground, he spoke over the intercom. "I can't shut down and block the emergency pad, so I need to find a place to park this machine. Don't wait for me." Jake lifted off and orbited over the area, spotting a fenced in construction lot. It was a parking area for bulldozers and trucks with plenty of room and no obstacles or power poles. He did a brief overflight and made a quick set down as to avoid blowing dust around. Jake shut off the engine and noticed a large burly man in a yellow hardhat stroll from a construction shack toward the ship. Jake stepped from the ship. *Aw shit, all I need now is a hassle.*

The yard foreman stood with his arms folded across his chest as Jake approached. The man eyed Jake through sunglasses and spoke in a gruff voice. "I suppose you think because this is a heavy equipment yard, your snazzy-looking whirlybird qualifies for some special privilege."

Jake wanted to hurry and avoid a confrontation. He tried humor. "Well, like your dozers over there it has a blade, four of them to be exact."

The man gave a guffaw and eyed the helicopter. "Brass and ass hauler," he said.

"Excuse me?" Jake said, coping an impatient glance at his watch.

"This thing looks like it would carry generals and politicians," the foreman said in mock disgust.

"Yeah, I guess it could." *What the hell is this guy talking about?*

The man rolled up his sleeve, exposing a tattoo that said US Army. "First Air Cavalry. I was a crew chief on a real helicopter, Blackhawk.

No helicopter should be without an M-60 door gun." He looked at Jake. "So why is this pansy looking bird in my equipment yard?"

"Just dropped my friends off at the ER pad. A dirtbag shot one of my employees, a teenager and we need to be with her. I can't leave the helicopter on the hospital pad so this is the best place I could find. Sorry about the dust I kicked up."

The man nodded. "Did somebody dump the shooter?"

"Well, yeah, I did. Had no choice."

The man grunted an approval. "Good." He gave a loud shrill whistle with his fingers and another worker came over. "Ray, take this guy over to the ER with the truck." He looked at Jake. "I'll watch the chopper; take all the time you need."

Jake shook hands with the man and grinned. "Thanks, take the ship for a spin if you want."

The foreman replied straight faced. "Better not, they're packed at the ER."

Logan helped Jake pass through several hospital security checkpoints. "Jessie's still in surgery."

"What's her condition?" Jake asked, walking off the elevator.

"Not sure, they rushed her into surgery without saying much. ER doc said the bullet penetrated her side, busted ribs, lots of blood loss. They didn't comment further. Nat and Valerie are with Mrs. O'Hara. Poor woman is a wreck. She's hangin' by a thread, Jake. Nat dialed me in on the family issues. What a mess. She's got no real medical insurance and she may get evicted from her house. She lost her son, now her daughter is critical. Jesus, that sucks."

"It sure does. And we still don't really know who's behind all this. But that FBI agent sure perked up when I said the word 'Russian.' "

"Nat's right, there's more to this then what you were told." Logan pointed. "That wrangler kid, what's his name, Fremont? He's been sitting in the corner chewing a hole in his cowboy hat. Hasn't left the surgery door since they brought Jessie in. Guess there's something between the two."

"Not sure, but Val would know." Jake spotted the women. "There they are."

Valerie and Natalie sat on either side of Nancy O'Hara, each holding the woman's hands, Nancy's cheeks were a mix of mascara and tears. She looked overwhelmed and worried sick. Valerie saw Jake. "Hi, I guess you found a parking spot."

"Construction yard, not too far away." He glanced at Nat, then knelt down in front of Jessie's mother. "Mrs. O'Hara, I'm Jake Cahill, Valerie's husband. I run the ranch. May I speak to you, alone?"

Nat looked at Jeff who looked at Val. Nat silently mouthed the words. "What's that about?" Jeff shrugged his shoulders with a 'beats me' look. Jake extended his hand and led Mrs. O'Hara away from others. He saw the lines of stress etched across her face and the deep rings under sad eyes. He spoke with a strong and reassuring tone, "Mrs. O' Hara, Jessie will survive this. She will be okay. Your only concern right now is Jessie. Not the medical bills, your job, rent or anything else. That is all taken care of. Concern yourself only with Jessie."

Nancy O'Hara's looked at Jake with surprise. "Mr. Cahill, you and your wife have been more than generous. And I'm not worried about anything else except my daughter's life."

"Nancy, Jessie was our employee when she got kidnapped and injured. If it weren't for us maybe your daughter wouldn't be in surgery. We are going to help in any way possible." His green eyes held a mischievous look. "If we didn't, then you could sue the hell out of us! My God, your attorney, Natalie Sherwin is a shark! This isn't about you. It's covering my ass from liability!" Jake broke into a wide grin. Valerie looked down the hallway as Jake hugged Nancy O' Hara. She smiled at her hubby. *Always the rescuer.*

Jake and Nancy O'Hara walked back to the others as a doctor came out from the surgery door wearing a sweat-stained gown. "Who's Jessie's mother?" Nancy raised her hand, "That's me, these are my friends."

The doctor gave a perfunctory glance at the group. "Jessie suffered trauma and a bullet wound to her side. We stopped the hemorrhaging. She has fractured ribs and internal injuries."

The surgeon paused. "Whoever gave the first aid saved her life. Jessie is strong and young. She will recover but will need a lot of time to recoup from this." Nancy O'Hara covered her face and cried. "Mrs. O Hara, your daughter is under sedation, but you can go see her."

Tim Fremont sat alone, listening to the doctor's diagnosis. Jake strolled over and sat down next to the bleary-eyed young wrangler. He put his arm around Tim's shoulder. "Thanks, Tim, for riding shotgun on the medevac. You helped keep our cowgirl alive."

He looked up with red eyes. "I guess she'll be okay, right?"

"She will, but it will be a long trail to full recovery. Only her Mom can see her right now. We came by helicopter. You want a lift back to the ranch?"

"Thanks, but I'd like to stay here if that's okay. I know I should be back helping Doug."

"Right now, your job is to bulldog Jessie and her Mom. Be there for them. Copy?"

Tim smiled. "Will do, Jake."

CHAPTER 45

F ish and Wildlife Warden Paul Davis waited up the street just out of sight of Wade Keeler's quarry. Within minutes two Lincoln PD units drove up. One of the officers with a canine stepped from the car. "Davis?"

Paul raised his hand. "Yeah, that's me. I've got the warrant."

The officers made introductions between agencies. The canine handler, name of Schonely, opened up his computer tablet. "Take a look at the drone video. Looks pretty quiet. There's one guy washing down the dust and that's it. The place has a 'closed' sign on the gate. We haven't seen any movement yesterday or today. Plus, no infrared signatures except that old guy with the hose. I think your boys have fled. We've got officers in the back just in case."

Davis nodded. "It is odd that everybody has the day off. Okay, let's take a careful look around. The warrant is to search the property, specifically the enclosures and trailers." Paul Davis considered the tenuous warrant. He had convinced the magistrate that between Cahill's observations, a reluctant informant, and Keeler and Stovall's past records, there was sufficient probable cause for an evidence search.

The officers cautiously approached the entrance. The old man hosing down the cement apron saw the uniformed men and walked toward the gate. He was Hispanic, in his late 60s with a slow and weary gait. Despite a work worn face he smiled and spoke in Spanish.

"I know that guy," said Schonely. "He does odd jobs in town." The officer spoke to the man in Spanish. After a short conversation the old man opened the gate. Schonely then translated for Davis. "He usually comes in on Tuesday's and washes the place down, but everybody's gone."

"How the hell did he get in?" asked Davis.

The officer pointed to a hole in the fence. "Says he has a job to do and Keeler owes him money, so he snuck through the fence. I told him we had to search the place. He doesn't care, just wants his money. He said Keeler screwed him again."

"Jesus," said the other police officer. "This Keeler guy must be a real piece of work. How much is owed to this guy?"

"About 20 dollars."

Davis pulled out his wallet and gave the old man 40 bucks. "Tell him thank you and he can go home."

Once in the compound the officers went directly to the trailers. They deactivated the security systems and entered. Davis walked into the rear trailer and saw the sad evidence. The double wide was filled with mounted heads and bodies of bear, deer, and mountain lions. Just about every animal that lived in the Sierras was affixed on the wall or sitting on the shelves. Davis looked at the worktable and saw baskets of eagle feathers. "Goddamn this guy," he uttered, looking at the racks of animal trophies. Davis opened the large freezer, now filled with bear organs.

One of the officers stared at the collection. "This guy is one hell of a taxidermist."

"No, he's not," said Davis in a disgusted voice. "He's a filthy ass poacher. All these animals were either taken out of season or were illegal to shoot. That freezer over there is filled with animal organs destined for Asia. This guy is a freak."

Paul Davis regained his calm. "Let's look around, take photos and get this stuff impounded." The other officers left to search the rest of the compound. Davis stood alone in the trailer staring with revulsion at the animal carnage. He turned when he saw Placer County Sheriff's Deputy, Matt Plahy, standing at the door.

"Matt, you're a bit out of your patrol area, aren't you?" said Davis his eyes still fixed on crates of dead, now stuffed animals.

"Just a tad. I heard you were serving a warrant on this place." Plahy looked around. "What a mess. This guy is a sicko. And all this is illegal?"

Davis nodded. "Yep, as well as the eagle feathers and the freezer full of animal guts. All to be sold overseas. The only thing missing is the asshole responsible for this."

"Who's the guy you're looking for?"

Davis opened more cabinets staring at the boxes of ammunition and knives. "His name is Wade Keeler. He runs this quarry. Has a couple of principles that help him. One shithead is a guy named Kenny Stovall."

"Keeler and Stovall, you sure?"

"Yep, got the probable cause and the warrant. Now I have the contraband but no suspects."

"Paul, I guess you didn't hear about the crazy shootout at that mountain ranch, Tierra del Puma."

Paul Davis looked up with surprise on his face. His thoughts flashed instantly to Jake Cahill. "Oh shit, what happened? That should have made the news or at least the police network."

"Uh huh, should have, but the FBI is involved, and events got squashed. I got this from one of the officers at scene. Apparently, so the story goes, the owner of the ranch had a gunfight with some treasure hunters who shot one of his employees. Then they tried to kill him and his wife. The owner dumped two guys and the third was found dead. They said two other guys got killed in a crazy vehicle pursuit through the mountains. Like I say, this is coming second hand."

"Sonofabitch," Davis said slowly. "No, I didn't hear about it. And the ranch owner, is he okay?"

He and his wife are fine, but some other shit went down and the feds put a blanket over it. That's all I heard."

Davis shook his head. "That's unreal."

"There's more, Paul. And the reason I stopped by. Three of the dead guys have names. One is a Kenny Stovall and the other is a Mason Reems."

Davis jawed dropped. "I'll be damned. The Stovall guy is on my warrant. Don't know anything about this Reems character. What about Keeler, was he up there?"

"He's the third guy. The word I got is they found his body in a stream. His guts were ripped out by a mountain lion."

"You're kidding? Damn, this is bizarre."

"I figured you would find that fascinating. One hell of a coincidence, that's for sure. Maybe you can reach out to the feds since your suspects are their suspects. They aren't talking to us except to say it was a gang of violent misfits looking for a crashed plane loaded with money or drugs." Plahy gave a slight chuckle. "Man, those assholes sure picked the wrong rancher to fuck with."

Paul Davis thought back to Jake Cahill's angry words about wanting to find the poachers and kill them, if he could. "Yeah, they sure as hell did."

"So, Paul, not to change the subject, but do wildlife cops have to track down this cougar and destroy it, given it's a man eater now?"

"No, we don't know the circumstances and I really don't care to know. I'm sure the owner of the ranch will handle it."

"Makes sense. Okay, I'm going to look around a bit. See ya outside."

Paul Davis looked at the animal heads mounted on the walls. Their dead eyes eerily stared back at him. He spoke in a hushed tone. "Maybe you got justice after all."

CHAPTER 46

TWO WEEKS LATER
NEAR TUNNEL 6
DONNER SUMMIT
DONNER, CA

Jake parked his truck near the old Donner Ski Lodge. The area was the jump off point for hikers to pick up the Pacific Crest Trail or to explore the old snow sheds and tunnels, the remnants of the original transcontinental railroad. He saw the pearl white SUV parked several feet away. He checked his watch. *She's punctual, that's for sure.* The air at 7000 feet had a brisk breeze that hurried the white cumulus clouds over Donner Summit.

Joy Lee stood alone, silently reading the plaque posted near the parking lot. It seemed an incongruous location, as if erected as a last-minute idea. It commemorated the work of the Chinese laborers who chiseled and tunneled a path for the first transcontinental railroad through the daunting geology of the High Sierra. It was a small, forgotten tribute to the hundreds who worked and died on the job. She glanced up as Jake approached and smiled. "Thank you for meeting me, Jacob."

"No problem. I was driving down from the ranch heading to Sacramento when I received your text." His eyes absorbed the striking scenery of Donner Pass; the granite slopes that contrasted with the dark somber waters of Donner Lake. The old railroad track bed and snow sheds rested precariously on the cliff above the lake. "You picked a beautiful place to meet."

Lee half smiled and pointed to the plaque. "I believe that some of my distant relatives died here building Tunnel 6 and that rock wall on the side of the mountain. That might be speculation since nobody kept a record of the Chinese deaths. Still, it could be true." She looked at Jake, "I was heading to the Reno Office. I'm back on my usual casework, literary piracy. Not as exciting as a missing airplane and the associated entanglements of national security. How are you Jacob? How are your wife, friends, and Jessie O'Hara?"

"Thanks for asking. We're all good. Jessie should get released from the hospital shortly. Then it will be a long road of physical therapy, but she's young and tough. Some of your colleagues interviewed her and my wife." Jake met Lee's eyes. "We played ball and accepted the cover story. Let's see, a gang of thugs killed Jessie's brother, kidnapped her because she knew the whereabouts of a smuggler's plane loaded with heroin and money. Then Val and I and our friends encounter them on the ranch and had a shootout. The other guys fled and got killed in a car accident. Wow, nice plot. Should be a movie. What actor plays me, Joy?" he said, with mock seriousness. "And how did you explain the canisters to Jessie?"

Joy Lee gave a slight smile. "They told her it was part of a computer system stolen along with the drugs. Our National Security people handled that aspect of things. My participation in this case has concluded. Now, it's back to finding copyright violations." A tinge of bitterness rang in her voice.

"Didn't mean to sound flippant," said Jake. "It just seems there's always some cover-up story and people pretending to be something they aren't. But considering the national security dynamic, I guess it's typical, though I'm not sure a smart teenager like Jessie will buy this tale."

"Jacob, you are not flippant, just straightforward. I told you that I would be honest with you. Therefore, I am here today to share additional information that you should not be privy to, however." She hesitated. "I know you will not compromise my integrity or what the Bureau is working on." She locked eyes with Cahill waiting for an answer.

"Joy Lee, nothing goes farther than between you and me. That includes wife, attorney or friends. I understand the position you're putting yourself in for my sake."

"Very well. Information points to a Russian espionage scheme. We believe they contracted with elements of the Russian Mafia or some offshoot to transport the device out of the country. The Americans involved included a Wade Keeler, now deceased along with his associates." She gave a wry grin. "You cancelled out our opportunity to interview them. But we think Keeler was the connection to illegal chop shops and selling non-taxed diesel fuel at his quarry. This Rodin individual acted as the liaison who oversaw other Russian illegal operations including a recycle center."

Jake Cahill's voice turned icy cold. "I would kill them again considering what they did."

Lee waited until the fury in Cahill's green eyes subsided, then spoke. "The investigation is in progress and complicated. It is strange for Russian organizations to trust people not of their blood. A lucky break came from the Department of Fish and Wildlife about an international poaching ring. That tied back to Keeler and his affiliations with the Russians. However, like the many compartments of a Russian doll box, all of this remains obfuscated and tangled." Joy Lee watched as Cahill's anger faded away with a nod of acceptance.

"That figures. I saw these filters and roadblocks play out when I dealt with cartels doing undercover work on the LAPD."

"I'm sure you did. There is more and just as nebulous. This case could involve a man known only as the Wolf. It is the moniker for an unknown person associated with sex trafficking, drugs and a host of other illegal activities. All that remains vague. But as I mentioned, I'm no longer involved."

Jake shook his head. Nothing shocked him anymore about the brutal and unscrupulous actions of people and organizations. "And here I thought living on the ranch would isolate my family from this evil," he said with a tone of resignation. He reached for her hand. "Thank you, Joy. Perhaps we will see each other again."

Joy Lee smiled. "Unless you understand copyright law, then I doubt our paths will cross. I'm being transferred to the LA Office after my trip to Reno. Take care of yourself and your family. Jacob, you are fortunate in many ways." She cast a last glance to the plaque, then walked to her car and left.

CHAPTER 47

DOWNTOWN
RENO, NV

J oy Lee planned extra time before her meeting at the Bureau office. She pulled into the full-service auto mat located on the outskirts of town. Lee strolled to the customer lounge where several people waited for their vehicles to be hand dried. She sat next to a man in a business suit seemingly engrossed in reading his computer tablet, oblivious to the noises of the car wash. He casually looked up, glanced around then spoke to Joy in Mandarin.

"We picked up the camera when you stopped at the rest area on Highway 80. We were afraid that some opportunist would steal it off the front seat before us. But you timed it well."

"And do I get to know the results?"

"The authenticity was confirmed. It is the energy system. Your efforts have saved us years of research and given us par with the Americans. The clumsiness of the Russians has left them far behind, again. They remain a gangster country on the decline."

"And me?"

"Enjoy Los Angeles and continue your work at the FBI. We will awaken you if another situation develops, or you may reach us should you discover something of importance, as you did with this. But for now, enjoy your career."

"I have but one other question. The agent in Ridgecrest, have you located him?"

"No, we must assume he was killed by the Russians or perhaps the Americans." The man paused. "We know you had a relationship with him. We are sorry. But perhaps it was not meant to be." A horn beeped and the man stood up. "I must go as my car is ready."

Joy Lee sat alone feeling introspective. She had lost someone she cared for. Inevitable in this profession, she thought. But such inevitabilities did not soften the grief. However, life and the jobs would go on. Lies and prevarication had become second nature to her. Falsehoods were a survival skill. Her goal was national security, but not for the country that Jake Cahill believed in. In some ways she envied the man. He had someone to love and a home called Tierra del Puma. Her thoughts were interrupted by the quick honk of a car. It was time to go to work.

CHAPTER 48

UC MED CENTER
SACRAMENTO

V alerie peeked into Jessie's hospital room. Nancy O'Hara stood combing her daughter's hair. Jessie lay in bed; tubes stuck in her arms. There were bandages on her side, but the color in her cheeks had returned.

"Hi, am I interrupting?" Valerie said, with a warm smile.

Jessie's eyes brightened.

Nancy O'Hara turned and set the hairbrush down. "Hi Valerie, no in fact I was just leaving." She glanced at her watch, then to Jessie. "I better get to work." She kissed Jessie on the forehead. "I'll be back tonight, sweetie."

"Mom, that's okay. Go home, you look tired. I'm fine and definitely not going anywhere."

After her mother departed Valerie noticed several bouquets of flowers on the bed stand. "Wow, somebody thinks you're pretty special."

Jessie grimaced trying to adjust her position in bed. Valerie helped her to sit up.

"They're from Tim Fremont. He comes in daily." She said matter-of-factly.

"That's sweet of him. Now we know why he wanted to work at the winery. Had to be something or someone important for that cowboy to leave the ranch," she said, adjusting Jessie's pillow.

Jessie glanced over at the floral bouquets. "Those are wildflowers from the ranch. He must drive up and back every day. I like them a lot."

Valerie sensed Tim's fondness for Jessie. She wasn't sure if the feeling was mutual. "He means well and thinks you're special, which you are."

"He's nice. Plus, friends from the winery came by too, including Buzz," she said with a grin.

Valerie chuckled. "Buzz" was Gene Murdoch, the handyman and all-around fix-it guy at Sierra Puma. His part-time job away from work involved the removal of wild critters from people's homes. Rattlesnakes were his specialty. The kids working at Sierra Puma nicknamed him "Buzz" and he loved it. Tim and Jessie got along well with the man's rough sawn personality. Val had even seen Jessie laugh when the three of them worked on projects at the winery.

Valerie looked around the room with raised eyebrows. "Hopefully, he didn't bring any creepy crawlers with him. So, when are you getting released?"

"The doctors told Mom, maybe in a few days. But I have to take lots of physical therapy. They said it's a lengthy process to a full recovery."

"And Jessie, you'll have a full recovery."

"Did you know the FBI talked to me about those horrible men?"

"I heard that. They interviewed us too."

Jessie shifted around in the bed. "They told me those monsters were a group of foreign guys looking for a lost airplane that carried drugs and some supercomputer part stolen from a company. And that they disguised themselves as treasure hunters."

Valerie knew the fabricated cover story. "They told us the same. It's hard to fathom all of this."

Jessie looked out the window. "They were hideous, especially that creep, Rodin. They scared me really bad. I knew they would kill me." She looked back at Valerie recalling those horrible hours in the car. "I peed my pants."

Val grinned. "And you think I wasn't sacred when they face-planted me on the hood of the truck? Nobody should ever go through something like that. It's okay to pee your pants." Valerie thought back to the deadly night in LA when she threw up after nearly getting strangled to death by an insane killer. She shivered at the memory.

Jessie's expression turned glum. "When I was in the car with that Rodin filth, he mentioned a guy with some weird name like Cerkin or something like that. They threatened to drug me and..." She chocked on the words. "Make me a whore. I saw the syringe."

Valerie closed her eyes at the sickness of it all. She grabbed Jessie's hand. "Did you tell the FBI about this?"

"I did, but they didn't say much. But I know it's about some sex slave stuff. I read about that. Maybe those monsters were just threatening me, but it scared me even more."

"Jessie, the FBI doesn't dismiss that kind of talk." Valerie hugged the frightened teenager. "It's over Jessie, you're safe." She changed the subject. "When you get better, you're going back to Tierra del Puma. Jake has a few mustangs that need some riding and TLC. Jessie, Team Cahill has your back. Given time, this will all fade away."

Jessie bit her lower lip as if she wanted to say something, but the words wedged in her throat. Valerie caught the hesitancy in her expression. "What is it Jessie?"

Jessie's voice broke with tears. "Valerie. I'm so sorry for all the hassle I've caused you and Jake. I almost got you killed. I didn't mean to betray your trust when I took notes off your desk. It's just..." She covered her face and sobbed. "I miss Sean, I miss my brother. He understood me. They killed him. I know they did." She choked on the words, trying to explain what she meant. "Sean knew why I am the way I am."

"Jessie," Val said softy, holding the girl's hand. "What did he understand? You want to tell me?" Jessie O'Hara's eyes streamed tears as she told Valerie about the shadows of depression that could never go away.

Jake walked down the hospital corridor as Valerie came out from Jessie's room.

"Hi, got tied up talking to Joy Lee. She's being transferred to LA. Guess her part is over, but not the investigation." He looked at Valerie's sad expression. "Hey, you all right? What's up, is Jessie okay?"

Valerie dabbed her eyes and grabbed Jake's hand. "She's good and not so good. It's been a rough ride her entire life. She's asleep now. It's time for us to go home."

CHAPTER 49

THREE WEEKS LATER
SIERRA PUMA VINEYARD
AUBURN, CA

A gentle breeze tempered the noontime sun. The two women sat beneath the patio umbrella sipping a chilled iced tea and enjoying the day's freshness and blue sky.

Natalie brushed a strand of blonde hair from her face. "So, how are you doing, Mrs. Cahill?"

Valerie slowly set her glass down. "Getting better as the time passes. Natalie, I wasn't about to let those heathens kill Jessie or me. Something made me fight. I was even more afraid for Jake than myself."

Natalie stared at the woman sitting across from her. "You had help, didn't you, Val? And I'm not talking from Jake. There was something else going on, wasn't there?"

Valerie smiled. "I can never explain it. Not that anybody would believe it anyway." She hesitated as if to find the right words. "Those whispers in the wind heard me, Natalie. Jake knows now, he saw things that defy reason." She sighed. "Oh well, it just is."

Natalie reached across the table and touched Valerie's hand. "I knew you were part of Tierra del Puma the day Jake told me he was in love with you. You carry the legend in your soul. Like you say, it just is."

Valerie smiled appreciatively. "Change of subject, how are you after this nightmare?"

"Still in disbelief. State of shock is a better term." She tapped her fingernails on the glass, recalling the near-death attack on her and Logan. "Jeffery instantly sensed that something was wrong when that pickup approached us. He acted so quickly and pushed me under the dash. Then the windshield exploded." She paused to find her voice. "He saved my life, Val, he reacted by instinct."

"Jake said it's a sixth sense that cops develop and never lose. Lucky for us, given the other flaws our men have," she said laughing. The women clinked their glasses together.

Natalie grew serious. "I learned something besides what the FBI told Jake and what he said to us in the helicopter."

"Can you talk about it, considering the confidentiality?"

"Only to this extent, which is all I learned. Dad's legal partner has some old connections within government. There's a story going around that a top-secret device got stolen from a military weapons base in California and later recovered from a plane that crashed in the Sierras. Now, isn't that interesting?"

"That's beyond crazy and one more odd coincidence we can't explain." Valerie stared out at the vineyards, lost in contemplation. "So, what's your Jeffery been up to these past few weeks?"

"Jake made an offer on Nancy O'Hara's house that the landlord couldn't refuse. Hey, you look puzzled. He told you, right?"

"My husband, as usual, forgets to share details or is brief in his remarks on some things. Is laconic the right word?"

"That's Jake. Ah, well, he had Jeffery remodel the house. That's what he's doing now. And from what I understand, Mrs. O'Hara is now working for you, right?"

"That I do know. She's working in the restaurant. Like her daughter, a hard charger. With time, maybe all this family tragedy will fade a bit. Though I'm not sure time can really heal all things."

"And how's Jessie? I heard you guys gave her a nice bonus. Are you sure she'll come back to work?" Nat said, smiling.

"It was the least we could do. I haven't spoken to her for a while. She's doing physical therapy and then wanted reset time. She's carrying some emotional baggage." Valerie didn't elaborate on details.

"I sensed that when I first spoke to Nancy O'Hara. I hope she works things out." Natalie glanced around at the large waterfalls that nosily tumbled into several ponds. "This is a nice ambiance. I like the water features."

"Your Jeffery did a beautiful job on the design and construction."

Natalie gave Val a crafty grin. "Hmm, I bet this would be a perfect place for a wedding."

"I think it's an ideal setting," Valerie said, returning a smile.

"After all of the craziness, Jeffery said we should make a contract to take care of each other. A contract with the words 'I do' written in it. I know you'll be around, will Jake?"

The sound of a helicopter interrupted their conversation. Valerie looked skyward. "He will, but right now my flyboy is northbound taking some scientists to Mt. Lassen. His current Walter Mitty fantasy is being a flying geologist."

"He hasn't grown up Val."

The helicopter noise slowly faded. "I hope he never does." She grinned, thinking about her man who didn't like surprises.

CHAPTER 50

G ene Murdoch casually strolled out of his house holding his travel cup filled with black coffee. Murdoch scratched the top of his gray crew cut and then readjusted his ball cap. At 55 years old, the former Marine kept himself in good shape. Slightly less than 6 feet tall, he carried more muscle than fat. Murdoch worked as the handyman at Sierra Puma Winery. He normally wore blue overalls at the winery, but it was his day off. This morning the uniform consisted of jeans and a T-shirt that said, "Don't tread on me" complete with an image of a rattlesnake. Gene "Buzz" Murdoch's part-time gig was snake handler. He laughed when the two kids at the winery, Fremont and that red-haired girl, gave him the sobriquet "Buzz". They were all curious why anyone was crazy enough to hunt rattlesnakes. Out of curiosity, Fremont tagged along on a snake removal job. "Buzz, you must be nuts to have a job like that," said Tim watching Buzz catch and bag a rattler. Gene chuckled. "Not nuts, Tim, just a Marine." Murdoch had traveled around the world with the Corps visiting lots of shitty places that had some of the meanest and most poisonous vipers he had ever seen.

Gene Murdoch had an okay job at Sierra Puma winery-no squawks, but it got boring. Then he'd discovered sections of the Sierra foothills had too many rattlesnakes. The way Murdoch thought; too many people, not too many snakes. But the word got out that Murdoch would make house calls. He would locate and fearlessly bag the buzzing, slithering intruder and take it away. People paid well for the service versus trying to take a shovel to some five-foot-long coiled rattler. Gene had to chuckle knowing that more times than not, the pissed off snake either struck at the ignorant person or made good an escape, usually to a place the scared homeowner didn't want to go in pursuit of. So, they called "Mean Gene the Snake Machine." Murdoch's business developed into a profitable part-time gig. Gene wasn't stupid or careless. As in handling weapons in the Marine Corps, he treated the fanged reptiles with respect and caution. And, he carried a host of capturing equipment that fitted nicely into the fully enclosed utility trailer pulled by a shiny red F-250 4-wheel drive truck. A logo on the side of the truck said, "The Slither Slammer."

Gene swallowed the last of the java and did his usual pre-departure inspection. He had several calls scheduled for this morning. Murdoch checked the cab for his gear followed by a quick walk around of the vehicles. He reached the back of the trailer and stopped. The lock on the doors were unlatched. "What the hell?" he said. He looked at the hasp and lock. It appeared he simply forgot to push the lock down and secure it. Murdoch furled his brows, thinking that wasn't like him. But it was a wild night of drinking with a bunch of his retired Marine Corps buddies so maybe he didn't secure the lock. Murdoch slowly opened the trailer door, always alert for escapees that might have crawled out of the containers. The inside of the trailer appeared clean and undisturbed. The occasional electric shaver buzz told him his captives remained secured. He closed the trailer door and secured the lock. Seconds later he jumped in the truck, tuned in his favorite country western music station, and headed to his first call.

CHAPTER 51

I t wasn't unusual to see an occasional cargo drone flying over the foothills making household deliveries. Though still in the infancy stage, a small package drone service seemed inevitable. Given the drone could be remotely operated from miles away, it provided flexibility and saved driving time given some homes were set back from major roads.

This pilotless device flew higher and faster than most airborne delivery drones. Its noise footprint was barely audible as it flashed over houses with a cardboard box suspended beneath its frame. The drone made a few turns as it tracked to its destination. It slowed and did a high orbit over the large, well-gated estate that set some distance off the paved road. The onboard cameras scanned the area to confirm it reached the right address. Then the craft descended and hovered in front of the partially open garage, depositing a flimsy box that hit the ground and fell apart. The drone shot vertical and sped south.

Minutes later the drone descended into a steep canyon, where far below a remote stretch of the American River pushed its way through the rugged, near inaccessible canyon. The drone jerked downward in a dive and smashed into the canyon wall. Pieces tumbled down into thick brush and the turbulent rapids of the river. Two people stood atop the cliff looking down at the crash site. The youthful cowboy crushed the remote control and tossed it over the cliff. He turned to the teenage girl beside him. "There, done deal and over with."

She gazed down at the river and then said with concern, "Are you sure it was the right address?"

"I grew up here. My friends and I used to mountain bike around this area until the jerk and his asshole buddies ran us off with a gun. I heard his name mentioned by the guys that brush clear his property. They said he's an arrogant foreign guy; a rude, cheapskate piece of shit." The young man gave a grin of satisfaction. "The warm weather is perfect for this. Surprising what you can learn from our handyman." He put his arm around the girl and helped her limp back to his Toyota pickup. Suitcases and camping gear filled the bed of the truck.

Once buckled in she looked at him with a worried expression. "Tim, before we go you should know something." Her eyes got moist and voice cracked with emotion. "Years back, when I was young my father let one of his drunk buddies..." she hesitated, gulped hard and wiped away more tears. "He touched me, did things as my father watched. Then they threatened me not to tell." She turned away and stared out the window. "I just want you to know. I want you to know that I'm damaged goods, inside and out. My chest is scarred, and I have demons from what he did to me, and what those men did when they kidnapped me." She wiped her eyes and looked back at him. "I'm damaged Tim and I'm not sure you will ever understand me. I don't understand myself. I'm not sure how this will work, you and me."

Tim Fremont put his finger on the nose of the red haired, freckle faced girl and gave her a warm smile. "Jessie, in my eyes you are perfect, the most beautiful and courageous woman I ever met. No one will ever harm you again. I promise. We'll drive north and explore Oregon. We'll be together and learn together. I love you, no matter what happens." Jessie O'Hara smiled, and for the first time in her life it was a smile from the heart.

She kissed the young cowboy. "Let's go find a new adventure."

CHAPTER 52

CHERENKOV RESIDENCE
AUBURN, CA

Nikolai Cherenkov threw on golf shorts and walked around the house bare-footed. It was evening but the house remained unusually warm from the day. He took another sip of vodka and studied the coded message. They wanted him home. He had diplomatic immunity and by morning he would be out of the country. Cherenkov let the paper drop on the table and grunted. Life, he realized, changed because of the stupid errors of others, outsiders. Now a possibility existed such mistakes could trace backward. There would be questions. But they considered the 'Wolf' too valuable for retirement. His ruthless talents and discipline to the code had use in other places.

Cherenkov set his glass down and went to the garage to retrieve his suitcase. He strolled through the kitchen to the adjoining laundry room and opened the door to the darkened garage. His hand fumbled for the light switch when his foot stepped on something that moved. There was a buzz, followed by an instant and horrific burning sensation on his leg. He felt another sharp twinge on his leg and more excruciating, fiery pain. He stumbled back into the laundry room, his hand frantically searching for the light switch. The stabbing anguish in his legs quickly spread through his body as his heart rate soared. He hit the light switch and looked down. The two rattlesnakes had followed him into the laundry room. "Goddamn it!" he screamed, then stumbled as a visceral wave of panic washed over him. His body began to convulse, unable to fight the rapidly spreading venom. Saliva foamed out of his mouth and a piercing pain ripped through his heart. He clutched his chest in agony and collapsed. Cherenkov, the Wolf, lay dead on the floor as the pit vipers slithered over his body into the warm house.

CHAPTER 53

CAHILL RESIDENCE
TIERRA DEL PUMA

Jake sat at the large dining room table, writing. As he had done for his entire life, he kept a diary of events and personal perspectives. Journaling was a family tradition that began with the first generation of Cahill's. He capped the fountain pen that belonged to his late mother and wondered if and who would ever read his words. Jake had become the finale of the Cahill legacy. His thoughts were still adrift when Valerie came into the room carrying a box. "Hey, there, what ya thinking?" she said, rubbing the back of his neck.

He looked at her, then at the package. "I'm thinking what might be in that box."

"Come sit with me in the living room and I'll tell you. It's a surprise."

As usual, they sat on the floor, their backs leaning against the old leather recliners once owned by Valerie's late grandparents. She handed him the box. "Here, this is for you, and don't shake it!"

He eyed the box, feeling its weight. "What is it?"

"Don't ask, just open it."

Jake carefully untied the wrapping and his eyes widened. "Wow!" he said, staring at the model replica of the helicopter he flew on the LAPD. It was virtually identical, down to the decals and tail number. "This is amazing. Val where did you get this?" he said, astonished by the perfect craftsmanship.

She smiled, enjoying the satisfaction the gift created. "An old guy in Nevada City carved it. You should see his shop, it's incredible. Jake, I know you're not into police memorabilia, but I think this is special, for both of us."

He read the small plaque on the pedestal of the model. "The carriage on our first date. Love, Valerie."

Jake felt the lump in his throat. He stared at the model, recalling the beginning of a new chapter in his life. Jake had flown a police copter back from Texas. He had been returning to Los Angeles and made a fuel stop at a remote airport in the tiny town of Quiet Mesa, New Mexico. It was there he met her, sitting forlornly in the airport lounge. The bankrupt commuter airline had stranded her.

She had just settled the estate of her late grandmother and needed to return to her home in LA. Within 20 minutes of chatting, they had both taken a chance on each other. Jake convinced her to hitch a ride in the helicopter and share an adventurous flight across the Southwest. The flight ended in LA, the connection between them did not. A relationship developed, but not without both of them running into harm's way. However, they fell in love and discovered they both had ties to Tierra del Puma. Valerie Paige added Cahill to her name.

Jake reached over and kissed his wife. "This...," he said, holding the model and speaking softly, "is all about us."

She beamed a warm smile hearing his words. "I'm glad you like it."

"Indeed, I do." Jake turned the model over and saw the imprint inscription. "Hand carved by Cal Greenwood." He stared at the name than asked, "Val, where did you say this shop is located?"

CHAPTER 54

LATE AFTERNOON
NEVADA CITY, CA

Jake and Valerie strolled down the streets of old town Nevada City. They went slow, gazing in the shop windows. "Jake did that model suddenly make you want to be a collector?" she said, as they approached the model store.

"No, I just want to meet the talented guy that carved this. Craftsmen like that are a unique breed."

"Do I see a future woodworking shop at the ranch?" she said, holding his hand.

"We already have workshops at the ranch. Besides, I need to learn how to cook and use our expensive chef's kitchen."

"Well, I suppose there are such things as miracles." She pointed to the shop. "Here it is. Check out this old-fashioned ringing bell. The entire place is retro." They entered the little store as Jake stared in wonder at all the models.

Valerie walked straight to the back counter as Jake followed, distracted by the number of aircraft replicas that covered the shop from floor to ceiling. Cal Greenwood came from the back room wearing his gold rim glasses, and dressed in his work apron, replete with pocket protector. Valerie smiled, noticing he still seemed a bit unkempt, but his eyes sparkled at the sight of her. "Well, this is a surprise. Hello again Mrs. Cahill. And this must be the aviator, Jake, right?" Greenwood wiped his hand on the apron and extended it over the counter.

Jake felt a firm grasp from the man. "It's a pleasure to meet you, Mr. Greenwood." Jake looked around. "What an incredible store, or should I say hangar?"

"It's Cal. Yep, lots of airplanes here. Lucky for me I sell quite a few."

"Cal, I wanted to thank you for that helicopter model you made. The craftsmanship is impeccable. You, Sir, are quite the gifted artist."

Greenwood chuckled. "Thank you, but your lovely wife was very specific." He winked at Valerie. "I just followed her detailed instructions."

"You sure put heart and soul into it," Jake said, eyeing the other handmade models in the glass case. "So, Cal, did you ever fly?"

"A long time ago, but not anymore, too old. And not commercially or in those crazy helicopters you fly. Just small private planes."

Jake nodded, staring at one model in the case. "Small planes are sometimes more fun than the bigger machines. I still enjoy the thrill of stick and rudder flying, looking out the window and watching the wing create that magic of lift. And flying over the Sierra is beautiful as long as you can clear the peaks." Jake grinned. "Don't you agree?"

"Yep, something special for sure, especially clearing mountain tops."

Valerie listened, sensing something in Jake's conversation. *Just pilot talk,* she thought.

Jake pointed to a model in the case. "Now, there's a classic, a beautiful little airplane. That's a Cessna 170, right?"

Greenwood nodded as he pulled out the model. "You know old planes, son. I painted it with the original Cessna paint colors."

"It's perfect, Cal."

Greenwood held the model in his hands, admiring it. "She was a fine plane," he said, wistfully.

Jake studied the old man's expression. "So, Cal, being an aviation buff, maybe you can help me identify this item I found."

"I can try." Greenwood readjusted the glasses on his nose.

Jake reached in his pocket and handed Cal the E6B computer that he had discovered in the old wrecked plane that lay jammed in the crevasse.

Greenwood studied the instrument with washed-out markings. "Hmm, that's an old whiz wheel flight computer. They still sell versions of them today. Most are digital or an app on a phone or tablet. This, however, is the genuine article. Truly a pilot's wheel of answers," he said, admiring the faded gadget.

Cal started to give it back, but Jake pushed the object back into the old man's hand. "Figured that's what it was, but can you make out that dull inscription on the back? It's tough to read." Greenwood squinted at the barely visible, scratched letters that spelled, "C. Greenwood."

"Sweet Jesus," Cal Greenwood said, barely above a whisper. He clutched the E6B in the palm of his hand and stared at it.

Valerie held a confused look on her face, unaware of what Jake handed the man. Greenwood remained silent as he contemplated the little device. He looked up at Jake. "Where did you find this?"

"Next to an old broken up Cessna 170 resting in a crevasse near a place called Tear Drop Pass. I bet it has some history."

Greenwood kept hold of the E6B and glanced at the clock on the wall. "I'm closing the shop. Might you folks be interested in coming to my house? It's out back, just across the street. I want to tell you a story."

Valerie saw a melancholy expression cross Greenwood's face. She looked at Jake who replied, "Cal, it would be a privilege. And I'll tell you how I found it. Fair enough?"

"That it is, son." Greenwood locked the front door and turned off the lights. "Come through the back." Jake and Val followed the old craftsman as he tossed off his work apron, still holding the little device.

The house was a fully restored old Victorian, bordered by a white picket fence. Jake noted the perfect detail of the home with its gingerbread trim and sharp-edged rooflines. The front steps creaked underfoot as they made their way to the large porch. "Spent my life keeping this old place in good shape. Got rid of the rotten wood but can't get rid of the loneliness," he said as they followed him through the oak front door. The interior of the house had a vintage style that reflected a coziness of another time. The hardwood floors were original and well maintained.

Greenwood led the Cahills through the foyer, past a grandfather clock that seemed as old as the house, and into a small living room. A few pictures adorned the fireplace mantel. A large braided area rug added softness to the room. Valerie noticed the ornate crown molding that accented the ceilings. The furnishings were sparse, two overstuffed chairs and a couch. It was neat in a man's sort of way, she thought, but lacked what she considered a woman's touch. A few magazines lay scattered on the table next to an empty plate. *He eats by himself.*

Greenwood pointed to the couch. "Have a seat." He glanced at the grandfather clock that softy chimed. "About time for a wee bit of good scotch. Can I get you one?"

Jake grinned. "That would be great."

"Mrs. Cahill, may I get you a scotch or a glass of wine? I have a bottle of excellent chardonnay. It's local stuff from an Auburn winery."

She grinned. "No thank you. I know from experience that when pilots get together and drink scotch, it mandates a designated driver, which is me."

"Aviation talk and scotch. You know pilots only too well." Greenwood disappeared into the kitchen.

Valerie whispered to Jake. "What's going on, what other airplane? What aren't you telling me, again?"

He winked and patted her knee. "We're about to find out."

Cal returned with two small glasses. The amber drink was mixed with water. "Hope you like water with your scotch." He patted his stomach. "A bit hard to take it straight anymore." He raised his glass. "Cheers." Greenwood eased back into the chair. He picked up the E6B, gave it another glance and looked at Jake. "I'd like to know how you found this."

"It's a crazy story." Jake said, tasting the scotch. "This is single blend stuff."

Cal grinned. "Son, is there another type?"

Jake began his story, giving Greenwood a sanitized version of the events. "I own the Tierra del Puma ranch, miles north of Truckee. It's a lot of acreage and covers the eastside of Tear Drop Pass. Last winter an airplane crashed up there. This spring we found part of the plane. That started us searching for the rest of it. Figured since nobody reported a plane missing, it could have been a smuggler's plane. They don't get reported lost too often."

Greenwood took another nip of his drink and smiled. "No, they don't-solo flights."

"True. We finally found it. And it was just that; a smuggler's plane never reported lost." Jake massaged the story a bit further. "All that got resolved after locating the plane, *that* plane, anyway." Jake took another slow swallow of scotch. Valerie sat there, intrigued, waiting for the next part of a story she had never heard.

Jake set his glass down. "While hiking down from the pass, I slipped and fell into a gigantic hole, a volcanic fissure of sorts. Low and behold, I ended up next to an old airplane sitting on its tail with the wings twisted forward. Not much left but dull aluminum bones. Pretty obvious it had been there for a long time. That's when I found the pilot's E6B. I cleaned it up and saw your name on it. I didn't connect the name until Valerie gave me that fantastic model with your name on the base plate." Jake grinned at Greenwood. "It all registered when I saw the Cessna model in your shop and how you looked at it. It's a model of the plane up at Tear Drop Pass. Your face gave you away when you saw the name on the E6B." Jake leaned back on the couch. "So, that's my part of the story. We would love to hear the history behind all of this. If it's something you want to talk about."

Cal Greenwood slowly exhaled and looked up at the ceiling then back at Jake. "Only one person knew about this. She held all my secrets, and that was a long time ago. I'm in my 80s now so I guess it's safe to share the story with the right people." Greenwood stared at Valerie, meeting her eyes. "The day you walked into my shop you rekindled the embers of forgotten memories. Right then I knew there was more to come. And that Mrs. Cahill, is a splendid thing." Cal Greenwood began his story.

"I grew up around here in the foothills. Had a lousy upbringing and owned nothing except an attitude and some talent for carpentry work and fixing motorcycles. I was always getting into trouble and dropped out of school. I was a bum with a cocky attitude. But I loved motorcycles and then airplanes. So, I did some odd job construction work." He grinned. "And stole motorcycle parts to get enough money for flying lessons. I ended up buying an old Cessna 170 from a crooked guy happy to leave town. The plane needed some work. Well, I wasn't an airplane mechanic, but I knew engines and had good mechanical aptitude. I got motivated and fixed the plane myself." He looked at Jake. "Probably sounds scary, a motorcycle mechanic fixing planes."

"Well, we don't do it that way anymore. But talented motorcycle mechanics are hard to find these days," Jake said with a grin.

Greenwood chuckled. "I wanted to get my Air Frame and Powerplant license but had no money. Still, I kept the plane flying and in good shape. All illegal, but hell, I never once had a problem with that little bird. I kept it parked in Grass Valley. Nobody talked or asked questions. Then things changed. I got greedy and even cockier. I was a loner, didn't have many friends and lived in a junky little trailer in the hills. So, I started carrying freight around and running certain errands for people. That altered my life."

"What changed?" asked Valerie.

"Met some guy that had an enormous bag of money, what you might call a drug dealer. He offered me some major dollars if I would fly him down south to a place near Baker, California. It's the middle of nowhere, miles off the major highway that leads to Las Vegas. Don't know what's there now. Back then it was a smuggler's drop zone with lots of dry lakes to land on, which I did. The Cessna was perfect for that, being a tail dragger and the prop sitting high off the ground. I didn't tell the guy I had never landed on a dry lake, much less flown that far south." Greenwood gave a chuckle. "He was desperate for an airlift and knew even less about flying than I did! So, I told him I was a pro at this type of flying."

Jake had to smile at the remark. "The confidence curve exceeded the skill curve. That's caught me a few times."

"Caught us all, at one time or another. So, I get this dummy down there with his duffle bag of bucks. The plan was to meet his supplier, buy more dope, and fly it home. Then I would have enough money to impress the only person who believed in me; Peggy." He paused and cleared the lump from his throat. "A sweet looker who lived with her parents in this very house. She thought I was crazy but still believed I had good in me." He sniffed. "Hell, can you imagine that? For the first time in my life somebody had faith in me."

Greenwood looked at Valerie and continued. "Told her I was going to make good money on this flyin' job. Afterwards, we could do something together-make a go of it. Well, she wanted no part of it and said she might not be around when I got back. Hell, not only was I overconfident, I was overly optimistic. She only said maybe. That's how I operated in life, thinking there's always a chance."

"What happened at the dope meet?" asked Jake, recalling his undercover days and how things went bad in a flash.

"It went to shit. I landed on some dry lake at dusk. I had a full moon, so taking off wasn't a problem. My guy walked over to these Mexican fellas as I stood off by the plane. The next thing I heard is a bunch of gunshots. Then, a couple rounds whack the tail of my Cessna. I flatten out and kiss the ground. After that it got really quiet, I mean dead quiet. I crawled out from under the plane, real slow like. With the moonlight I could see off in the distance. All these guys were lying on the ground. I walked over, scared shitless. Damn it all, they killed each other. Everybody was dead! I panicked and ran back to the plane, fired that baby up and took off!"

"You got lucky, Cal."

"Lucky? Dang, my little Saint Christopher medal was workin' overtime with more to come. So now I'm flying northbound for home. Then it hits me. I got a duffel bag full of cash in the backseat. The owner of the bag is dead. I start thinking that nobody would know about this. I could get home, stay low and hide the money. Then, when I was sure there wasn't any blowback, I'd have myself a nest egg. And just maybe, Peggy would see me as a different man." He shook his head. "That's me, thinking big with a small brain, and in this case with a small plane. After some fuel stops, I made it to the base of the Sierra. Then, the weather gets crappy and I can't get through Donner Pass. So, I turn north, then west over what I guess is now your ranch."

"Been in the family nearly 200 years."

"Interesting, I just assumed more Sierra Nevada mountains covered in snow. Anyway, I banked west, and the weather got grim with clouds. Then came the snow. The visibility started dropping and the terrain rising to meet the clouds. I knew about Tear Drop Pass. I crossed over it several times before, in pleasant weather. But I also knew the weather up there could change in a heartbeat. Legend has it that ancient spirits play catch with the clouds. Might be bullshit, but damn if it didn't happen that day."

Valerie tossed a wry grin to Jake.

"You got trapped?" asked Jake.

"Trapped and scared. I was flying with near zero visibility and about ready to lose control of the plane. Suddenly, I'm not flying anymore! My wheels had somehow gently touched a snow-covered slope, all at the right attitude. Talk about another miracle. I was in a white out condition and landed without knowing it!"

"Pretty lucky, Cal."

"And one for the books. I touched down on a slope, that I knew. But I couldn't see a damn thing. Then the plane slides backwards. Now, I'm ridin' an aluminum sled and expecting to go over a cliff. A second later I come to one helluva stop and pointing straight up. The plane fell into that crevasse. I struggled to get out of the wreckage before it torched off. Ha, that would have been hard since I was damn near on empty tanks. I unbuckled and fell out of the busted cockpit. I grabbed the money duffel and started climbing my way out of that trench. Then the hard part started."

"Were you hurt?" asked Valerie.

"Cut up, bloody, and bruised. My arm hurt like a son of a bitch, but I was in my 20s. Thought I was invincible."

"I know someone like that, and he isn't 20 either." She grinned looking at her husband.

"I sling the duffel over my shoulders still thinking I'm gonna be a rich guy. That is, if I could trek over Tear Drop Pass and down towards Grass Valley. That looked to be a long, hard hike. But it was better than sitting on my ass and freezing to death."

"Cal, that's a brutal climb, how did you manage it in the deep snow?" asked Jake.

"With determination and some help. After 30 minutes pushing through the freezing wind and deep snow I gave up. The wind turned snowflakes into glass shards. Got totally exhausted, with nothing left inside of me. I gave up, figured- what's the use? Nobody knew where I was at, what I was doing, or cared. About then, I opened my wallet and looked at a picture of Peggy. I begged her for that photo when we first met." Greenwood looked at Valerie. "Her smile and eyes gave me the motivation to keep pushing on. I prayed she would be there when I got out of that mess. Then something really strange happened." Cal Greenwood hesitated, scratching his face as if contemplating his next words.

Valerie and Jake spoke in unison. "What happened?"

"The howling wind just stopped. I mean quit. No snow. Nothing. It got quiet, like a soft winter silence when you snowshoe in the backcountry. Now I could see the mountain peak off to the left. Then a warm wind brushed across my face and..."

He stopped and stared at Jake and Valerie. "This is the crazy part. I thought I heard whispers of little kids. Figured I was suffering from hypothermia. A minute later they stopped. I kept climbing, hoping to get up further before I collapsed. The next thing I see are cougar tracks in front of me. Now *that* got my blood pumping. I followed the deep prints, which saved a lot of effort from cutting my own snow trail."

"Mr. Greenwood, did you see the lion?" asked Val, shooting quick a gaze at Jake then back to Greenwood.

"Nope, never saw the animal. I just used its tracks to get me through the deep snow. But those tracks took me to a path towards the ridge top. That made the last part of the hike a lot easier. Doubt I would have made it if I hadn't followed those big paw prints. Thanks to that cougar I made it over the pass. Well, a day later and eating the last of my candy bars, I found a paved road and hitch-hiked home; duffel bag and all." Greenwood took another sip of scotch and set his glass down.

"And nobody the wiser?" asked Jake.

"Nobody knew. Peggy waited for me and her folks took me in." Greenwood's voice faltered with emotion. "My parents had long ago moved away, leaving me to fend for myself. They didn't give a damn about me. Can't say that I blamed them considering what a rebel I was. But Peggy saw something in me. I told her about the money, but not her folks. We hid the cash and waited. Nobody ever asked about the plane. I told everyone it got sold in Nevada." Greenwood shook his head. "Years later, somebody, maybe other drug runners started a rumor about a lost smuggler plane in the Sierra. Guess that rumor hung on. I sort of figured my plane got buried forever." He gave a thoughtful glance at the old E6B. "Time altered that idea, didn't it?"

Jake let the old man reflect for a moment. "Cal, your plane and story rests on Tierra del Puma. Your secrets will remain hidden forever."

"Thank you, Jake. That means a lot to this old man. Some history should stay buried in the past."

"Mr. Greenwood, what happened after you got back?" asked Valerie, curious about the woman in his life.

"I started doing odd jobs and carpentry work. Made a pretty good living at it. Then Peggy's dad taught me woodcarving. I also fixed motorcycles; just didn't sell stolen parts. Later, I stuck with woodworking."

"You do have a talent, Mr. Greenwood. These models and this house are testimony to that," Val said with a warm smile.

"Well, Peggy and I got married. Because of their health her folks moved to Sacramento and sold us this house." He grinned. "Then with our duffle bag savings we bought the model shop. Peggy suggested I hand carve models. We called the shop PAC, as in Peggy And Cal. That went well for lots of years. Me and Peggy had a great life in this town. She opened a hair salon. We were busy and happy." He took a deep breath. "But all that changed." Cal Greenwood closed his eyes and blinked to hold back tears. "Damn, been a lot of years but I still get choked up." He cleared his throat, struggling with the words. "I lost my beautiful Peggy to cancer. I lost the only person who ever believed in me. We lived by a simple plan; she counted on me and I counted on her." He covered his eyes trying to hide the heartbreak.

Valerie walked over and gently touched his arm. "Mr. Greenwood, we are so sorry. There's never closure, just time."

Greenwood patted her hand. "I suppose." He sniffed, regaining his composure. "Mrs. Cahill, meeting you wasn't a chance encounter. I know that now." Valerie and Jake gave each other a quizzical look. Greenwood stood up and went into another room, returning with a small photograph. He handed it to Jake. "I carried this in my wallet when I crashed. It's Peggy when she was young. Her picture got me home. That girl had spirit and magic in her heart."

Jake accepted the old photo. His eyes widened as he stared at the picture of the youthful woman. He handed it over to Valerie, waiting to see her expression. Valerie looked at the photo and gasped. "Oh my God," she said, covering her mouth in surprise. The picture was a near identical image of herself. "I don't believe this."

Greenwood reached over and gently retrieved the photo from her hand. "I nearly had a heart attack the first day you came in the shop. You were my Peggy; you came back to me. For a moment I flew back in time. They say everybody has a twin, a doppelganger. You and Peggy made that match." He sighed and stared longingly at the old picture. The soft ticking of the grandfather clock accented the silence and the end of the story. Jake broke the stillness.

"Cal, would you like to see your plane? I can get you up to Tear Drop."

Greenwood had a sad smile. "No Jake, I'll just keep this little metal memento and set it next to the picture of Peggy. That's all I need." He looked at Valarie. "Mrs. Cahill, seeing you brought back memories of the sweetest human being I ever met. Made me feel young again." He stood up. "I better let you young folks get on with your lives. Thank you for allowing an old man to tell his story for the first time." He hugged Valerie and shook Jake's hand as they left the old house.

The Cahill's strolled down the street, hand in hand, passing by the shops. Both were lost in thought as the evening brought a chill. "I would never have believed that story if he didn't tell it himself," said Jake shaking his head. "And the picture of his Peggy. It was you Val. That's unreal. And him talking about whispers in the wind, lion tracks that's..." Valerie interrupted him.

"Jake, remember what your mom once said, some things at Tierra del Puma remain unexplainable. I know that darling, and now so do you." She tapped her finger on his chest. "And by the way, I would appreciate it, Mr. Cahill, that you get into the habit of telling me a bit more about things. We might be soul mates, but some verbal communication would help on details such as finding the other airplane and that little pilot device," she said grinning.

"My bad, I'll get better." He looped his arm around hers as they continued walking. After passing more shops, she stopped and peered into a shop's front window. Above the door was a sign that said, "Mother Lode Quilts."

"Jake, look at all the quilts in there, aren't they beautiful?"

Jake tried to sound interested. "They look beautiful."

She pointed to a small quilt, colored in pink with patterns of horseshoes on it. "That's cute, I love the cowgirl theme."

Jake nodded, "Definitely lots of detail."

Valerie put her index finger on her chin, "Hmm, you know what I'm thinking?"

"No, what?"

"I'm thinking Sarah would like that?"

Jake got lost. "Sarah, who is that?"

She looked up at him with a sparkle in her bright blue eyes. "You know, Sarah was your great, great, great grandfather's wife. The first owners of Tierra del Puma."

"Yeah, that I know."

"And Sarah is my middle name."

"Got that too," he said.

"I decided that Sarah will be the name of our daughter."

She glowed with a warm smile looking at Jake's frozen expression. His astonishment turned into a wide grin. "And you say that I don't tell you everything!"

"Jake, why do you think I've been so busy finishing things at the winery? I want to make sure I'll have plenty of the time at the ranch. I have lots to teach our Sarah about the legend of Tierra del Puma."

Jake Cahill swallowed hard, his eyes got moist and the smile wouldn't leave his face. He wrapped his arms around her. "Did I ever tell you that I love you?"

Valerie looked up at him and then rested her head on his chest. "Tell me again flyboy; tell me over and over."

EPILOGUE

Valerie walked alone to the top of the promontory. The sun had dropped below the jagged mountain peak that stood as a sentry across the meadow. The last vestiges of sunlight cast a fiery orange on the clouds resting on the horizon. In those moments between sunset and twilight it was quiet and tranquil. She looked west, toward the dark summit and spoke softly. "She is of me. Will you protect her?" The mountain stillness gave way to a warm breeze that gently swirled about her. A smile crossed her face; she had the answer.

CPSIA information can be obtained
at www.ICGtesting.com
Printed in the USA
BVHW070412090221
599638BV00006B/1344